James Grant

Legends of the Black Watch

Or, Forty-second Highlanders

James Grant

Legends of the Black Watch
Or, Forty-second Highlanders

ISBN/EAN: 9783744766036

Printed in Europe, USA, Canada, Australia, Japan

Cover: Foto ©Andreas Hilbeck / pixelio.de

More available books at **www.hansebooks.com**

LEGENDS

OF

THE BLACK WATCH:

OR,

Forty-second Highlanders.

BY

JAMES GRANT,

AUTHOR OF

" THE ROMANCE OF WAR," "HOLLYWOOD HALL," ETC., ETC.

NEW EDITION.

LONDON:
ROUTLEDGE, WARNE, AND ROUTLEDGE,
FARRINGDON STREET.
NEW YORK: 56, WALKER STREET.
1860.

LONDON
SAVILL AND EDWARDS, PRINTERS,
CHANDOS STREET.

PREFACE.

WOVEN up with an occasional legend or superstition gleaned among the mountains from whence its soldiers came, the warlike details and many of the names which occur in the following pages, belong to the military history of the country and of the brave Regiment whose title is given to our Book.

It is generally acknowledged that but for the retention of the kilt in the British service, and for the high character of those regiments who wear it, the military *name* of Scotland had been long since forgotten in Europe, and her national existence had been as completely ignored during the Wars of Wellington as in those of Marlborough ; nor in times more recent had the electric wire announced that, when the cloud of Russian horse came on at Balaclava and our allies fled, " the Scots stood firm."

The kilt alone indicated *their* country, as our Scots Lowland regiments are clad like the rest of the Line. The martial and picturesque costume of

the ancient clans which is now so completely identified with modern Scotland, is one of the few rem-
nants of the past that remain to her; and it is
remarkable that it has survived so long; for it was
the garb of those adventurous Greeks who fought
under Xenophon, and of those hardy warriors who
spread the terror of the Roman name from the
shores of the Euphrates on the east, to those of the
Caledonian Firths upon the west.

It was the best public service of the great Pitt
when he first rallied round the British throne, as
soldiers of the Highland Regiments, the men of that
warlike race, who had been so long inimical to the
House of Hanover.

"I sought for merit wherever it was to be found,"
said he; "it is my boast that I was the first minister
who looked for it and found it on the mountains of
the north. I called it forth, and drew into your service a hardy and intrepid race of men, who, when
left by your jealousy, became a prey to the artifice of
your enemies, and who, in the war before the last,
had well nigh gone to have overturned the State.
These men in the last war were brought to combat
by your side; they served with fidelity as they fought
with honour, and conquered for you in every part of
the world."

Highlander and Lowlander are now so mingled by

intermarriage that there is scarcely a subject in the northern kingdom without more or less Celtic blood in his or her veins; and to this mixture of race, which unites the fire and impatience of the former to the steady perseverance of the latter, Scotland owes her present prosperity.

The Clans are passing away, and with them a thousand great and glorious historical and romantic associations; while, by the rapid spread of education, even their language cannot long survive; " but when time shall have drawn its veil over the past as over the present—when the *last* broadsword shall have been broken on the anvil, and the shreds of the *last* plaid tossed to the winds upon the cairn, or been bleached within the raven's nest, posterity may look back with regret to a people who have so marked the history, the poetry, and the achievements of a distant age;" and who, in the ranks of the British army, have stood foremost in the line of battle and given place to none!

26, Danube Street, Edinburgh,
October, 1859.

CONTENTS.

LEGENDS

OF

THE BLACK WATCH.

I.

THE STORY OF FARQUHAR SHAW.

THIS soldier, whose name, from the circumstances connected with his remarkable story, daring courage, and terrible fate, is still remembered in the regiment, in the early history of which he bears so prominent a part, was one of the first who enlisted in Captain Campbell of Finab's independent band of the *Reicudan Dhu*, or Black Watch, when the six separate companies composing this Highland force were established along the Highland Border in 1729, to repress the predatory spirit of certain tribes, and to prevent the levy of black mail. The companies were independent, and at that time wore the clan tartan of their captains, who were Simon Frazer, the celebrated Lord Lovat; Sir Duncan Campbell of Lochnell; Grant of Ballindalloch; Alister Campbell of Finab, whose father fought at Darien; Ian Campbell of Carrick, and Deors Monro of Culcairn.

The privates of these companies were all men of a superior station, being mostly cadets of good families —gentlemen of the old Celtic and patriarchal lines,

and of baronial proprietors. In the Highlands, the
only genuine mark of aristocracy was descent from
the founder of the tribe ; all who claimed this were
styled *uislain,* or gentlemen, and, as such, when off
duty, were deemed the equal of the highest chief in
the land. Great care was taken by the six captains
to secure men of undoubted courage, of good stature,
stately deportment, and handsome figure. Thus, in all
the old Highland regiments, but more especially the
Reicudan Dhu, equality of blood and similarity of
descent, secured familiarity and regard between the
officers and their men—for the latter deemed themselves inferior to no man who breathed the air of
heaven. Hence, according to an English engineer
officer, who frequently saw these independent companies, "many of those private gentlemen-soldiers
have gillies or servants to attend upon them in their
quarters, and upon a march, to carry their provisions,
baggage, and firelocks."

Such was the composition of the corps, now first
embodied among that remarkable people, the Scottish
Highlanders—" a people," says the Historian of Great
Britain, " untouched by the Roman or Saxon in-
vasions on the south, and by those of the Danes on
the east and · west skirts of their country—the *un-
mixed remains* of that vast Celtic empire, which
once stretched from the Pillars of Hercules to Arch-
angel."

The Reicudan Dhu were armed with the usual
weapons and accoutrements of the line ; but, in addition to these, had the arms of their native country—
the broadsword, target, pistol, and long dagger, while
the sergeants carried the old Celtic *tuagh,* or Lochaber
axe. It was distinctly understood by all who enlisted
in this new force, that their military duties were

to be confined *within* the Highland Border, where, from the wild, predatory spirit of those clans which dwelt next the Lowlands, it was known that they would find more than enough of military service of the most harassing kind. In the conflicts which daily ensued among the mountains—in the sudden marches by night; the desperate brawls among Caterans, who were armed to the teeth, fierce as nature and outlawry could make them, and who dwelt in wild and pathless fastnesses secluded amid rocks, woods, and morasses, there were few who in courage, energy, daring, and activity equalled Farquhar Shaw, a gentleman from the Braes of Lochaber, who was esteemed the *premier* private in the company of Campbell of Finab, which was then quartered in that district ; for each company had its permanent cantonment and scene of operations during the eleven years which succeeded the first formation of the Reicudan Dhu.

Farquhar was a perfect swordsman, and deadly shot alike with the musket and pistol; and his strength was such, that he had been known to twist a horse-shoe, and drive his *skene dhu* to the hilt in a pine log ; while his activity and power of enduring hunger, thirst, heat, cold and fatigue, became a proverb among the companies of the Watch : for thus had he been reared and trained by his father, a genuine old Celtic gentleman and warrior, whose memory went back to the days when Dundee led the valiant and true to the field of Rinrory, and in whose arms the viscount fell from his horse in the moment of victory, and was borne to the house of Urrard to die. He was a true Highlander of the old school ; for an *old school* has existed in all ages and everywhere, even among the Arabs, the children of Ish-

mael, in the desert; for they, too, have an olden time
to which they look back with regret, as being nobler,
better, braver, and purer than the present. Thus, the
father of Farquhar Shaw was a grim *duinewassal*,
who never broke bread or saw the sun rise without
uncovering his head and invoking the names of "God,
the Blessed Mary, and St. Colme of the Isle;" who
never sat down to a meal without opening wide
his gates, that the poor and needy might enter
freely; who never refused the use of his purse and
sword to a friend or kinsman, and was never seen un-
armed, even in his own dining-room; who never
wronged any man; but who *never* suffered a wrong
or affront to pass, without sharp and speedy vengeance; and who, rather than acknowledge the
supremacy of the House of Hanover, died sword in
hand at the rising in Glensheil. For this act, his
estates were seized by the House of Breadalbane, and
his only son, Farquhar, became a private soldier in
the ranks of the Black Watch.

It may easily be supposed, that the son of such a
father was imbued with all his cavalier spirit, his
loyalty and enthusiasm, and that his mind was filled
by all the military, legendary, and romantic memories
of his native mountains, the land of the Celts, which,
as a fine Irish ballad says, was THEIRS

Ere the Roman or the Saxon, the Norman or the Dane,
Had first set foot in Britain, or trampled heaps of slain,
Whose manhood saw the Druid rite, at forest tree and rock—
And savage tribes of Britain round the shrines of Zernebok;
Which for generations witnessed all the glories of the Gael,
Since their Celtic sires sang war-songs round the sacred fires of
    Baal.

When it was resolved by Government to form the
six independent Highland companies into one regi-

ment, Farquhar Shaw was left on the sick list at the cottage of a widow, named Mhona Cameron, near Inverlochy, having been wounded in a skirmish with Caterans in Glennevis, and he writhed on his sickbed when his comrades, under Finab, marched for the Birks of Aberfeldy, the muster-place of the whole, where the companies were to be united into one battalion, under the celebrated John Earl of Crawford and Lindesay, the last of his ancient race, a hero covered with wounds and honours won in the services of Britain and Russia.

Weak, wan, and wasted though he was (for his wound, a slash from a pole-axe, had been a severe one), Farquhar almost sprang from bed when he heard the notes of their retiring pipes dying away, as they marched through Maryburgh, and round by the margin of Lochiel. His spirit of honour was ruffled, moreover, by a rumour, spread by his enemies the Caterans, against whom he had fought repeatedly, that he was growing faint-hearted . at the prospect of the service of the Black Watch being extended beyond the Highland Border. As rumours to this effect were already finding credence in the glens, the fierce, proud heart of Farquhar burned within him with indignation and unmerited shame.

At last, one night, an old crone, who came stealthily to the cottage in which he was residing, informed him that, by the same outlaws who were seeking to deprive him of his honour, a subtle plan had been laid to surround his temporary dwelling, and put him to death, in revenge for certain wounds inflicted by his sword upon their comrades.

The energy and activity of the Black Watch had long since driven the Caterans to despair, and nothing but the anticipation of killing Farquhar comfortably, and chopping him into ounce pieces at leisure, enabled them to survive their troubles with anything like Christian fortitude and resignation.

"And this is their plan, mother?" said Farquhar to the crone.

"To burn the cottage, and you with it."

"Dioul! say you so, Mother Mhona," he exclaimed; "then 'tis time I were betaking me to the hills. Better have a cool bed for a few nights on the sweet-scented heather, than be roasted in a burning cottage, like a fox in its hole."

In vain the cotters besought him to seek concealment elsewhere; or to tarry until he had gained his full strength.

"Were I in the prime of strength, I would stay here," said Farquhar; "and when sleeping on my sword and target, would fear nothing. If these dogs of Caterans came, they should be welcome to my life, if I could not redeem it by the three best lives in their band; but I am weak as a growing boy, and so shall be off to the free mountain side, and seek the path that leads to the Birks of Aberfeldy."

"But the Birks are far from here, Farquhar," urged old Mhona.

"*Attempt*, and *Did-not*, were the worst of Fingal's hounds," replied the soldier. "Farquhar will owe you a day in harvest for all your kindness; but his comrades wait, and go he must! Would it not be a strange thing and a shameful, too, if all the Reicudan Dhu should march down into the flat, bare land of the Lowland clowns, and Farquhar not be with them? What would Finab, his captain, think? and what would all in Brae Lochaber say?"

"Yet pause," continued the crones.

" Pause ! Dhia ! my father's bones will soon be clattering in their grave, far away in green Glensheil, where he died for King James, Mhona."

" Beware," continued the old woman, " lest you go for ever, Farquhar."

" It is longer to *for ever* than to Beltane, and by that day I must be at the Birks of Aberfeldy."

Then, seeing that he was determined, the crones muttered among themselves that the *tarvecoill* would fall upon him ; but Farquhar Shaw, though far from being free of his native superstitions, laughed aloud ; for the tarvecoill is a black cloud, which, if seen on a new-year's eve, is said to portend stormy weather ; hence it is a proverb for a misfortune about to happen.

" You were unwise to become a soldier, Farquhar," was their last argument.

" Why ?"

" The tongue may tie a knot which the teeth cannot untie."

" As your husbands' tongues did, when they married you all, poor men !" was the . good-natured retort of Farquhar. " But fear not for me ; ere the snow begins to melt on Ben Nevis, and the sweet wallflower to bloom on the black Castle of Inverlochy, I will be with you all again," he added, while belting his tartan-plaid about him, slinging his target on his shoulder, and whistling upon Bran, his favourite stag-hound ; he then set out to join the regiment, by the nearest route, on the skirts of Ben Nevis, resolving to pass the head of Lochlevin, through Larochmohr, and the deep glens that lead towards the Braes of Rannoch, a long, desolate, and perilous journey, but with his sword, his pistols, and gigantic hound to guard him, his plaid for a covering,

and the purple heather for a bed wherever he halted,
Farquhar feared nothing.

His faithful dog Bran, which had shared his couch
and plaid since the time when it was a puppy, was a
noble specimen of the Scottish hound, which was
used of old in the chase of the white bull, the wolf,
and the deer, and which is in reality the progenitor
of the common greyhound ; for the breed has de-
generated in warmer climates than the stern north.
Bran (so named from Bran of old) was of such size,
strength, and courage, that he was able to drag down
the strongest deer ; and, in the last encounter with
the Caterans of Glen Nevis, he had saved the life
of Farquhar, by tearing almost to pieces one who
would have slain him, as he lay wounded on the
field.   His hair was rough and grey ; his limbs
were muscular and wiry ; his chest was broad and
deep ; his keen eyes were bright as those of an
eagle.   Such dogs as Bran bear a prominent place in
Highland song and story.   They were remarkable
for their sagacity and love of their master, and their
solemn and dirge-like howl was ever deemed ominous
and predictive of death and woe.

Bran and his master were inseparable.   The noble
dog had long been invaluable to him when on hunting expeditions, and now since he had become a
soldier in the Reicudan Dhu, Bran was always on
guard with him, and the sharer of all his duties ; thus
Farquhar was wont to assert, "that for watchfulness
on sentry, Bran's two ears were worth all the rest in
the Black Watch put together."

The sun had set before Farquhar left the green
thatched clachan, and already the bases of the purple
mountains were dark, though a red glow lingered on
their heath-clad summits.   Lest some of the Cateran

band, of whose malevolence he was now the object, might already have knowledge or suspicion of his departure and be watching him with lynx-like eyes from behind some rock or bracken bush, he pursued for a time a path which led to the westward, until the darkness closed completely in ; and then, after casting round him a rapid and searching glance, he struck at once into the old secluded drove-way or Fingalian road, which descended through the deep gorge of Corriehoilzie towards the mouth of Glencoe.

On his left towered Ben Nevis—or "the Mountain of Heaven"—sublime and vast, four thousand three hundred feet and more in height, with its pale summits gleaming in the starlight, under a coating of eternal snow. On his right lay deep glens yawning between pathless mountains that arose in piles above each other, their sides torn and rent by a thousand watercourses, exhibiting rugged banks of rock and gravel, fringed by green waving bracken leaves and black whin bushes, or jagged by masses of stone, lying in piles and heaps, like the black, dreary, and Cyclopean ruins " of an earlier world." Before him lay the wilderness of Larochmohr, a scene of solitary and solemn grandeur, where, under the starlight, every feature of the landscape, every waving bush, or silver birch ; every bare scalp of porphyry, and every granite block torn by storms from the cliffs above ; every rugged watercourse, tearing in foam through its deep marl bed between the tufted heather, seemed shadowy, unearthly, and weird—dark and mysterious ; and all combined, were more than enough to impress with solemnity the thoughts of any man, but more especially those of a Highlander ; for the savage grandeur and solitude of that district

B

at such an hour—the gloaming—were alike, to use a paradox, soothing and terrific.

There was no moon. Large masses of crape-like vapour sailed across the blue sky, and by gradually veiling the stars, made yet darker the gloomy path which Farquhar had to traverse. Even the dog Bran seemed impressed by the unbroken stillness, and trotted close as a shadow by the bare legs of his master.

For a time Farquhar Shaw had thought only of the bloodthirsty Caterans, who in their mood of vengeance at the Black Watch in general, and at him in particular, would have hewn him to pieces without mercy; but now as the distance increased between himself and their haunts by the shores of the Lochy and Eil, other thoughts arose in his mind, which gradually became a prey to the superstition incident alike to his age and country, as all the wild tales he had heard of that sequestered district, and indeed of that identical glen which he was then traversing, crowded upon his memory, until he, Farquhar Shaw, who would have faced any six men sword in hand, or would have charged a grape-shotted battery without fear, actually sighed with apprehension at the waving of a hazel bush on the lone hill side.

Of many wild and terrible things this *locale* was alleged to be the scene, and with some of these the Highland reader may be as familiar as Farquhar.

A party of the Black Watch in the summer of 1738, had marched up the glen, under the command of Corporal Malcolm MacPherson (of whom more anon), with orders to seize a flock of sheep and arrest the proprietor, who was alleged to have "lifted" (*i.e.,* stolen) them from the Camerons of Lochiel. The soldiers found the flock to the number of three hundred, grazing

on a hill side, all fat black-faced sheep with fine long
wool, and seated near them, crook in hand, upon a
fragment of rock, they found the person (one of the
Caterans already referred to) who was alleged to have
stolen them.   He was a strange-looking old fellow,
with a long white beard that flowed below his girdle ;
he was attended by two huge black dogs of fierce
and repulsive aspect. He laughed scornfully when
arrested by the corporal, and hollowly the echoes of
his laughter rang among the rocks, while his giant
hounds bayed and erected their bristles, and their
eyes flashed as if emitting sparks of fire.

The soldiers now surrounded the sheep and drove
them down the hill side into the glen, from whence
they proceeded towards Maryburgh, with a piper
playing in front of the flock, for it is known that
sheep will readily follow the music of the pipe.   The
Black Watch were merry with their easy capture, but
none in MacPherson's party were so merry as the captured shepherd, whom, for security, the corporal had
fettered to the left hand of his brother Samuel ; and
in this order they proceeded for three miles, until they
reached a running stream ; when, lo ! the whole of
the three hundred fat sheep and the black dogs
turned into clods of brown earth; and, with a wild
mocking laugh that seemed to pass away on the
wind which swept the mountain waste, their shepherd
vanished, and no trace of his presence remained but
the empty ring of the fetters which dangled from
the left wrist of Samuel MacPherson, who felt every
hair on his head bristle under his bonnet with terror
and affright.

This sombre glen was also the abode of the *Daoine
Shic*, or Good Neighbours, as they are named in the
Lowlands; and of this fact the wife of the pay-

sergeant of Farquhar's own company could bear terrible evidence. These imps are alleged to have a strange love for abstracting young girls and women great with child, and leaving in their places bundles of dry branches or withered reeds in the resemblance of the person thus abstracted, but to all appearance dead or in a trance ; they are also exceeding partial to having their own bantlings nursed by human mothers.

The wife of the sergeant (who was Duncan Campbell of the family of Duncaves) was without children, but was ever longing to possess one, and had drunk of all the holy wells in the neighbourhood without finding herself much benefited thereby. On a summer evening when the twilight was lingering on the hills, she was seated at her cottage door gazing listlessly on the waters of the Eil, which were reddened by the last flush of the west, when suddenly a little man and woman of strange aspect appeared before her— so suddenly that they seemed to have sprung from the ground—and offered her a child to nurse. Her husband, the sergeant, was absent on duty at Dumbarton ; the poor lonely woman had no one to consult, or from whom to seek permission, and she at once accepted the charge as one long coveted.

"Take this pot of ointment," said the man, impressively, giving Moina Campbell a box made of shells, "and be careful from time to time to touch the eyelids of our child therewith."

"Accept this purse of money," said the woman, giving her a small bag of green silk ; "'tis our payment in advance, and anon we will come again."

The quaint little father and mother then each blew a breath upon the face of the child and disappeared, or as the sergeant's wife said, seemed to melt away

into the twilight haze. The money given by the
woman was gold and silver ; but Moina knew not its
value, for the coins were ancient, and bore the head
of King Constantine IV. The child was a strange,
pale and wan little creature, with keen, bright, and
melancholy eyes ; its lean freakish hands were almost
transparent, and it was ever sad and moaning. Yet
in the care of the sergeant's wife it throve bravely,
and always after its eyes were touched with the ointment it laughed, crowed, screamed, and exhibited
such wild joy that it became almost convulsed.

This occurred so often that Moina felt tempted to
apply the ointment to her own eyes, when lo ! she
perceived a group of the dwarfish Daoine Shie— little
men in trunk hose and sugar-loaf hats, and little
women in hoop petticoats all of a green colour—
dancing round her, and making grimaces and antic
gestures to amuse the child, which to her horror she
was now convinced was a bantling of the spirits who
dwelt in Larochmohr !

What was she to do ? To offend or seem to fear
them was dangerous, and though she was now daily
tormented by seeing these green imps about her, she
affected unconsciousness and seemed to observe them
not ; but prayed in her heart for her husband's speedy
return, and to be relieved of her fairy charge, to whom
she faithfully performed her trust, for in time the
child grew strong and beautiful ; and when, again on
a twilight eve, the parents came to claim it, the
woman wept as it was taken from her, for she had
learned to love the little creature, though it belonged
neither to heaven nor earth.

Some months after, Moina Campbell, more lonely
now than ever, was passing through Larochmohr,
when suddenly within the circle of a large green fairy

ring, she saw thousands, yea myriads of little imps in
green trunk hose and with sugar-loaf hats, dancing
and making merry, and amid them were the child
she had nursed and its parents also, and in terror and
distress she addressed herself to them.

The tiny voices within the charmed circle were
hushed in an instant, and all the little men and
women became filled with anger. Their little faces
grew red, and their little eyes flashed fire.

"How do _you_ see us?" demanded the father of
the fairy child, thrusting his little conical hat fiercely
over his right eye.

"Did I not nurse your child, my friend?" said
Moina, trembling.

"But how do you _see us?_" screamed a thousand
little voices.

Moina trembled, and was silent.

"Oho!" exclaimed all the tiny voices, like a breeze
of wind, "she has been using our ointment, the insolent mortal!"

"I can alter that," said one fairy man (who being
three feet high was a giant among his fellows), as he
blew upward in her face, and in an instant all the
green multitude vanished from her sight; she saw
only the fairy ring and the green bare sides of the
silent glen. Of all the myriads she had seen, not
one was visible now.*

"Fear not, Moina," cried a little voice from the
hill side, "for your husband will prosper." It was
the fairy child who spoke.

---

* This, and the two legends which follow, were related to me
by a Highlander, who asserted, with the utmost good faith, that
they happened in Glendochart; but I have since seen an Arabian
tale, which somewhat resembles the adventure of the sergeant's
wife.

"But his fate will follow him," added another voice, angrily.

Full of fear the poor woman returned to her cottage, from which, to her astonishment, she had been absent ten days and nights; but she saw her husband no more: in the meantime he had embarked for a foreign land, being gazetted to an ensigncy; thus so far the fairy promise of his prospering proved true.*

Another story flitted through Farquhar's mind, and troubled him quite as much as its predecessors. In a shieling here a friend of his, when hunting, one night sought shelter. Finding a fire already lighted therein he became alarmed, and clambering into the roof sat upon the cross rafters to wait the event, and ere long there entered a little old man two feet in height. His head, hands, and feet were enormously large for the size of his person; his nose was long, crooked, and of a scarlet hue; his eyes brilliant as diamonds, and they glared in the light of the fire. He took from his back a bundle of reeds, and tying them together, proceeded to blow upon them from his huge mouth and distended cheeks, and as he blew, a skin crept over the dry bundle, which gradually began to assume the appearance of a human face and form.

These proceedings were more than the huntsman on his perch above could endure, and filled by dread that the process below might end in a troublesome likeness of himself, he dropped a sixpence into his pistol (for everything evil is proof to *lead*) and fired straight at the huge head of the spirit or gnome, which vanished with a shriek, tearing away in his

---

* His "fate" would seem to have followed him, too; for he was killed at Ticonderoga, when captain-lieutenant of the Black Watch.—See *Stewart's Sketches*.

wrath and flight the whole of the turf wall on one
side of the shieling, which was thus in a moment reduced to ruin.

These memories, and a thousand others of spectral
Druids and tall ghastly warriors, through whose thin
forms the twinkling stars would shine (but these
orbs were hidden now) as they hovered by grey
cairns and the grassy graves of old, crowded on the
mind of Farquhar; for there were then, and even
now *are*, more ghosts, devils, and hobgoblins in the
Scottish Highlands than ever were laid of yore in
the Red Sea. Nor need we be surprised at this
superstition in the early days of the Black Watch,
when Dr. Henry tells us, in 1831, that within the last
twenty years, when a couple agreed to marry in
Orkney, they went to the Temple of the Moon, which
was semicircular, and there, on her knees, the woman
solemnly invoked the spirit of Woden!

Farquhar, as he strode on, comforted himself with
the reflection that those who are born at night—as
his mother had a hundred times told him he had
been—*never saw spirits;* so he took a good dram
from his hunting-flask, and belted his plaid tighter
about him, after making a sign of the cross three
times, as a protection against all the diablerie of the
district, but chiefly against a certain malignant fiend
or spirit, who was wont to howl at night among the
rocks of Larochmohr, to hurl storms of snow into the
deep vale of Corriehoilzie, and toss huge blocks of
granite into the deep blue waters of Loch Leven.
He shouted on Bran, whistled the march of the Black
Watch, "to keep his spirits cheery," and pushed on
his way up the mountains, while the broad rain drops
of a coming tempest plashed heavily in his face.

He looked up to the "Hill of Heaven." The night

clouds were gathering round its awful summit, wheeling, eddying, and floating in whirlwinds from the
dark chasms of rock that yawn in its sides. The
growling of the thunder among the riven peaks of
granite overhead announced that a tempest was at
hand; but though Farquhar Shaw had come of a
brave and adventurous race, and feared nothing
earthly, he could not repress a shudder lest the
mournful gusts of the rising wind might bear with
them the cry of the Tar' Uisc, the terrible Water
Bull, or the shrieks of the spirit of the storm!

The lonely man continued to toil up that wilderness till he reached the shoulder of the mountain,
where, on his right, opened the black narrow gorge,
in the deep bosom of which lay Loch Leven, and, on
his left, opened the glens that led towards Loch Treig,
the haunt of Damh mohr a Vonalia, or Enchanted Stag,
which was alleged to live for ever, and be proof to
mortal weapons; and now, like a tornado of the
tropics, the storm burst forth in all its fury!

The wind seemed to shriek around the mountain
summits and to bellow in the gorges below, while the
thunder hurtled across the sky, and the lightning,
green and ghastly, flashed about the rocks of Loch
Leven, shedding, ever and anon, for an instant, a
sudden gleam upon its narrow stripe of water, and on
the brawling torrents that roared down the mountain
sides, and were swelling fast to floods, as the rain,
which had long been falling on the frozen summit of
Ben Nevis, now descended in a broad and blinding
torrent that was swept by the stormy wind over hill
and over valley. As Farquhar staggered on, a gleam
of lightning revealed to him a little turf shieling
under the brow of a pine-covered rock, and making a
vigorous effort to withstand the roaring wind, which

tore over the bare waste with all the force and might
of a solid and palpable body, he reached it on his
hands and knees. After securing the rude door,
which was composed of three cross bars, he flung
himself on the earthen floor of the hut, breathless and
exhausted, while Bran, his dog, as if awed by the ele-
mental war without, crept close beside him.

As Farquhar's thoughts reverted to all that he had
heard of the district, he felt all a Highlander's native
horror of remaining in the *dark* in a place so weird
and wild ; and on finding near him a quantity of dry
wood—bog-pine and oak, stored up, doubtless, by
some thrifty and provident shepherd—he produced
his flint and tinder-box, struck a light, and, with all
the readiness of a soldier and huntsman, kindled a fire
in a corner of the shieling, being determined that if it
was the place where, about "the hour when church-
yards yawn and graves give up their dead," the
brownies were alleged to assemble, they should not
come upon him unseen or unawares.

Having a venison steak in his haversack, he placed
it on the embers to broil, heaped fresh fuel on his fire,
and drawing his plaid round Bran and himself, wearied
by the toil of his journey on foot in such a night, and
over such a country, he gradually dropped asleep,
heedless alike of the storm which raved and bellowed
in the dark glens below, and round the bare scalps of
the vast mountain whose mighty shadows, when falling
eastward at eve, darken even the Great Glen of
Albyn.

In his sleep, the thoughts of Farquhar Shaw wandered to his comrades, then at the Birks of Aberfeldy.
He dreamt that a long time—how long he knew
not—had elapsed since he had been in their ranks ;
but he saw the Laird of Finab, his captain, surveying

him with a gloomy brow, while the faces of friends and comrades were averted from him.

"Why is this—how is this?" he demanded.

Then he was told that the Reicudan Dhu were disgraced by the desertion of three of its soldiers, who, on that day, were to die, and the regiment was paraded to witness their fate. The scene with all its solemnity and all its terrors grew vividly before him; he heard the lamenting wail of the pipe as the three doomed men marched slowly past, each behind his black coffin, and the scene of this catastrophe was far, far away, he knew not where; but it seemed to be in a strange country, and then the scene, the sights, and the voices of the people, were foreign to him. In the background, above the glittering bayonets and blue bonnets of the Black Watch, rose a lofty castle of foreign aspect, having a square keep or tower, with four turrets, the vanes of which were shining in the early morning sun. In his ears floated the drowsy hum of a vast and increasing multitude.

Farquhar trembled in every limb as the doomed men passed so near him that he could see their breasts heave as they breathed; but their faces were concealed from him, for each had his head muffled in his plaid, according to the old Highland fashion, when imploring mercy or quarter.

Lots were cast with great solemnity for the firing party or executioners, and, to his horror, Farquhar found himself one of the twelve men chosen for this, to every soldier, most obnoxious duty!

When the time came for firing, and the three unfortunates were kneeling opposite, each within his coffin, and each with his head muffled in a plaid, Farquhar mentally resolved to close his eyes and fire at random against the wall of the castle opposite;

but some mysterious and irresistible impulse compelled him to look for a moment, and lo ! the plaid
had fallen from the face of one of the doomed men,
and, to his horror, the dreamer beheld *himself!*

His own face was before him, but ghastly and pale,
and his own eyes seemed to be glaring back upon him
with affright, while their aspect was wild, sad, and
haggard. The musket dropped from his hand, a weakness seemed to overspread his limbs, and writhing in
agony at the terrible sight, while a cold perspiration
rolled in bead-drops over his clammy brow, the
dreamer started, and awoke, when a terrible voice,
low but distinct, muttered in his ear—

"*Farquhar Shaw, bithidth duil ri fear feachd,
ach chu bhi duil ri fear lic!*"*

He leaped to his feet with a cry of terror, and
found that he was *not* alone, as a little old woman was
crouching near the embers of his fire, while Bran, his
eyes glaring, his bristles erect, was growling at her
with a fierce angry sound, that rivalled the bellowing
of the storm, which still continued to rave without.

The aspect of this hag was strange. In the light
of the fire which brightened occasionally as the wind
swept through the crannies of the shieling, her eyes
glittered, or rather glared like fiery sparks ; her
nose was hooked and sharp ; her mouth like an ugly
gash ; her hue was livid and pale. Her outward attire
was a species of yellow mantle, which enveloped her
whole form ; and her hands, which played or twisted
nervously in the generous warmth of the glowing
embers, resembled a bundle of freakish knots, or the
talons of an aged bird. She muttered to herself at times,

---

* A man may return from an expedition ; but there is no hope
that he may return from the grave.—*A Gaelic Proverb.*

and after turning her terrible red eyes twice or thrice
covertly and wickedly towards Farquhar, she suddenly
snatched the venison steak from amid the flames,
and, with a chuckle of satisfaction, devoured it
steaming hot, and covered as it was with burning
cinders.

On Farquhar secretly making a sign of the cross,
when beholding this strange proceeding, she turned
sharply with a savage expression towards him, and
rose to her full stature, which was not more than
three feet; and he felt, he knew not why, his heart
tremble; for his spirit was already perturbed by the
effect of his terrible dream, and clutching the steel
collar of Bran (who was preparing to spring at this
strange visitor, and seemed to like her aspect as little
as his master) he said—

"Woman, who are you?"

"A traveller like yourself, perhaps. But who are
you?" she asked in a croaking voice.

"Do you know our proverb in Lochaber—

> What sent the messengers to *hell,*
> But asking what they knew full well?"

was the reply of Farquhar, as he made a vigorous
effort to restrain Bran, whose growls and fury were
fast becoming quite appalling; and at this proverb
the eyes of the hag seemed to blaze with fresh anger,
while her figure became more than ever erect.

"Oich! oich!" grumbled Farquhar, "I would as
readily have had the devil as this ugly hag. I have
got a shelter, certainly; but with her 'tis out of the
cauldron and into the fire. Had she been a brown-
eyed lass, to a share of my plaid she had been welcome; but this wrinkled cailloch——down, Bran,
down!" he added aloud, as the strong hound strained

in his collar, and tasked his master's hand and arm
to keep him from springing at the intruder.

"Is this kind or manly of you," she asked, "to
keep a wild brute that behaves thus, and to a woman
too? Turn him out into the storm; the wind and
rain will soon cool his wicked blood."

"Thank you; but in that you must excuse me.
Bran and I are as brothers."

"Turn him out, I say," screamed the hag, "or
worse may befall him!"

"I shall not turn him out, woman," said Farquhar,
firmly, while surveying the stranger with some uneasi-
ness; for, to his startled gaze, she seemed to have
grown *taller* within the last five minutes. "You have
a share of our shelter, and you have had all our supper; but to turn out poor Bran—no, no, that would
never do."

To this Bran added a roar of rage, and the fear or
fury which blazed in the eyes of the woman fully
responded to those of the now infuriated staghound.
The glances of each made those of the other more and
more fierce.

"Down, Bran; down, I say," said Farquhar. "What
the devil hath possessed the dog? I never saw him
behave thus before. He must be savage, mother, that
you left him none of the savoury venison steak; for
all the supper we had was that road-collop from one
of MacGillony's brown cattle."

"MacGillony," muttered the hag, spreading her
talon-like hands over the embers; "I know him well."

"You!" exclaimed Farquhar.

"I have said so," she replied with a grin.

"He was a mighty hunter five hundred years ago,
who lived and died on the Grampians!"

"And what are five hundred years to me, who saw

the waters of the deluge pour through Corriehoilzie, and subside from the slope of Ben Nevis ?"

"This is a very good joke, mother," said poor Farquhar, attempting to laugh, while the hideous old woman, who was so small when he first saw her as to be almost a dwarf, was now, palpably, veritably, and without doubt, nearly a head taller than himself; and watchfully he continued to gaze on her, keeping one hand on his dirk and the other on the collar of Bran, whose growls were louder now than the storm that careered through the rocky glen below.

"Woman !" said Farquhar, boldly, "my mind misgives me—there is something about you that I little like ; I have just had a dreadful dream."

"A morning dream, too !" chuckled the hag with an elfish grin.

"So I connect your presence here with it."

"Be it so."

"What may that terrible dream foretell?" pondered Farquhar; "for morning dreams are but warnings and presages unsolved. The blessings of God and all his saints be about mo !"

At these words the beldame uttered a loud laugh.

"You are, I presume, a Protestant?" said Farquhar, uneasily.

At this suggestion she laughed louder still, but seemed to grow more and more in stature, till Farquhar became well-nigh sick at heart with astonishment and fear, and began to revolve in his mind the possibility of reaching the door of the shieling and rushing out into the storm, there to commit himself to Providence and the elements. Besides, as her stature grew, her eyes waxed redder and brighter, and her malevolent hilarity increased.

It was a fiend, a demon of the wild, by whom he

was now visited and tormented in that sequestered
hut.

His heart sank, and as her terrible eyes seemed to
glare upon him, and pierce his very soul, a cold perspiration burst over all his person.

"Why do you grasp your dirk, Farquhar—ha!
ha!" she asked.

"For the same reason that I hold Bran—to be
ready. Am I not one of the King's Reicudan Dhu?
But how know you my name?"

"'Tis a trifle to me, who knew MacGillony."

"From whence came you to-night?"

"From the Isle of Wolves," she replied, with a
shout of laughter.

"A story as likely as the rest," said Farquhar, "for
that isle is in the Western sea, near unto Coll, the
country of the Clan Gillian. You must travel fast."

"Those usually do who travel on the skirts of the wind."

"Woman!" exclaimed Farquhar, leaping up with
an emotion of terror which he could no longer con-
trol, for her stature now overtopped his own, and ere
long her hideous head would touch the rafters of the
hut; "thou art either a liar or a fiend! which shall
I deem thee?"

"Whichever pleases you most," she replied, starting to her feet.

"Bran, to the proof!" cried Farquhar, drawing
his dirk, and preparing to let slip the now maddened
hound; "at her, Bran, and hold her down. Good,
dog—brave dog! oich, he has a slippery handful that
grasps an eel by the tail! at her, Bran, for thou art
strong as Cuchullin."

Uttering a roar of rage, the savage dog made a
wild bound at the hag, who, with a yell of spite and
defiance, and with a wondrous activity, by one spring,

left the shieling, and dashing the frail door to fragments in her passage, rushed out into the dark and tempestuous night, pursued by the infuriated but baffled Bran—baffled now, though the fleetest hound on the Braes of Lochaber.

They vanished together in the obscurity, while Farquhar gazed from the door breathless and terrified. The storm still howled in the valley, where the darkness was opaque and dense, save when a solitary gleam of lightning flashed on the ghastly rocks and narrow defile of Loch Leven ; and the roar of the bellowing wind as it tore through the rocky gorges and deep granite chasms, had in its sound something more than usually terrific. But, hark ! other sounds came upon the skirts of that hurrying storm.

The shrieks of a fiend, if they could be termed so ; —for they were shrill and high, like cries of pain and laughter mingled. Then came the loud deep baying, with the yells of a dog, as if in rage and pain, while a thousand sparks, like those of a rocket, glittered for a moment in the blackness of the glen below. The heart of Farquhar Shaw seemed to stand still for a time, while, dirk in hand, he continued to peer into the dense obscurity. Again came the cries of Bran, but nearer and nearer now ; and in an instant more, the noble hound sprang, with a loud whine, to his master's side, and sank at his feet. It was Bran, the fleet, the strong, the faithful and the brave ; but in what a condition ! Torn, lacerated, covered with blood and frightful wounds—disembowelled and dying ; for the poor animal had only strength to loll out his hot tongue in an attempt to lick his master's hand before he expired.

"Mother Mary," said Farquhar, taking off his bonnet, inspired with horror and religious awe, "keep

C

thy blessed hand over me, for my dog has fought with a demon!" . . . . . .

It may be imagined how Farquhar passed the remainder of that morning—sleepless and full of terrible thoughts, for the palpable memory of his dream, and the episode which followed it, were food enough for reflection.

With dawn, the storm subsided. The sun arose in a cloudless sky; the blue mists were wreathed round the brows of Ben Nevis, and a beautiful rainbow seemed to spring from the side of the mountain far beyond the waters of Loch Leven; the dun deer were cropping the wet glistening herbage among the grey rocks; the little birds sang early, and the proud eagle and ferocious gled were soaring towards the rising sun; thus all nature gave promise of a serene summer day.

With his dirk, Farquhar dug a grave for Bran, and lined it with soft and fragrant heather, and there he covered him up and piled a cairn, at which he gave many a sad and backward glance (for it marked where a faithful friend and companion lay) as he ascended the huge mountains of rock, which, on one hand, led to the *Uisc Dhu*, or Vale of the Black Water, and on the other, by the tremendous steep named the Devil's Staircase, to the mouth of Glencoe.

In due time he reached the regiment at its cantonments on the Birks of Aberfeldy, where the independent companies, for the first time were exercised as a battalion by their Lieutenant-Colonel, Sir Robert Munro of Culcairn, who, six years afterwards, was slain at the battle of Falkirk.

Farquhar's terrible dream and adventure in that Highland wilderness were ever before him, and the events subsequent to the formation of the Black

Watch into a battalion, with the excitement produced among its soldiers by an unexpected order *to march into England*, served to confirm the gloom that preyed upon his spirits.

The story of how the Black Watch were deceived is well known in the Highlands, though it is only one of the many acts of treachery performed in those days by the British Government in their transactions with the people of that country, when seeking to lessen the adherents of the Stuart cause, and ensnare them into regiments for service in distant lands; hence the many dangerous mutinies which occurred after the enrolment of all the *old* Highland corps.

This unexpected order to march into England caused such a dangerous ferment in the Black Watch, as being a violation of the principles and promise under which it was enrolled, and on which so many Highland gentlemen of good family enlisted in its ranks, that the Lord President Duncan Forbes of Culloden, warned General Clayton, the Scottish Commander-in-Chief, of the evil effects likely to occur if this breach of faith was persisted in ; and to prevent the corps from revolting *en masse*, that officer informed the soldiers that they were to enter England "solely to be seen by King George, who had never seen a Highland soldier, and had been graciously pleased to express, or feel great curiosity on the subject."

Cajoled and flattered by this falsehood, the soldiers of the Reicudan Dhu, *all unaware that shipping was ordered to convey them to Flanders*, began their march for England, in the end of March, 1743 ; and if other proof be wanting that they were deluded, the following announcement in the *Caledonian Mercury* of that year affords it :—

"On Wednesday last, the Lord Sempills Regiment of Highlanders began their march for England, *in order to be reviewed by his Majesty.*"

Everywhere on the march throughout the north of England, they were received with cordiality and hospitality by the people, to whom their garb, aspect, and equipment were a source of interest, and in return, the gentlemen and soldiers of the Reicudan Dhu behaved to the admiration of their officers and of all magistrates ; but as they drew nearer to London, according to Major Grose, they were exposed to the malevolent mockery and the national "taunts of the true-bred English clowns, and became gloomy and sullen.   Animated even to the humblest private with the feelings of gentlemen," continues this English officer, "they could ill brook the rudeness of boors, nor could they patiently submit to affronts in a country to which they had been called by the *invitation* of their sovereign."

On the 30th April, the regiment reached London, and on the 14th May was reviewed on Finchley Common, by Marshal Wade, before a vast concourse of spectators ; but the King, whom they expected to be present, had sailed from Greenwich for Hanover on the same night they entered the English metropolis. Herein they found themselves deceived ; for "the King had told them a lie," and the spark thus kindled was soon fanned into a flame.

After the review at Finchley Common, Farquhar Shaw and Corporal Malcolm MacPherson were drinking in a tavern, when three English gentlemen entered, and seating themselves at the same table, entered into conversation, by praising the regiment, their garb, their country, and saying those compliments which are so apt to win the heart of a Scotchman when far from home ; and the glens of the Gael seemed then indeed, far, far away, to the imagination of the simple souls who manned the Black Watch in 1743.

Both Farquhar and the corporal being gentlemen, wore the wing'of the eagle in their bonnets, and were well educated, and spoke English with tolerable fluency.

" I would that his Majesty had seen us, however," said the corporal ; " we have had a long march south from our own country on a bootless errand."

" Can you possibly be so simple as to believe that the King cared a rush on the subject ?" asked a gentleman, with an incredulous smile ; for he and his companions, like many others who hovered about these new soldiers, were Jacobites and political incendiaries.

" What mean you, sir ?" demanded MacPherson, with surprise.

" Why, you simpleton, that story of the King wishing to see you was all a tale of a tub—a snare."

" A snare !" •

" Yes—a pretext of the ministry to lure you to this distance from your own country, and then transport you bodily for life."

" To where ?"

" Oh, that matters little—perhaps to the American plantations."

" Or, to Botany Bay," suggested another, maliciously ; " but take another jorum of brandy, and fear nothing; wherever you go, it can't well be a worse place than your own country."

" Thanks, gentlemen," replied Farquhar, loftily,

while his hands played nervously with his dirk; "we want no more of your brandy."

"Believe me, sirs," resumed their informant and tormentor, "the real object of the ministry is to get as many fighting men, Jacobites and so forth, out of the Highlands as possible. This is merely part of a new system of government."

"Sirs," exclaimed Farquhar, drawing his dirk with an air of gravity and determination which caused his new friends at once to put the table between him and them, "will you swear this upon the dirk ?"

"How—why ?"

"Upon the Holy Iron—we know no oath more binding," continued the Highlander, with an expression of quiet entreaty.

"I'll swear it by the Holy Poker, or anything you please," replied the Englishman, re-assured on finding the Celt had no hostile intentions. " 'Tis all a fact," he continued, winking to his companions, "for so my good friend Phil Yorke, the Lord Chancellor, who expects soon to be Earl of Hardwick, informed me."

The eyes of the corporal flashed with indignation; and Farquhar struck his forehead as the memory of his terrible dream in the haunted glen rushed upon his memory.

"Oh! yes," said a third gentleman, anxious to add his mite to the growing mischief; "it is all a Whig plot of which you are the victims, as our kind ministry hope that you will all die off like sheep with the rot; or like the Marine Corps; or the Invalids, the old 41st, in Jamaica."

"They dare not deceive us!" exclaimed MacPherson, striking the basket-hilt of his claymore

"Dare not!"

" No."

" Indeed—why ?"

" For in the country of the clans fifty thousand claymores would be on the grindstone to avenge us !"

A laugh followed this outburst.

" King George made you rods to scourge your own countrymen, and now, as useless rods, you are to be flung into the fire," said the first speaker, tauntingly.

" By God and Mary !" began MacPherson, again laying a hand on his sword with sombre fury.

" Peace, Malcolm," interposed Farquhar; " the Saxon is right, and we have been fooled. Bithidh gach ni mar is aill Dhiu. (All things must be as God will have them.) Let us seek the Reicudan Dhu, and woe to the Saxon clowns and to that German churl, their King, if they have deceived us !"

On the march back to London, MacPherson and Farquhar Shaw brooded over what they had heard at Finchley; while to other members of the regiment similar communications had been made, and thus, ere nightfall, every soldier of the Black Watch felt assured that he had been entrapped by a royal false-hood, which the sudden, and to them unaccountable, departure of George II. to Hanover seemed beyond all doubt to confirm.

" In those whom he knows," according to General Stewart, " a Highlander will repose perfect confi-dence, and if they are his superiors will be obedient and respectful; but ere a stranger can obtain this *confidence*, he must show that he *merits* it. When once it is given, it is constant and unreserved; but if confidence be lost, no man is more suspicious. Every officer of a Highland regiment, on his first joining the corps, must have observed in his little transactions with the men how minute and strict they are in every item ; but when once confidence is established, scrutiny ceases, and his word or nod of assent is as good as his bond. In the case in question (the Black Watch), notwithstanding the arts which were practised to mislead the men, they proceeded to no violence, but believing themselves deceived and betrayed, the only remedy that occurred to them was to get back to their own country."

The memory of the commercial ruin at Darien, and of the massacre at Glencoe (the Cawnpore of King William), were too fresh in every Scottish breast not to make the flame of discontent and mistrust spread like wildfire ; and thus, long before the bell of St. Paul's had tolled the hour of midnight, the conviction that he had been BETRAYED was firmly rooted in the mind of every soldier of the Black Watch, and measures to baffle those who had deluded and lured them so far from their native mountains were at once proposed, and as quickly acted upon.

At this crisis, the dream of Farquhar was constantly before him, as a foreboding of the terrors to come, and he strove to thrust it from him ; but the words of that terrible warning—a man may return from an expedition, but never from the grave—seemed ever in his ears !

On the night after the review, the whole regiment, except its officers, most of whom knew what was on the *tapis*, assembled at twelve o'clock on a waste common near Highgate. The whole were in heavy marching order ; and by direction of Corporal Malcolm MacPherson, after carefully priming and loading with ball-cartridge, they commenced their march in silence and secresy and with all speed for Scotland—a wild, daring, and romantic attempt, for they were heedless and ignorant of the vast extent of hostile country that lay between them and their homes, and scarcely knew the route to pursue. They had now but three common ideas;—to keep together, to resist to the last, and to march *north.*

With some skill and penetration they avoided the two great highways, and marched by night from wood to wood, concealing themselves by day so well, that for some time no one knew how or where they had gone, though, by the Lords Justices orders had been issued to all officers commanding troops between London and the Scottish Borders to overtake or intercept them ; but the 19th May arrived before tidings reached the metropolis that the Black Watch, one thousand strong, had passed Northampton, and a body of Marshal Wade's Horse (now better known as the 3rd or Prince of Wales's Dragoon Guards) overtook them, when faint by forced and rapid marches, by want of food, of sleep and shelter, the unfortunate regiment had entered Ladywood, about four miles from the market town of Oundle-on-the-Nen, and had, as usual, concealed themselves in a spacious thicket, which, by nine o'clock in the evening, was completely environed by strong columns of English cavalry under General Blakeney.

Captain Ball, of Wade's Horse, approached their bivouac in the dusk, bearer of a flag of truce, and was received by the poor fellows with every respect, and Farquhar Shaw, as interpreter for his comrades, heard his demands, which were, " that the whole battalion should lay down its arms, and surrender at discretion as mutineers."

" Hitherto we have conducted ourselves quietly and peacefully in the land of those who have deluded and wronged us, even as they wronged and deluded our forefathers," replied Farquhar ; " but it may not be so for one day more. Look upon us, sir; we are famished, worn, and desperate. It would move the heart of a stone to know all we have suffered by hunger and by thirst, even in this land of plenty."

"The remedy is easy," said the captain.

"Name it, sir."

"Submit."

"We have no such word in our mother-tongue, then how shall I translate it to my comrades, so many of whom are gentlemen ?"

"That is your affair, not mine. I give you but the terms dictated by General Blakeney."

"Let the general send us a written promise."

"Written ?" reiterated the captain, haughtily.

"By his own hand," continued the Highlander, emphatically; "for here in this land of strangers we know not whom to trust when our King has deceived us."

"And to what must the general pledge himself ?"

"That our arms shall not be taken away, and that a free pardon be given to all."

"Otherwise——"

"We will rather be cut to pieces."

"This is your decision ?"

"It is," replied Farquhar, sternly.

"Be assured it is a rash one."

"I weigh my words, Saxon, ere I speak them. No man among us will betray his comrade ; we are all for one and one for all in the ranks of the Reicudan Dhu !"

The captain reported the result of his mission to the general, who, being well aware that the Highlanders had been entrapped by the Government on one hand, and inflamed to revolt by Jacobite emissaries on the other, was humanely willing to temporize with them, and sent the captain to them once more.

"Surrender yourselves prisoners," said Ball; "lay down your arms, and the general will use all his influence in your favour with the Lords Justices."

"We know of no Lords Justices," they replied. "We acknowledge no authority but the officers who speak our mother-tongue, and our native chiefs who share our blood. To be without arms, in our country, is in itself to be dishonoured."

"Is this still the resolution of your comrades?" asked Captain Ball.

"It is, on my honour as a gentleman and soldier," replied Farquhar.

The English captain smiled at these words, for he knew not the men with whom he had to deal.

"Hitherto, my comrade," said he, "I have been your friend, and the friend of the regiment, and am still anxious to do all I can to save you; but, if you continue in open revolt one hour longer, surrounded as you all are by the King's troops, not a man of you can survive the attack, and be assured that even I, for one, will give quarter to none! Consider well my words—you may survive banishment for a time, but from the grave there is no return."

"The words of my dream!" exclaimed Farquhar, in an agitated tone of voice; "*Bithidh duil ri fear feachd, ach cha bhi duil ri fear lic.* God and Mary, how come they from the lips of this Saxon captain?"

The excitement of the regiment was now so great that Captain Ball requested of Farquhar that two Highlanders should conduct him safely from the wood. Two duinewassals of the Clan Chattan, both corporals, named MacPherson, stepped forward, blew

the priming from their pans, and accompanied him to
the outposts of his own men—the Saxon *Seidar
Dearg,* or Red English soldiers, as the Celts named
them.

Here, on parting from them, the good captain renewed his entreaties and promises, which so far won
the confidence of the corporals, that, after returning to the regiment, the whole body, in consequence
of their statements, agreed to lay down their arms
and submit the event to Providence and a court-martial of officers, believing implicitly in the justice of
their cause and the ultimate adherence of the Government to the letters of *local* service under which they
had enlisted.

Farquhar Shaw and the two corporals of the Clan
Chattan nobly offered their own lives as a ransom for
the honour and liberties of the regiment, but their
offer was declined ; for so overwhelming was the force
against them, that all in the battalion were alike at
the mercy of the ministry.   On capitulating, they
were at once surrounded by strong bodies of horse,
foot, and artillery, with their field-pieces grape-
shotted; and the most severe measures were faith-
lessly and cruelly resorted to by those in authority
and those in whom they trusted.   While, in defiance
of all stipulation and treaty with the Highlanders, the
main body of the regiment was marched under escort
towards Kent, to embark for Flanders, two hundred privates, chiefly gentlemen or cadets of good
family, were selected from its ranks and sentenced to
banishment, or service for life in Minorca, Georgia,
and the Leeward Isles.   The two corporals, Samuel
and Malcolm MacPherson, with Farquhar Shaw, were
marched back to London, to meet a more speedy, and
to men of such spirit as theirs, a more welcome fate.

The examinations of some of these poor fellows prove how they had been deluded into service for the Line.

"I did not desert, sirs," said John Stuart, a gentleman of the House of Urrard, and private in Campbell of Carrick's company. "I repel the insinuation," he continued, with pride; "I wished only to go back to my father's roof and to my own glen, because the inhospitable Saxon churls abused my country and ridiculed my dress. We had no leader; we placed no man over the rest."

"I am neither a Catholic nor a false Lowland Whig," said another private—Gregor Grant, of the family of Rothiemurchus; "but I am a true man, and ready to serve the King, though his actions have proved him a liar! You have said, sirs, that I am afraid to go to Flanders. I am a Highlander, and never yet saw the man I was afraid of. The Saxons told me I was to be transported to the American plantations to work with black slaves. Such was not our bargain with King George. We were but a Watch to serve along the Highland Border, and to keep broken clans from the Braes of Lochaber."

"We were resolved not to be tricked," added Farquhar Shaw. "We will meet the French or Spaniards in any land you please; but we will die, sirs, rather than go, like Saxon rogues, to hoe sugar in the plantations."

"What is your faith?" asked the president of the court-martial.

"The faith of my fathers a thousand years before the hateful sound of the Saxon drum was heard upon the Highland Border!"

"You mean that you have lived——"

"As, please God and the Blessed Mary, I shall die

—a Catholic and a Highland gentleman ; stooping to none and fearing none——"

" *None*, say you ?"

"Save Him who sits upon the right hand of His Father in Heaven."

As Farquhar said this with solemn energy, all the prisoners took off their bonnets and bowed their heads with a religious reverence which deeply impressed the court, but failed to save them.

On the march to the Tower of London, Farquhar was the most resolute and composed of his companions in fetters and misfortune ; but on coming in sight of that ancient fortress, his firmness forsook him, the blood rushed back upon his heart, and he became deadly pale ; for in a moment he recognised the castle of his strange dream—the castle having a square tower, with four vanes and turrets—and then the whole scene of his foreboding vision, when far away in lone Lochaber, came again upon his memory, while the voice of the warning spirit hovered again in his ear, and he knew that the hour of his end was pursuing him !

And now, amid crowds of country clowns and a rabble from the lowest purlieus of London, who mocked and reviled them, the poor Highlanders were marched through the streets of that mighty metropolis (to them, who had been reared in the mountain solitudes of the Gaël, a place of countless wonders !) and were thrust into the Tower as prisoners under sentence.

Early on the morning of the 12th July, 1743, when the sun was yet below the dim horizon, and a frowsy fog that lingered on the river was mingling with the city's smoke to spread a gloom over the midsummer morning, all London seemed to be pouring from her many avenues towards Tower Hill, where an episode of no ordinary interest was promised to the sight-loving Cockneys—a veritable military execution, with all its stern terrors and grim solemnity.

All the troops in London were under arms, and long before daybreak had taken possession of an ample space enclosing Tower Hill; and there, conspicuous above all by their high and absurd sugar-loaf caps, were the brilliantly accoutred English and Scots Horse Grenadier Guards, the former under Viscount Cobham, and the latter under Lieutenant-General John Earl of Rothes, K.T., and Governor of Duncannon; the Coldstream Guards; the Scots Fusiliers; and a sombre mass in the Highland garb of dark-green tartan, whom they surrounded with fixed bayonets.

These last were the two hundred men of the Reicudan Dhu selected for banishment, previous to which they were compelled to behold the death, or—as they justly deemed it—the deliberate murder under trust, of three brave gentlemen, their comrades.

The gates of the Tower revolved, and then the craped and muffled drums of the Scots Fusilier Guards were heard beating a dead march before those who were "to return to Lochaber no more." Between two lines of Yeomen of the Guard, who faced inwards, the three prisoners came slowly forth, surrounded by an escort with fixed bayonets, each doomed man marching behind his coffin, which was borne on the shoulders of four soldiers. On approaching the parade, each politely raised his bonnet and bowed to the assembled multitude.

"Courage, gentlemen," said Farquhar Shaw; "I see no gallows here. I thank God we shall not die a dog's death!"

"'Tis well," replied MacPherson, "for honour is more precious than refined gold."

The murmur of the multitude gradually subsided
and died away, like a breeze that passes through a
forest, leaving it silent and still, and then not a sound
was heard but the baleful rolling of the muffled drums
and the shrill but sweet cadence of the fifes. Then
came the word, *Halt!* breaking sharply the silence
of the crowded arena, and the hollow sound of the
three empty coffins, as they were laid on the ground,
at the distance of thirty paces from the firing party.

Now the elder brother patted the shoulder of the
other, as he smiled and said—

"Courage—a little time and all will be over—our
spirits shall be with those of our brave forefathers."

"No coronach will be cried over us here, and no
cairn will mark in other times where we sleep in the
land of the stranger."

"Brother," replied the other, in the same forcible
language, "we can well spare alike the coronach and
the cairn, when to our kinsmen we can bequeath the
dear task of avenging us!"

"If that bequest be valued, then we shall not die
in vain."

Once again they all raised their bonnets and uttered
a pious invocation; for now the sun was up, and in the
Highland fashion—a fashion old as the days of Baal—
they greeted him.

"Are you ready?" asked the provost-marshal.

"All ready," replied Farquhar; "*moch-cirigh
'luain, a ni'n t-suain 'mhairt.*"*

This, to them, fatal 12th of July was a *Monday;* so
the proverb was solemnly applicable.

Wan, pale, and careworn they looked, but their
eyes were bright, their steps steady, their bearing

* Early rising on *Monday* gives a sound sleep on *Tuesday.*—
See MacIntosh's *Gaelic Proverbs*

erect and dignified. They felt themselves victims and martyrs, whose fate would find a terrible echo in the Scottish Highlands; and need I add, that echo *was heard*, when two years afterwards Prince Charles unfurled his standard in Glenfinnan? Thus inspired by pride of birth, of character, and of country—by inborn bravery and conscious innocence, at this awful crisis, they gazed around them without quailing, and exhibited a self-possession which excited the pity and admiration of all who beheld them.

The clock struck the fatal hour at last!

"It is my doom," exclaimed Farquhar; "the hour of my end hath followed me."

They all embraced each other, and declined having their eyes bound up, but stood boldly, each at the foot of his coffin, confronting the levelled muskets of thirty privates of the Grenadier Guards, and they died like the brave men they had lived. One brief paragraph in *St. James's Chronicle* thus records their fate.

"On Monday, the 12th, at six o'clock in the morning, Samuel and Malcolm MacPherson, corporals, and Farquhar Shaw, a private-man, three of the Highland deserters, were shot upon the parade of the Tower pursuant to the sentence of the court martial. The rest of the Highland prisoners were drawn out to see the execution, and joined in their prayers with great earnestness. They behaved with perfect resolution and propriety. Their bodies were put into three coffins by three of the prisoners, *their clansmen and namesakes*, and buried in one grave, near the place of execution."

Such is the matter-of-fact record of a terrible fate!

To the slaughter of these soldiers, and the wicked

D

breach of faith perpetrated by the Government, may
be traced much of that distrust which characterized
the Seaforth Highlanders and other clan regiments
in their mutinies and. revolts in later years; and
nothing inspired greater hatred in the hearts of those
who "rose" for Prince Charles in 1745, than the
story of the deception and *murder*) for so they named
it) of the three soldiers of the Reicudan Dhu by King
George at London.   "There must have been something more than common in the case and character of
these unfortunate men," to quote the good and gallant old General Stewart of Garth, "as Lord John
Murray, who was afterwards colonel of the regiment,
had portraits of them hung in his dining-room."

This was the first episode in the history of the
Black Watch, which soon after covered itself with
glory by the fury of its charge at Fontenoy, and on
the field of Dettingen exulted that among the dead
who lay there was General Clayton, "the Sassenach"
whose specious story first lured them from the Birks
of Aberfeldy.

II.

THE SEVEN GRENADIERS.

"As the regiment expects to be engaged with the enemy to-morrow, the women and baggage will be sent to the rear. For this duty, Ensign James. Campbell, of Glenfalloch."

Such was the order which was circulated in the camp of the 42nd Highlanders (then known as the Black Watch) on the evening of the 28th April, 1745, previous to the Duke of Cumberland's attack on the French outposts in front of Fontenoy. Our battalion (writes one of our old officers) was to form the advanced guard on this occasion, and had been ordered to the village of Veson, where a bivouac was formed, while Ensign Campbell, of Glenfalloch, the same who was afterwards wounded at Fontenoy, marched the baggage, with all the sorrowing women of the corps, beyond Maulpré, as our operations were for the purpose of relieving Tournay, then besieged by a powerful French army under Marshal Count de Saxe, and valiantly defended by eight thousand Dutchmen under the veteran Baron Dorth. It was the will of Heaven in those days that we should fight for none but the Dutch and Hanoverians.

I had been appointed captain-lieutenant to the Black Watch from the old 26th, or Angus's Foot, and having overtaken the corps on its march between the

gloomy old town of Liege and the barrier fortress of
Maestricht, the aspect and bearing of the Highlanders
—we had then only *one* regiment of them in the service—seemed new and strange, even barbaric to my
eyes ; for, as a Lowlander, I had been ever accustomed to associate the tartan with fierce rapine and
armed insurrection.   Yet their bearing was stately,
free, and noble ; for our ranks were filled by the
sons of Highland gentlemen, and of these the most
distinguished for stature, strength, and bravery were
the seven sons of Captain Maclean, a cadet of the
house of Duairt, who led our grenadiers. The very
flower of these were the seven tall Macleans, who,
since the regiment had been *first* mustered at the
beautiful Birks of Aberfeldy, in May, 1740, had
shone foremost in every encounter with the enemy.

Captain Campbell, of Finab, and I seated ourselves
beside the Celtic patriarch who commanded our
grenadier company, and near him were his seven
sons lounging on the grass, all tall and muscular
men, bearded to the eyes, athletic, and weather-
beaten by hunting and fighting in the Highlands,
and inured alike to danger and to toil. Though gentlemen volunteers, they wore the uniform of the privates, a looped-up scarlet jacket and waistcoat faced
with buff and laced with white,* a tartan plaid of
twelve yards plaited round the body and thrown over
the left shoulder ; a flat blue bonnet with the fesse-
chequé of the house of Stuart round it, and an
eagle's feather therein, to indicate the wearer's birth.
The whole regiment carried claymores in addition to
their muskets, and to these weapons every soldier
added, if he chose, a dirk, skene, pair of pistols, and

* The regiment was not made royal until 1758.

target, in the fashion of the Highlands; thus our front rank men were usually as fully equipped as any that stepped on the muir of Culloden. Our sword-belts were black, and the cartouch-box was slung in front by a waist-belt. In addition to all this warlike paraphernalia, our grenadiers carried each a hatchet and pouch of hand-grenades. The servicelike, formidable, and *cap-à-pie* aspect of the regiment had impressed me deeply; but Captain Maclean and his seven sons more than all, as they lay grouped near the watchfire, in the red light of which their bearded visages, keen eyes, and burnished weapons were glinting and glowing.

The beard of old Maclean was white as snow, and flowed over his tartan plaid and scarlet waistcoat, imparting to his appearance a greater peculiarity, as all gentlemen were then closely shaven. As Finab and I seated ourselves by his fire, he raised his bonnet and bade us welcome with a courtly air, which consorted ill with his sharp west Highland accent. His eye was clear and bold in expression, his voice was commanding and loud, as in one whose will had never been disputed. Close by was his inseparable henchman and foster-brother Ronald MacAra, the colour-sergeant of his company, an aged Celt of grim presence and gigantic proportions, whose face had been nearly cloven by a blow from a Lochaber axe at the battle of Dunblane.

"Welcome, gentlemen," said old Maclean, "a hundred thousand welcomes to a share of our supper, a savoury *roud collop*, as we call it at home. It was a fine fat sheep that my son Dougal *found* astray in a field near Maulpré; and here is a braw little demijohn of Belgian wine, which Alaster borrowed from a boor close by. These other five lads are also my

sons, Dunacha, Deors, Findlay Bane, Farquhar Gorm,
and Angus Dhu, all grenadiers in the King's service,
and hoping each one to be like myself a captain and
to cock their feathers among the best in the Black
Watch. Attend to our comrades, my braw lads."

The *lads*, the least of whom was six feet in height,
assisted us to a share of the sheep, which was broil-
ing merrily on the glowing embers, and from which
their comrades, who crowded round, partook freely,
cutting off the slices, as they sputtered and browned,
by their long dirks and sharp skenes. The seven
grenadiers were all fine and hearty fellows, who trun-
dled Alaster's demijohn of wine from hand to hand
round the red roaring fire, on which the grim henchman or colour-sergeant heaped up, from time to time,
the doors and rafters of an adjacent house, and there
we continued to carouse, sing, and tell stories, until
the night was far advanced.

The month was April, and the night was a glorious
one; all our bivouac was visible as if at noonday.
The hum of voices, the scrap of a song, a careless
laugh, the neigh of a horse, or the jangle of a
bridle alone broke the silence of the moonlit sky;
though at times we heard the murmur of a stream
that stole towards the Scheldt, like a silver current
through the fields of sprouting corn, and under banks
where the purple foxglove, the pink wild rose, and the
green bramble hung in heavy masses.

And could aught be more picturesque than our
Highland bivouac, lighted up by wavering watchfires
and the brilliant queen of night—the Celtic soldiers
muffled in their dark-green plaids, their rough bare
knees, hardy as the stems of the mountain pine, and
alike impervious to the summer heat and winter cold,
lying asleep upon their "umbered arms," or seated in

groups, singing old songs, or telling wild stories of those distant glens from which, as *Seidaran Dearg* or "Red Soldiers," the chances of the Belgian war had brought them here.

I was delighted with the old chief and his sons—they were so free and gay in manner, so frank and bold in bearing, while there was something alike noble and patriarchal in the circumstance of their stately old father leading a company of brave hearts, nearly all of whom were men of his own name and kindred. The fire had been freshly heaped with billets and fagots, the demijohn still bled freely; we had just concluded a merry chorus, which made the Uhlan videttes on the distant plain prick up their ears and listen, and we had reached that jovial point when a little wit goes a very long way, when Sergeant Ronald MacAra, the old henchman, approached Captain Maclean, and placing a hand upon his shoulder with that kind but respectful familiarity which his relation as a foster-brother sanctioned, said with impressive solemnity—

"For the love of the blessed God, see that ye do not fight the stranger to-morrow with your stomach fasting."

The ruddy face of the old soldier grew pale.

"No, Ronald," said he ; "our race has already paid dear for neglecting that strange warning."

"God and Mary forbid!" muttered two of his sons, crossing themselves devoutly.

"Keep something for me in your havresac, Ronald," said the captain, "and call me before the drums beat for marching ; keep something for the laddies, too—for the Lord forfend that ever son of mine should draw his blade with a fasting stomach under his belt."

" A wise precaution, Maclean," said old Captain
Campbell of Finab; " but Gude kens we have often
had to draw our blades here in Low Germanie, and
fall on, without other breakfast than a tightened
waist-belt."

" True; but it was by omitting to break his fast
that my worthy ancestor Sir Lauchlan Maclean lost
his life in Mull, and hence the warning of Sergeant
MacAra, my fosterer."

" How came that to pass?" I asked with surprise;
for the impressive manner of these Celts was strange
and new to me.

" 'Tis a story as well as any other, and I care not
if I tell you, gentlemen," said the old captain of
grenadiers. " Dunacha, throw some more sticks on
the fire—Angus, pass round the black-jack, my son,
while I tell of the doleful battle of Groynard. The
presence of the Lord be about us, but *that* was a
black day, and a dreary one for the house of Duairt
and the Clan Gillian to boot!"

After this preamble and collecting his thoughts a
little, the captain commenced the following strange
story :—

History will tell you, gentlemen, that in the early
part of the reign of his Majesty James VI. there arose
a deadly feud between my people, the Clan Gillian
in Mull, and the Clan Donald of Islay, concerning
the claim which, from times beyond the memory of
man, we had, or believed we had ('tis all one in the
Highlands) to the Rhinns of Islay. For many a
year our people and the Macdonalds invaded, harried,
hacked, hewed, and shot each other; the axe and
bow, the pistol and claymore were never relinquished
for one entire week, but we were never nearer our

end, for I must admit that our antagonists were a brave tribe, though in boyhood—such is the absurdity of a transmitted feud—I was taught to hate them more than death. I have been told that there was not a man of either of the hostile tribes but had lost his nearest and dearest kinsmen in that ungodly contest.

But now a crisis was coming.

My worthy ancestor, Sir Lauchlan Maclean of Duairt, was a soldier of high renown and bravery— one whose skill in war was acknowledged by all who saw him lead the Clan Gillian to victory at the great battle of Bénrinnes, where twelve thousand Scottish Protestants measured swords with Lord Huntly's Catholics on the banks of the Livat, and there decided their religious differences like pretty men. Well, Sir Lauchlan, through the great favour in which he was held at court, obtained from the King's own hand at Holyrood a charter or warrant empowering him to take possession not only of those devilish Rhinns, but of the whole island of Islay—the patrimony and home of the Lords of the Isles—what think you of that, sirs? All Islay with Eilan-na-Corlle, or the Island of Council, the great castle in Loch Finlaggan, the Rock of the Silver Rent, the Rock of the Rent-in-Kind, with everything that flew over Islay, walked on its hills, or swam in its lakes, to him and his heirs for ever, heritably and irredeemably, until the day of doom.

This seemed a severe stroke of fortune to the poor Clan Donald, the more so as their chief, Angus of Kintyre, was aged and frail, and had not drawn a sword since last he fought our people in his seventieth year, and now he was eighty. His son, Sir James, was as yet unknown as a soldier, while Sir Lauchlan was in the noon of his strength and manhood—second

to none that stepped on heather or ever wore the
tartan : hence, full of hope and confident of success,
he rejected with scorn the offers of mediation made
by neighbouring chiefs; for old Angus had many
friends, and my forefathers' claims were, to say the
least of them, rather unjust. Sir Lauchlan summoned
all the clan, his friends and kinsmen, to meet him in
arms and with their galleys on a certain day to sail
for Islay, when he hoped to crush the Clan Donald
for ever in one decisive battle.

On the evening before the muster, mounted and
alone he rode from Duairt to consult a witch who
dwelt in an uncouth den known among us as "the
cave of the Grey Woman." It was not without some
misgivings that my ancestor paid this visit ; but the
advice and auguries of this woman, Aileen Glas, had
never failed our race in times of war and peril.

As he drew near her dwelling, the night was closing
in ; the wind shook the' boughs of the forest, and as
he looked back, they resembled the long green waves
of a sea of foliage rolling up the narrow glen. The
"gloaming" darkened fast, and the silent dew distilled from the drooping leaves ; the golden cups of
the broom and the calices of the heather-bells were
shrinking with many a summer fly and honey-bee
concealed in their petals, for night was descending on
the stormy shores and boisterous hills of Mull—boisterous indeed, for there the hollow winds rave and
howl from peak to peak, and wreath up the mist into
many a strange and many a fearful shape, till the
ghosts of Ossian seem again to tower above Benmore
and Bentaluidh.

Sir Lauchlan rode rapidly up the narrowing glen,
till he found the cave of the Grey Woman before him.
It yawned dark, lofty, and profound ; so, dismounting,

he tied his horse to a tree, and with his target and claymore advanced boldly, but with no small trouble, as the darkness was now intense, and the ascent to the cavern was rocky and difficult. Above his head rose its capacious arch, fringed by matted ivy and the light waving mountain ash that covered all the upper rocks, the splintered peaks of which shot up against the starless sky in abrupt and jagged outline. Clambering up, he entered with a stately step, though his heart beat fast with anxiety; before him lay a dark abyss of blackness and vacancy, opening into the bowels of the mountain; and though lightly shod in cuarans of soft deer hide, he could hear his footsteps echoing afar off.

At last a red light began to gleam before him, playing in fitful flashes upon the wet slimy walls of the den, and on the huge stalactites that hung like rough Gothic pendants from the roof, and were formed by the filtrations of calcareous rills that stole noiselessly down between the chasms and crannies in the walls of rock.

Aileen Glas was said to have been born in the mossy isle of Calligrey, in a hut built among the stones of the temple of Annat, the ruined shrine of a Druidical goddess. Annat presided over the young maidens of the Western Isles, and there still remains her well, in which they are said to have purified themselves. In that well Aileen was baptized by the Red Priest of Applecross, and hence her magical power.

As Maclean stepped on, he perceived the Grey Woman, a withered, shrivelled, and frightful hag, whose nose was hooked like an eagle's beak, and on whose chin was a grey tuft, like a thistle's beard—a mere anatomy of bones and skin—seated before a heap

of blazing turf and sticks, but asleep, and reclining
against the wall of rock. A tattered plaid of our clan
tartan was over her head, the grey hair of which hung
in twisted elflocks round her bony visage. An urchin
—a hideous hedgehog—nestled in her fleshless bosom,
and its diminutive eyes shone like red beads in the
light. On one side lay a heap of withered herbs, a
human skull cloven in battle, and the spulebane of a
sea-wolf; on the other side was an old iron three-
legged pot used in her incantations. Therein sat a
huge, rough, and wild-eyed polecat, which spat at the
intruder, and woke up a large, sleepy bat that swung
by his tail from a withered branch which projected
from a fissure of the rock.

The Grey Woman awoke also, and, without moving,
fixed her green basilisk eyes on Sir Lauchlan's face,
saying sharply—

" What want ye, Duairt ?"

" Your advice, good Aileen Glas," replied the chief,
meekly, for he was awed by her aspect.

" Advice !" shrieked the Grey Woman. " Is it a
spell you seek, to insure success, that you may do a
greater wrong unto the hapless and guiltless Clan
Donald of Islay ?"

" I seek to do them no wrong, Aileen. The Rhinns
are ours by right, and Islay is ours by the King's own
charter ?"

" The *people* were there before kings or charters
were known in the land. God gave the hills and the
isles to the children of the Gael, and His curse will
fall on all who seek to dispossess them by virtue of
sheepskins and waxen seals. Did not a Lord of the
Isles say that he little valued a right which depended
on the possession of a scrap of parchment ? Beware,

Lauchlan Maclean! beware! for the hand of fate is upon you!"

Scared by her words and her fury, as her shrill voice awoke the inmost recesses of the vault, Sir Lauchlan said—

"In the name of the mother of God, Aileen Glas, I beseech you to be composed, and to tell me of what I must beware!"

She snatched up the spulebane of the wolf, and, after looking through it by holding it between her and the fire, cast it aside with a shriek, saying—

"Lauchlan of Duairt, listen to me, for never may you hear my voice again!"

"It may be so, Aileen; we sail for Islay to-morrow!"

"Well, do not land upon a *Thursday*, and do not drink of the well that flows at the head of Loch Groynard, for I can see that *one* Maclean will be slain there, and *lie headless!* Away! leave me now! In the glen you will meet those who will tell you more!" and she muffled her face in her plaid as Sir Lauchlan left her.

"I can easily avoid a landing on Thursday, and a draught of that devilish well too; but whom shall I meet in the glen?" thought he, as he mounted and galloped homewards to Duairt, glad the horrid interview was over. As he rode round the base of Benmore, the waning moon began to show half her disc above the black shoulder of the mighty mountain, and a pale light played along the broad waves of Loch-nakeal, which lay on his left, and were rolled in foam against the bold headlands and columnar ridges, which are covered with coats of ivy and tufted by remains of oak and ash woods that overhung the salt

billows of that western sea, where the scart, the mew,
and the heron were screaming.

On, on rode our chief, treasuring the words of Grey
Aileen in his heart, and soon he saw the lights in his
own castle of Duairt glittering before him about a
mile off, and anon he could perceive the outline of
the great keep as it towered in the pale moonlight on
its high cliff that breasts the Sound of Mull.   But
hark! the voice of a woman made him pause.

He checked his horse and looked around him.

Under an old and blasted oak-tree, the leafless and
gnarled branches of which seemed white and ghastly
in the cold moonlight, stood the figure of a woman
arrayed in a pale-coloured dress that shimmered and
gleamed as the moon's half-disc dipped behind the
sharp rocky cone of Bentaluidh.   The figure, which
was thin and tall, was enveloped in a garment that
resembled a shroud.   It came forward with one lean
arm uplifted, as if to stay the onward progress of
Maclean, whose rearing horse swerved, trembled, and
perspired with fear.   Nearer she came, and, as the
starlight glinted on her features, they seemed pallid,
ghastly, hollow, and wasted; the lips were shrunken
from the teeth, the eyes shone like two pieces of glass,
and, to his horror, Sir Lauchlan recognised his old
nurse Mharee, who had been buried in the preceding
year, and whom, with his own hands, he had laid in
her grave, close by the wall of Torosay Kirk, the bell
of which at that moment tolled the eleventh hour
of the night.   Gathering courage from despair, he
asked—

"In the name of Him who died for us, Mharee,
what want you here to-night?"

"Oh, my son!" said she, "for such indeed I may
call you (for did not these breasts, on which the worms

are now preying, give you suck?) this expedition
against the men of Islay is full of mighty consequences
to you and all Clan Gillian!"

"I am sure of that, Mharee," replied Maclean,
with a sinking heart; "but we go to gather
glory and triumph, to spread the honour and the
terror of our name, and to win a fairer patrimony
to bequeath, with our swords, to the children who suc-
ceed us."

"Lauchlan Maclean! by the bones of your father
and the fame of your mother, I conjure you to abandon this wicked war, to sheath your sword, to burn
the King's charter, and to leave the Clan Donald in
peace, for Islay is the land of their inheritance."

"To what disgrace would you counsel me, Mharee?
to be a coward and a liar in the face of the King, of
my kindred and clansmen? Come weal, come woe,
to-morrow my birlinns shall spread their sails upon
the sea that leads to Islay, though I and all my
people go but to their graves: by the cross of Maclean
I have sworn it!"

"So be it then; but if go you will, I warn you not
to cross the threshold of Duairt with a *fasting
stomach*, or sore evil, Lauchlan, will come of it to all
thy kin and thee!"

With these strange words, the figure faded away
like a moonbeam, and nothing was seen but the bare,
blasted tree stretching its naked arms across the
narrow way. Some time elapsed before Maclean recovered from his terror and astonishment to find his
horse dashing up the ascent which led to the Castle
of Duairt, where his pale face and wild manner
caused many questions and excited much comment;
but he kept his own counsel, resolving *not* to march
on the morrow before breakfast, *not* to land on a Thurs-

day, and *not* to drink of any well in Islay, if other
liquor could be found for love or money.

Next morning great were the hurry, din, and pre-
paration in Duairt, and long before cockcrow the
shore of Loch Linnhe was covered by armed men,
with their brass targets and burnished claymores,
axes, bows, and Spanish muskets; their helmets and
lurichs sparkled in the dawn, and when the sun arose
above the hills of Lorn, the white sails of the birlinns,
with banners flying and pipers playing at the prow,
covered all the sea around the Castle of Duairt.   Sir
Lauchlan in person superintended the embarkation
of his followers, and if there was one, there were seven
hundred good claymores among them—not a bonnet
less !   Every man, as he left Duairt, had a ration of
bannock, cheese, and venison given to him, with a
good dram to put under his belt, for such is our
Highland custom before setting out on an expedition.

But such was the enthusiasm, such were the cheers,
the congratulations and hopes uttered aloud, the
yelling of pipes, the twangling of clairsachs and
quaffing of toasts with blade and bicker held aloft,
that it was not until he was on board his great war
birlinn, with all her canvas spread to catch the
northern gale which blew towards the peaks of Jura,
that the fated chieftain found that, in attending to
his people, he had forgotten to regale himself, and,
contrary to the solemn warning of the spirit, had
actually commenced his hazardous expedition with a
" fasting stomach !"

" Dhia !" cried he to my grand-uncle Lauchlan
Barroch ; " I am lost, nephew," and he related the
vision of last night.

" If that be all," replied my grand-uncle, who was
his brother's son, "rest easy, for here have I and

Ronald of the Drums marched too, with nothing under our belts but the cold north wind."

Still my ancestor felt far from easy; but he forgot it before night, when a heavy gale came on, and the birlinns were scattered on the waters of the darkening deep like a flock of gulls; and it was in vain that he fired his pateraroes as signals to keep together.

The storm increased, and while some of the little fleet narrowly escaped being sucked (like the Danish prince of old) into the roaring whirlpool of Coirv-reckan, many were blown to the Isle of Colonsay and others to the Sound of Jura. Many days—all days of storm with nights of pitchy blackness—followed, and on the first *Thursday* of the next week the little fleet of birlinns made the low green shores and sandy inlets of Islay, and saw the rising sun gild the woods and hills that rise upon its eastern coast. Still the stormy wind ploughed up the sea; the sun was en-veloped in watery clouds, and the tempest-tossed Clan Gillian gladly steered their vessels (oh, fatality!) into the salt Loch of Groynard, a shallow bay on the north-west of the isle, where, with a shout of triumph, they ran the keels into the sand and leaped ashore with brandished swords, and formed their ranks, all barelegged, in the water.

But long ere this the crian tarigh, or cross of fire, had blazed upon the hills of Islay!

Under their young chief, Sir James, the whole Clan Donald, many of whom had been trained to service in the Irish wars, were drawn up in array of battle at the head of Loch Groynard; and there, with all their weapons glittering from the purple heather, they hovered like a cloud of battle. As the hostile bands drew near, some gentlemen of the Clan Donald, to prevent the effusion of Christian blood, prevailed

E

upon Sir James to promise that he would resign one
half of Islay to Maclean during his life, provided he
would acknowledge that he held it for personal service
to the Clan Donald, in the same manner as our forefathers had held the Rhinns of Islay.

But, rendered furious on finding that he had doubly
transgressed the wizard warnings he received, Sir
Lauchlan laughed the proposition to scorn. Then the
young chief offered to submit the matter in dispute to
any impartial umpires Duairt might choose, with the
proviso that, if *they* should disagree, his Majesty the
King should be their arbiter.

But my ancestor drew off his glove, and, taking a
handful of water from a fountain that gurgled from a
rock near him, exclaimed—

"May this water prove my poison, if I will have
any arbiter but my sword, or any terms but an absolute surrender of the whole island!"

Then my grand-uncle Lauchlan Barroch uttered a
cry of terror—for Duairt in his anger had forgotten
the prediction, and drank of "*the well* at the head of
Loch Groynard, where *one* Maclean was to fall"—
and there, in ten minutes after, he was slain by a
MacDonald, who by a single blow of a claymore swept
his head off his shoulders.

Long and bloody was the battle that ensued when
the MacDonalds rushed down the hill to close with
the Clan Gillian, who were routed, leaving eighty
duinewassals and two hundred soldiers, with their
chief, dead upon the field. Ronald Maclean of the
Drums—a little tower upon the peninsula of Loch
Suinard—was shot by an arrow, and not one who left
Duairt with "a fasting stomach," escaped;—why,
God alone knows; for though my grand-uncle
Lauchlan Barroch retreated with a remnant of our

people to the birlinns, he was mortally wounded by
a musket-shot. Of the Clan Donald, only thirty men
were killed and sixty wounded. Among the latter
was their young chief—afterwards a general of the
Scots Brigade in Holland—who was found on the
field with an arrow in his breast.

I have heard my mother say that all that night
the watchman on the keep of Duairt heard cries and
moans coming from the seaward, though the castle
was more than fifty miles distant from Groynard ; for
it seemed as if the spirits of the air brought the
sounds of battle on their wings from the fatal shore
of Islay. Late that night, the hoofs of a galloping
horse were heard reverberating in the glen and ringing on the roadway that led to Duairt ; and soon a
horse and rider were seen in the moonlight approaching rapidly, the hoofs of the steed striking fire from
the flinty path.

"A messenger approaches !" cried the watchman,
and in an instant the lady of Duairt and all her
household were at the gate ; but how great was their
terror when they perceived that the approaching
horseman was headless, though wearing the arms,
plaid, and trews of a chief ! Up, up the ascent came
the terrible vision, galloping in the pale moonlight,
but passing on, it disappeared in the glen which led
to the blasted oak where Sir Lauchlan had received
his last unearthly warning.

Be this story false or true, there are in our regiment a hundred brave men of trust and honour, who
can swear to having seen this spectre gallop up to
Duairt gate on the anniversary of the battle of Groynard, or when any calamity overhangs the Clan Gillian. Sir Lauchlan—the heavens be his bed to-night !
—sleeps in Torosay Kirk, yet that headless horseman

may appear to-morrow on the shore of Mull, for many a bonnet will be on the turf, many a plaid in our ranks dyed red in the wearer's blood—and I have seven sons in the field! But our fate is in the hands of God, so let our hearts be stout and true, for He will never fail us, though we may be false to ourselves. Hand round the demijohn, Findlay, my brave lad—and rouse the brands, Farquhar, for the moon has sunk behind the hills, and our fire is getting low.

So ended this legend of Celtic diablerie, to which I had listened attentively, for the air and manner of the venerable narrator were very impressive, as he devoutly believed it all; but Captain Campbell of Finab, who affected to consider it, as he said, "a tale of a tub," was as much startled as I by the issue of the next day's engagement with the enemy.

By dawn next day the wild pibroch "Come to me and I will give you flesh," that fierce invitation to the wolf and raven, rang in the allied bivouac, as his Royal Highness the Duke of Cumberland took post at Maulpré in view of the French position, and ordered a squadron of each regiment, with six battalions of foot, five hundred pioneers, a body of Austrian hussars, and six pieces of cannon, all under the command of the veteran Lieutenant-General Sir James Campbell, K.B., Governor of the Castle of Edinburgh, to drive the enemy out of the defiles of the wood of Barri. This movement was the prelude to the disastrous battle of Fontenoy, where Campbell was killed.

The Guards and we—the old Black Watch—began the engagement at Veson—the well-known affair of outposts. There the Dauphin commanded, and his soldiers were the flower of the French line, a splendid brigade, all clad in white coats laced with gold, long ruffles, tied perriwigs, and little plumed hats. They were intrenched breast high, and defended by an abattis.

We fell furiously on; the Scottish Foot-guards with their clubbed muskets and fixed bayonets; the Black Watch with swords, pistols, and dirks, and the struggle was terrible, as the action ensued at a place which was swept by the fire of a redoubt mounted with cannon and manned by six hundred of the noble Regiment de Picardie. Old Captain Maclean, at the head of his grenadiers and with his seven sons by his side, rushed up the glacis to storm the palisades.

"Open pouches—blow fuses—dirk and claymore, fall on!" were his rapid orders, as the hand-grenades fell like a hissing shower over the breastwork, from which a sheet of lead tore through the ranks of our stormers. Maclean fell at the foot of the palisades with one hand upon them and the other on his sword. All his sons perished with him, falling over each other in a gory heap as they strove to protect his body. The last who fell was the youngest, Angus Dhu, who, after slaying a French field officer, had driven a bayonet into his head, thrusting it through the ears; using it as a lever, he strove furiously to twist, tear, or wrench off the Frenchman's skull as a trophy of vengeance; for the young Celt was beside himself with grief and rage, when a volley of bullets from the white-coated Regiment de Picardie laid him on the grass to rise no more, just as Sir James Campbell carried the intrenchment sword in hand, and totally routed or destroyed the soldiers of the Dauphin.

Whether old Captain Maclean and his sons marched that morning without breaking their fast—a fatal omission apparently in any of the Clan Gillian—I have no means of ascertaining ; but, as Ronald Mac Ara, who bore their provisions, was killed by a stray bullet about daybreak, it was generally believed so by the regiment, as this faithful henchman of the captain was found dead with a full havresac under his right arm, and the weird story of the seven fated grenadiers was long remembered by the Black Watch, when the greater events of the rout at Fontenoy and the evacuation of Flanders were forgotten.

III.

THE LOST REGIMENT.

A LOVE STORY.

I HAVE been told that a better or a braver fellow than Louis Charters of ours never drew a sword. He was, as the regimental records show, captain of our 7th company, and major in the army when the corps embarked for service in the *Illinois* in 1763; but prior to that his story was a strange and romantic one. Louis was a cadet of one of the oldest houses in Scotland, the Charters of Amisfield; thus he was a lineal descendant of the famous Red Riever. Early in life he had been gazetted to an ensigncy in Montgomery's Highlanders, the *old* 77th, when that corps was raised in 1757 by Colonel Archibald Montgomery (afterwards Earl of Eglinton and Governor of Dumbarton), among the Frasers, Macdonalds, Camerons, Macleans, and other Jacobite clans.

Charters was a handsome and enthusiastic soldier, full of the old chivalry and romance of the Highlands; but, at the time he joined the Black Watch, with the remnant of Montgomery's regiment, which volunteered into our ranks in 1763, he was a pale, moody, and disappointed man, who had no hope in the service, but that it might procure him an honourable death under the balls of an enemy.

The story of Louis Charters was as follows :—

In January, 1757, he was recruiting at Perth for
the 77th, when it was his good, or perhaps ill fortune,
to become attached to a young lady possessed of great
attractions, whom he had met at a ball, and who was
the only daughter of the Laird of Tullynairn, a
gentleman of property in the vicinity of the " Fair
City."

Emmy Stuart was four-and-twenty, and Louis was
three years her senior.   She was tall and beautiful in
face and figure ; her hair was chesnut, her eyes hazel,
and there was a charming droop in their lids which
enhanced all her varieties of expression, especially the
droll, and lent to them a seductive beauty, most dangerous to the peace of all who engaged in a two-
handed flirtation with her ; for although that word was
unknown to the fair maids of Perth in those days, yet
they flirted nevertheless, and none more than the
lively Emmy Stuart.

Though her charming figure was almost hidden by
her frightful hoop petticoat, and her beautiful hair by
white powder—but that, if possible, increased the
brilliance of her eyes and complexion—none knew
better than Emmy the piquant mode of arranging her
capuchin, of holding a vinaigrette under her pretty
pink nostrils; and your great-grandmother, my good
reader, never surpassed her in the secret art of putting
those devilish little patches on her soft cheek, or about
her bright roguish eyes, in such a manner as to give
double point to those glances of drollery or disdain in
which all ladies then excelled ; or, worse still, an
amorous languish, levelled à la Francaise, in such a
mode as would have demolished a whole battalion ;
while the adorable *embonpoint* of her figure was
somewhat increased by the arrangement of her busk,
her jewelled necklace, her embossed gold watch and

étui, which no lady was ever without, and which Emmy of course carried at her waist.

When she left the assembly, there was always such a crush of gay gallants about the door to see her depart, that Louis seldom got her safely into her sedan or coach without swords being drawn, and some unfortunate being run through the body, or having a few inches of a flaming link thrust down his throat ; for the " fine fellows " of those days were not over-particular in their mode of resentment when a pretty woman was concerned. The " Blood," or " Buck," or " Maccaroni," of the last century was a very different fellow from the peaceful unmitigated " snob " of the present day.

It was no wonder that Louis loved Emmy ; the only marvel would have been had he proved invulnerable ; so he fell before a glance of her bright hazel eyes, as Dunkirk fell before the allied armies. But Emmy was so gay in manner, distinguishing none in particular, that Charters was often in an agony of anxiety to learn whether she would ever love him ; and moreover, there was one of ours, a Captain Douglas, recruiting in Perth, who possessed a most annoyingly handsome person, and who hovered more about the beautiful Emmy than our friend of the 77th could have wished. To make the matter worse, Douglas was an old lover, having met Emmy at a ball three years before, and been shot clean through the heart by one of her most seductive glances.

Emmy was so full of repartee and drollery, that though Charters was always making the most desperate love to her, he was compelled to mask his approaches under cover of pretty banter, or mere flirtation ; thus leaving him an honourable retreat in case of a sharp repulse ; for he could not yet trust himself to opening the trenches in earnest, lest she might laugh at him, as she had done at others; and Louis knew enough of the world to be aware, that a lover once laughed at *is lost*, and may as well quit the field.

So passed away the summer of—I am sorry to give so antique an epoch—1757. The snow began to powder the bare scalps of the Highland frontier; the woods of Scone and Kinnoull became stripped and leafless, and their russet spoils where whirled along the green inches and the reedy banks of the Tay; then the hoar frost wove its thistle blades on the windows in the morning, and our lovers found that a period was put to their rambles in the evening, when the sun was setting behind the darkening mountains of the west.

Now came the time to ballot for partners for the winter season; and then it was that Louis first learned to his joy that he was not altogether indifferent to the laughing belle. The fashion of balloting for partners was a very curious one, and now it is happily abolished in Scottish society; for only imagine one's sensations, good reader, on being condemned to dance everything with the same girl, and with her only, during a whole winter season! Besides, as the devil would be sure to have it so, one would always have the girl one did not want. The laws respecting partners were strictly enforced, and when once settled or fairly handfasted to a dancing girl for the season, a gentleman was on no account permitted to change, even for a single night, on pain of being shot or run through the body by her nearest male relative.

In the beginning of the winter season, the appointment for partners usually took place in each little coterie before the opening of the first ball or assembly. A gentleman's triple-cocked beaver was unflapped, and the fans of all the ladies present were slily put therein; the gentlemen were then blindfolded, and each selected a fan; then·she to whom it belonged, however ill they might be paired or assorted, was his partner for the season. Such was the strange law, most rigidly enforced in the days of Miss Nicholas, who was then the mirror of fashion and presiding goddess of the Edinburgh assemblies.

When the time for balloting came, great was the anxiety of poor Louis Charters lest his beloved Emmy might fall to the lot of that provoking fellow Douglas of ours; but judge of his joy when Emmy told him, with the most arch and beautiful smile that ever lighted up a pair of lovely hazel eyes, how to distinguish *her fan* from amid the eighteen or twenty that were deposited in the hat.

"Now, my dear Mr. Charters," said she in a whisper, "I never pretended to be ferociously honest, and thus my unfortunate little tongue is always getting me into some frightful scrape; but I shall give you a token by which you will know *my* fan. Does that make you supremely happy?"

"Happy, Emmy? Dear Emmy, more than ever you will give mo credit for!"

"Do not be sure of that, and do not make a scene. Quick now, lest some one anticipate you."

"But the fan——"

"Has a silver ball in lieu of a tassel. Now go and prosper."

Thus indicated, he soon selected the fan and drew it forth, to the annoyance of Douglas, who beheld him present it to the fair owner; and her hazel eye sparkled with joy as Charters kissed her hand with a matchless air of ardour and respect. Honest Charters felt quite tipsy with joy. Emmy had now shown

that he was *not* without interest to her; and was not
this a charming admission from a young beauty, who
could command any number of wedding-rings at any
hour she pleased?   Thus, according to the witty Sir
Alexander Boswell, who (for one of his squibs) was
shot one morning by Stuart of Dunearn,

> " Each lady's fan a chosen Damon bore,
> With care selected many a day before."

With the dancing of a whole season before them,
the reader may easily imagine the result. All the
tabbies, gossips, and coteries of the fair city had long
since assigned them to each other; and though the
mere magic of linking two names constantly together
has done much to cajole boys and girls into a love for
each other, no such magic was required here, for
Emmy, I have said, was four-and-twenty, and Louis
was three years her senior.

Finding himself completely outwitted, and that the
fan of a demoiselle of somewhat mature age and
rather unattractive appearance had fallen to his lot,
Willy Douglas " evacuated Flanders," *i.e.*, forsook the
ballroom, and bent all his energies to recruiting for
the second battalion of the Black Watch, leaving the
fair field completely to his more successful rival.

But though assigned to Charters by the fashion of
the time, and by her own pretty manœuvre, as a
partner for the season, our gay coquette would not
yet acknowledge herself conquered ; and Charters felt
with some anxiety that she was amusing herself with
him, and that the time was drawing near when he
would have to rejoin his regiment, which was then
expecting the route for America, over the fortunes of
which the clouds of war were gathering. Besides,
Emmy had a thousand little whims and teasing ways

about her, all of which it was his daily pleasure, and sometimes his task, to gratify and to soothe; and often they had a quarrel—a real quarrel—for two whole days. These were two centuries to Louis; but then it was of course made up again; and Emmy, like an Empress, gave him her dimpled hand to kiss, reminding him, with a coy smile, that

"A lover's quarrel was but love renewed."

"True, Emmy; but I would infinitely prefer a love that required no renewal," said Charters, with a sigh.

"How tiresome you become! You often make me think of Willy Douglas. Well, and where shall we find this remarkable love you speak of?"

"Ah, Emmy, you read it in every eye that turns to yours; it fills the very air you breathe, and sheds a purity and a beauty over everything."

"Then you always see beauty here?"

"Oh, Emmy, I always see *you*, and you only; but you are still bantering."

"Do you know, Captain Charters, that I do not think it polite to tell a woman that she is beautiful?" said Emmy, pretending to pout, while her eyelids drooped, and she played with her fan.

"To tell any ordinary woman that she was beautiful, might offend her, if she was sensible; but to tell you so, though you have the sense of a thousand, must be pleasing, because you are conscious of your great beauty, Emmy, and know its fatal power—but alas! too well."

"What!" exclaimed Emmy, her eyes flashing with triumph and fun, "I am beautiful, then?"

"Too much so for my peace. Beautiful! Oh, Emmy Stuart, you are dangerously so. But you trifle with me cruelly, Emmy. Think how time is

gliding away—and a day must come when I shall bo
no longer here."

Her charming eyelids drooped again,

"A time—well, but remember there is an Italian
poet who says,

> All time is lost that is not spent in love."

Charters gazed at her anxiously, and after a mo-
mentary pause, with all his soul in his eyes and on
his tongue, he said :—

"Listen to me, dearest Emmy. Of all things necessary to conduce to man's happiness, love is tho
principal. It purifies and sheds a glory, a halo over
everything, but chiefly around the beloved object
herself. It awakens and matures every slumbering
virtue in the heart, and causes us to become as pure
and noble as a man may be, to make him more worthy
of the woman we love. Such, dear Emmy, is my
love for you."

This time Emmy heard him in silence, with downcast eyes, a blush playing upon her beautiful cheek,
a smile hovering on her alluring little mouth, with
her breast heaving and her pretty fingers playing
nervously with her fan and the frills of her busk.

This conversation may be taken as a specimen of a
hundred that our lovers had on every convenient
opportunity, when Louis was all truthful earnestness
—devotion and anxiety pervading his voice and manner; while Emmy was all fun, drollery, and coquetry,
yet loving him nevertheless.

But a crisis came, when Charters received, by the
hand of his chief friend, Lieutenant Alaster Mackenzie, of the house of Seaforth, a command to rejoin his
regiment, then under orders to embark at Greenock,
to share in the expedition which Brigadier-General

Forbes of Pittencrief was to lead against Fort du Quesne, one of the three great enterprises undertaken in 1758 against the French possessions in North America. How futile were the tears of Emmy now!

"Though divided by the sea, dear Louis, our hope will be one, like our love," she sobbed in his ear.

"Think—think of me often, very often, as I shall think of you."

"I do not doubt you, Louis. I now judge of your long, faithful, and noble affection by my own. Oh, Louis! I have been foolish and wilful; I have pained you often; but you will forgive your poor Emmy now; she judges of your love by her own."

It was now too late to think of marriage. Emmy, subdued by the prospect of a sudden and long separation from her winning and handsome lover, and by a knowledge of the dangers that lay before him by sea and land, the French bullet, the Indian arrow— all the risks of war and pestilence—was almost broken-hearted on his departure. The usual rings and locks of hair, the customary embraces, were exchanged; the usual adieus and promises—solemn and sobbing promises of mutual fidelity—were given, and so they parted; and with sad Emmy's kiss yet lingering on his lips, and her undried tears on his cheek, poor Charters found himself marching at the head of his party of fifty recruits, while the drum and fife woke the echoes in the romantic Wicks of Baiglie, as he bade a long adieu to beautiful Perth, the home of his Emmy, and joined the headquarters of Montgomery's Highlanders at Greenock.

But amid all the bustle of the embarkation in transports and ships of war—such rough sea-going ships as Smollet has portrayed in his " Roderick Random "—Charters saw ever before him the happy,

bright, and beautiful Emmy of the past year of joy ;
or as he had last seen her, pale, crushed, and drooping in tears upon his breast—her coquetry, her drollery, her laughter, all evaporated, and the true loving
and trusting woman alone remaining—her eyes full
of affection, and her voice tremulous with emotion.

Louis sailed for America with one of the finest regiments ever sent forth by Scotland, which, in the war that
preceded the declaration of American independence,
gave to the British ranks more than sixty thousand
soldiers*—few, indeed, of whom ever returned to lay
their bones in the land of their fathers.

Montgomery's Highlanders consisted of thirteen
companies, making a total of 1460 men, including 65
sergeants who were armed with Lochaber axes, and
30 pipers armed with target and claymore.

Once more among his comrades, the spirit of Charters rose again ; a hundred kindly old regimental sympathies were awakened in his breast, and, though the keen
regret of his recent parting was fresh in his memory,
yet in the conversation of Alaster Mackenzie (who
shared his confidence), and in his military duty, he found
a relief from bitterness—a refuge which was denied to
poor Emmy, who was left to the solitude of her own
thoughts and the bitter solace of her own tears, amid
those familiar scenes which only conduced to add

---

* See " Present Conduct of the Chieftains Considered."
Edinburgh : 1773. " Thus it appears," says an anti-ministerial
pamphlet, published in 1763, " that out of 756 officers *commanding* in the Army, garrisons, &c., 210 are Scots : and out of
1930 in the Navy, 536 are Scots." The table was thus :—

Scots Generals	29			Scots Admirals	7	
„ Colonels	39	Army.		„ Captains	81	Navy.
„ Lieut.-Colonels	81			„ Masters	33	
„ Majors	61			„ Lieutenants	271	
				„ Surgeons	144	

poignancy to her grief, and served hourly to recal some memory of the absent, and those hours of love and pleasure that had fled, perhaps never to return.

Meanwhile, Charters had not a thought or hope, desire or aim, but to do his duty nobly in the field, to obtain promotion, and to return to wed Emmy. A year—two years—yea, even three, though an eternity to a lover, would soon pass amid the bustle and excitement of war and of foreign service. Three years at most, then, would find him again at the side of Emmy, hand in hand as of old. But, alas! as poor Robert Burns says pithily—

> "The best-laid schemes of mice and men
> Gang aft ajee."

Though our lovers had resolved that nothing should exceed the regularity of their correspondence, and that the largest sheets of foolscap should be duly filled with all they could wish each other to say, in those days when regular mails, steamers, telegraphs, and penny postage were yet concealed in Time's capacious wallet, neither Emmy nor Charters had quite calculated upon the devious routes or the strange and wild districts into which the troops were to penetrate, or the chances of the Western war, with all its alternate glories and disasters.

After a lapse of two long and weary months, by a sailing vessel poor Emmy received a letter from Louis, and, in the hushed silence of her own apartment, the humbled coquette wept over every word of it—and read it again and again—for it seemed to come like the beloved voice of the writer from a vast distance and from that land of danger. Then when she looked at the date and saw that it was a month—a whole

F

month—ago, and when she thought of the new terrors each day brought forth, she trembled and her
heart grew sick ; then a paroxysm of tears was her
only relief, for she was a creature of a nervous and
highly excitable temperament.

It described the long and dreary voyage to America
in the crowded and comfortless transport—one thought
ever in his soul—the thought of her ; one scene ever
around him—sea and sky.   It detailed the hurried
disembarkation and forced march of General Forbes's
little army of 6200 soldiers from Philadelphia in the
beginning of July, through a vast tract of country,
little known to civilized men ; all but impenetrable
or impassable, as the roads were mere war paths, that
lay through dense untrodden forests or deep morasses
and over lofty mountains, where wild, active, and
ferocious Indians, by musket, tomahawk, scalping-
knife, and poisoned arrow, co-operated with the
French in harassing our troops at every rood of the
way.   He told how many of the strongest and
healthiest of Montgomery's Highlanders perished
amid the toils and horrors they encountered ; but
how still *he* bore up, animated by the memory of her,
by that love which was a second life to him, and by
the darling hope that, with God's help, he would survive the campaign and all its miseries, and would find
himself again, as of old, seated by the side of his beloved Emmy, with her cheek on his shoulder and her
dear little hand clasped in his.   He sent her some
Indian beads, a few forget-me-nots that grew amid
the grass within his tent ; he sent her another lock
of his hair, and prayed kind God to bless for the
sake of the poor absent heart that loved her so
well.

And here ended this sorrowful letter, which was

dated from the camp of the Scottish Brigadier, who halted at Raystown, ninety miles on the march from Fort du Quesne. Thus, by the time Emmy received it, the fort must have been attacked and lost or won.

"Attacked!"—How breathlessly and with what protracted agony did she long for intelligence—for another letter or for the War-office lists! But days, weeks, months rolled on; the snow descended on the Highland mountains; the woods of Kinnoull were again leafless; again the broad Inches of Perth wore the white mantle of winter; the Tay was frozen hard as flint between its banks and between the piers of the old wooden bridge; there now came no mails from America; no letter reached her; and poor Emmy, though surrounded by admirers as of old, felt all the misery of that deferred hope which "maketh the heart sick."

Meanwhile Louis, at the head of his company of Montgomery's Highlanders, accompanied the force of Brigadier Forbes, who, in September, despatched from Raystown Colonel Bouquet to a place called Loyal Henning, to reconnoitre the approach to Fort du Quesne. The colonel's force consisted of 2000 men; of these he despatched in advance 500 Provincials and 400 of Montgomery's regiment, under Major James Grant of Ballindalloch, whose second in command was Captain Charters. Despite the advice of the latter, Grant, a brave but reckless and imprudent officer, advanced boldly towards Fort du Quesne with all his pipes playing and drums beating, as if he was approaching a friendly town. Now the French officer who commanded in the fort was a determined fellow. He it was who had behaved with such heroism at the recent siege of Savannah, where he had been sergeant-

F 2

major of Dillon's Regiment of the Irish Brigade in
the service of King Louis. When the Comte d'Estaing
madly proposed to take the fortress by a *coup-de-
main*, M. le Comte Dillon, anxious to signalize his
Irishmen, proposed a reward of a hundred guineas to
the first grenadier who should plant a fascine in the
fosse, which was swept by the whole fire of the garrison ; but his purse was proffered in vain, for not an
Irishman would advance. Confounded by this, Dillon
was upbraiding them with cowardice, when the ser-
geant-major said—

"Monsieur le Comte, had you not held out a sum
of money as an incentive, your grenadiers would one
and all have rushed to the assault !"

The count put his purse in his pocket.

"Forward !" cried he—forward went the Irish
grenadiers, and out of 194 who composed the company, 104 left their bodies in the breach.

But to resume : the moment the soldiers of Grant
were within range, the French cannon opened upon
them, and under cover of this fire, the infantry made
a furious sortie.

"Sling your muskets ! Dirk and claymore !" cried
the major as the foe came on. A terrible conflict
ensued, the Highlanders fighting with their swords
and daggers, and the Provincials with their fixed
bayonets ; the French gave way, but, unable to reach
the fort, they dispersed and sought shelter in the vast
forest which spread in every direction round it. Here
they were joined by a strong body of Indians, and
returning, from amid the leafy jungles and dense
foliage they opened a murderous fire upon Major
Grant's detachment, which had halted to refresh,
when suddenly summoned to arms.

A yell pierced the sky ! It was the Indian warwhoop, startling the green leaves of that lone American forest, and waking the echoes of the distant hills that overlook the plain of the Alleghany; thousands of Red Indian warriors, horrible in their native ugliness, their streaky war paint, jangling mocassins and tufted feathers, naked and muscular, savage as tigers and supple as eels, with their barbed spears, scalping-knives, tomahawks, and French muskets, burst like a living flood upon the soldiers of Ballindalloch. The Provincials immediately endeavoured to form square, but were broken, brained, scalped, and trod under foot, as if a brigade of horse had swept over them. While, in the old fashion of their native land, the undaunted 77th men endeavoured to meet the foe, foot to foot and hand to hand, with the broadsword, but in vain. Grant ordered them to throw aside their knapsacks, plaids, and coats, and betake themselves to the claymore, and the claymore only. For three hours a desultory and disastrous combat was maintained—every stump and tree, every bush, rock, and stone being battled for with deadly energy and all the horrors of Indian warfare—yells, whoops, the tomahawk and the knife—were added to those of Europe, and before the remnant of our Highlanders effected an escape, Captains MacDonald and Munro, Lieutenants Alaster, William and Robert Mackenzie, and Colin Campbell, were killed and scalped, with many of their men. Ensign Alaster Grant lost a hand by a poisoned arrow; but of all who fell, Charters most deeply regretted Alaster Mackenzie, his friend and confidant, to save whom, after a shot had pierced his breast, he made a desperate effort and slew three Indians by three consecutive blows; but this succour came too late, and Mackenzie's scalp was torn off before he breathed his last. .

"Stand by your colours, comrades, till death!"
were his last words. "Farewell, dear Charters—may
God protect you for your Emmy's sake—we'll meet
again!"

"Again!"

"Yes—again—in heaven!" he answered, and expired with his sword in his hand, like a brave and
pious soldier.

The Red men were like incarnate fiends, and, amid
groans, yells, prayers, and entreaties, were seen on
their knees in frenzy, drinking blood from the spout-
ing veins and bleeding scalps of their victims. The
combat was a mere massacre, and seemed as if all hell
had burst its gates and held jubilee in that wild forest
of the savage West. The Provincials were destroyed.
Grant, with nineteen officers, fell into the hands of
the French; and of his Highlanders only 150 succeeded in effecting a retreat to Loyal Henning, under
the command of Louis Charters, to whose skill,
bravery, and energy, they unanimously attributed
their escape. Many of their comrades who were captured died under agonies such as Indians, Turks, or
devils alone could have devised; and the story of one
—Private Allan MacPherson—who escaped a cruel
death by pretending that his *neck* was sword-proof, as
related by the Abbé Reynal, and General Stewart of
Garth, is well known.

James Grant of Ballindalloch died a general in the
army in 1806; but he never forgot the horrors of his
rashness at Fort du Quesne, which was abandoned to
Brigadier Forbes on the 24th November; by this he
was deprived of a revenge, and to win it Charters had
volunteered to lead the forlorn-hope. Poor General
Forbes died on the retreat.

Charters's regiment served next in General Amherst's army at Ticonderoga, at Crown Point, and on the Lake Expedition, where he saved the life of Ensign Grant—now known as Alaster the One-handed —by bearing him off the field when wounded; but during all those desultory and sanguinary operations, he never heard from Emmy, nor did she hear from him. He suffered much; he nearly perished in the snow on one occasion with a whole detachment; he was wounded in the left shoulder on that night of horrors at Ticonderoga, and had a narrow escape from a cannon-ball in the fight with a French ship, when proceeding on the expedition to Dominique under Lord Rollo and Sir James Douglas; but though the ball spared his head, the *wind* of it raised a large inflamed spot, which gave him great trouble and pain. He was with his corps at the conquest of the Havannah; he was at the capture of Newfoundland with the 45th and the Highlanders of Fraser, and he served with honour in a hundred minor achievements of the brave Highlanders of Montgomery.

Renewed or recruited thrice from the Highland clans, the old 77th covered themselves with glory, and of all the Scottish corps in the King's service, there was none from which the soldiers more nobly and rigidly transmitted to their aged parents in Scotland the savings of their poor pay or the prize money gained by their blood in the Havannah. In one of his (unanswered) letters to Emmy Stuart, Louis says, " I have known some of our poor fellows, my dear girl, who almost starved themselves for this purpose."

One of the majors being killed at the storming of the Moro, his widow, in consideration of his great services, was permitted to sell his commission. Louis was now senior captain, and the regiment knew well that he, having only his pay, was unable to purchase it: but so greatly was he beloved by the soldiers, many of whom, in America, had thrown themselves before the sharp tomahawks and poisoned arrows of the Indians to save him, that they subscribed each Highlander so many days' pay to purchase his majority; and the plunder of the rich Havannah having put these brave souls in good funds, the money was all fairly laid on the drum-head in one hour, when the corps was on evening parade in the citadel of El Fuerte.

Such a noble instance of *camaraderie* and true soldierly sentiment never occurred in the British service but once before; and then it was also in an old Scottish regiment which had served, I believe, in the wars of Queen Anne, before the amalgamation of the forces of the two kingdoms.*

This was the most noble tribute his soldiers could pay to Charters, who was duly gazetted when the regiment was stationed at New York in the summer of 1763, to enjoy a little repose after the toils of the past war.

The services and adventures so briefly glanced at here, had thus spread over a period of five years—to Louis, long and weary years—during which he had never heard of Emmy but once; and now he had no relic of her to remind him of those delightful days of peace and love that had fled apparently for ever. The ring she had given him, warm from her pretty hand, had been torn from his finger by plunderers as he lay wounded and helpless on the ramparts of Fort Loudon, on the confines of far Virginia; her fan was lost when his baggage was taken on the retreat from Fort du Quesne; the locket with her hair had been

* See "Advice to Officers." Perth, 1795.

rent from him, when he was taken prisoner and stripped by the French, in the attack on Martinique. He was changed in appearance too; his hair once black as night was already seamed by many a silvery thread, yet he was only two-and-thirty. His face was gaunt and wan, and bronzed by the Indian sun and keen American frost. His eyes, like the eyes of all inured to facing death and danger, pestilence and the bullet, were fierce at times, and keen and haggard; and when tidings came, or it was mooted at mess, that the war-worn regiment of Montgomery was once again to see the Scottish shore, poor Louis looked wistfully into his glass, and doubted whether Emmy would know him; for between the French and the Cherokees he had acquired somewhat the aspect of a brigand.

Peace was proclaimed at last, and the Government made an offer to the regiment, that such officers and men as might choose to settle in America should have grants of land proportioned to their rank and services. The rest might return to Scotland or volunteer into other corps. A few remained among the colonists, and on the revolt of America in 1775, were the *first men* to join the standard of George III., who ordered them to be embodied as the 84th or Royal Regiment of Highland Emigrants. The rest— most of whom volunteered to join the Black Watch —with the band, pipes, and colours, under Louis Charters, embarked at New York, and, full of hope and joy, with three hearty cheers, as their ship cleft the waters of the Hudson and bore through the Narrows, saw the future capital of the western world sink in the distance and disappear astern.

Five years! . . . . .

"Emmy must now be nearly nine-and-twenty!"

thought Louis; "in a month from this time I shall
see her—shall hear her voice—shall be beside her
again, assuring her that I am the same Louis Charters of other days."

But month after month passed away, and six
elapsed after the sailing of the transport from New
York had been duly notified by the London and the
Edinburgh Gazettes, and yet no tidings reached
Britain of the missing regiment of Montgomery.

During all these five long years—those sixty months
—those one thousand eight hundred and twenty-five
days, every one of which had been counted by poor
Louis—how fared it with the beautiful Emmy Stuart,
who was still the belle of the fair city?

So far as the defective newspapers of those days,
when Edinburgh had only *three* (and those of London
seldom came north), supplied intelligence, she had
traced the operations of Montgomery's Highlanders
in the Canadas, the States, on the Lakes, and in the
West Indies, in the despatches of Brigadier Forbes,
of Colonel Bouquet, Lord Rollo, and others; she had
frequently seen the name of her lover mentioned, as
having distinguished himself, and twice as having
been left wounded on the field. I need not dwell on
her days and nights of sickening sorrow and suspense,
which no friendship could alleviate.

Save once, no letter from Louis had ever reached
her; yet poor Louis had written many: from among
frozen camps and· bloody fields—from wet bivouacs,
and places such as Emmy's gentle mind could never
conceive—had he written to ·her the outpourings of
his heart, believing that in due time Emmy would be
gazing fondly on the words his hand had traced, and
endeavouring to conjure up the tones in which he
would have said all that distance and separation com-

pelled him to commit to paper; but, by a strange
fatality, these letters never reached her; yet Emmy,
the belle, the coquette, remained true, for she knew
the chances of war; and that, until the regiment returned home and he proved false, she could not desert
her lover.

But Willy Douglas of the Black Watch, who had
been all this time comfortably recruiting about Perth
and Dunkeld (thanks to his uncle, the Duke of
Douglas), was wont to remind her that the 40th
Regiment had been more than *forty* years abroad,*
and the battalion of Montgomery might be quite as
long away.

After three years had passed without letters arriving, Emmy still mourned and loved Louis more than
ever; while well-meaning friends, who never thought
of consulting the army list, assured her that he was
killed; but it availed them nought.

Then five years elapsed, and in all that time there
came no letter; yet, when taunted that Louis had
forgotten her, she replied as Cleopatra did to Alexis
when he advised her to deem her lover cruel, incon-
stant, and ungrateful :—

> " I cannot, if I could ; these thoughts were vain ;
> Faithless, ungrateful, cruel if he be,
> I still must love him !"

But time changes all things. A pleasing and sad
recollection was now beginning to replace her lively
affection for Charters. Tired of worshipping one
who had become little more than a beautiful statue,
her admirers had disappeared gradually, till the
assiduous Douglas alone remained in the position

* Fact in 1764.

of a tacit and privileged dangler. Willy was an
honest-hearted fellow, and with his real love for
Emmy there was mingled much of pity for what she
suffered on account of his " devilish neglectful rival,"
as he termed Charters. Emmy had long been insensible to his addresses ; but as Douglas, who was very
prepossessing, was the nephew of the last Duke of
Douglas, and had a handsome fortune, her father
frequently, earnestly, and affectionately urged her to
accept his proposals ; while her mother reminded her
that she was past eight-and-twenty now ; and added,
that in a new and more fortunate attachment—in
the love that is supposed to follow marriage—she
would forget the sorrows of the past. But Emmy,
though knowing that this was all mere sophistry, was
about to give a silent acquiescence to their schemes,
when, turning over the leaves of an old periodical,
one day, in a dreamy and listless mood, her eye fell
on the following :—

" A union of fortunes, *not* a union of hearts, is the
thing generally aimed at in marriage, and, by those
who esteem themselves *prudent* people, is thought
the only rational view. There is no divine ordinance
more *frequently disobeyed than that wherein God
forbids human sacrifices, for in no other light can
most modern marriages be viewed. Brazen images,
indeed, are not the objects of their worship ; a purer
metal is their deity. Every one who reads in ancient
history of human sacrifices, exclaims against the
horrid practice and trembles at the narrative, though
there is scarcely one of the female readers, if she is of
a marriageable age, who is not ready to deck her
person, like an adorned victim, in the hope of
tempting some *golden idol* to receive a free-will
offering."

Emmy thought of Douglas's fortune, and the book fell from her hand.

" No, no," she said with a shudder ; " I shall not be the adorned victim offered up to this golden idol ;" and from that hour she resolved to decline his addresses.

On the day succeeding this brave resolution came tidings "that the remnant of Montgomery's Highlanders, under the command of Major Louis Charters, had sailed from New York six weeks ago, and were daily expected at Greenock, from whence that gallant corps had sailed for the wars of the Far West in 1758."

Now came Emmy's hour of triumph, and already Louis seemed before her, loving, trusting, and true ; and hourly she expected to have, in his own handwriting, assurance of all her heart desired ; but, alas ! time rolled on—days became weeks—weeks became months, and no tidings reached Britain of the Highlanders of Montgomery.

"The lost regiment" was spoken of from time to time, till even friends, comrades, and relations grew tired of futile surmises, and their unaccountable disappearance became like a tale that is told—or a fragment of old and forgotten intelligence.

For a time a sickening and painful suspense had been kept alive by occasional reports of pieces of wreck, with red coats and tartan fluttering about them, having been espied in the Atlantic ; vessels waterlogged and abandoned were passed by solitary ships, and averred to be the missing transport ; craft answering her description had been seen to founder in tempests off the banks of Newfoundland ; but after eight months had elapsed nothing was heard of what was emphatically called *the lost regiment.*

Emmy mourned now for Louis as for one who was dead—one who, after all his toil and valour, suffering and constancy (she felt assured.he had been constant), was sleeping in the great ocean that had divided them so long.

Tired of all this, her friends had arrayed her in mourning as for one who was really dead; and to carry out a plan of realizing this conviction, her father had erected in the church of St. John a hand-some marble tablet to the memory of Charters; and this cold white slab *in memoriam* met Emmy's heavy eyes every time she raised them from her prayer-book on Sunday. So at last.Louis was dead —she felt convinced of it, and, with a reluctant and foreboding mind, she consented to a marriage with Captain Douglas of the Black Watch—a consent in which she had but one thought, that in making this terrible sacrifice she was only seeking to soothe the anxiety and gratify the solicitations of her mother, who was now well up in the vale of years, and who loved her tenderly.

Emmy was placid and content; but though even cheerful in appearance, she was not happy; for her cheek was ever pale and her soft hazel eyes, with their half-drooping lids, failed to veil a restlessness that seemed to search for something vague and unde-fined.

They were married. We will pass over the appear-ance of the bride, her pale beauty, her rich lace, the splendour of all the accessories by which the wealth of her father, of her husband, and the solicitude of her kind friends surrounded her, and come to *the crisis* in our story—a crisis in which a lamentable fatality seemed to rule the destinies of the chief actors in our little drama.

The minister of St. John's Church had just pronounced the nuptial blessing, and the pale bride was in her mother's arms, while the officers of the Black Watch were crowding round Douglas with their hearty congratulations; a buzz of voices had filled the large withdrawing room, as a hum of gladness succeeded the solemn but impressive monotony of the marriage service, when the sharp rattle of drums and the shrill sound of the fifes ringing in the Southgate of Perth struck upon their ears, and the measured march of feet, mingling with the rising huzzahs of the people, woke the echoes of every close and wynd.

A foreboding smote the heart of Captain Douglas. He sprang to a window and saw the gleam of arms— the glitter of bayonets and Lochaber axes, with the waving of plumed bonnets above the heads of a crowd which poured along the sunny vista of the Southgate; and, as the troops passed, led by a mounted officer whose left arm was in a sling—a bronzed, warworn, and weatherbeaten band—their tartans were recognised as well as the tattered colours which streamed in ribbons on the wind, and their name went from mouth to mouth :—

"The Lost Regiment—the Highlanders of Montgomery!"

A low cry burst from Emmy; she threw up her clasped hands, and sank in a dead faint at her mother's feet. All was consternation in the house of Stuart of Tullynairn; and the marriage guests gazed at the passing soldiers, as at some fascinating but unreal pageant—but on they marched, cheering, to the barracks, with drums beating and pipes playing; and now the mounted officer, who had been gazing wistfully at the crowded windows, stoops from his saddle and whispers a few words to another—Alaster the

One-handed, now a captain—then he turns his horse, and, dismounting at the door, is heard to ascend the stair ; and in another moment, Louis Charters, sallow, thin, and hollow-eyed, by long toil and suffering, his left arm in a sling and his right cheek scarred by a shot, stands amid all these gaily-attired guests in his fighting jacket, the scarlet of which had long since become threadbare and purple.

He immediately approached Emmy, who had now partially recovered and gazed at him, as one might gaze at a spectre, when Douglas threw himself forward with a hand on his sword.

" What is the meaning of all this ?" said Louis, who grew ashy pale, and whose voice sank into Emmy's soul ; " have you all forgotten me—Louis Charters of Montgomery's Regiment ?"

" No," replied Douglas, " but your presence here at such a time is most unfeeling and inopportune."

" Unfeeling and inopportune—I—Miss Stuart—Emmy—"

" Miss Stuart has just been made my wedded wife ; thus any remarks you have to make, sir, you will please address to *me*."

Louis started as if a scorpion had stung him, and his trembling hand sought the hilt of his sword ; here the old minister addressed him kindly, imploringly, and the guests crowded between them, but he dashed them all aside and turned from the house, without a word or glance from Emmy.   Poor Emmy ! dismay had frozen her, and mute despair glared in her haggard yet still beautiful eyes.

" Half an hour earlier and I had saved her and saved myself !" exclaimed Charters, bitterly ; " the half-hour I loitered in Strathearn !" for he had halted there to refresh his weary soldiers.

And now to explain this sudden reappearance.

Tempest-tossed and under jurymasts, after long beating against adverse winds, the transport; with the remnant of his regiment, had been driven to 37 and 40 degrees of north latitude, and was stranded on the small isles of Corvo and Flores, two of the most western and detached of the Azores. There they had been lingering among the Portuguese for seven months, unknown to and unheard of by our Government; and it was not until Charters, leaving Alaster Grant in command at Corvo, had visited Angra, the capital of the island, and urged the necessity of having his soldiers transmitted home, that he procured a ship at Ponta del Gada, the largest town of these islands, and sailing with the still reduced remnant of his corps—for many had perished with the foundered transport—he landed at Greenock, from whence he was ordered at once to join the 2nd battalion of the Black Watch, into which his soldiers had volunteered, and which, by a strange fatality, was quartered in Perth—the home of his Emmy, and the place where for five long years he had garnered up his thoughts and dearest hopes.

The reader may imagine the emotions of poor Emmy on finding that her lover lived, and that her heart was thus cruelly wrenched away from all it had treasured and cherished for years. Then, as if to aggravate her sorrow, our battalion marched the next day for foreign service, and Louis again embarked for America, the land of his toil, without relentless fate permitting Emmy to excuse or explain herself.

Douglas left the corps and took his wife to Paris, where he fell in a duel with a Jacobite refugee.

Emmy lived to be a very old woman, but she never smiled again.

G

Thus were two fond hearts separated for ever.

Three months after Louis landed in America, he died of a broken heart say some ; of the marsh fever say others. He was then on the march with a detachment of ours up the Mississippi, a long route of 1500 miles, to take possession of Fort Charters in the Illinois. His friend, a Captain Grant—Alaster the One-handed—performed the last offices for him, and saw him rolled in a blanket, and buried at the foot of a cotton-tree, where the muskets of the Black Watch made the echoes of the vast prairie ring as they poured three farewell volleys over the last home of a brave but lonely heart.

IV.

THE MASSACRE AT FORT WILLIAM HENRY.

When the Black Watch sailed for America, in 1756, to serve under the heroic Wolfe and fight against the Marquis of Montcalm, the lieutenant of the 7th company was Roderick MacGillivray, known in the ranks by his local patronymic, Roderick Ruadh (or the Red) of Glenarrow, a gentleman of the Clan Chattan, who, eleven years before, had been a captain in the army of Prince Charles Edward, and had served throughout the memorable campaign of 1745-6. In his heart Roderick MacGillivray had no love either for the service or sovereign of Britain, whom he considered as the butcher of his countrymen, and the usurper of their crown ; but his estate of Glenarrow had been forfeited ; he was penniless, and having a young wife to maintain, he was glad to accept a commission in the Royal Highlanders—a favour he procured through the interest of one who has already been mentioned in these pages, Louis Charters, who served at Fort du Quesne, as already related in the legend of the " Lost Regiment."

In those days there were many soldiers in the ranks of our regiment who had served in the army of Prince Charles, and who deemed his father, James VIII., the undoubted sovereign of these realms, by that

G 2

hereditary right, which, as their Celtic proverb has it, "will face the rocks," and which they deemed as sacred and immutable as if the breath of God had ordained it. Thus they served George II., *not* because they wavered in their loyalty to their native kings, but because they hated his enemies the French, whom they knew to have betrayed the cause of the clans, and in the hope that a time would yet come when the standard which Tullybardine, the loyal and true, unfurled in Glenfinnan, would again wave over a field in which God would defend the right.

And such thoughts and hopes as these were the theme of many a poor soldier of the Reicudan Dhu, in their tents and bivouacs, on the plains of Flanders, on the Heights of Abraham, and by the vast and then untrodden shores of the American lakes.

Similar thoughts, and the memory of all he had endured at the hands of the victorious party, together with the confiscation of his estate, which had descended to him through twelve generations of martial ancestors, made Roderick MacGillivray a grave and somewhat sombre man. He had fought valiantly in the first line at Culloden, where he was one of the guard, the *Leine Chrios* (*i.e.* Shirt of Mail, or Children of the Belt) around the Laird of Dunmacglas,* who led the MacIntoshes, and who was next day murdered by the English soldiers, when found all but dead of wounds upon the field, where they dashed out his brains by the butts of their muskets as he lay in the arms of his distracted wife.

After that day, MacGillivray became a fugitive and outlaw, but was happy enough to be one of those

* The Fort of the Greyman's Son.

eight brave men who, with MacDonald of Glenala-
dale—the faithful, the gentle, and the true Glenala-
dale—watched, guarded, and tended by night and by
day the unfortunate Prince Charles in the wild
cavern of Coire-gaoth among the beautiful Braes of
Glenmorriston.   There these starving and outlawed
men made a bed of heather for the royal fugitive, and
there he slept and lurked in perfect security, though
thirty thousand pounds were set upon his head by
George II., and though the Saxon drum was heard,
where the flames of rapine were seen rising on the
vast steeps of Corryarrack.

The memory of those stirring days—this com-
panionship with the son of his exiled King, with
Prionse Tearlach Righ nan Ghael, words that were
said and promises made, with all that winning charm
of manner, for which the princes of the House of
Stuart were so remarkable, sank deep in Roderick's
heart ; and there were times when in his soul he
panted for the hour when again the White Rose
would shed its bloom upon the wasted Highland hills,
when the swift vengeance of the loyal would fall on
the faithless clans of the west, and the shrill wild
pibroch of the Clan Chattan would ring in fierce
triumph above the burial mounds at Culloden.

And so he hoped and thought, and watched and
waited, but that new day of battle never came !

His secret aspirations were shared to the full by
his young wife, Mary MacDonald, who was a grand-
daughter of MacViclan, the chieftain of Glencoe, the
terrible Williamite episode in whose history can yet
make the brow of every Highlander darken.   But
Mary was gentle and timid ; she had seen too much
of war and bloodshed, of butchery and terror in her
girlhood, during the time that followed Culloden ; and

though she prayed in her innocent little heart for the restoration of Scotland's exiled kings, it was in peace she would have wished it achieved.

In the ancient fashion of the Highlands, Roderick on the day of their marriage had bestowed on Mary— in addition to the espousal ring—an antique brooch ; one of those old marriage gifts which were usually given on such occasions. It had been worn by many matrons of his house, and thus became invested with many deep and endearing memories : association, old tales of the love, the spirit and virtue of the dead, hallowed the gift, for it had shone on many a soft breast that had long since mouldered in the dust. Being circular, it was the mystic emblem of eternity, and bore the crest of the Clan Gillibhreac—a cat, with the significant motto in the old Gaelic letter—

" Touch not the cat without the glove ;"

and as her own life Mary prized this old bridal brooch, the dearest gift her husband could bestow upon her.

When MacGillivray joined the regiment, Mary was in her twentieth year. She was pale and more than pretty, having that dazzling white skin for which the women of her clan are said to excel all others in Scotland ; but of old the same was said of the Camp-bells and the Drummonds. Her hair was black ; her eyes, deep and quiet, were dark hazel, and her features were unexceptionable. She was neither brilliant nor beautiful, but there was a sweetness and delicacy in her smile and manner that touched and won the hearts of all who knew her. There was a sadness, too, in her air and tone, for the most of her kindred had perished in the Glencoe massacre, or at Culloden. She was thus alone in the world, with none to shield or shelter her but her husband—he who was now beginning a life of war and peril—the savage war and double peril of a campaign in America, a wild and untrodden land of barbarous hordes and mighty forests. She shrank with a terror of the prospect before them, and viewed with dismay the many lesser horrors which surrounded her in a crowded transport of those days.

MacGillivray sailed on board the *Mercury*, the master of which was James Cooke, afterwards the celebrated navigator.

"Twain of heart and of purpose," husband and wife were to each other all in all; and the Celtic soldiers, who knew their story well, said in their own forcible language, that if the bullet of a Frenchman or the arrow of an Indian brought death to Roderick Ruadh, the daughter of MacVicIan would not survive him long.

Each scarcely knew how deep was the love of the other; for the Scots are not a demonstrative people, and the most powerful emotions of the heart are those which they have been taught, perhaps erroneously, to conceal; but of this negative quality we find less in the more impulsive Celt. The ardour of love had now been succeeded by the affection of marriage, and the sincerity of friendship had replaced the glow of passion; but Roderick's enthusiasm in the estimate of perfect excellence by which he judged his own little wife was only equalled by the standard which she had formed for him. To make her happy was to be himself happy, and it was the study of his life to surround her with such comforts as a camp and barrack or transport afforded upon the pay of a lieutenant of the line in the days of George II. "England," says honest *Harry Coverdale*, "expects every man to do his duty, and occasionally recompenses him for it with honourable starvation." And such was indeed a subaltern's pay in 1757.

In their new mode of existence all seclusion was destroyed ; and amid the whirl of a military life, the hurry of embarkation for foreign service, and in the narrow recess allotted to her in the transport, odious by the odour of tar, tobacco, and bilge water, poor Mary sighed for the hum of the summer bee, and for the free, pure breeze that waved the heather bells in Glencoe, or for her husband's once happy home in Glenarrow, roofless and ruined now, as the flames and the devastators of the ducal butcher had left it.

"We have lost all, Mary," said Roderick, bitterly, as one evening she sat on deck, nestled in his plaid, and whispering of these things and of other times ; "all but the name of our fathers have gone to the Campbells of Breadalbane, for they have become the lords of all."

"But a time shall come, Roderick, when these usurpations and another still greater shall end, and then the Clan Donald, the MacGregors, the MacIntyres of Glen O, and the race of MacVicar, like the King, shall enjoy their own again."

"Mhari, laoghe mo chri—Mary, calf of my heart," replied the husband, folding her, with a smile, to his breast ; "but this will never be——"

"Until the *fatal plaid* floats down Loch Fyne," she added, with a smile.

There is a Highland prophecy, that a time is coming when a plaid of many colours shall float down Loch Fyne from the Ara to the Firth of Clyde, and then the eagles from a thousand hills shall assemble, and each take therefrom a piece of his own colour ;

and this is to be the day of general restoration by the Campbells of all of which they have dispossessed the clans of the west. ·

Under Colonel Francis Grant of Grant (afterwards a lieutenant-general) the regiment landed in America, where the peculiar garb of the Highlanders astonished the Indians, who, during the march to Albany, "flocked from all quarters to see these strangers, who they believed were of the same extraction as themselves, and therefore received as brothers;" for the long hunting-shirt of the Indians resembled the kilt, as their moccassins did the gartered hose, their striped blanket the shoulder plaid, and they too had round shields and knives, like the target and dirk of the Celt; hence, according to General Stewart, "the Indians were delighted to see a European regiment in a costume so similar to their own."

At this period our officers wore a narrow gold braiding round their jackets, but all epaulettes and lace had been laid aside to render them less conspicuous to the Canadian riflemen. The sergeants laced their coats with silver, and still carried the terrible *tuagh* or Lochaber axe, the head of which was fitted for hooking, hewing, or spearing an enemy.

After remaining in quarters at Albany for some months, during the winter and spring of 1757, the Black Watch were exercised in bush-fighting and sharpshooting; and amid the dense copsewood or jungle which covered the western margin of the Hudson, on the rugged, stern, and sterile banks of the Mohawk, among woods of stunted pine, dwarf shrubs, and sedge grass, they soon revived the skill they had attained as hardy hunters, deerstalkers, and deadly shots on their native hills; but when they fairly took the field, their ardour and impatience often lured them within the fire of the more wary and cunning Indians who served the Marquis of Montcalm.

So expert, brave, and active did the soldiers of the Black Watch prove themselves in skirmishing, that when, in the beginning of summer, a plan was formed to reduce Louisbourg, and they joined the army destined for that purpose under Major-General Abercrombie, a detachment of fifty chosen men, under the orders of MacGillivray of Glenarrow, departed to reinforce the little garrison in Fort William Henry, on the southern bank of the beautiful Lake George, a sheet of clear water, which is thirty-three miles long and two miles broad, and which, on its northern quarter, near Ticonderoga (that place of fatal memory to the Royal Highlanders), discharges itself into Lake Champlain. It is surrounded by high mountains of the most romantic beauty.

Here, then, lay a garrison of nearly three thousand British soldiers, commanded by Colonel Munro, a veteran Highland officer of great courage and experience, who had for some time successfully protected the frontier of the English colonies, and by his cannon covered the waters of the lake, the double purpose for which the fort had been built. Before the departure of MacGillivray, a serious *malheur* had occurred near this place.

Munro having heard that the French advanced guard, composed of regulars and Indians, had reached Ticonderoga, sent Colonel John Parker, with four hundred soldiers, down the lake in bay-boats to beat up their quarters; but three of his boat crews being captured, his design became known to M. Beauchatel, the officer in command. Parker was lured into an ambush, and the most dreadful scene of massacre and scalping ensued. His detachment was literally cut to pieces, only two officers and seventy privates escaping, of the four hundred who left the garrison of Munro.

It was on a beautiful evening when MacGillivray's party of Highlanders, marching from the mountains that look down on Lake Champlain, came suddenly in view of Lake George. They had their muskets slung, and were encumbered by their knapsacks, havresacks, canteens, and blankets, and the live-long day had toiled to reach the fort ere night fell; for to halt in that woody district, teeming as it was with the savage Iroquois of Montcalm, would have been a measure fraught with danger and death. MacGillivray came in rear of his little band, leading by the bridle a stout pony, on the pad of which his wife was mounted, for she was ever the object of his tenderest solicitude. This pony was a sturdy little nag, but the long march from Albany had somewhat impaired its vigour, and now it was beginning to fail when almost at the end of the journey.

With the detachment of MacGillivray were two of his comrades in the late civil war, Alaster Mac-Gregor, from Glengyle, and Ewen Chisholm, one of the faithful men of Glenmorriston, who guarded the Prince in the Coire-gaoth.

The sun was setting, and his gorgeous disc seemed for a time to linger among clouds of saffron, crimson, and purple, that were piled in glowing masses above the wooded hills, some of which were a thousand feet in height, and surrounded the waters and islets of Lake George—named by the Indians of old the Horican, and by the Pilgrim Fathers the Lake of the Sacrament; for, charmed by the limpid purity of the water and the sylvan beauty of the scenery, it had been selected, especially by the Jesuits, as a place for procuring the element of baptism. But now for the old Indian name had been substituted that of his Majesty George II. ; while, to awe the Mohawks, the Oneidas, the Tuscaroras, and to keep the French in check, Fort William Henry—named after another prince of the House of Brunswick—had been built, as related, upon the southern margin of the lake.

Like all American forts, it was formed with earthen ramparts, covered by rich green turf, and defended by tall stockades of dry white timber.   Within were seen the shingle-covered roofs of the low barrack buildings, tarred and painted black, and all glistening in the sunshine.   Two of the lower bastions were faced with stone and washed by the azure water of Lake George, while a deep fosse secured the fort-on the landward, and dangerous morasses protected its flanks. Beyond lay a cleared space, where the timber of the old primeval forest had been cut down for garrison purposes.   The bayonets of the sentinels flashed like · stars on the green ramparts ever and anon, while some thirty or forty lines of steady horizontal light marked where the setting sun shone on the iron guns that peered through the embrasures, or frowned *en barbette* above the slope of the parapets.

The gaudy Union Jack hung unwaved upon its staff. As evening closed in, masses of vapour ascended from the bosom of the deep blue water, and wreathed like white and golden scarfs about the summits of the mountains, whose tops were mellowed in the distance, and those rocky bluffs that start forward from the wooded slopes, as if to break the harmony of the scenery by a few darker and bolder features.   As the last vestige of the sun sank, and its rays alone remained to play upon the clouds above and the ripples of the Horican below, the boom of the evening gun was heard pealing through the wilderness with a hundred solemn reverberations; and as the flag descended from its staff on the fort, a sound on the soft and ambient air came floating up the mountain-side.

"The drummers are beating the evening *retreat,* Mary," said MacGillivray to his wife, who was looking pale and weary; "in half-an-hour we shall be with old Munro."

"Yonder fort is like some place I have seen before," said she, pressing her husband's hand.

"Aye, Lady Glenarrow," responded Ewen Chisholm, coming close with the easy familiarity of a Highlander—a familiarity that is destitute of all assurance; "you are thinking of Fort George, for there are the same palisades and the same fashion of ramparts washed by the waves of the Moray Firth; but oich! oich! we miss green Ard-na-saor."

"And the Black Isle, and the Chanonry-ness, Ewen," added MacGillivray.

"Yes, yes," said Mary, thoughtfully, to the soldiers in their own language; "the land is beautiful; but it is not *home.* Then what is it to us?"

"Yet," said Ewen, "here is a badge for your bonnet, MacGillivray, and, though of American growth, you cannot despise it."

"Thanks, Ewen," said the officer, with a kindling eye, as he placed the gift in his bonnet.

It was a sprig of the red whortleberry, the *badge* of those of his name in Scotland, where they are styled the *Clann Gillibhreac,* "or the Sons of the Freckled Man."

The elm, the ash, the cypress, the chesnut, the pine, and the beech, all mingled their varied foliage above the narrow track or Indian trail the soldiers were pursuing, while a thousand flowers and shrubs, to them unknown, flourished in all the rich luxuriance of this new world into which they were penetrating, and the musk-rat, the racoon, and the fox scampered before them from tree to tree as they proceeded.

"Hark!" exclaimed Alaster MacGregor, a wary old forester, "something on two feet stirs in the bush!"

"Dioul! and see, Alaster, the objects are close enough," added the officer.

At a part of the wood where it became more open by the trees having been cut away, and where the ground shelved abruptly down to the depth of eighty or a hundred feet, they suddenly came in view of two Indians gliding stealthily from stem to stem, as if seeking to elude observation. Their wild and horrid aspect caused the timid wife of MacGillivray to utter a faint cry of terror, while the whole detachment halted simultaneously to observe them, and began instinctively to handle their muskets.

"They are Iroquois," whispered MacGillivray to his sergeant; "I was told that Montcalm had filled all the woods around Lake George with the cursed tribes of that race."

"One of them is carrying something," replied the sergeant, as he shred away by his Lochaber axe a magnificent azalea, the flowers and foliage of which obscured his view.

"It is a child—a poor little child," exclaimed Mary, piteously. "Listen to its cry of despair!"

"The child of a white man, by Heaven!" added MacGillivray. "Come hither you that are the best shots, and bring yonder rascals down; but fire one at a time, lest we needlessly alarm the fort, or, what is worse, bring all the tribes of the Iroquois upon us."

Both these savages were nearly nude. Their skins had the deep and tawny red of their race, but were streaked with war paint. One was daubed over red and blue, and the other who bore the child was striped with white lines, and these glaring upon a background so sombre, gave him the horrible aspect of a walking skeleton. Their heads were closely shaved, or by some other process divested of all hair, save the scalp-lock, in which was tied a tuft of eagles' feathers. Each had the terrible tomahawk and scalping-knife glittering at his gay wampum girdle, and each bore a French musket ornamented with brass rings. One wore over his shoulder the fur of a wild animal; the other had nothing across his bare, brawny chest but the buff belt of a cartridge-box. By their weapons they were at once known to be allies of the Marquis de Montcalm, who with a policy, alike dangerous and ungenerous, had armed the six nations of the Iroquois against the British.

On finding themselves perceived, the savages uttered a wild laugh of derision, and the skeleton— he who bore the child, a poor little boy of some three or four years—waved him thrice round his head, as if with the intention of dashing out his brains against a tree; then, suddenly seeming to change his mind, he deliberately deposited him on the ground, and grasping a handful of the boy's golden hair in his brown fingers, drew his scalping-knife from the tail-piece of a musk-rat, the skin of which formed his hunting-pouch: but now a wild cry of entreaty from Mary MacGillivray made him pause.

"Ewen Chisholm—Alaster, shoot—shoot, at all hazards!" exclaimed her husband.

Ewen knelt down, took a deliberate aim, and then paused, for the Iroquois was also on his knees, and had artfully interposed the child between his person and the soldiers.

"Fire, Ewen, I command you; fire at all hazards!" reiterated MacGillivray, impetuously; "'tis better for the poor child to die by a bullet than by an Indian's knife—a poisoned one, perhaps."

The Iroquois raised his arm for the purpose of giving the knife one vigorous sweep round the scalp of the child, who was frozen with fear; but at that moment Ewen fired. The ball pierced the red skin near the shoulder; with a yell of rage he dropped his weapon, and plunging into the woods disappeared. A shot from the musket of Alaster MacGregor brought down his companion, who though one of his legs was broken, endeavoured to crawl away, but was overtaken by the soldiers, and roughly dragged up the slope to the forest path. The rescued child clung to his preservers, and to the neck of Mary MacGillivray, who placed him on her saddle-bow, and with that motherly tenderness and those caresses which come so naturally from a kind and amiable woman, endeavoured to calm the terrors his late adventure had excited.

With a sudden glare of defiance, the wounded Iroquois surveyed those captors at whose hands he expected immediate immolation.

Several bayonets were directed against him, and more than one musket was clubbed butt-end uppermost to close his career, when Mary interposed and begged that his life might be spared, on which the Highlanders drew back. The glittering eyes of the

Iroquois were fixed upon her, and though he knew not the language in which she spoke, he was aware that to her intercession he owed his life, and smiled; for, Indian like, he despised the manhood of men who could be swayed by a woman. Thus he evinced neither surprise nor gratitude, nor even pain, though his wounded limb bled freely, and must have occasioned him exquisite torment. By Mary's desire the limb was bound up, and in a few minutes the astonished savage found himself placed across four muskets, and borne towards the fort, which was now little more than a quarter of a mile distant. From time to time he glanced keenly and sharply into the adjacent thickets, as if expecting a rescue, but none appeared; and on finding himself clear of the forest he doubtless gave himself up for lost.

"We are close to the gates," said MacGillivray to the piper; "play up, Alisdair Bane."

"Bodoich n' m briogois?" suggested the piper, assuming his drones.

The officer assented, and soon the far-stretching dingles of American forest were ringing to the stirring notes of Lord Breadalbane's march, while the tones of the instrument seemed to astonish and excite the terror of the Indian, in front of whom the piper was strutting with that lofty port peculiar to his profession. Considering this to be probably a prelude to his being scalped and slain, the Iroquois smiled disdainfully, remembered that he was a warrior, and relapsed into his previous state of apathetic indifference, resolved that in the death of torment for which he doubted not he was reserved, to perish with the phlegmatic coolness and iron resolution of his race.

These Iroquois were a confederation of tribes, who supported each other in battle in a manner not unlike the sixteen confederated clans known in Scotland as the Clan Chattan. The chief of the Iroquois were the Mohawks, who resided on the Mohawk River and the banks of those lakes which still bear their name, and from thence they extended their conquests beyond the Mississippi and the St. Lawrence, sub-duing the Eries, the Hurons, the Ottawas and five other tribes, till they became the terror of their enemies by their ferocity and valour ; but even these were forced to yield at last to British rule.*

The report of the musket-shots had reached the fort, where the mainguard and a strong inlying piquet were under arms when the Highlanders marched in. They were received by their countryman Colonel Munro, who, to his astonishment and joy, discovered in the little fellow who nestled in the arms of the mounted lady, his own son and only child Eachin (or Hector), who had been abstracted—but how, none could tell—from the gate of the fort by some of the lurking Indians.

The colonel was a brave and veteran officer, who had recently been deprived, by death, of a young wife. She had left him this little boy, and the heart of the soldier was filled with lively gratitude for the rescue of one whom he prized more than life. After pouring out his thanks to MacGillivray, he turned sternly towards the Iroquois. A sudden glow of anger for the narrow escape of the child made him unsheath his sword, with the intention of passing it through the heart of the Indian, to destroy him, as

* In the Army List of the 15th September, 1816, will be found among *officers* having the local rank of *Major* in Canada, " John Norton, *alias* Teyoninhakawaren, Captain and leader of the Indians of the Five Nations."

one might slay a reptile or wild animal; but again Mary interposed, saying,—

"For my sake, spare him, Colonel Munro."

"I cannot refuse you anything, madam," replied the old soldier, courteously, lowering the point of his sword; "and I would that you had something of greater value to ask of me than the life of a wretched Iroquois; but it shall be spared—ay, and his wound shall be dressed, if such is your wish."

"Thanks, dear colonel."

"But, bear in mind, madam," continued Munro, pressing his little boy close to his breast, "that were the case reversed and we at the mercy of the Iroquois, even as this tawny villain is at ours, we should be stripped, bound to trees, and put to death by such torments as devils alone could devise. And now, MacGillivray, though doubtless weary with your long march, ere you refresh, tell me (for here amid the wilds of the Horican, we hear nothing but the whoop of the wild Iroquois, the yells of the Mohawks, and, now and then, a rattle of musketry) what news of the war?"   .

"The Earl of Loudon has marched to besiege Louisbourg!"

"And delayed his attack upon Crown Point?"

"Yes."

"I expected so much. Since the capture of Oswego, the French have remained masters of the lakes, and collecting the Indians, force or lure them, like the Iroquois, to serve King Louis, and thus all our settlements on the Mohawk River and the German Flats have been destroyed and the land laid as waste and desolate as—"

"The Braes of Lochaber after Culloden," said Mac Gillivray, with a louring eye.

"While here with red coats on us, let us think
no more of Culloden," replied Munro in a low
voice. "But what news of Montcalm? Our scouts
assert he is moving up this way to besiege me."

"At Abercrombie's head-quarters, all say that,
elated by recent advantages, Louis de St. Veran,
and his second in command, the Baron de
Beauchatel, are desirous of attempting something
great."

"And that something—"

"Will be the destruction of Fort William Henry,
as it covers the frontiers and commands Lake
George."

"But does the commander-in-chief expect that I,
with only three thousand regulars, will be able to
withstand the whole French army?" asked Munro,
with a stern and anxious whisper.

"No—General Webb—"

"Old Dan Webb of the 48th?"

"With a column of infantry, was to leave head-
quarters a day or two after us to succour you, and
Fort Edward is to be the base of his operations.
Meanwhile, I with my fifty Highland marksmen,
pushed on as a species of avant-garde."

"Then both Webb and Montcalm are *en route* for
this locality?"

"'Tis a race, and he who wins may win Fort William Henry."

"In three days a great game shall have been
played here, perhaps," said Munro, thoughtfully;
"but to God and our own valour we must commit the
event; and now, madam, a hundred pardons for
leaving you here so long," he added, bowing to Mary,
and with that old air of Scoto-French gallantry which
Scott has so well portrayed in his "Baron of Brad-

THE MASSACRE AT FORT WILLIAM HENRY. 113

wardine," he drew the glove from his right hand, and
raised his little triangular hat; "permit me to lead
you to my quarters until your own are prepared, and
we shall have a cheerful evening's chat about poor
old Scotland, and the homes we may never see again.
When I first heard the sound of your pipe rising up
from the dingles of yonder forest, and saw the tartans
waving as your Highlanders marched up the gate, I
cannot describe the emotions that filled my heart.
The thoughts of home and other times came throng-
ing thick and fast upon my memory—kinsmen and
friends, father, mother, and wife—voices and faces of
years long passed away, of the loved, the lost, and the
dead, were there with the memory of *all* that the
voice of the war-pipe rouses in the heart of an exiled
Scotsman; but enough of this! And now, to you,
madam, and to you, MacGillivray, as we say in the
land of hills and eagles, a hundred thousand welcomes
to Fort William Henry!"

The wounded Iroquois was consigned to the temporary hospital of the fort; the newly arrived Highlanders were "told off" (as the phrase is) to their
quarters, and in one hour after, when the last roll of
the drum at the tattoo had died away, and when
the rising moon shone over the wooded mountains
on the clear glassy water and green islets of Lake
George, all was still in Fort William Henry, and
nothing seemed moving but the bayonets flashing
back the rays of silver on their tips, as the muffled sentinels trod to and fro upon the palisadoed
ramparts.

The fatigue of her journey northwards from Albany
to Lake George had proved too much for the delicate
wife of MacGillivray, as at this time she was on the
eve of adding a little stranger to the number of the

garrison, and thus the solicitude of her husband for her health and safety, in a crowded fort, prepared for a desperate siege, and situated in a wild district, now swarming with hostile Indians, became at times alike deep and painful. The issue of the coming strife, none could foretell, and Roderick knew that if aught fatal happened to him, Mary and her babe—the babe he might not be spared to see—would be alone, in this far world of the west, exposed to penury, to perils and horrors, which his mind could neither contemplate nor conceive.

The first and second day after their arrival passed without any alarm.

On the third, Mary visited the wounded Indian, and gave him some little comforts prepared by her own hands. His limb had been simply fractured, and the wound, which was not so severe as had been at first supposed, was now healing rapidly. He received her with a bright smile of recognition—perhaps of gratitude, for he remembered that she had twice saved his life—first from the bayonets of the Highlanders, and secondly from the sword of Colonel Munro. His features were rather regular and handsome, and save for their deep tawny tint and strong lines, not unlike those of many Europeans. He received her presents, and then relapsed into moody and sullen silence ; but Mary, whose tender nature felt pity for the poor Indian who was deemed and treated little better than a dog by those around him, had learned some of the native language from an old Ottawa woman who had acted as her servant in Albany; and now she made an effort to address the savage in that singular mixture of Canadian-French, English, and Indian, which formed the usual medium of communication with the natives. She asked his name.

"Orono," he replied in a husky voice, while his eyes brightened, and a red deeper even than the war-paint and the glass beads he wore, spread under his tawny skin.

"And he who accompanied you?"

"Ossong, a Mohawk warrior, and a brave one! Before the door of his wigwam a hundred scalps of the Yengees are drying in the wind."

Mary uttered a faint exclamation of horror, but the savage smiled, and said—

"Are no men ever killed in your country?"

"And what meant you to do with the child?"

The stealthy and cunning eyes of Orono lowered for a moment; then, as a gleam of unutterable ferocity spread over his striped visage, he answered—

"To have kept him till we could get the grey scalp of the white chief his father."

"And then——"

"We would have given him to an old pawaw, as a son, to replace one slain by the white chief two moons ago; but I will pardon him all wrong for the sake of you, the pale-face who have been so kind to me."

As he said this the Indian took the tiny white hand of Mary in his strong brown muscular fingers, and attempted to place it on his bare head near the scalp-lock, in token of amity and future service; but she shrank back in terror and with a repugnance which she could not repress, and once more the malevolent gleam which always filled her with dread, shone in the glittering eyes of the Red Indian.

"Have you a wife, Orono?" she asked, to conciliate him.

"Orono *had* a wife," replied the Indian, sadly; "a girl of the Oneidas, and he had two little children for whom she boiled the rice and maize, and wove bright belts of wampum. Orono had a mother too, who shared his wigwam by the sunny bank of the Horican ; but three moons ago the red warriors came, his wigwam was burned, his cattle taken, the trees were cut down, and the mother, the squaw, and the children of Orono were all destroyed, as we would destroy the big snakes in the reeds or the otter in the swamps. And they slew his father—an aged warrior, a man of many moons, and many, many days, who remembered when first the great fire-spouting canoes of the Yengees, with their huge white sails, came over the salt lake from beyond the rising sun ; but they slew him also—all, all ! Father, mother, squaw, and papoose—cattle and dog ; nothing was left but a little heap of cinders to mark where the wigwam stood : all were gone, like the flowers of last summer—gone to the happy hunting grounds of the Iroquois," he added, pointing westward.

"And poor Orono is left quite alone !" said Mary, patting his shoulder kindly, for the story of the Indian impressed her by its resemblance to the fate of her own family in Glencoe, and to many an episode of murder and outrage after Culloden; "alone," she added, "in this great selfish world !"

"To revenge them ; and for this I have trod on the pipe of peace and dug up the war-hatchet !" he replied in a voice like the hiss of a snake, while his eyes glared like two red carbuncles in the dusk of the evening, as Mary retired in dismay.

Ere the night was finally set in her tender sympathies for her new friend received a severe shock. To her husband, who had just returned from a reconnoitring expedition, she was relating her interview with Orono, when the sharp report of two muskets echoed among the logwood edifices which formed the barracks of the fort. Mary grew deadly pale, and clung to Roderick.

"The French!" was his first thought, as he broke away, snatched his claymore, and hurried to the barrack-square, where he heard that a soldier of the Royal American Regiment had been assassinated.

Orono the Indian had abstracted a knife from the basket of his late unsuspecting visitor, and springing unseen upon the sentinel at the hospital door had slain him, swept the blade once round his head above the ears, and torn away his scalp. Then though weak and wounded, with his knife in one hand, and the ghastly trophy reeking in the other, he had bounded over the palisades like an evil spirit, glided through the wet ditch like an eel, and, escaping the musket-shots of two sentinels on the summit of the glacis, reached the darkening forest, where all trace of him was instantly lost in the thickness of the foliage and the gloom of a moonless evening.

"And so, dear Mary, with this terrible episode closes your little romance," said MacGillivray, with a kind smile, as he put an arm round her.

" I devoutly hope so,"said she, shuddering, and feeling, she knew not why, a horrible impression that she would yet see more of this Indian, whose lithe but herculean form, sternly sombre face, glittering eyes, and scalp-lock were ever before her.

"The black traitor, to reward our kindness thus ! 'Tis a thousand pities, dearest, you saved him from our men on the march, and from old Munro's sword in the fort ; for these wretches are no better than wild beasts. Thus it matters little whether we kill them now or a month hence."

"Oh, Roderick !" exclaimed Mary, with her hazel eyes full of tears ; "how can *you* talk thus ?"

"Why ?"

"For so said King William's warrant to massacre my people in Glencoe; and so said that order which was written on the night before Culloden."

"True, true ; the poor Indian only fights for the land God gave his fathers, even as ours, Mary, was given to the children of the Gael," replied Roderick, as the usual current of his bitter thoughts returned ; "and a time there was Mary (God keep thee from harm !) when I little thought to find myself so far from my father's grave, wearing the black cockade of the Hanoverian in my bonnet, and the red uniform of those men who trampled on the white rose at Culloden, and murdered the aged men, the women, and the little ones of your race, under cloud of night, at the behest of a bloodthirsty Dutchman !"

"Still speaking of Glencoe and Culloden !" said Colonel Munro, joining them, as they sat on the bastion, at the base of which rippled the waters of Lake George, then flushed red with the last light of sunset.

"Yes, Munro ; I am thinking of the time when the kilt alone was seen upon the Highland mountains, and when the breeches of the Lowlander—the *brat-galla* (*i.e.* foreigner's rag)—were unknown among us."

"Let us have no more of these sour memories, and if my fair friend will favour me with that song which she sang to my little boy last evening, it may lighten the tedium of a time which to me, after being caged up here for six months, seems insufferably weary."

Mary coloured, and glanced round timidly, for

several officers of the garrison who had been lounging on the parapets drew near, and she knew few songs save those of her native hills, and consequently they were in a language totally unintelligible to the gentlemen of the Royal Americans and Parker's Foot ; but on being pressed by the colonel and his little one, who nestled at her feet, she sang the only English song with which she was acquainted. It was a paraphrase of one of the psalms,* and was then a favourite with the Jacobites, who sang it to a beautiful and plaintive old Highland air.

On Gallia's shore we sat and wept,
  When Scotland we thought on,
Robbed of her bravest sons, and all
  Her ancient spirit gone !

"Revenge!" the sons of Gallia said,
  "Revenge your wasted land;
Already your insulting foes
  Crowd the Batavian strand !

"How shall the sons of Freedom e'er
  For foreign conquest fight ?
For power how wield the sword, deprived
  Of liberty and right ?

"If thee, O Scotland ! we forget,
  Even to our latest breath,
May foul dishonour stain our name,
  And bring a coward's death.

"May sad remorse for fancied guilt
  Our future days employ,
If all thy sacred rights are not
  Above our chiefest joy.

* Psalm cxxxvii.

" And thou, proud Gaul, O faithless friend,
   Thy ruin is not far;
May God, on thy devoted head,
   Pour all the woes of war!

" When thou, thy slaughtered little ones,
   And outraged dames shalt see;
Such help, such pity mayest thou have,
   As Scotland had from thee!"

       *   *   *   *

As Mary sang, many loiterers of the Black Watch had joined the little group around her, and listened as if turned to stone. The veteran colonel of the Royal Americans, who had been long, long from the land of his birth, felt his grave iron nature melted. He sat on the parapet of the gun-battery, with his chin placed in his right hand, and his left nervously grasping the hilt of his sword. His keen grey eyes, which roved uneasily from one object to another, began at last to moisten and fill, and then tears ran down the furrows of his cheeks—old dry channels worn by war and time, but all unused to such visitors.

The *air* rather than the words moved MacGillivray and his soldiers who listened. Their heads were bowed and their eyes were sad, for their hearts and souls, their memory and their love, were far away— away to the land where, at that hour, the silver moon was casting the shadows of the heath-clad mountains on the grassy glens below; away to the Braes of Lochaber, the shores of Lochiel, and the deep blue lochs that form a chain of watery links in the great glen of Caledonia; away to the land of the clans, the soil from whence their fathers sprang, and where their graves lay under the old sepulchral yew, or by

the Druid clachan of ages past and gone ; away from
the lone woods and mighty wilds of that Far West,
which in the next century was to become the home of
their children, where the expatriated men of Sutherland, Barra, and Breadalbane were to find a refuge
from the avaricious dukes, the canting marquises, and
grinding factors of the Western Highlands, and from
their infamous system of modern oppression, tyranny,
and misrule, which has decreed that the poor have no
right to the soil of their native country.

All were hushed and still in the group as the
Highland girl sang—for, though a wedded wife, and
on the eve of being a mother, Mary was but a girl
yet—when hark ! the report of a musket on the
outer bastion broke the stillness of the evening hour,
and an officer of the mainguard rushed, sword in hand,
towards the startled listeners.

"Munro,", he exclaimed ; "Colonel Munro—a
column of French are in sight, and already within
range of cannon-shot."

"So close, Captain Dacres?"

"And in great strength," added the officer.

"And the Indians—those diabolical Iroquois?"

"Fill the woods on every side—they are already at
the foot of the glacis. Hark !" continued Captain
Dacres, as a confused volley was heard, "the main-
guard are opening a fire on their advanced files."

The colonel kissed his child, and with an impressive glance consigned it to the care of Mary.

" Fall in, Sixtieth !" he exclaimed, rushing into the
barracks, where the alarm was now general. " Mac-
Gillivray, get your lads of the Black Watch under
arms, and let them pick me off those brown devils as
fast as they can load and fire again. Gentlemen, to
your companies ; we shall have grim work to do

before another sun sets on the waters of the Horican."

In ten minutes the troops in the little garrison were all under arms, for the men came rushing, cross-belted, to their colours, while the log huts echoed again and again to the long roll of the alarm drum—that peculiar roll, which, when heard in camp or garrison, makes the blood of all quicken, as it is the well-known warning "to arms;" and now the pipes of Alisdair Bane (a pupil of Murrich Dhu, or Black Murdoch MacInnon, the old piper of Glenarrow) lent their pibroch to swell the warlike din, while the troops loaded, and fresh casks of ball-cartridge were staved and distributed by the sergeants in rear of each company.

The artillerymen stood by their guns, with rammer, sponge, and lighted matches; the battalions of the Royal Americans and of the unfortunate Colonel Parker, a corps of Provincials, and the fifty Celts of the Black Watch, soon manned the ramparts, from whence, in the dim twilight of eve, the white uniforms of the regiments of Bearn, Guienne, and Languedoc, who formed the flower of Montcalm's army, and the bronze-like figures of the gliding Iroquois, who formed the scourge of ours, were seen at times between the green masses of foliage that fringed the calm, deep waters of Lake George, which lay motionless as a vast mirror of polished steel.

"Away to the bomb-proofs, Mary; this is no scene for you," said MacGillivray, giving his weeping and terrified wife a tender embrace; "the vaults are your only place of safety. Would to God," he added, giving her a farewell kiss, "that you were safe at home, laoighe mo chri, even with the humblest of our cottars in Glenarrow. The thought of you alone causes my heart to fail, and makes a coward of me, Mary. Alaster MacGregor, conduct her to the bomb-proofs, and join us again."

The soldier led her to the vaults in which the whole of the women and children of the garrison were enclosed for safety from shot and shell, and where they nestled together in fear and trembling, preparing lint and bandages for the wounded ; and scarcely had Alaster rejoined his commander, when a red flash and a stream of white smoke came from the darkening wood, and the first cannon of the French sent a sixteen-pound shot crashing through the log barracks and slew a captain of the Royal Americans.

Then a hearty hurrah of defiance rose from the garrison of Munro, and the fiendish yells and war-whooping of the Iroquois were heard in the echoing woods.

MacGillivray envied the lightness of heart possessed at this crisis by his unmarried comrades, who had neither wife nor child to excite their anxiety, compassion, or fear—men who, careless and soldier like, seemed to live for the present, without regret for the past or dread of the future ; but such is the life of a soldier, while as we have it in "Don Juan"—

"Nought so bothers
The hearts of the heroic in a charge,
As leaving a small family at large."

At the head of all the forces he could collect, ten thousand regular infantry of France, and hordes of the wild Iroquois, Louis de St. Veran, Marquis of Montcalm, and his second in command, the Baron de Beauchatel, Chevalier of St. Louis, now invested Fort William Henry, and pushed the siege with a vigour

that was all the greater because General Webb, with
four thousand British troops, was posted at some distance, for the purpose of protecting Munro's garrison,
a duty about which he did not give himself the smallest
concern whatever.

Before daybreak next morning, the French artillery opened heavily on the turf ramparts, the wooden
palisades and log huts of the fort; while a fire of
musketry was maintained upon it from every available point, and the Indian marksmen, from behind
every tree, rock, and bush, or tuft of sedge-grass that
afforded an opportunity for concealing their dingy
forms, shot with deadly precision at the officers, and
all who in any way exposed or signalized themselves.
Munro and his soldiers fought with ardour, and
defended themselves with confidence, never doubting
that General Webb would soon advance to their sup-
port, and by a brisk attack in the rear, compel the
marquis to abandon the siege. From their gun-bat-
teries and stockades, they maintained an unceasing
fire, and thus the slaughter on both sides became
desperate and severe.

In the gloomy vault to which the humanity and
prudence of Colonel Munro had consigned the women
and children of his garrison, the timid wife of Mac
Gillivray could hear the roar of musketry, with the
incessant booming of the heavy artillery on every
side, and ever and anon the hiss or crash of the exploding shells. These and other dreadful sounds
paralysed her; for she had but one thought—the
safety of her husband; and appalled by the united
horrors of the siege, she almost forgot to pray, and
sat with her arms round the child of Munro, pale,
sad, and silent—awed and bewildered.

Meanwhile Roderick, with his party of the Black

Watch, proved invaluable to Munro. As the dis-
patch of the latter has it, "Being all expert marksmen and deadly shots, they manned a line of loopholed
stockades, which faced a wood full of the Iroquois, of
whom they slew an incredible number; for if the foot
or hand, or even the scalp lock of a warrior became
visible for a moment to these quicksighted deerstalkers from the Highland hills, it revealed where
the rest of his body could be covered by their levelled
barrels; thus there were soon more dead than living
warriors in the bush where the braves of the Five
Nations had posted themselves, and the yells and
screams of rage uttered by the survivors in their
anticipations of vengeance, were like nothing one
could imagine but the cries of the damned."

Among the savages who swarmed thick as bees
upon the skirts of the forest, MacGillivray repeatedly
recognised the ghastly warrior Ossong, who was
painted over with white stripes; and his comrade
Orono, who had so recently made an escape from
the fort, and who was conspicuous alike by his
bravery and the tuft of eagle's feathers in his scalp-
lock.

MacGillivray relinquished his claymore for a musket,
and, as Munro said, "Knocked over more Red Indians
in an hour, than he could have done red deer in a
week, at home."

On the second day, just as the firing was about to
re-commence, a French officer, bearing a flag of truce,
and accompanied by a drummer beating a parley,
appeared before the gates, and was received by Mac
Gillivray, who conducted him, blindfolded by a hand-
kerchief, to the presence of Munro. He was a tall
and handsome man, about forty years of age, and
wore the white uniform of the Grenadiers of Guienne,

with the order of St. Louis, and had a white flowing peruke, *à la Louis XV.*

"Your name, monsieur?" said Munro, bowing low.

"The Sieur Fontbrune, Baron of Beauchatel," replied he, bowing to the diamond buckles at his knees, and then presenting his box of rappee.

"Indeed—the second in command to the Marquis of Montcalm!"

"The same, and Colonel of the Regiment of Guienne."

"We are greatly honoured."

"Nay," responded the courteous French noble, "the honour is mine in having the privilege of conferring with an officer of such valour as M. le Colonel Munro."

"And your purpose?" asked the latter, drily.

"The delivery of this letter."

In presence of the senior officers of his garrison, Munro opened and read this communication from the French marquis, in which the latter wrote, that he deemed himself obliged by the common dictates of humanity to request that M. le Colonel Munro would surrender the fort, and cease, by a futile resistance, to provoke the savage Iroquois, who accompanied the French army in such vast and unmanageable hordes.

"A detachment of your garrison, under Colonel Parker, has lately (he continued) experienced their cruelty. I have it yet in my power to restrain and oblige them to observe a capitulation, as comparatively few of them have been hitherto killed. Your persisting in the defence of your fort can only retard its fate a few days, and must of necessity expose an unfortunate garrison, who cannot possibly receive relief, when we consider the *precautions* taken to prevent it. I demand a decisive answer; and for this purpose have sent the Sieur do Fontbrune, one of my staff. You may implicitly credit all that ho tells you.

"MONTCALM."

"I will never surrender while we have a shot left," exclaimed Munro, furiously. "What say you, gentlemen?"

"That we and our soldiers will stand by you, Colonel, to the last gasp!" replied Captain Dacres.

"This, then, is your decision, messieurs?" said M. Beauchatel, playing with the ringlets of his peruke.

"It is—it is," was the answer on all hands.

"A most unwise one, permit me to say," urged the baron.

"To yield when General Webb is within less than one day's march of us, would be a treason to tho King and a disgrace to ourselves."

The French baron smiled with provoking coolness, and said,

"General Webb beholds our preparations and approaches with an apparent indifference that originates either in infamous cowardice or miserable infatuation. In short, M. le Colonel, he has abandoned you."

"M. le Baron," replied Munro, with some heat, "General Webb is a British officer, and I have no doubt will fully maintain his reputation. If ho has not already advanced to raise the siege, he must deem it better for tho King's service to remain in position

I 2

where he is; but, ere long, you will hear his cannon opening on your rear."

"Pardieu, you delude yourself."

"I do not, M. le Baron, and you may inform the Marquis de Montcalm, that he had better have continued to amuse himself with mounting guard at Versailles and Marli, than by beating up our quarters here on the Canadian lakes."

"Oh, he and I have mounted guard at Mons and Tournay, at Lisle and Fontenoy, Colonel, where men don't play at soldiers, as here in America," replied the Frenchman, smiling; "but adieu, mon ami—adieu."

"Farewell—MacGillivray, conduct M. le Baron beyond the gates."

So ended this parley, and in less than five minutes the din of cannon and musketry, with the warwhoop of the Indians, again rang along the echoing shores of the Horican, and once more the white smoke shrouded alike the defences and defenders of Fort William Henry.

The Baron de Beauchatel led the Regiment of Guienne close up to the stockades, which were lined by the fifty Highlanders of the Black Watch, and though exposed to a withering fire, he bravely and furiously strove to destroy the barrier by axes and sledge hammers. MacGillivray thrice covered the Baron with his deadly aim; but, inspired by some mysterious emotion, the origin of which at that time he could not fathom, he spared him and levelled his weapon at others. Filled with rage by the resistance they experienced, the soldiers of the Regiment of Guienne encouraged each other by shouts of

"Vive le Roi! Tue—tue les sauvages d'Ecosse! à la baionette! à la baionette!"

They soon fell into confusion; but the brave Beauchatel continued to brandish his sword and shout the *mot de ralliement* of his corps, for it was then usual in the French service to have a war-cry or regimental rallying-word.

"Notre Dame! Notre Dame de frappemort!" (Our holy Lady, who strikes home!) he was heard crying again and again; for the Virgin was the patroness of the Grenadiers of Guienne; but neither the spell of her name nor the fiery spirit of Beauchatel enabled the soldiers to withstand the fire-of the Highlanders, whose position was impregnable; and on Captain Dacres' company of the 60th opening a flank fusilade upon them, they were swept back into the forest, leaving a mound of white-coated killed and wounded before the stockades they had so valiantly attempted to destroy.

Alaster MacGregor received a wound from a French soldier, who, on finding himself dying, crawled on his hands and knees close up to the stockade, and, with the last effort of expiring nature, fired his musket through a loophole and fell back dead.

"A brave fellow!" exclaimed MacGillivray.

"Yes," added Alaster, as the blood dripped from his left cheek: "but I wish he had departed this life five minutes sooner."

A third and fourth day of conflict passed away, and the loss by killed and wounded became severe in Fort William Henry; five hundred dead men were already lying within the narrow compass of its batteries; but still there was no sign of Webb's brigade advancing to the rescue. Munro began to have serious doubts of the issue, with secret regrets that he had not accepted the first offers of the Marquis de Montcalm, for the blood of the Iroquois was now at boiling heat, in their longing to revenge the fall of so many of their braves, who, notwithstanding all their caution and cunning, had perished under the deadly aim of the Highland marksmen, and lay in dusky piles among the long wavy sedge grass and luxuriant foliage of the forest; but though he confined these thoughts to his own breast, his garrison began to have the same misgivings.

One day, telescope in hand, he was eagerly sweeping the distant landscape in the direction where it was known that General Webb was posted, when Dacres, of his own regiment, approached him.   Not a bayonet or musket-barrel were seen to glitter, or a standard to wave in the hazy distance in token of coming aid, and he sharply closed the glass with a sigh and turned away; so Dacres addressed him.

"When smoking a pipe in the bomb-proofs this morning—by the bye, my dear colonel, I am always thoughtful during that operation—it occurred to me that General Webb——"

"Well, sir—well," said Munro, irritably.

"Remains very long in position without advancing to our relief."

"I am too well aware of that, sir."

"But what does such conduct mean?"

"God and himself alone know," replied Munro, while his keen grey eye flashed with passion; "he would seem to be in league with the enemy against us; ay, in league with Montcalm, and the words of Beauchatel seemed to infer some previous knowledge of his intentions, and hence perhaps the friendly warning about the Indians; but we have cast the die with them. If in the course of one day more Webb comes not to our aid ——"

"By Heaven, I will pistol him with my own hand;

that is, if I survive this affair!" exclaimed MacGillivray, who joined them.

"Nay, sir," replied the colonel, "I shall claim that task, if task it be ; but hark ! there is a salvo."

A tremendous shock now shook the fort, as a camarade battery of ten 32-pounders commenced a discharge against it, and showers of destructive bomb-belles from small mortars were poured into the heart of the place. Many of these little engines of destruction bounded from the shingle roofs of the barracks and burst in the waters of the lake ; others were exploding in all directions, with a sound like the roar of artillery, forcing the soldiers, who crept and cowered in rear of the parapets and palisades, to lie close, while the heavy *hum* of the round shot, with that peculiar sound which terminates its course by piercing the ground, or crashing through a building, and the sharper *whish* of the musket-balls, filled up all the intervals by noises fraught with alarm. The barracks and storehouses were soon unroofed and ruined, for the camarade battery proved very destructive ; the stockades were soon swept away in showers of white splinters before its discharges, which resembled nothing but a whirlwind of shot and shell, while vast masses of the earthen works were also torn down, leaving the defenders exposed to the deadly rifles of the lurking Indians. The cannon of Munro were alike defective and dangerous to his soldiers; for two 18-pounders, two 32-pounders, and two 9-pounders burst in succession, destroying all who were near them, and at last the colonel received intimation that only seventeen bombs remained in the magazine.

On the *sixth* day, there was still no appearance of General Daniel Webb (who was Colonel of the 48th, or Northamptonshire Foot), though his column was

within hearing of the firing, being at Fort Edward,
which was only six miles distant; and now the spirit
of the garrison began to sink ; but in that dejected
band there was no heart more heavy than MacGillivray's, for the condition of his wife at such a terrible
crisis filled him with the deepest anxiety and the most
tender solicitude.

At last Munro, finding the futility of further resist-
ing forces so overwhelming, and that all hope of succour from Webb was hopeless, on the 9th day of
August, 1757, lowered his standard, and sent forth
MacGillivray to the French camp, bearer of a flag of
truce, to confer on the terms of a surrender.

Immediately on leaving the gates, he was received
by the Baron de Beauchatel and a party of the Grenadiers of Guienne, who surrounded him with fixed
bayonets, as a protection from the infuriated Iroquois,
who crowded near in naked hordes, leaping, dancing,
screaming like incarnate fiends, and brandishing their
tomahawks, seeking only an opening in the close files of
the French escort to slay, scalp, and hew him to pieces.
Thus he was conducted to the tent of Louis Marquis de
Montcalm de St. Veran, Maréchal du Camp, and Lieutenant-General of the Armies of His Most Christian
Majesty in America. Before the tent were posted the
colours of the Regiments of Bearn and Languedoc,
and around it were a guard of grenadiers in white
coats, with the long periwigs and smart little triangular hats of the French line. These received the
flag of truce with presented arms, while the drums
beat a march.   ·   •

Montcalm, then in his forty-fifth year, came forth,
and, presenting his hand to MacGillivray, conducted
him within. Then followed several officers of the

staff whom, with M. de Beauchatel, he had invited to the conference.

"You perceive, now," said the baron, "that I proved a true prophet!"

"In what manner, monsieur?" asked MacGillivray.

"When I affirmed that M. le Général Webb would leave Munro to his own resources. Ma foi! but he is a brave fellow, Munro."

"M. le Marquis," said MacGillivray, with an air of hauteur, "I am here to stipulate that our garrison shall be permitted to march out with their arms——"

"Unloaded——"

"Be it so; but as Christian men you cannot refuse us arms in a land so wild as this; the officers to have their baggage, and the men their kits; that a detachment of French troops shall escort us to within two miles of the gates of Fort Edward, and that your interpreter attached to the savages will make this treaty known to the Iroquois."

"I gladly agree to these conditions," replied Montcalm, "though I fear the *latter portion* will be achieved with difficulty; for the comprehension of these Red Iroquois is not very clear, and they will despise me for burying the war-hatchet and smoking the pipe of peace, for permitting you to depart with your scalps on, and so forth; but they must be forced to understand and observe our treaty. For the space of eighteen months every officer and soldier now in Fort William Henry must not bear arms against the Most Christian King. M. le Colonèl Munro must give me hostages for the safe return of my troops who are to form your escort; and say to him, that in testimony of my esteem for his valour and spirit as a soldier, I shall present him with one cannon, a

6-pounder, to be delivered at the moment the grenadiers of my own regiment receive the gates of the fort, and his troops are ready to depart."

"Our wounded and sick, of whom we have many——"

"I shall send under guard to General Webb at Fort Edward."

"Thanks, marquis."

The terms were soon drawn up and signed by the staff officers of both forces ; by Munro in the name of the British Commander-in-Chief, and by Montcalm in the name of the Marquis de Vaudreuil, Governor-General, and Lieutenant-General of New France ; and after ably concluding this negotiation, so important for his comrades, MacGillivray returned to the fort just as the red round moon began to rise like a bloody targe above the eastern skirts of the forest, and to tinge with its quivering rays the placid waters of Lake George.

The first who received him at the gate was his "dear wee Mary," as he called her, trembling and in tears for his safety. During the whole time of his visit to the camp of Montcalm, the yelling and whooping of the Indians had filled the fort and the woods with horrid sounds.

The next day passed before Munro had all prepared to leave the shattered ramparts he had defended so well.

It was on a gorgeous August evening when his war-worn and weary garrison paraded, prior to their final departure. The western clouds, as they floated across the sky, were tinged with violet and saffron hues. The forest and the grass wore their most brilliant green, and Lake George its deepest blue. The large golden butter-cups that spotted all the verdant glacis

of the ramparts, within which so many brave men
were lying stark and stiffened in their blood, and the
bright-coloured wildflowers that grew amid the waters
of the fosse and by the margin of the lake which
filled it, were unclosing their petals, to catch the
coming dew, and wore their gayest tints.

The whole aspect of the scenery, and of the soft
balmy evening, were little in accordance with the
horrors that were passed, and those which were soon
to ensue!

Already the grenadiers of Montcalm, with all the
formality of friends, had received the gates and various posts from the guards of the Royal Americans;
the white banner of France, under a royal salute, had
replaced the Union Jack, and at that moment sharply
beat the drums, as the garrison began to march out,
with their *unloaded* muskets slung and their colours
cased—the Royal Americans, Parker's Foot, and the
little band of our old friends, the Black Watch (now
less by sixteen men than on the day of their arrival),
with the piper and MacGillivray at their head, de-
filing from the fort in close column of subdivisions,
while the French escort was under arms to receive
them in line by a general salute, with drummers beating on the flanks.

A faint cheer was heard within the fort. It came
from the log huts where the wounded lay. They,
poor fellows! were left to the care of the enemy, together with the unburied bodies of those who would
never hear a sound again until the last trumpet
shakes the earth with its peal.

The veteran Colonel Munro, tall and erect, with his
quaint Kevenhuller hat and old-fashioned wig of the
days of Malplacquet, marched at the head of his crest-
fallen column; he was on foot, with his sword drawn,

and led by the hand the child, his son, as being the
only object he cared about preserving in that hour of
bitterness and defeat.

Seated on the tumbril of the 6-pounder, with two
other ladies (one of whom had lost her husband in the
siege), was the wife of MacGillivray, awe-stricken and
all unused to such stern and stirring scenes as she had
daily witnessed in Fort William Henry. Her *marriage brooch*, almost the only ornament she possessed,
she had concealed in the folds or tresses of her long
black hair, lest it should excite the cupidity of
any French soldier or Indian, for she had an equal
dread, and nearly an equal repugnance for them
both.

A slender escort of French soldiers with their
bayonets fixed protected Munro's garrison on both
flanks ; but as they proceeded into the forest, the
savages continued to assemble in dark hordes, till
their numbers, their gestures, and yells of rage became seriously alarming. They were animated by
the blindest frenzy on finding themselves deluded of
their plunder and the blood—the red reeking scalps
of the hated Yengees—by a treaty which they could
not and cared not to understand. They were rehearsing to each other the bravery and worth, the
names and number of their warriors who had perished,
and all continued to scream and shout, but none cared
to begin the work of destruction while so near the
tents of the pale faces of France.

" Push on—push on, for God's sake, gentlemen and
comrades !"

" Forward, my friends—let us lose no time in reaching Fort Edward."

"Step out, comrades—step out, you fellows in
front."

"Throw off your knapsacks—let these greedy hounds have them."

"Better lose an old kit than a young life.",

"On, on—push on, boys!"

Such were the cries that were heard along the column as the rear urged on the front, and the dark yelling hordes of the infernal Iroquois blackened all the woods and grew denser and closer, until at last they insolently jostled and crushed the French guard among the impeded ranks of those they were escorting.

"This is intolerable—let us attack those dogs," said MacGillivray.

"Beware—beware!" exclaimed Munro; "if once blood be shed or the warwhoop raised, all will be over with us."

The leader of this hostile display was the savage whom we have already introduced as Ossong. A Lenni Lennape, he was almost the last of his ferocious tribe, which, with the Miami, had been conquered and exterminated by the Iroquois, with whom he had now completely identified himself. His aspect was frightful! His forehead was low; with a short nose of great breadth; his ears were huge, and set high upon his head; his mouth was large, with teeth sharp and serrated like those of some voracious fish. His mantle of woven grass was trimmed with scores of human scalp-locks salted and dried, while rows of human teeth intermingled with glass beads and gilt regimental buttons and British coins (the relics of Colonel Parker's force) covered all his brown expansive chest. On his brawny shoulders hung the skin of a black bear; in front, he wore the fur of a racoon; his girdle, moccassins, and arms were ornamented with brilliant wampum beads, which rattled as he walked, and he brandished alternately a rifle, a tomahawk, and scalping-knife.

Two or three soldiers had already been dragged out of the ranks and slain to increase the general alarm; but as yet the *warwhoop* had not been raised.

Perceiving a savage near him, who was placing his hands to his mouth and puffing out his cheeks, previous to raising that dreadful signal for a general onslaught, MacGillivray, unable longer to restrain the fury which boiled within him, drew the Highland *tack* (*i.e.* steel pistol) from his belt and shot him dead.

" Rash man," exclaimed Munro, " we are lost !"

" Fix your bayonets, my lads, and bear back this naked rabble !" said MacGillivray, drawing his sword. " Remember, colonel, you are a kinsman of the House of Foulis; in an hour like this belie not your name !"

A thousand throats now uttered the horrible whoop of the Iroquois, and from a myriad echoes the vast forest encircling the shores of the Horican replied.

It was the death-knell of the *Yengees;* and now ensued that frightful episode of the war known in American history as the Massacre of Fort William Henry.

" In the name of God and the King, keep together, 60th—shoulder to shoulder, Royal Americans !" cried Munro; but his soldiers, crushed and impeded by the pressure, strove in vain to free their muskets and bear back the human tide that closed upon them. In the confusion poor old Munro lost his child, and with him all his soldierly coolness and self-possession. He became a prey to grief and distraction.

" Lochmoy ! Lochmoy ! stand by MacGillivray !" were the shouts of the Black Watch, as they flung aside their muskets, knapsacks, and cantines, and, unsheathing their dirks and claymores, closed hand-to-hand with the Iroquois, and hewed them down like children on every side.

" Dhia ! O Dhia ! my wife !" was the first thought of MacGillivray ; and when last he saw Mary she was standing erect on the tumbril, the horses of which had been shot, wringing her hands in an attitude of despair, as the brown tide of the Iroquois swept round her like a living sea ; and the last she saw of her husband was his form towering above all others, when combating bravely and making frantic efforts, with Alaster MacGregor, Ewen Chisholm, Bane the piper, and other Celtic swordsmen, to reach her; but by a horde of savages they were driven into the forest, and she saw them no more.

The French guard offered but a feeble resistance, and fled ; then ensued a thousand episodes replete with horror ! On all hands the unfortunate survivors of the siege were hewn down, slashed, stabbed, toma-hawked, and scalped. Shrieks, groans, screams, prayers, and wild entreaties for mercy, with the occa-sional explosions of musketry, rang through the forest ; but above all other sounds, on earth or in the sky of heaven, rose the appalling whoop of the un-glutted Iroquois.

One of Mary's companions—the widow—was lite-rally hewn to pieces in a moment, while her children were whirled round by the feet, and had their brains dashed out against the trees ; her other friend, the wife of Captain Dacres, a fair-haired and pretty young Englishwoman, was torn from her side. The glitter-ing hatchet of one Indian cleft her head to the nose, while another caught her body as it was falling, and by a single sweep of his knife shred off her scalp, and waved the silken curls as a trophy above his head.

Mary was to be their next victim; but ere they could drag her down she flung herself at the feet of Ossong, and, clasping his moccassined legs, said in his own language—

"I will pray the Great Spirit that he pardon you my death; but do not torture me; do not make me suffer—I am a weak woman, and about to become a mother."

Ossong grinned hideously, and grasping her by the hair raised his scalping-knife; but at that moment his hand was grasped from behind. He turned furiously, and was confronted by Orono.

"Spare her!" said the latter, in his guttural tones.

"For what? My ears are not as the ears of an ass, therefore I hear not follies; nor of a fox, therefore I hear no lies!" responded the fierce savage; "spare her for what?"

"The wigwam of Orono."

Ossong laughed scornfully, and turned away in search of other victims, which he found but too readily.

Mary clung to her preserver. She gave a wild and haggard glance over that forest scene, in the recesses of which the shrieks of the destroyer and destroyed were already dying away—over that wilderness of red-coated dead, of mothers and their children, gashed, hewn and dismembered, scalped and mutilated—over the debris of scattered muskets, torn standards, and broken drums, rifled baggage, open knapsacks, hats, and powdered wigs—everywhere blood, death, and disorder! Then the light seemed to go out of her eyes; she became senseless, and remembered no more.

Saved by the French, Colonels Munro and Young

with three hundred fugitives reached Albany; and General Webb, when all was over, sent out five hundred men from Fort Edward to glean up survivors and bury the dead. Our soldiers perished in the forest in scores under every species of torture, wounds, thirst and fatigue; many were flayed and roasted alive by the Iroquois; others were stripped nude, scalped, and made a mark for bullets or tomahawks till death relieved them of their misery.

"Thus," says Smollett, "ended (with the fall of Fort William Henry) the third campaign in America, where, with an evident superiority over the enemy, an army of twenty thousand regular troops, a great number of provincial forces, and a prodigious naval power—not less than twenty ships of the line—we abandoned our allies, exposed our people, suffered them to be cruelly massacred in sight of our troops, and relinquished a large and valuable tract of country, to the eternal disgrace and reproach of the British name!"

Three of the Black Watch alone escaped this massacre—viz., Ewen Chisholm, with Alaster MacGregor —whose adventures were somewhat remarkable—and another, of whom hereafter.

Duncan MacGregor, a soldier from Glengyle, and as some averred a son of the venerable *Glhun Dhu,* who was captain of Doune Castle under Prince Charles, fell mortally wounded by a bullet from the rifle of an Indian in the woods. On finding himself dying, he begged his clansman Alaster to convey his little all— a few pounds of back pay and prize-money—to his aged and widowed mother. Faithful to the trust reposed in him by his expiring friend, this poor fellow bore the money about with him, untouched, throughout the most arduous struggles of the American cam-

K

paign, during a long captivity in France, and amid
the urgent necessities of nearly ten years of privation,
until he reached Glengyle, and then he handed to the
mother of his comrade the money, still wrapped in the
moccassin of a Pawnee, whom he had slain at Fort
William Henry.

Ewen Chisholm, one of the eight faithful men of
the Coire-gaoth in Glenmorriston, survived the war in
America, but was slain when the Black Watch was at
Guadaloupe, in 1759 ; and his death is thus recorded
in the *Edinburgh Chronicle* for that year, which
contains a letter from Ensign Grant—known as Alaster the One-handed—detailing the circumstance :—

" When the troops were to embark, the outposts
were called in.   This soldier (Chisholm) had been
placed as a single sentinel by his captain. When summoned to come off, he refused, unless his captain who
had appointed him his post would personally give him
orders.   He was told that his captain and most of
the troops were embarked, and that unless he came
off he would be taken prisoner ; he still refused, and
said he would keep his station.   When the troops
were all on board the ships, they saw a party of forty
or fifty men coming towards him ; he retired a little,
and setting his back to a tree, fired his gun at them,
then, throwing it aside, he drew his sword, rushed
amongst them, and after making considerable havoc
was cut to pieces."

Such was the end of Ewen Chisholm ; but to resume :—

The noon of the next day—the 11th August—was
passed before Mary became fully alive to the desolate
nature of her position—to all that she had lost and
suffered—and to the circumstance that in her delirium she had become the mother of a little daughter.

She was lying on a bed of soft furs of various kinds, within a hut formed by branches and matting tied to poles, and covered with broad pieces of bark. Upon these poles hung various Indian weapons, at the sight of which she closed her swimming eyes as the memory of her husband and the horrors of yesterday rushed upon her. An old Indian woman, hideous as a tawny skin full of wrinkles and streaked with paint could make her, sat near, squatted on the ground like a Burmese idol; but this ancient squaw was nursing the new-born infant tenderly, and with care placed it in the bosom of Mary, who wept and moaned with sorrow and joy as she pressed it in her arms, and the new emotions of a mother woke within her; but again the light seemed to pass from her eyes, and a faintness came over her. Then starting, she sought to shake it off that she might look upon her child, and strive to trace the features of Roderick in her face; but the weakness she suffered was too great—she sank back upon the bed of furs, and lay still, and to all appearance asleep, though tears were oozing fast from her long black lashes.

Close by, behind a matting, crouched an Indian warrior. This person was Orono concealing himself, for the honest creature felt instinctively, that at such a critical time his presence or his aspect might very naturally excite the terror of the desolate patient. Two terrible questions were ever on the tongue and in the heart of the latter.

" Was Roderick safe ?"

If so, how were she and her babe to join him ?

At last she remembered Orono, who had preserved her, and on the third day, though weak, and though she knew it not—dying—she inquired of the squaw where he was.

"Here," replied the watchful Indian, stepping forward, while his eyes beamed with pleasure, on finding that he was not forgotten.

"My husband, Orono—know you aught of my husband?"

The Indian shook his head.

"When did you last see him?" she asked, imploringly.

"Fighting against a hundred braves in the forest, where the pawaws of the French have put up two trees, *thus*," said he, crossing his fingers to indicate a cross made by the Jesuits near the Horican.

"Alas! my mother taught me that the way of the cross was the way to heaven. Oh, my husband!—and that at the foot of that cross I should give up my whole heart. God, who bringeth good out of evil, will order all things for the best; but can this be, if my husband, my friend, my protector, the father of my babe, be slain? May he not have been preserved for himself and this little one? Oh, yes—God is kind. His will is adorable," continued the poor girl, kissing her babe in a wild rapture of resignation and despair.

She recalled with sorrow and horror the many whom she had seen so barbarously destroyed, and others whom she believed to have perished; the brave soldiers, the kind old colonel, and the poor little boy, his son, to whom she had been almost a mother, during the terrors of the recent siege. Their voices lingered in her ear; their faces hovered before her.

Orono visited the place where he had last seen the "white chief," as he not inaptly named MacGillivray; but could discover no trace of him. Many of the dead had already been interred by the soldiers of

Montcalm, who now possessed the shattered remains of Fort William Henry; others had been devoured by wild animals. No body answering the description of Roderick had been, found or seen among the slain by the Iroquois. He was known to have a gold bracelet of Mary's, rivetted round his sword arm; but that might have been cut off, or buried with him, undiscovered.

Mary felt a great repugnance for the old squaw; yet the poor Indian was kind and attentive in her own barbarous fashion; and the patient, while her heart was swollen almost to bursting, conversed with her, in the hope of obtaining surer protection for her little one, and discovering some traces of its father.

" What would it avail you, were he found ?" asked the squaw.

" Why ?"

"The Red warriors would immediately take his scalp, for the oracles of the pawaws have driven them mad. After three days of conjuration, they have told us—"

" They—are the pawaws a tribe of the Iroquois ?"

" They are our wise men—our oracles."

" And they told—what ?"

" That the devils would not hinder the pale faces from being masters of our country. We have fought bravely ; but the brandy, the gold and silver of the Yengees are more powerful than the prophesies of the lying pawaws or the knives of our warriors."

" Every Red man in the land has dug up the war-hatchet," said a strange guttural voice ; " the print of the white moccasins will soon be effaced on the prairies and in the woods—their graves alone will re-main—their scalps and their bones."

The old squaw started nimbly forward, and poor Mary pressed her little naked babe closer to her breast, on seeing the towering form of Ossong, streaked with his ghastly war paint, appear between her and the door of the wretched wigwam in which she lay so helplessly at his mercy.

" What seek *you* in the dwelling of Orono ?" demanded the Indian woman with some asperity.

" Neither the squaw nor the papoose of the white man," replied Ossong, scornfully.

" It is well. You are in your native land, and can find the bones of your fathers ; but here the poor squaw of the white chief is a stranger."

" And Orono will protect her," added the other savage, who bore that name, stepping proudly forward.

" The pawaws say our fathers come from the rising sun, and that we must go towards the place of its setting—that *there* is the future home of the Red man," said Ossong, as a savage glare lit up his eyes and he played with his scalping-knife ; " shall even one pale face be permitted to live, if such things are said ? Go—Orono has become a woman !"

With this taunt, the most bitter that can be made to an Indian, Ossong waved his hand,. and strode away with a sombre air of fury and disdain.

As he left the hut, a glittering ornament which hung at his neck caught the eye of Mary. She uttered a faint cry, for she was weak and feeble, and while clutching her babe in one arm, strove to raise her attenuated form with the other. She endeavoured to call back Ossong ; but her voice failed, and she sank dispairingly on her bed of skins. Among the gewgaws which covered the broad breast of Ossong, to her horror, she had discovered the gilt regimental gorget of her husband, which she knew too well, by its silver thistle, as there had been no other officer of Highlanders but he in Fort William Henry.

The eyes of Orono gleamed brightly; he, too, had detected the cause of her agitation, and he said,

"It is an ornament of the pale chief, worn by Ossong."

"It was my husband's! Oh, Orono, ask him—for pity, ask him, where, when, how he obtained possession of it."

"Ossong is fierce as a Pequot," said the Iroquois, sadly.

"Ask him, lest I die!" exclaimed Mary, passionately.

"Ossong is a strong and fierce warrior," replied the savage, gently; "I will steal it for you, if I can. Ossong is cruel. Listen; he found a pale face on the shore of the Horican; he was wounded and feeble, so Ossong stripped and bound him to a gum-tree, where he roasted him with sedge-grass, and, before death, forced him to eat his own ears, which were cut off by a scalping-knife."

"Oh, my husband!" exclaimed Mary, in despair; "and a fiend such as this has had his hands on you!"

"I fear me," said Orono, shaking his head, "that he you weep for has gone to where the sun hides itself at night."

"What mean you, Orono?"

"Away beyond the great prairies of the buffaloes—to the place of sleep—the wigwam of grass, where the Indian sleeps sounder than even the fire-water of the white man can make him."

" Alas ! you mean the grave ?"

The Iroquois nodded his head, and relapsed into silence, while with a low moan at a suggestion which seemed to fulfil her own fears, and seemed only too probable, Mary fell back and became, to all appearance, insensible.

Several days passed, during which she hovered between time and eternity; but nothing, even in civilized life, could surpass the watchful kindness and attention of the poor but grateful savage on whose mercy she found herself thrown. *How* Ossong became possessed of the regimental gorget—whether he had found it in the wood, or torn it from her husband's neck when dead, Orono could never discover, as his tawny compatriot was animated in no measured degree by the worst attributes of the American Indian—craft, timidity, fickleness, ferocity, revenge, and quickness of apprehension. Hence there were no means of wresting the important — perhaps dreadful — secret from him. He was soon after shot in a skirmish by the soldiers of Fort Edward, and the story of the gilded badge perished with him.

" Oh, never to see my dear, dear husband again—never, in this dreary world ! It is a terrible blow—a dreadful and soul-crushing conviction !" Mary continued to exclaim, " God has required many sacrifices of me ; but that Roderick should never see the wee pet-lamb I have brought into this vale of woe is the bitterest thought of all ; and to what a fate shall I leave it ! My heart is like a stone—my brain a chaos."

" Remain and be the squaw of Orono ; he is good and gentle, and will love the lonely pale face, and will teach her to hoe rice," said the enterprising proprietor of the wigwam, who also possessed a valuable property in wampum and scalp-locks.

"Remain here! a month, yea, a week of this will kill me, Orono. Remain here, and so far away from my country—from the deep glens where the heather blooms so sweetly! I cannot stay, Orono," continued the poor girl, wildly. "I have been taught to love my native land by the voices of my father, who fell in battle, of my mother, who died of sorrow, and of my brave husband, who perished in this hated wilderness!"

"Orono understands," said the Indian, quietly; "he, too, loves the hunting-grounds of the Iroquois; but he will protect the poor pale face and her child."

Seeing her weep bitterly, after a pause, during which he regarded her attentively—

"Orono," said he, "is but a poor Indian warrior and knows not the God of the pale faces; but may he speak?"

"Say on."

"Turn to the Great Spirit of the Iroquois, who dwells far away beyond the lakes and the prairies; be resigned to his will. The lightning is not swifter than his wrath; the hunting-grounds are not greater than his goodness. This Great Spirit knows every leaf in the woods—every ripple on the waters; and doubtless he has removed the white chief from evils more terrible than yonder battle by the Horican; for sudden death is good."

"How think you so?"

"I know not; but the pawaws say so."

Here was a subject for one who could reflect; but the heart of Mary seemed to have died within her.

" Oh yes," continued the Indian, patting her white
shoulder gently with his strong brown hand, and
pointing south ; " he is gone to the abode of the Great
Spirit, to the happy hunting-grounds, where the souls
of all brave warriors go, and where they seem to live
again."

" Oh that I were with him."

" Orono has no squaw now ; but the Oneida girl
who slept on his breast is there."

" Orono," said the widow, touched by his tone,
and gathering hope from his protection, "is a good
warrior."

" He is a brave one !" replied the Iroquois, proudly.

" It is better to be good than brave ; and you *are*
good."

" Orono is grateful to the squaw of the white chief,
and has given his promise to protect her ; so the
strongest and tallest braves of the Iroquois must
respect that promise. My brothers say, Let the pale
face die——"

" She will not trouble you long," said Mary, weeping over her child, for which she had neither proper
nurture nor little garments, nor even the rites of
baptism.

"Are we to perish, they cry, that pale faces may
gather, and dig, and sow,· on the sacred banks of
the Horican ? Are they sent here to inherit the home
of the Indian, the hunting-ground of his fathers, and
the great solemn barrows where their bones lie by the
Oswego and the Mississippi, as if the Great Spirit
loved them better than his children the Iroquois."

From this day fever of mind and body—an illness
for which she had neither nurse, physician, nor comforts around her—prostrated the faculties of the poor
widow, for such she deemed herself. As each link in

the chain of life is broken by death, we are united more closely to those which remain; but to poor Mary all seemed a hopeless blank. The *last link* was a child, whose feeble life and doubtful future filled her with dismay.

Now that Roderick was gone, her heart seemed to follow him. She clung with fonder affection to the world that was to come, and where she was to meet him; but her babe, could she selfishly forsake it? Her heart was sorely lacerated. Eternity seemed close—terribly *close* to her; and her husband being there, instituted to her a more endearing tie between this world and that mysterious "bourne from whence no traveller returns." She had no terror of this journey, for he whom she loved with all the strength of her soul had gone before and awaited her there. At times she fancied that he chid her delay; she felt drawn towards that spirit-world by a chord of affection which made her now yearn for it, as before she had wept and yearned for her Highland home.

But her babe—so innocent and so deserted—could she die and leave it among the Iroquois?

How did Roderick die—where? Peacefully or in torture? Was he buried, or lying still unentombed?

These dreadful questions and thoughts were ever before her in the intervals of waking from her fits of delirium, which often lasted for hours; and her snatches of sleep were filled by horrible dreams.

In these intervals a new hope dawned in her heart. Her husband might have escaped and gained Fort Edward or the army of Montcalm, and she might yet reach him with her child if protected by Orono. This idea gave a new and exciting impulse to her already overwrought frame; but it came, alas! too late, for, a few days after the birth of her little one,

she too surely felt herself dying—dying there with
none to hear her story, or to whom she could bequeath
her helpless babe—a thought sufficient alone to kill
her. With the last effort of her strength she took
from her now matted hair the Celtic marriage brooch
(the old palladium of her husband's family) which
she had kept there concealed since the day of their
departure from Fort William Henry, and fixing it to
a fragment of her own dress, which she had wrapped
round· the infant, pointed to it, that Orono might
deem it an amulet or talisman—"a great medicine"—
and expired !

    *   *   •   •

It was about the time of sunset, and before inter-
ring the body in a deep grave which he had scooped
at the foot of a gum-tree, and lined with soft furs,
Orono sat silent and watching in his wigwam. Near
the dead mother her unconscious child slept peacefully. The poor Indian was perhaps praying, and
feeling thankful in his heart that he had discharged
a debt of gratitude, and would yet do more by conveying the little orphan to the nearest white settle-
ment, and there leaving her to her fate.

The evening was beautiful, like those which preceded the siege and the massacre. A mellow sunset
was deepening on the hills that overlook the waters
of Lake George, and the setting beams played with a
wavering radiance on the green foliage that was tossed
like verdant plumage by the evening wind, and on the
ripples that ran before it over the bosom of that lovely
lake. All was still within the Indian hut where the
dead woman lay, with her long black lashes resting
on the pallid cheek from which they never more
would rise ; and with her pure, pale profile, sharply
defined against the coarse grass matting that screened

her wretched couch. Crouching on one side was the old squaw, appalled by the marble hue of the strange corpse ; on the other sat Orono, divested of his plume and all his ornaments in token of grief, with his deep glittering eyes fixed on the rocky bluffs which seemed to start forward from the copse-covered slopes, and were then tinted with a deep purple by the sinking sun.

As the last rays died away from the volcanic peaks, the Indian started up and prepared to inter the remains of poor Mary, when the glittering epaulettes and appointments of a French officer, who was leading his horse by the bridle, appeared at the door of the wigwam.

He was the Baron de Beauchatel, with the gold cross of St. Louis dangling on the lapelle of the gay white uniform of the Grenadiers of Guienne. Having lost his way in the forest, he now sought a guide to the camp of Montcalm ; but the dead mother caught his eye at the moment he peered into the obscurity of the hut.

"Mon Dieu ! what have we here ?" he asked, with surprise.

"The squaw and papoose of a pale chief," replied the apparently unmoved Indian.

"Dead—a lady, too !" exclaimed the French officer, stooping over her with a commiseration that was greatly increased when he discovered that she was young and beautiful. He gently pressed her thin white hand, and lifted her soft black hair. "And this is her child ?"

Orono nodded.

"Almost newly born—how calmly it sleeps ! The poor infant—alone in this wilderness—Tête Dieu ! it is frightful ! Tell me all about this, Iroquois, and I will reward you handsomely with a new English clasp-knife, a bottle of eau de vie, a blanket, or whatever else your refined taste teaches you to prize most."

In his own language, by turns soft and guttural, Orono related to the baron all that he knew of the white woman; that she had twice saved his life, and that he, in gratitude, had protected her from the Iroquois; but he had no power over the Great Spirit.

The baron was a humane and gallant French officer of the old days of the monarchy. He had been a gay fellow some few years before, and had been sent to America (according to Parisian gossip) because he had been too favourably noticed by Madame de Pompadour; but he had a good and tender heart; thus, the story of the poor mother, and the helplessness of her orphan, stirred him deeply. By the whole aspect of the dead, and the remains of her attire, he suspected that her rank and position in life had been good—a lady at least. A ring upon the fourth finger of her left hand, bearing the name of her husband in Gaelic, he gently removed; he then cut off some of her fine black hair, and, after making a few memoranda descriptive of her person, he bargained with the Indian that he should give up the child for a few francs. This the Iroquois at once agreed to do, and, with the assistance of the baron, Mary was wrapped in furs and buried under a tree on the sequestered shore of the Horican.

To Beauchatel it seemed strange and repugnant that a Christian woman should be laid there without a prayer or a blessing, on the rough mould that covered her pale attenuated form, her pains and her sorrows; but it was long since *he* had prayed; yet, with an impulse of piety, he cut on the bark of the tree, which covered the place where she lay, a large cross, and raising his hat retired.

The act was in itself a prayer!

"Can I now do aught for you?" he asked of Orono. The Indian mournfully shook his head, and then said,

"Give me a new musket, for the time is coming— the time that has been foretold."

"By whom?"

"The sachems, the pawaws, and the old men of the Iroquois."

"And what shall happen, *mon camarade?*"

"The warriors of the Six Nations will break the pipe of peace and dig up the great war-hatchet."

"Against whom?"

"All who come from the land of the rising sun."

"Be it so," said the baron, shrugging his shoulders, and looking with some anxiety towards the long shadows, that darkened in the forest vistas; "you shall have your musket; but give me the child, *mon ami;* and now for the camp of Louis de St. Veran!"

    ＊   ＊   ＊   ＊

Let us change the scene.

It is 1778, exactly twenty-one years after the events recorded as having happened at Fort William Henry. We are now in France, in the sunny province of Guienne, and near the gay city of Bordeaux.

A lady, young and beautiful, is seated at one of the lofty open windows of the turreted Chateau de Fontbrune, which crowns the summit of a wooded eminence on the right bank of the Garonne. Her eyes and hair are dark; her complexion soft and brilliant. Her attire, as she is in the country, partakes of the picturesque fashion of the last days of Louis XV. She reclines on a velvet fauteuil, and forcibly reminds us of a languid little beauty in

one of Watteau's pictures waiting for some one to
make love to her.   As a poet of the time has it, her
attire

> " Was whimsically traversed o'er,
> Here a knot and there a flower;
> Like her little heart that dances,
> Full of maggots—full of fancies;
> Flowing loosely down her back,
> Fell with art the graceful sacque;
> Ornamented well with gimping,
> Flounces, furbelows, and crimping,
> While her ruffles, many a row,
> Guard her elbows, white as snow,
> Knots below and points above,
> Emblem of the ties of love."

Her cheek rested on her hand, and heedless of the
too familiar splendour of the apartment in which she
was seated, she impatiently drew back the blue
satin hangings, which were festooned by cords and
tassels of silver, and setting her round dimpled chin
into the white palm of her pretty little hand, gazed
languidly upon the beautiful landscape that spread,
as it were, at her feet.

The vine-covered district of the Bordelais, through
which wound the Garonne ; Bourdeaux, clustering on
its left bank in the form of a crescent, with its old
walls and towers of the Middle Ages ; its nineteen
gates, through which the tide of human life was
ebbing and flowing ; its long rows of trees casting
their lengthening shadows to the eastward ; the
huge grey ramparts of the venerable Chateau de
Trompette ; the palace of the Dukes of Guienne ; the
church of St. Michel and the cathedral of St. André,
with its two tall and splendid spires, which pierced
the saffron-tinted sky like stone needles ; and then
the majestic river sweeping past towards the sea, all

bathed in the broad light of a glorious June sunset. But Therese had seen all this a thousand times before, and it ceased to interest her now.

In the lap of this noble lady reposed a pretty, but saucy and snubnosed Bologna spaniel, with the long ears and black silky hair of which the white fingers of one hand played involuntarily. Statues, bronzes, buhl tables, vases of flowers, and a hundred beautiful trifles, decorated this little room, which was her boudoir—her own peculiar sanctum sanctorum—and the windows of which overlooked a bastion, whereon were sixteen antique brass cannon ; for the Chateau de Fontbrune, in which we have now the honour of finding ourselves, was an old baronial house, which, after being fortified by Louis de Foix, had given shelter to Charles VII., and been beleaguered by the Maréchal de Matignon.

The productions of the popular men of the day strewed the apartment. The poems of Bernis, the comedies of the Abbé Boissy, the music of Lulli, with drawings and pictures without end, lay near, while a vaudeville by Panard was open upon the piano. Mademoiselle had evidently been sorely puzzled in her efforts to get through the long hours of this day of June, 1778.

"Oh, Nanon !" she exclaimed to her attendant, a pretty girl of eighteen, who sat near her on a tabourette, sewing ; "I am *so* ennuyé—for in this dreary old chateau, which I am not permitted to leave, and to which no one comes but prosy old colonels and stupid magistrates, such as M. le Maire, or M. le Maitre du Palais, or still worse, those horrid counsellors of the Court of Admiralty, there is so little to rouse one from sad thoughts and drowsy lethargy."

L

"Try another chapter of that new romance by M. de Marivaux."

"Ah, *merci !* he is a most tiresome fellow, Nanon, and odious, too,"

" Odious?"

" Yes."

" How, Mademoiselle Therese ?"

" I judge from his memoir of himself."

" Explain, mademoiselle."

" He was once in love with a young lady—"

"*Once,* only—then he is no true romance writer."

" She had black hair, hazel eyes and long lashes, divine little hands and feet—in fact, the counterpart of myself, as the old Abbé de Boissy told me—and was on the point of paying his most solemn and magnificent addresses to her ; when, happening to enter her boudoir one day unexpectedly, he found—"

"Not a lover?" exclaimed Nanon, becoming suddenly interested ; "not a student or mousquetaire, I hope ?"

"*Ma foi !* no—nothing half so pleasant."

" What, then ?"

" Mademoiselle studying smiles and postures before her mirror."

" And this—"

"So shocked the staid and proper M. de Marivaux, that his passion passed away in a moment, and he took to novel writing."

" It was no passion whatever, mademoiselle," replied Nanon, disgusted to find that a lady should lose a lover by the same arts which she practised daily to win one ; and now ensued another long pause.

This young lady—so beautiful, so tenderly nurtured, so accomplished, and so splendidly jewelled—was the richest heiress in Bordeaux, a ward of the young King Louis XVI., *fiancée* of the Comte

d'Arcot, a high military noble, who had covered himself with distinction in India, and was now on his way
home with a fabulous sum in livres, and, of course,
with the liver complaint. But this noble demoiselle,
successor of M. le Baron Beauchatel, Seigneur de
Fontbrune and of St. Emilion, Seneschal of Bourdeaux, and Commandant of the Chateau de Trompette, was the foundling of the Iroquois wigwam, the
orphan child of Roderick MacGillivray and of that
lonely and despairing mother who found her grave,
uncoffined, in the savage solitude on the southern
shore of the Horican.

And now to solve this mystery.

Beauchatel had conveyed the infant girl to Fort
William Henry, and consigned her to the care of the
baroness, a lady of gentle and amiable disposition.
In pity for the helplessness of the child, she undertook its care, at first as a mere duty of humanity, but
as months passed on, her regard became a strong love
for this lonely little waif—a love all the stronger that
she was herself without children, and had long ceased
to hope that she would ever be a mother; so it
seemed as if Heaven had sent this infant to fill up the
void in her heart. She named her *Therese,* after herself; for she had been Mademoiselle Therese de St.
Veran, a sister of the Marquis de Montcalm, and consequently was a lady of Nismes. Soon after her return to France with Beauchatel she died, and her last
request was, that he would continue to protect the
orphan which fate had so strangely committed to his
care. The good and faithful soldier had learned to
love the little girl as if she had been his own, and
being without kinsmen or heirs to his title and estates,
he obtained from the young King Louis XVI., then
in the fourth year of his unhappy reign, as a reward

for his services and those of his ancestors, permission
to adopt her in legal form. The necessary docu-
ments were accordingly drawn up, sealed, signed, and
registered ; and thus the poor foundling of the Canadian forest, the child of Roderick MacGillivray of
the Black Watch, became the heiress of the Chateau
de Fontbrune and of the Seigneurie of Saint Emilion.

On returning from America, the baron had served
five years under M. Law de Lauriston in the East,
upholding the interests of the French India Company against the Nabob of Bengal and the British,
under Lord Clive. There he had met and become
acquainted with Count d'Arcot, for whom he had con-
ceived a sudden and vehement friendship—so much
so, that, after his return to France, he resolved that,
bongré malgré, his young ward should marry this
soldier of fortune ; for such he was, having been
created Count d'Arcot and Knight of St. Louis for
his bravery at the recapture of that city of Hindostan,
the capital of the Carnatic.

Poor Therese had been told the sad story of the
mother she had never known, and of whom no relics
remained but some silky black hair, a ring, and that
singular brooch—an ornament so unlike anything she
had ever seen, and which was graven with a legend
in a language to her so strange and barbarous ; and
her heart yearned for a further knowledge of whom she
was, and whence she came, and for that mother's kiss,
of which, though it had been planted a thousand
times upon her little lips, she had no memory ; and
at times she mourned for that father she had never
seen. Then it seemed so odd, so strange, so grievous
that she could have any other father than the dear,
kind old baron, for whom she had a love and reverence so filial and so strong.

But to resume.

"The evening lags, as if the sun would never set," yawned the petulant little beauty. "What shall we do with ourselves—speak, you provoking Nanon?"

"Play," was the pithy reply.

"I have played everything that came last from Paris, and my piano is now frightfully out of tune—the chords are fallen."

"Read."

"I have read MM. Marivaux, Bernis, and Jean Jacques de Rousseau till I am sick of them."

"Draw."

"It makes my head ache, and the Abbé Boissy says it will spoil my eyes, in which he seems to take a poetical interest."

"Sing."

"Nanon, you bore me!"

"Suppose we pray, then?"

"Ma foi!—that would not be very amusing when one is dull and dreary."

"Order out the grey pads and ride."

"M. Beauchatel never allows that, as you know well, Nanon, save when he is with me; and we shall have enough of our horses, I have no doubt, when this odious old count, whom I am to marry, and whom I already hate, and whom I am resolved to tease to death, arrives here."

"I shall retire, mademoiselle."

"You shall not!"

"I fear you find me poor company," urged Nanon, demurely.

"Poor or bad company are better than none——"

"Here in this huge chateau, perhaps; but one would not think so in the midst of a wood."

" Here I am left all day with no thoughts to rouse me but of that horrible old Comte d'Arcot, who is certainly coming from India, and to whom I am to be given like a box of rupees or a bale of sugar."

" It is a long way to India," said Nanon ; " away round the end of the world at Cape Finisterre, and perhaps—perhaps——"

" Say on, Nanon."

" He may be drowned by the way."

" Ah ! don't say so, Nanon !"

" Storms may arise, as they frequently do, and then ships are wrecked.   There was M. la Perouse, who sailed away out into the wide ocean in the days of the late King Louis XV., and has never been heard of since.   If stout young sailors drown, surely an old soldier like Comte d'Arcot may."

" I am almost wicked enough to wish it."

" I think I see something that will amuse you, mademoiselle."

" Mon Dieu ! I am glad of that—what is it ?"

" A party of soldiers."

" Where ?—oh, I do so love to see soldiers !"

" 'Tis a guard conveying prisoners to the Chateau de Trompette, and now they are about to cross the Garonne by boats."

The lady gazed from the window, and saw a mass of armed soldiers marching quickly down the opposite slope towards the river.   As they issued from under the green vine trellis which shaded the roads for miles in every direction, she could distinctly discern the scarlet coats of the prisoners contrasting with the white of the French linesmen who formed the escort, and had their bayonets fixed.

" Red uniforms—they are British prisoners of war !" exclaimed Nanon; " oh, mademoiselle, we have gained a battle somewhere, and beaten the English, as we always do."

"Poor, poor fellows!" sighed Therese; "ah, Nanon, I feel sad when I see them, for M. le Baron says my mother was one of these people: yet it seems so strange that I should ever have had any other than Therese de St. Veran—dear Madame la Baronesse, whom the Blessed Virgin has taken to herself."

"See how they crowd into that little boat! Oh, mon Dieu! the brave reckless fellows—it will never hold them all!"

"And the stream is deep and rapid there."

See—see, O Dieu! what has happened!" shrieked Nanon.

"Overturned—the boat has overturned."

"No—'tis a man overboard!—he is in the stream, and drowning!"

"Oh, I cannot look· upon this!" said Therese, shrinking back and burying her face in her hands, while loud cries of alarm ascended from the river to the windows of the chateau; but Nanon, whose nervous temperament was less delicate than that of her mistress, continued to gaze steadily.

Two men were swimming or splashing in the water. One had fallen overboard; the other had plunged in to succour or save him; but both were swept away by the stream. In short, the former was soon drowned, and the latter rescued with the utmost difficulty. When dragged on shore he was quite insensible; but the officer in command of the escort, having no time to spare, desired four of his men to form a litter with their muskets, and bear him to the Chateau de Fontbrune, as the nearest place where the usual means might be adopted for the restoration of life.

The half-drowned man, who had perilled life so
gallantly to save the unfortunate soldier, was an
officer, and moreover, one that was sure to win favour
in French eyes, being young, handsome, and an
Officier d'Ecossais, as Nanon reported minutely to
her startled mistress, who had promptly all her
household in attendance on the sufferer, though she
dared not peep into his room in person. At last
Nanon brought the joyous intelligence that he was
" recovering, and had opened a pair of *such* beautiful
eyes !"—so here was a stirring episode for our young
demoiselle, who, a half hour before, had been so dull
and *ennuyé* that she was weary of her own charming
self and all the world beside.

France and Britain were still, as we last left them
twenty-one years ago, engaged in the lively and profit-
able occupation of fighting battles, battering fleets and
burning towns in America, where the subject of taxa-
tion had occasioned hostilities between the mother
country and her colonies, whose forces, led by Washing-
ton, were aided in the strife by the armies and fleets
of France, Spain, and Holland.

Some days elapsed before the young officer, who
was on his parole of honour, had sufficiently recovered
to appear on the terrace of the chateau, where
Mademoiselle Therese and the gossiping Nanon received him in due form. He was pale and thin from
the effects of a wound, his long sea voyage, and the
severe treatment to which prisoners of war were
usually subjected in those days ; but all this only
served to make him the more interesting to the two
girls, who were quite flattered by the presence of the
chance visitor fortune had sent them to enliven the
old chateau. His uniform was sorely dilapidated ;
the lace and epaulettes of his scarlet coat were

blackened by powder and long service, and it consorted oddly with a pair of French hussar pantaloons. Still, notwithstanding these disadvantages, his bearing was free, gallant, and gentlemanly; and in very good French he thanked the lady of Fontbrune for her humanity and hospitality.

" May I ask your name, monsieur ?" asked Therese, timidly.

" Munro—Hector Munro."

" And your regiment ?"

" The Black Watch—Ecossais."

" Oh, indeed," said Therese, with her dark eyes brightening; for to belong to a Scottish regiment in those days (and even in the *present*) was as sure a guide to French favour as if he could have answered, " The Irish Brigade."

" And you were taken prisoner——"

" In America, mademoiselle, on the Acushnet River, where my regiment was serving with the brigades of grenadiers and light infantry then ordered to destroy a number of pirates who made New Plymouth their haunt. This we achieved successfully, but not without severe loss."

" Were you not dreadfully frightened ?"

" I was then under fire for the *first* time," said the young officer, smiling.

" And how did you feel—oh, pray tell me ?"

" A tightening of the breast—a long-drawn breath, as the *first* shot whizzed past my ear ; another as the first cannon-ball seemed to scream in the air overhead, and then I rushed on fearless, filled by a fierce and tumultuous joy. I heard only the din of the bagpipes and the cheers of my comrades. But I lost my way in the wood, and falling among a detachment of the Regiment of Languedoc, was made a prisoner.

With many others in the same predicament, I was
soon shipped off for France, and so have the honour
to appear before you."

"And who was the soldier for whom you risked
your life?"

"A sergeant of the Regiment of Languedoc."

"A Frenchman!"

"Yes, mademoiselle; the same man who made me
prisoner in America."

"Ah, mon Dieu! and you tried to save him! How
noble!"

"Mademoiselle, my father, who was a brave old
soldier, taught me that when the sword was in the
scabbard *all men are brothers.*"

"And your rank?"

"Lieutenant; and now," he added, bitterly, "I may
remain a prisoner for ten years perhaps, with my
hopes blighted, my promotion stopped, and my pay
gone."

"It is very sad," replied Therese, casting down her
fine eyes, which she feared might betray the interest
she already felt in the young prisoner of war; "but
when the baron comes home from Paris—he will be
here in three days—we shall see what can be done
for you."

Three days—poor little Therese! by that time she
was irrevocably in love with young Munro, and
Nanon left nothing undone or unsaid to convince her
that the passion was quite mutual. Though they did
not meet at meals, they, were constantly together on
the terraces and in the gardens of the chateau; thus
it was impossible for this young man to spend his
time in the society of such a girl as Therese, in the
full bloom of her youth and beauty (a *fair bloom* that
belonged not to France), without feeling his heart in-

fluenced; while her artless and charming manner, which by turns was playful, sad, earnest, or winning, lured him into a passion against which his better judgment strove in vain ; for he knew the danger and absurdity of a subaltern—a prisoner of war—a lad without rank, home, friends, or subsistence—and more than all, in that land of tyranny, bastilles, and lettres de cachet, engaging in a love affair with a lady of rank and wealth.

"In three days," thought he, "this deuced old baron returns ; but in three days I shall be well enough to be out of the sick list, to march off from here, and report myself at the Chateau de Trompette."

According to the author of *Dream Life*, "Youthful passion is a giant ! It overleaps all the dreams and all the resolves of our better and quieter nature, and madly drives toward some wild issue that lives only in its own frenzy. How little account does passion take of goodness ! It is not within the cycle of its revolution—it is below—it is tamer—it is older—it wears no wings."

So the evening of the *sixth* day passed into twilight, and found M. Hector Munro, of his Britannic Majesty's 42nd Highlanders, still lingering by the side of Therese in the garden of that delightful old chateau by the " silvery Garonne," when the ominous sound of horses' hoofs, and of wheels rasping on the gravel under the antique porte cochère, announced the return of the Baron de Beauchatel !

Therese grew deadly pale.

"Your father—he has arrived, and I must bid you farewell," said Munro, kissing her trembling hands with sudden emotion.

"Stay, monsieur," said Therese, in an imploring

voice.   So "monsieur" stayed; to go was impossible.

"M. le Baron !" exclaimed Nanon, rushing towards them, while her round black eyes dilated with excitement; "M. le Baron, and oh, mon Dieu, M. le Comte d'Arcot is with him !"

"M. d'Arcot !" murmured poor Therese, and stood rooted to the spot, the statue of terror and grief; for, after six days such as the last, to meet an old and previously unknown *fiancé* with the cordiality requisite, was more than poor human nature could bear or achieve.

The baron, who was considerably changed in person since we last had the pleasure of seeing him, having become stout and paunchy, abrupt and irritable in manner, now approached, leading, and indeed almost pulling forward a tall, thin, and soldier-like Chevalier of St. Louis, whose form and face seemed wasted by inward thought and care, by exposure to the burning sun of India and the toils of war, rather than by lapse of time; yet he seemed quite old, though in reality not much more than fifty years of age. His hair, which he wore unpowdered, was white as snow, and was simply tied behind by a black ribbon. He wore the undress uniform of a French Maréchal du Camp, and leaned a little on his cane as he walked.

"Mademoiselle de Beauchatel—my daughter—M. le Comte d'Arcot," said the baron, introducing them, and kissing Therese.

"M. le Comte is most welcome to Fontbrune," said Therese, presenting her trembling hand to the tall old soldier, who kissed it respectfully; and after a few polite commonplaces, muttered hurriedly, on the calmness of the evening, the beauty of the chateau, its gardens, the scenery, &c., she drew aside to wipe away her tears, and desire Nanon to conceal Munro or get him quietly away.

"What think you of her?" asked the baron, covertly.

"She is most lovely; but now, my dear Beauchatel, though I have come to visit you, pray forget your project of the marriage."

"Forget the object nearest my heart!" exclaimed the impetuous baron.

"To unite an old veteran, a man of a withered heart, to a blooming young girl—December to May —it is absurd, my dear baron!" replied the Maréchal du Camp, laughing.

"Absurd—parbleu! do not say so."

"I assure you it is."

"When you know her, you will be charmed."

"I do not doubt it," replied D'Arcot; "but oh! what is this that moves me? Her face seems more than familiar to me, and recals some old friend or relative."

"Impossible, comte; you have been more than twenty years in India, and she is barely twenty-one."

Therese came forward again, and the comte began to examine her features with a fixed and earnest gaze, which filled her timid heart with inexpressible fear and confusion.

At that moment the baron's eye caught the red coat of poor Munro, who had withdrawn a little way back, and was irresolute whether to advance or retire on finding himself so suddenly *de trop* where hitherto he had been so much at home.

"Oh, *sacre bleu!*" exclaimed Beauchatel, drawing his sword in a sudden gust of fury and suspicion, as he rushed upon the stranger; "whom have we here?"

Therese uttered a cry and sprang forward; but she was less alert than Count d'Arcot, who, at that moment, threw himself between the baron and the object of his jealous anger.

"Permit *me* to arrange this matter," said the Maréchal du Camp, unsheathing his sword; "officer, answer me truly on your honour—on your life—how long you have been here."

"Six days, M. le Comte."

"Oh, *sang Dieu!*" swore the baron, pirouetting about in a fresh gust of fury; "six whole days."

"How came you here?"

"On a litter, insensible—being half-drowned, in attempting to save the life of a French soldier in the Garonne."

"You are a prisoner—"

"On my parole," interrupted Munro, bowing.

"One of those who were landed at Castillon from America, and were *en route* for the Chateau de Trompette?"

"Exactly, M. le Comte."

"You are named—"

"Munro—Hector Munro, lieutenant in the 42nd Highlanders."

"The old Black Watch!" said the Maréchal du Camp, sheathing his sword, while an inexplicable expression came over his grave features; "I once knew well an officer who bore the good old name of Munro."

"My father, perhaps," said the prisoner, anxiously; "he was a brave soldier."

"*Was*—he is, then, dead?"

"He fell in action against the Spaniards!"

"Where?"

"At the storming of the Moro Castle."

" And what was his rank ?"

" Colonel of his Britannic Majesty's 60th Regiment of Infantry."

" Or Royal Americans ?" continued the count, with a kindling eye.

" The same, M. le Comte."

" Did he command at Fort William Henry, where the defeated troops were so shamefully abandoned by General Webb, and were afterwards massacred by the Iroquois ?"

" He did. I was saved from that massacre by the wife of a French soldier. It was my second narrow escape from the Iroquois, then ; for once before two Indians bore me into the forest, and my life was spared by the luckiest chance in the world."

" You must have been very young," said Beauchatel ; " I too, served there, and am quite an old fellow now."

" I was a mere child, messieurs, in those days."

" Ah, they will soon be friends now !" thought Therese ; " already they are comrades."

" And you were saved—" resumed D'Arcot.

" By an officer named MacGillivray, who was on his march to join that ill-fated garrison with a party of the Black Watch, the same regiment to which I have now the honour to belong. Then followed that unparalleled massacre, the memory of which seems like a horrible dream to me."

" And to me, too, boy ; for I, also, was at the siege of Fort William Henry, and I was that lieutenant of the Black Watch who saved you from the Iroquois," said Count d'Arcot, taking the hand of Munro in his ; " I had, then, a wife — perhaps a child," he added in a troubled voice ; " but both lie buried in the forest by the shore of Lake George !"

"Your wife, M. le Comte," said Beauchatel; "how did she die?"

"Not as the leaves die when the summer is over; for she was torn from me by the hands of the accursed Iroquois—my beloved Mary! After the lapse of one and twenty years, baron, her image, so noble, so gentle, and so womanly, fills up my past, as once it filled my future. I was taken prisoner, as you know, and joining the French army in sheer disgust of the British, whose conduct, under Webb, maddened me, I have attained in India the rank I now bear, and which I never could have won in the armies of the House of Hanover."

"Stay—*peste!* a sudden light breaks in upon me!" exclaimed the baron, smiting his forehead; "ah, *mon Dieu! mon Dieu!* if it should be!"

"What?"

"Excuse me, messieurs, for one moment; a thought has struck me!" said the impulsive Frenchman, and rushing into the house, he returned in a few moments, bearing in his hands an antique oak casquet, in which he kept his commissions, his diplomas, orders of knighthood, and other objects of value; and, drawing therefrom the brooch which had been found upon the dress of Therese when a child, he placed it in the hands of the count.

As Roderick MacGillivray, now M. le Comte d'Arcot, Governor of Pondicherry, Maréchal du Camp, and Colonel of the Regiment du Roi, a man grown old by war and thought and time, saw the ancient and well-known heirloom of his house—the marriage-brooch of the brides of Glenarrow—the same mystic symbol which, in youth, he had bestowed upon his wife, a sudden tremor came over him, and a flush and then a pallor crossed his wrinkled face.

" *Lochmoy !*" he muttered in his native language, which he had so long unused ; "*touch not the cut without the glove.* Oh my God ! whence came this trinket, Beauchatel ?"

" I found it fastened to the dress of a newly-born babe in the forest near Lake George—a babe that lay on the breast of its dead mother, in the wigwam of an Iroquois, and on her finger was this ring, inscribed—"

" Roderaick Ruadh MacGillibhreac—my own name, and my gift it was to Mary, the grand-daughter of the murdered MacIan of Glencoe," exclaimed Mac Gillivray, in an agonized voice, as his eyes filled with tears ; "and you buried her—"

" By my own hands, at the foot of a tree, which I marked with a cross—"

" God bless thee, my brave and honest Beauchatel !" exclaimed Roderick.

" And there she lies in peace."

" But the babe, baron—the little babe ?"

" Therese—she stands before you."

The veteran Comte d'Arcot opened his arms, and the pale and agitated girl found herself pressed to the breast of her newly-discovered father.

* * * *

Our readers may guess the sequel.

Hector Munro of the Black Watch remained a prisoner of war in France until the autumn of 1782, when a general peace was concluded. He was on parole not to pass beyond two miles from the gates of the Chateau de Trompette. As the mansion of Therese was within that boundary, he found his limits ample enough, and long before that auspicious day when the cannon on the ramparts of Bourdeaux announced the peace of the two countries, and the

M

independence of America, he had become the son-in-
law of Count d'Arcot.

The latter, soon after, seeing the approaching storm
of the Revolution, transferred himself and all his property to Britain, and thus escaped the fate of the
loyal and gallant Beauchatel, whose noble chateau
was destroyed, and whose fate is thus recorded in a
despatch of the Comte d'Artois, dated Coblentz, 10th
June, 1793.—

"M. Beauchatel rivalled his forefathers in glory
and in faith. He died in battle, at the head of his
Emigrant Regiment, and lies in the trenches of Lisle,
a fitting grave for the *premier Chevalier de St.
Louis.*"

V.

THE WIFE OF THE RED COMYN.

MY GRANDFATHER'S STORY.

THE old gentleman had served in the 42nd Highlanders, or old Black Watch, in early life, and could
spin to us endless yarns of the bloody affair of Ticonderoga, where the regiment had no less than six
hundred and forty-seven officers and soldiers killed
or wounded ; the expedition to the Lakes ; the surrender of Montreal ; the siege of the Moro, and the
scalping, flaying alive, the tomahawking, and other
little pleasantries incidental to the relief of Fort Pitt
in 1763 ; and of that devilish business with the Red
Indians amid the swamps and rocks at Bushy Run,
all of which were " familiar in our mouths as household words ;" while, to the venerable narrator, the
smell of gunpowder, the flavour of Ferintosh,' or the
skirl of a bagpipe were like the *elixir vitæ* of the
ancients, and seemed to renew his youth, strength, and
spirit for a time ; and thus the fire of other years
would flash up within him, like the last gleam of a
sinking lamp, as we sat by our bogwood fire in the
long winter nights of the North.

In the year 1768, his regiment was cantoned in
Galway, where it was reviewed by Major-General
Armiger, and the old gentleman was wont to boast,
that except two Lowland Scots, every soldier in its
ranks was from the clans that dwell northward of the

M 2

Tay, "and happily for the corps," he used to add, "these two were knocked on the head during the onfall at Long Island." The regiment, then for the *third* time in Ireland, remained there for seven years. During 1772, it was employed in suppressing tumults occasioned by the complicating interests and adverse views of the Catholic and Protestant landlords and tenants in Antrim and elsewhere ; and in this delicate service their Highlanders were found particularly useful, from the knowledge of the language and their gentle bearing towards the people, whom by old tradition they believed to be sprung from the same stock as themselves. Though some of the Highland tribes have a proverb which says, *cha b'ionann O'Brién is na Gaël*—that O'Brien and the Gael are *not* alike, yet they found many sympathies in common—to wit, a love of fun and breaking heads; a jealousy of the English ; an aversion to still-hunting, and a just, laudable, and commendable antipathy to all gaugers and tax-gatherers.

For the ticklish service of settling disputes in the neighbourhood of Antrim, it pleased his Majesty George III. to order that an additional company of the Black Watch should be raised among the Breadalbane Campbells ; and it was soon seen, that though the slaughter of Ticonderoga had carried woe and desolation to many a lonely hearth and loving heart in the country of the clans, so far from extinguishing the military ardour of the Highland youth, it made them more than ever anxious to enrol themselves in the ranks of the *Reicudan Dhu*, for so was the regiment named, from the dark colours of its plumes and tartans, in contradistinction to the troops of the line, who wore scarlet coats, white waistcoats, pipeclayed breeches and flour-powdered wigs, with queues, pomatumed curls, and looped-up hats, having the true Blenheim cock and the star of Brunswick—*i.e.* the black leather cockade of the Protestant succession, which still survives on the chapeaux of the penny postman.

My grandfather was popular among the Breadalbane men, to please whom he had, at various times, hanged sundry MacNabs and MacAlpines, whose ideas of the eighth commandment were somewhat vague; thus on being sent into "the marquis's country" to recruit, he raised the required company in three days, and marched down from the hills of Glen Urchai with pipes playing, across the dreary Braes of Rannoch, and down by the Brig of Tay with a hundred of the handsomest men that ever became food for gunpowder, all clad in their native tartans, and well armed, each with his own sword, dirk and pistols, to which the Government added the usual arms and accoutrements of the line. From Perth, the captain was ordered to march his company to Glasgow, there to embark for Ireland; and proceeding *en route*, after leaving Falkirk and traversing the remains of the Torwood, he found himself, with his little command, approaching the burgh of Kirkintulloch one dreary November evening, just as the dusk was closing in, while the rain fell in torrents, and the wind swept in gusts through the pastoral hollows and hurled the wet and withered leaves furiously before it. There he was compelled to halt, and oblige the authorities to procure immediate quarters for a hundred Highlanders—a race of whom the westland Whigs had harboured a holy aversion and wholesome terror, since the epoch of the Great Montrose and his daredevil Cavaliers, one hundred and twenty years before.

"But what has all this to do with the Wife of the

Red Comyn ?" the reader may ask. I answer, everything—for had not my grandfather halted on that wet
November night in the ancient burgh of Kirkintulloch, that good lady—though she made some noise in
her time—had never been introduced to the reader's
notice. So patience yet awhile.

The soldiers were soon distributed among the people
by the town constable, and in a few minutes after
seeing the last man off to his billet, my grandfather
found himself standing before the gate of the Castle
of Kirkintulloch drenched through plaid and philabeg,
while the rain dripped gracefully from his long
feathers into the nape of his neck, and the water
spouted from his scabbard as from a syringe when he
sheathed his claymore.   Draggled and weary, he
knocked furiously against the gate of the huge mansion,
on which, as being the most important in the town,
he was billeted as commander of the forces.   Being a
Celt, 'and not blessed with overmuch patience, he
thrust his billet-order almost into the mouth of the
servant who opened the door, and then swaggered in
with all the air of a man who had heard the forty
days' cannonade at the Moro ; but a couple of good
drams from a jolly magnum bonum of Ferintosh,
which were given to him without delay, at once restored his equanimity, and, chucking the plump
housekeeper under the chin, my grandfather—or, as
I shall call him in future, the captain—proceeded up-
stairs.

This ancient Castle of Kirkintulloch, which had
been stormed by Edward I. of England, but re-taken
by the Scots, was a good specimen of the gloomy
mansions of the Middle Ages, when every Scotsman
was forced to keep watch and ward against his neigh-
bour, and, more than all, against Southern invasion ;

for it was built by the Comyns, who flourished in the
days of Malcolm III., and were Lords of Linton Roderick and of Badenoch, and who made a great
figure during the reigns of the three Alexanders and
Robert I.

In those turbulent times every Scotsman was a
soldier, and a brave one, too ; every house was a fortress, every fortress a citadel, and its inmates were a
garrison, while the urgent necessity for security caused
the Scottish baron literally to found his dwelling on a
rock.

A site alike remote and inaccessible was usually
selected, on the isle of some deep lake, or the brow
of a sequestered hill, and there the Scottish feudatory
raised the mansion in which his race were to dwell, to
be married and given in marriage, to be born and to
die, "while grass grew and water ran"—the strong
square peel-house, with its corbelled battlements,
through the openings of which missiles could be shot
securely ; its stone-flagged roof; its irregular slits or
windows, all strongly grated, though ninety or a
hundred feet from the base, and girdled by a bar-
bican, having an arched gate and flanking towers.
Such was unvaryingly the external aspect of the
dwelling of a Scottish baron, and such was the Castle
of Kirkintulloch.

Above the gate, which bristled with loopholes for
musketry, were the armorial bearings of Robert
Comyn, who was slain at the battle of Alnwick, and
the monogram of his descendant, the black Lord of
Badenoch, who married the Princess Marjorie,
daughter of King John Baliol, and whose son was
the last of his race.

After taking a draught from the cup of ale which was
filled for him, as for all other visitors, from a barrel

which stood in a recess of the entrance lobby, the
captain ascended the hollow-stepped stair to the
common hall of the venerable tower.

Internally the accommodation and construction
were of the plainest description. A narrow turn-
pike stair gave access to the various floors of the
keep. The first of these being the levelled rock on
which the edifice was founded, was vaulted, and contained the pit or dungeon, with cellars for the stores
necessary to a crowded household during the long
northern winter, and there was also a deep draw-well
hewn through the living rock. The next contained
the arched hall into which our wet and weary captain
was ushered with much formality. Its floor was
paved; the fireplace was of stone, and had ingle-seats
within its arch. The windows were deeply embayed,
and were secured by shutters within and iron bars
without. The sun, when it shone through the half-
darkened halls of those days, must have imparted to
the dwelling of the Scottish baron the aspect of a
prison; thus their prisons became dungeons, for the
good folks of the olden time knew no medium in
anything.

A gigantic fire blazed redly on the hearth, and by
its light the captain could discern a number of those
unfortunate wights who, as casual guests, trencher-
men, or boys-of-the-belt, in that year, 1772, shared
the old-fashioned hospitality of the Flemings of
Kirkintulloch; but not being of sufficient consequence to have separate apartments, lay rolled up
in their plaids on the benches, or among the stag-
hounds that nestled together on the warm hearthstone.

The reader may deem my description somewhat
minute, but the events which occurred to my vene-

rable kinsman in the old stronghold of the Comyns, and a tale which he heard there, served to impress every feature of it on his memory, and thus it bore a prominent place in his narrative.

As he entered the hall, a stout and jolly-looking old man, who sat with his sturdy legs stretched out before the fire, one hand supporting a long pipe in his mouth, the other resting on a silver tankard of mulled claret, rose up at his approach and bade him welcome. The fashion of this person's dress was old—for still the Scots are always a year or two behind every innovation; his red vest was deeply flapped, his coat of brown broadcloth was square-tailed, with enormous cuffs and silver buttons; he wore a brown bob periwig with a single row of curls round the bottom thereof; square buckles on his square-toed shoes, and a hat cocked with great exactness in the form of an equilateral triangle, completed the costume of the old chamberlain or castle bailie of the Laird of Kirkintulloch.

"A cold night, bailie," said the captain; "I am sorely chilled, having marched from the Torwood amid this tempest of wind and rain."

"The more are you welcome, sir, to the Castle of Kirkintulloch," replied the bailie, placing a chair; "and if a draught from this tankard of hot mulled claret will comfort you, take it and welcome, while something better is preparing."

"A thousand thanks, good bailie," replied the captain, as he drained the silver pot which came seething from the glowing hob.

Being thoroughly drenched, he begged the bailie would have him shown to an apartment where he might change certain portions of his attire. A boy in the livery of the Flemings, with their goat-head worked on his sleeves, appeared to conduct him, and, taking a candle, the lad, who was evidently displeased at being summoned from the warm fire of the kitchen, which in the Scoto-French fashion adjoined the hall, hurried up the staircase before the captain, leaving him to follow as he pleased.

I have already hinted that my grandfather was somewhat short-tempered, so he swore one of those hearty oaths which our army picked up so glibly in Flanders, adding, " Hollo ! you young devil—do you mean to leave me here in the dark ?"

Without heeding him, the lad sprang to the top of the stairs, and hastened across the landing-place into an apartment, leaving the captain to ascend by no other light than the feeble rays that fell from a candle in a tin sconce, which hung on the wall in the first turn of the spiral stair. Looking angrily up in search of his guide, the captain saw—or thought he saw—a lady cross the landing-place.

She was tall, and her white profile was stern and grave, and she was attended by the most diminutive black dwarf in the world—a little creature who appeared absolutely to perspire under the weight of her enormous train, which was of some dark rich stuff, but brilliantly brocaded with white stars. The captain paused and bowed very low, lifting up the end of his long claymore, believing that this stately dame might wish to descend ; but when he raised his head again she was gone ! Her disappearance was so sudden that he was confounded, and rubbed his eyes.

" Can the long march against a chill November wind have affected my vision ?" thought he ; " or has that brimming tankard of hot claret affected my nerves ? Impossible ! Tush—the dame has been scared by my draggled appearance, and has hastened

into one of these apartments ;" so the old gentleman
swore another Flemish oath, and reached the top of
the stairs.

The guide now reappeared, and he would certainly
have had his ears pulled, but the captain's mind was
strangely agitated by thoughts of the lady, whose tall
aristocratic figure, and pure, cold, and almost sublime
profile seemed to be still before him in the dusk.

He was shown into a handsome bed-chamber, which
was lighted by four candles in brass-mounted holders
of carved oak. The walls were hung with antique
leather, of a pale yellow colour, embossed with red
flowers ; the bed was very ancient, and resembled the
canopied tombs one occasionally sees in old churches.
Over the mantelpiece was a Latin legend, informing
the visitor that in this chamber the wife of the Red
Comyn had died a prisoner in the year of our redemp-
tion 1310.

" Four hundred and sixty-two years ago," quoth the
captain, after airing his subtraction a little ; " ugh !
how gloomy the place looks, compared to the cheerful
hall—so gloomy, indeed, that I shall be here as little
as possible before marching to-morrow."

He flung off his belted plaid, badgerskin sporran,
and sword-belt, wrung the water from his kilt and
from the curls of his periwig, smoothed his queue,
donned a pair of dry hose, and, after giving a casual
glance to the primings and charges of his pistols,
which were a pair of true steel-butted Doune pops,
from the armoury of old Thomas Caddel, he turned
to leave the chamber, from the ceiling of which a
dried kingfisher hung by a thread ; for it is an old
superstition that the bird will turn his bill to *that*
point from which the wind blows.

Taking one of the candles, the captain left the

chamber, and was about to descend, when by some
" glamour" he mistook the way; for being supperless,
I am convinced that the hot wine had affected his
head ; he stumbled against a door ; it flew open, and
he found himself in the dressing apartment of a lady,
whose face was turned towards him, and by the lights
on a side-table he perceived at a glance that she was
the same queenly dame who had recently crossed the
landing-place.   She gazed fixedly at the amazed intruder, as she stood before a mirror, with her round
polished shoulders turned towards him, and her jet
black hair gathered up in heavy masses on her slender
fingers, for she seemed in the act of dressing it. From
a faultless bust, her dark dress, brocaded with stars,
hung in magnificent folds to her feet, where, crouching
like a marmoset, the hideous little dwarf was sitting.
Her figure was beautiful, but so motionless and still,
as she gazed with eyes full of indignation and inquiry,
that the words of apology hung half arrested on the
lips of the bowing intruder, who, in another moment,
discovered that he had before him a—picture—only
a picture ; but one painted in the first style of
antique art.
   Nothing artistic could be more beautifully executed
than the upturned and polished arms, from which the
lace that foreign looms must have woven, hung in
loops upheld by diamonds.   A necklace of precious
stones encircled her neck, and a large band of the
same formed a coronet round her head, and gave an
imperial grace to her lofty beauty of feature and
of form.
   The captain gazed on it till the figure appeared to
come forward and the canvas to recede, till the eyes
seemed to fill with light and the proud lips to curl
with a scornful smile ; and then he turned away, for

the strange picture had a mysterious effect upon him,
and hastily he sought the hall, where a hot and
savoury supper smoked on the centre table, and where
the bailie or castellan of the absent proprietor impatiently awaited him.

"Come awa, sir—come awa; I thought you meant
to bide up-stairs a' night. Here are hot collops,
devilled turkey, stewed kidneys, mulled claret, port,
sherry, and whisky toddy—draw in a chair, sir, and
make yourself at hame."

"I have a hawk's appetite, bailie," said my kinsman, applying himself assiduously to the devil and
the sherry.

"And I ditto, double — for I have ridden in
from Stirling market to-day; try the cold gibelotte
pie."

"Thank you; I'll rather stick to my old friend—a
devilled bone smacks of the bivouac. Pass the sherry,
bailie. Thank you."

"Try the kidneys; they would serve a king."

"Thanks. By the bye, who is that noble lady now
residing here?"

"Noble lady?" reiterated the bailie, looking up
with his mouth full, and surprise in his flushed
face.

"Yes; she whom I passed, or rather who passed
me, on the staircase to-night." The bailie pushed
back his chair and plate.

"A lady, sir!" he stammered, while his eyes
opened wider.

"She in the black dress brocaded with white
stars."

"Gude hae mercy on us!—and a dwarf holding up
her tail?"

"The same."

"The Lord take us a' into his holy keeping ! Ye have seen *her ?*"

"Seen who?   What the devil do you mean?"

"*The wife of the Red Comyn !*"

"Come, that is good ; but I am too old a soldier, bailie, to believe all this."

"Keep us frae harm !" continued the old man, as his rubicund visage grew pale, and he glanced stealthily over his shoulder while lowering his voice ; "she hasna' been seen for these ten years past ; heaven send it portends nae evil to our family !"

"Our family," meant the house; so completely were the old Scottish domestics identified with those they served.

"Lord help you, sir," he continued, draining a hot jug of toddy almost at a draught ; "you have seen a wandering spirit."

"It may have been fancy, bailie ; but I certainly saw her picture, and that is tangible enough."

"That picture was painted two hundred years and mair after her death ; and there is a devilish story connected with it too."

"'Pon my honour, bailie, you quite interest me," said the captain, brewing a jug of smoking toddy, and drawing a chair nearer to the fire ; "the atmosphere of this place becomes full of diablerie.   Painted two hundred years *after* her death !   I hope the likeness is good ; but tell me all about it."

"She was the wife of the last Comyn to whom this castle belonged, and she was a woman possessing alike the pride and temper of Lucifer ; but they cost her dear, for she suffered a sore penance in the yellow bed-chamber up-stairs, and there 'tis said her spirit walks to this hour.   Now it chanced that in the days of King James IV., his Master Painter, the famous Sir

Thomas Galbraith, the pupil of Quentin Matsys, of Antwerp, and the friend of Leonardo da Vinci and of Titian Vecelli, came here during the lifetime of John Lord Fleming—the same who was so barbarously assassinated by the cursed Laird o' Drummelzier, wi whose folk we have a feud outstanding yet, like an auld debt—well, the King's painter slept, or rather, perhaps, passed the night in the yellow room, and from that time he was a changed man; from being rosy-faced, he became pale and wan, hollow-eyed and ghastly; from being as full of fun and frolic as the King himself, he became sad, woful and thoughtful, and he shut himself up in the haunted-room, where he worked day and night for a whole week, without eating, drinking, or sleeping, as folks aver, until *that* awful picture was finished; and whether it was done from the memory of *one* vision of the spirit, or whether the wife of the Red Comyn came to him nightly from hell, and sat for her portrait, I cannot say; but when finished by Sir Thomas Galbraith, it was the last work he did on earth, for he was found dead, seated before it, one morning, with a pallet on his left thumb and a brush in his right hand. Terror was on his dead face, and the marks of strangulation were round his throat; so the Flemings buried him in the auld Kirk of St. Ninian, at the Oxgang, where his grave is yet to be seen. I would fain have the picture burned, but the family set a high value upon it; yet I verily believe, if a puir presumptuous auld carle like me dare judge o' sic things, that its presence here may keep the spirit o' that awfu' woman hovering about the walls o' the auld castle she rendered accursed by her crimes !"

" Well, bailie, tell me the story and——"

" Mak' another browst o' toddy while the water is hot, sir," replied the castellan, as he stirred up the fire

with an enormous poker, and as the flames roared in
the tunnel-like chimney, the red sparks flew up in
pyramids.

" I am charged to the brim," said the captain ; " so
fire away, my friend, I am all impatience."

After a few preliminary hems, coughs, and flourishes,
with sips of toddy between, the bailie told the
captain the following strange story, which I give
in my own words, being vain enough to prefer them
to his.

In the beginning of the fourteenth century, the
Castle of Kirkintulloch was the principal residence of
John Comyn Lord of Badenoch, who, as nephew of
King John Baliol, was a competitor with Bruce for
the crown of Scotland, and he was called the *Red*
Comyn to distinguish him from his father, the *Black*
Comyn, who was so named from his swarthy com-
plexion.

In those days the country around this castle was
covered by forests of oak and pine, through the
secluded hollows of which the Kelvin and the Logie
crept with that slow and sluggish current which gives
them more the aspect of Flemish canals than streams
that roll from Scottish mountains. The rising burgh
was then roofed with stone, or thatched ; the Roman
fort on the Barhill was nearly entire, as when a thousand years before the soldiers of the Cæsars had relinquished it before the furious Scots ; and the how
ruined tower of Sir Robert Boyd, Baron of Kilmar-
nock, Hartshaw, Ardneil and Dalry, was still the
stronghold of his family, who were the sworn enemies
of the Baliols and all their adherents. So deep,
indeed, was their hatred, that they would not bury

their dead in the same church ; thus, while the Boyds were laid in the Chapel of St. Mary (which is now the parish kirk), the Comyns were interred in the Church of St. Ninian.

The Red Comyn was powerful, cunning, and dissembling ; being ambitious, and though he fought under Wallace at Falkirk, intensely selfish, he feared to lose his estates after that disastrous battle was lost ; and as usual with Scottish nobles, considering his own interest before the common weal or the national honour, he joined the English ranks, and fought against his own country in the army of the traitor-king, John Baliol.

He was a woful tyrant to the burgh of Kirkintulloch ; for, in defiance of the old laws of the land, he enforced the bludewit, the stingisdynt, the marchet, the herezeld, and other exactions now unknown within the ports of a Scottish town ; and as all pleas between burgesses and travelling merchants must be settled before the third flowing and ebbing of the tide, he usually decided them by whipping the burgess and confiscating the goods of the stranger. Moreover, although it had been ordained by the kings of old, that on any burgess departing on a pilgrimage to the Holy Land or other sacred place, his goods and family should be protected "vntill God brought him hame againe," the wives of the absent were often seized by Comyn, and their goods by his lady.

At his mills he exacted exorbitant mulctures, and he hung all who dared to complain ; if any ventured to grind wheat, mashloch, or rye with hand querns, they were also hanged ; and though it was statute and ordained that he who stole a halfpenny-worth of bread should be scourged, that he who stole a pair of

N

shoes should be pilloried, or eightpence worth should
have *one leg* cut off, the tyrant hanged them all.
Thus his Dule-tree was never without a man hanging
from it, with the black gleds flying round him ; for
Comyn ground alike to the dust'the burgesses within
the walls and the gudemen of the Newland Mailings
without ; so that it was generally said in Dumbarton-
shire, that the devil himself would be a gentler over-
ord than he ; and he was so hated that men remembered the dreadful fate of his father in Badenoch,
and it came to be whispered about that there was a
prophecy made by a weird woman, that he too should
die a violent death !

His wife, Lady Gwendoleyne, was esteemed one of
the most beautiful women in Scotland, and none had
outshone her at the Court of Queen Yolande, the
consort of Alexander III. Lovely beyond all com-
parison, tall, stately and magnificent in form, with
pale commanding features and dark eyes, indicative
rather of pride of birth and loftiness of mind than of
gentleness, she made the people—even those whom
her beauty dazzled, and her slightest smile would
have won for ever—shrink and quail before her, as
beneath the eye of some mysterious spirit ; for the
keen black eye of that imperious lady is said to have
been as dangerous in its beauty as it was terrible in
its expression.

She had been wedded early to the Red Lord of
Badenoch ; they had three daughters, the youngest
of whom (according to Andrew Wyntoun) was married to the traitorous MacDougal of Lorn. They had
also one son, who at the time this history opens,
A.D. 1306, was in his eighteenth year, and was said
to be a handsome, gallant, and high-spirited youth ;
but, unfortunately, devoted to the false Baliol, at

whose mock Court in the Castle of Perth he resided, and there he had been educated.

Notwithstanding her own unparalleled beauty, her husband's rank, power, and overweening authority, Lady Gwendoleyne was far from being happy! A thorn sharper than a poisoned arrow rankled in her heart, in the form of a restless jealousy of her husband, to whom she was passionately devoted, and whom she loved with all the ardour of her impulsive nature. And though he seemed to be, in manner, all that befitted a faithful and attached spouse, he was yet an object of suspicion to Gwendoleyne ; for some artful minion had skilfully sown the seeds of mistrust between them, and several of Comyn's unguarded actions and interferences with the wives of pilgrim-burgesses had given her every reason to deem her fears were just and true ; hence her fiery heart became a prey to furious passions and to bitter thoughts, and she looked about her, longing for some fitting object on which to vent her wrath.

Her husband's kinsman and her own dear friend, old Sir Alexander Baliol of Cavers, Great Chamberlain of Scotland, to whom she often hinted her complaints against Comyn and her suspicions of his infidelity, endeavoured to laugh away her fears.

"Madam," said he, on one occasion, "jealousy is the soul of a love which will brook no rival even for a moment. I mean not to hint that you love Red Comyn too much, but without this jealousy your love for him perhaps would die."

"You are too subtle a casuist for a woman, Sir Alexander of Cavers," replied the lady, cresting up her beautiful head ; "but you must be aware that the disposition and manners of Comyn, your kinsman, are at least but too well calculated to excite my suspicion

N 2

and distrust. To wit: his passionate and unconcealed admiration for female beauty; this is known over the whole country, and thrice, on vague suspicion, I have had to discard certain ladies of my household, and thus make their families deadly enemies of ours. And say, my good Lord Chamberlain, are these wandering sallies not shameful, when perpetrated by one who has a son now in his eighteenth year, and tall and handsome as himself?"

Sir Alexander thought of Comyn's gigantic red beard, and smiled when remembering the handsome youth, who had all his mother's beauty, without his father's ferocity of aspect and bearing.

" You smile, Sir Alexander !" said the fiery dame. " You smile—'tis very well, sir ! You know more of the Red Comyn and his secrets than you care to tell me, and that courtier's smile assures me that I am an injured wife——"

" I beg to assure you, Lady of Badenoch——"

" Assure me of nothing, Lord of Cavers, if you cannot assure me of your kinsman's faith and purity."

" Madam," said the old Lord Chamberlain, testily, "there are two kinds of jealousy—a pure fear by which the young and restless lover is animated—and a grovelling suspicion, which is jealousy in the worst sense of the term. Your suspicion wounds your self-esteem—it piques your honour—and is but a new phase of selfishness, for you suspect yourself an injured woman."

" And justly too, for Comyn's coldness to me during the last month cannot be accounted for but by some new fancy."

" Your husband is never jealous of *you*, madam."

" That only proves his indifference. 'Tis shamel, false, and unknightly; and I only trust that the pre-

sence of our boy, the young Sir John, whom the King
has just knighted, will in some degree recal my wandering husband to a sense of his own honour and the
honour of his wife and daughters."

"Madam, how often shall I assure you that the
husband of one so beautiful as you could never prove
false—I am an old man, your father's friend, and may
well say this."

"True, you are an old man, and were my father's
friend," resumed the lady, whose black eyes flashed
with dusky fire through their tears; "thus it is the
more culpable in you to be in my husband's wicked
secrets, and endeavouring thus to blind and to deceive
a loving and devoted wife. But woe to Comyn and
to you in that hour when I prove the falsehood of you
both!"

And gathering up her long silk kirtle, which was
worn without sleeves, but was so long in the skirt as
constantly to require upholding by one hand, she
swept away with the air of an offended queen, and
with her long and magnificent hair floating over her
shoulders from under a band of burnished gold.

"Alas!" thought the old chamberlain, shrugging
his shoulders, "how true it is, that love being jealous,
maketh a good eye look asquint."

In those days maidens of good family were received
into the houses of ladies of high rank to be delicately
nurtured and well educated; for which, strange as it
may now seem, a befitting fee or pension was paid.
Now, among the ladies of the *tabourette*, or *dames
d'honneur* of the Lady of Badenoch, were the daughters of many noble houses of the Baliol faction, and
who were consequently false to their country. Thus
she had Margaret, daughter of that Lord Abernethy
who basely accepted from the English King a com-

mission as Captain-General of the Scottish rebels ;
Muriel, daughter of Sir Gilbert de Umphreville, the
forfeited Earl of Angus ; Isabel, daughter of David
Lord Brechin, who was accused of a design to betray
Berwick to the English ; Rosamond and Alice, the
daughters of John Comyn, Earl of Buchan, and Lord
High Constable of Scotland, another prime traitor of
the Baliol faction ; and Yolande, daughter of William
de Gifford, Lord of Yester, in East Lothian.   All
these were beautiful girls, and, save the last, were
proud, haughty, and reserved ; for their manners and
bearing were all modelled exactly after those of Lady
Comyn.   Yolande de Gifford, whose father, though a
lord, had, strange to say, been true to Scotland, was
an orphan, and had been taken into the Castle of
Kirkintulloch at the request of Bernard, Abbot of
Arbroath, the Lord Chancellor, and almost in pity,
as all her father's lands in the shire of Haddington
had been seized by John Baliol.   She was the most
beautiful of Gwendoleyne's attendants, and perhaps
the most reserved and gentle, for she felt herself
friendless and alone among the selfish courtiers of the
Scottish King.   Blue eyed, golden haired, and softly
skinned, Yolande, who had been so named after her
godmother, the late queen (Yolande, Countess de
Dreux), was, indeed, the most gentle and loveable of
all gentle creatures, and she shrank under the bold
black eyes of Lady Gwendoleyne, as a sensitive plant
might shrink beneath a hot sun, or before the keen
north wind.

Yolande, when the tresses of her rich hair were
gathered in the golden crespinette then worn by ladies
of the Scottish Court, to show the contour of the neck
and shoulders ; when her blue kirtle, with its tight
sleeves, displayed her beautiful form, over which

floated her surquayne or velvet mantle, tied with
tassels at each shoulder, looked only second in beauty
to Lady Comyn herself, for they were nearly of a
height; and her pretty white fingers were the most
expert of all the ladies there at the weaving of those
endless waves of tapestry at which all noble demoi-
selles then worked daily for the comfort and decora-
tion of their dwellings and churches. Such was then
the industrious custom; and we are told that Matilda,
Queen of William the Conqueror of England, sewed
with her own fair hands sixty-seven yards representing
the history of the Conquest of South Britain, beginning with Harold's embassy to the Norman Court, and
ending with his death at Hastings.

After a long absence at King Edward's Court in
London, Red Comyn returned to Scotland, which
was then groaning under the yoke of the infamous
King John Baliol, the tool of the English, and a faction of traitorous Scottish nobles. On arriving at his
home, he gave presents to all the ladies of his household—to one a necklace, to another a bracelet, a
crespinette, a brooch, and so forth; but to Yolande
de Gifford he gave a golden ring.

A ring!

The restless suspicions of his lady had now discovered a clue to something real and tangible; and
now she had an object on which her vague jealousies
could settle with security. Yolande de Gifford, the
playmate of her absent son—the viper whom she had
taken into her bosom at the entreaty of the cunning
Abbot Bernard, was doubtless involved with her
husband in one of those intrigues which had
embittered her whole life, although she had never
been able to detect them or discover solid proofs.

"Let me be wary and watch well," said she to

herself; "should it be so, by the cross that stood on
Calvary, my Lord of Badenoch shall pay dear for his
fair-haired toy!"

Iago's words have been quoted a thousand times,
and none are more true; for

> "Trifles light as air
> Are to the jealous, confirmation strong
> As proofs of holy writ . . . . .
> Dangerous conceits are in their natures poisons,'
> Which, at the first, are scarce found to distaste,
> But, with a little act upon the blood,
> Burn like the mines of sulphur."

Lady Comyn suddenly discovered that the timid
Yolande had been abstracted and thoughtful, neglectful of her apportioned duties, and inattentive alike to
the conversation of her companions and the commands
of her mistress. Was not this a sign of love and of
secret thoughts? She frequently and bitterly repri-
manded her, till even the gentle Yolande could not
forget that she was the Lord Yester's only daughter,
and replied with honest pride and proper spirit, assert-
ing her own position and rank.

"This insolence and hauteur are alike unbe-
coming," said Lady Gwendoleyne; "and you shall
be banished, minion, from my hall and bower, though
the poorest convent in Scotland be your portionless
home!"

And assuredly this harsh threat would have been
put in execution, but for the determined intervention
of the Red Comyn, whose kindness to the orphan increased with his haughty wife's displeasure; and so
she set her little black dwarf, who was dumb, to watch
Yolande constantly. This dwarf was a present from
Sir Thomas of Charteris, the famous Red Rover and
pirate, who afterwards became Lord of Kinfouns, and

was conquered on the high seas by William Wallace.

About the time that great preparations were making for the return of her son, the young Sir John Comyn, whom—whether the youth was so disposed or not—she meant to wed to his cousin, Alicia Comyn, daughter of the Lord High Constable, she was again imparting her griefs to Sir Alexander of Cavers.

"Comyn goeth from bad to worse; he braves me now, and dares to keep his minion here, whether I will it or no. By God's teeth, sir, could I but discover aught to prove my suspicions right, I'd slay that pale-faced Yolande with Red Comyn's own dagger!"

"I beseech you, lady, to compose yourself, and to be assured that your suspicions are alike unjust and cruel; for they malign your husband and crush this friendless maiden to the dust."

"I tell you that I hate her!" responded the imperious dame, grinding her beautiful teeth, while her magnificent eyes flashed fire.

"Then get her married," said the Chamberlain of Scotland, pithily.

"Who in these selfish times will be mad enough to wed the penniless daughter of a forfeited house? Who would ask her love?"

"I for one, were I young as herself; but let her seek a husband according to the ancient law."

"Sir Alexander, you mock me again."

"Heaven forbid, fair kinswoman; I do but remind you of an Act of Parliament passed in the reign of the late Queen Margaret."

"Pshaw—the Maid of Norway—well?"

"Anent spinsters, like this Yolande."

" Well—well," continued Gwendoleyne, stamping
her pretty foot.

" In 1288, it was statute and ordained, 'that during
the reign of her Most Blessed Majesty, *ilk maiden
ladye of baith high and lowe estate shall have
libertie to bespeak ye man she likes :* albeit, if he re-
fuses to take her to be his wyf, he shall be mulctit of
ye sum of one hundred pounds or less, as his estate
may be, except and alwais, if he can make it appear
that he is betrothit to ane ither woman, when he
shall be free."

" Yolande is proud as myself, for she comes of a
race that would not stoop their crests to kings ; and
this is but mockery, my Lord Chamberlain, so—but
what is this now ?"

At that moment the little black dwarf crept close
to her side, pulled her skirt, and pointed towards the
chamber of Yolande Gifford. The yellow glossy eyes
of the stunted negro gleamed with malevolent light,
as, snatching up her train, the lady swept out of the
hall ; and the Chamberlain shrugged his shoulders
and blessed his stars that he was still a bachelor,
while he whistled merrily, and resumed his employment of teaching a hawk to shake its little bells and
coquette with its wings.

With all her pride and spirit, her furious will and
temper, so completely had the demon of jealousy
taken possession of her soul, that Gwendoleyne stooped
to the humility of eavesdropping ; and on hearing the
murmur of voices whispering in the chamber of
Yolande, she crept close to the thick arras that covered
the door, and listened with all her soul in her ears.

" Go, I implore you," she heard Yolande say, in a
stifled voice ; " alas ! if you are discovered here, what
will my tyrannical mistress say ?"

"Just what she pleases," replied a voice, and then there was a sound—*a kiss*—which set the listener's blood on fire.

"I am watched by that hateful imp her dwarf, and live in daily terror of her discovering all," continued the sobbing Yolande ; "and you know what her views are concerning yourself. Go—go—John Comyn, for the love of God and Saint Mary, go !"

"*John Comyn !*" muttered Lady Gwendoleyne ; "oh, wretch ! that I had a dagger here to avenge this double perfidy !"

A pause ensued.

"To-morrow evening be it, then—at the Roman Peel," said a low voice.

"When the moon is over Campsie Fells."

"You will not forget, beloved Yolande."

"Oh, no—no ; and let that meeting be our last, for another day will change the face of everything," wept Yolande.

Unable longer to restrain her fury, the white hand of Lady Comyn tore aside the arras, and she rushed into the apartment with all the aspect of an enraged Pythoness, while at the same moment the figure of a man vanished from the open window, and his steps were heard crashing through the bushes and trees without, as he retired hastily and in the dusk ; but Gwendoleyne saw—or thought she saw—enough. to be convinced that the fugitive was no other than her husband !

"Alas ! madam," cried Yolande, sinking on her knees in an agony of terror, "you have discovered us."

"At last—yes, at last !" exclaimed the fierce, exulting woman, in hoarse accents, as she savagely wreathed her slender fingers, which rage had endued with triple strength, in the golden hair of Yolande, and proceeded to drag her several times across the oak floor; "beggar! viper! outcast!—ha, ha, ha! thou shalt die now!" and she laughed as she tore out those beautiful tresses in handfuls, till the poor girl's shrieks died away, and she sank senseless at her feet. Then Gwendoleyne locked her up, and after tying the key of the chamber to her silver girdle, retired to her own apartment to still the fierce tumult that swelled her fiery heart, and to lay her plans of deeper and surer vengeance. Alas! they were but too soon formed and matured for pity or remorse to arrest them.

The night passed away, and though she had alternate fits of tenderness and tears, with gusts of jealous rage and passion, the morning found her cold, calm, inexorable, and resolved to have a terrible retribution on the Red Comyn for this attempt to deceive her; and the arrival of a hasty message from him, stating that he was compelled to depart with a slender train on public business to the town of Dumfries, only made her smile the more bitterly, as she thought she saw the game her truant husband meant to play; but she resolved to checkmate him.

"Dumfries, my Lord Chamberlain!" she said, with a scornful smile upon her lovely lip; "now what fool's errand takes him there?"

"To hold a conference with Sir Robert Bruce, the young Earl of Annandale," replied the other, in a low voice; "the Bruces have some bold project now in hand."

"A project."

"Ay, to root the English faction and all Baliol's people out of Scotland. Comyn hath known of this project long, and duly gives King John and King

Edward notice of its progress ; thus Bruce ere long must perish amid his own plots and follies."

"And without waiting for our boy's arrival from Perth, without even bidding me adieu, Comyn has gone to confer with him ?   'Tis well—I wish him speed on his journey.   But there is *a prophecy concerning him ;* so let him beware lest he perish by a violent death like his kinsman who died at Craigie, and who had no other grave than his own girdle."

"Now, grace me guide, lady, talk not thus," replied Sir Alexander, growing pale at her words, which referred to a terrible tale ; for it came to pass in the days of King Alexander III., that it was foretold by Thomas the Rhymer, that Comyn Earl of Buchan, who was ranger of the royal hunting forests of Plater, would die by a violent death ; so he mocked the seer, saying—

"Thou art Sir Thomas the Liar, rather than the Rhymer."

But the aged chief replied solemnly in verse, as was his wont when inspired by his mysterious power—

> "Though *Thomas the Liar* thou callest me,
> The sooth, Lord Earl, I tell to thee !
> By Aikeyside,
> Thy horse shall ride ;
> He shall stumble and thou shalt fa',
> Thy neckbane shall be broken in twa,
> And the hunting dogs thy bones shall gnaw !
> There, maugre all thy kin and thee,
> Thine own belt thy bier shall be !"

And so it came to pass soon after, for when the earl was hunting in the gloomy Den of Howie, as he galloped over the green hill of Arkeybrae, his horse became dazzled by the setting sun, and threw him with such violence that his brains were dashed out by some blocks of grey stone, which to this day are named Comyn's Craigie, and there his bones were found after his hounds had gnawed and torn them asunder.

"So, for God's love, dear lady," resumed the Lord of Cavers with a shudder, "refer no more to these dark and terrible predictions."

; The white lips of the haughty lady smiled, but a wild expression of rage and sorrow filled her eyes, and the glance she gave her kinsman was to him inexplicable, as she had not a doubt that this sudden journey was all a device of her husband to meet, or perhaps to elope, with Yolande. Dark and terrible were the silent thoughts of Gwendoleyne as the evening drew on. The old prophecy that like the Black Comyn, the Red one would *die by a violent death*, seemed ever before her in letters of fire; and she thought that now the time had come.

"How was I ever weak enough to expect that a fair-haired man could be true to me?" she muttered; "in all old Scripture tapestries are not Cain and Judas represented with large yellow beards, or red ones, like that of my husband Comyn! Oh, woe is me! and cursed be the hour I forsook Sir John the Grahame to become the wife of his home and the mother of his children!"

All that day she kept Yolande carefully under lock and key, and without food or drink, while the black dwarf watched the window and the corridor. The sunset faded on the green ridges of the Campsie Fells, evening darkened into sombre night, and the pale light of the moon, long before her rising, was spread across the blue and starry sky behind the hills of Lanarkshire. The woolly-leaved birches that fringed the banks of the Logie and Kelvin, diffused a rich fragrance as the dew of eve fell on them; and the lonely heron sent up its mournful cry at times, as it waded in the pools that gleamed below the castle walls.

Attired as Yolande, in a dress of *dark velvet starred with silver*, with her black locks gathered in a golden crespinette, a veil spread over her head and shoulders, and with her little white hand grasping the hilt of a jewelled dagger that was concealed in her bosom, the wife of the Red Comyn left the Castle of Kirkintulloch unseen by all, and by a little postern on the south, and, skirting the houses of the town, reached the trysting-place, the Caer-pen-tulloch, or old Roman fort at the west end of the hill. The fallen ramparts of the tower were eighty feet square, and the yellow broom, the green whin, the purple foxglove, and the sweet wallflower, all flourished together on the masses of fallen masonry which were covered by long grass that waved mournfully to and fro between the pale Gwendoleyne and the white starlight. The place seemed very silent, lonely, and desolate. All was intensely still, save the fierce beating of her heart, which teemed with passion, as her eyes did with tears she scorned to weep. Time stole away. The moments seemed like hours.

No one came! Could she have mistaken the place —the time?

Now the yellow moon began to peep above the distant hills, and its lustre glinted on the green mounds and shattered masonry of the ancient peel.

Up, up it came, and now its whole disc was gleaming above the dark mountain-ridge, and tipping each rock and peak with fire.

Gwendoleyne prayed in her heart that no one might

come—that she might have been deceived—that
Comyn, the father of her four children—but, hark !
the hoofs of a horse rang hollowly on the green turf,
and through the archway of the ruined enclosure rode
an armed man, who sang merrily the same march to
which, eight years after, Bruce marched his victorious
host to Bannockburn.

> "Hark to the tramp, from yonder camp,
> Whence the Scottish spearmen come !
> When they hear the bagpipe sounding,
> *Tuttie taittie* to the drum !"

" 'Tis the Red Comyn's favourite song !" said she,
shrinking aside ; " now mayest thou be accursed from
the bearing cloth in which thou wert baptized to that
shroud of blood in which thou shalt lie ! Now by
the soul of him who loved me well, the Grahame
who fell at Falkirk, and by the life of my son—my
dearest hope—I shall have a terrible vengeance !"

The knight, on whose head was a plumed chapel-de-
fer, with a mail coif that concealed the lower part of
his face, wore over his armour an embroidered coin-
tise, with the cognisance of the Comyns, two ostriches,
with the motto " Courage." He dismounted, and
after looking about him for a moment, discovered
Gwendoleyne, to whom he hastened with an exclamation of joy, and she recognised on the breast of the
surcoat some embroidery, on which she had but too
surely and too lately seen the white hands of Yolande
Gifford plying the needle ! What other proof of
perfidy was necessary ? ͏

An arm was thrown around her, and passionately
and joyously she was pressed to the breast of the new
comer. But while trembling with ungovernable fury
to find herself exposed to embraces intended for

Yolande, she drove her poniard in the heart of the lover twice, exclaiming,

"Die, villain and deceiver—die in your adultery—die!"

"*Mother—oh, mother!*" cried a voice, which froze the marrow in her bones; and the frantic and wretched Gwendoleyne discovered that she had slain—not the Red Comyn—but their beloved and only son.

The plumed *chapel-de-fer* rang as the wearer sank to the earth.

A gurgling sound was all that followed; the ruined tower swam round that miserable woman, and, multiplied by a thousand times, the horse of the murdered knight seemed to career around her; till borne down by misery, by a revulsion of feeling, by overtension of the heart, and by horror of what she had done, Gwendoleyne sank senseless on the body of her son.

The young Sir John Comyn had loved the orphan Yolande, and on his return had secretly wished to meet—perhaps, for all that we can learn now—to espouse her; but this terrible catastrophe ended his life and intentions together.

Meanwhile, like a true Scottish baron bent on selfish schemes of family ambition and degrading aggrandizement, Red Comyn had ridden fast to meet Robert Bruce, the younger, at Dumfries, and to concert with him a pretended plan to free Scotland from the English and from John Baliol; but of this scheme the red-headed traitor had duly informed King Edward from time to time. On Comyn's arrival in Nithsdale, the gallant Robert, afterwards King of Scotland, had fled in safety northward, by reversing his horse's hoofs, as the ground was covered with snow; and being furnished with clear proofs of his com-

O

patriot's villainy, he pursued him to the church of the
Minorites at Dumfries, whither he had fled for sanc-
tuary, being full of conscious guilt; but neither the house
of God nor its high altar could protect this perfidious
wretch, who was false to Scotland and her people;
and the prophecy that " Red Comyn should die by a
violent death " was terribly fulfilled; for there Bruce,
Lindsay, and Kirkpatrick buried their daggers in his
heart upon St. William's day, the 10th of February,
1306.

So perish all who are false to their country!

. He was the last Comyn of the house of Badenoch,
and was, moreover, the last of his race—a race which
Scotland well could spare.

Lady Gwendoleyne never spoke after she was borne
into the castle with the dead body of her son. She
lived for five years a close captive in that yellow chamber, and during those terrible five years a word, even of
prayer, never passed her lips; but a period was put
to her sufferings, for this proud and resentful beauty
died on the 10th day of February, 1310, at the hour
of three in the afternoon, the anniversary of the very
moment in which her husband died under the three
daggers in the Minorite Church of Dumfries.

She was buried before the Shrine of St. Ninian,
with all the grandeur of a princess and all the splendour of the Roman ritual; her son slept by her side,
and Sir Alexander of Cavers reared a stately monument above them; but that fierce woman's restless
spirit is still said to haunt the Castle of Kirkintulloch and the Roman ruins at the west end of the
town; for it is supposed that she will never find repose or peace until the day of doom.

Such was the story told to the captain by the castellan of the old fortress of Kirkintulloch, scarcely one stone of which now stands upon another, as it was removed about the beginning of the present century.

"And Yolande Gifford—what of her?" asked the captain.

"She did not die of love or grief either, but lived to be a very old woman, and passed away in about her eightieth year, when Robert III. was King, a prioress of the Bernardine nuns of St. Mary —a convent of which you may still see the ruins on the north bank of the Avon, about a mile above Linlithgow Bridge."

"A melancholy story!" said the captain; "what a devil of a wife that Gwendolcyne must have been —but no better than such an infamous traitor as Comyn deserved!"

"Beware ye, sir," said the castle bailie, lowering his voice, and looking furtively round him; "she is said to walk about—ay, at this very hour, and may pay you a visit that you may never get the better of."

"I'll be hanged, bailie, if I go up-stairs to-night— or this morning, rather," said my grandfather, laughing; "I would rather face the Dons at the Moro again, than meet that dame in black velvet with her devil of a dwarf—so make a fresh browst and stir up the fire."

The clock struck four.

"Four!" said the soldier; "four already; and we march in an hour!"

The bailie, who was a jolly old fellow, brewed a fresh jorum of hot toddy—by this time they had under their girdles ten jugs each; and my grandfather now began to spin *his* yarns, and detailed the slaughter

of Ticonderoga, the scalping and flaying at Fort
Pitt, the storming of the Moro, where British mus-
ket-butts and the pates of the Dons tested the hard-
ness of each other; he proceeded on the expedition
up the Lakes, and had just opened the trenches
before Montreal, when he found himself at the bottom of his tenth jug, the fire out, the bailie asleep
in his easy-chair, and heard the warning drum beaten
in the streets of Kirkintulloch—the warning for the
march, while the grey dawn stole through the ancient
windows.

It was daylight now, and fearless alike of Dame
Gwendoleyne and her dwarf, my grandfather sallied
down-stairs, and propping himself between his claymore and the walls of the houses, or an occasional
pump-well as he passed it, reached the muster-place,
and holding himself very erect, gave, with great
emphasis, the command to "march." His detachment marched accordingly, and—here ends our story
for the present.

VI.

STORY OF THE GREY MOUSQUETAIRE.

A FRAGMENT OF THE SEVEN YEARS' WAR.

AMONG the captains of "Ours" who had the honour of serving in the Seven Years' War was one named Allan Robertson, a gentleman of the clan Donnoquhy, and a cadet of the loyal house of Struan, who bore the singular soubriquet of the *Mousquetaire Gris*, and whose adventures during the early part of his military career were very remarkable.

In his latter years, when leading a quiet "half-pay life" in the Scottish capital, Allan was known to all the military loungers about "Poole's Coffee-house," at the east end of Prince's Street, then the great rendezvous of the military idler, as a warlike octogenarian—a silver-haired remnant of other days—and as a brave and warm-hearted old Highlander, who was so devoted to the memory of the 42nd, that he never saw those two numerical figures, even on a street door, without lifting his hat, and saying, "God bless the old number!" for his heart swelled at everything that reminded him of the venerable Black Watch.

The manner in which Allan joined the regiment was in itself romantic and singular.

Among the French army at the famous battle of Minden, in the year 1759, when the Household troops were led by Prince Xavier of Saxony, brother of the French Queen, no cavalry distinguished themselves more by the fury and valour of their reiterated charges than the *Compagnie Franche*, or "Free Company" of the Chevalier Jules de Cœurdefer, and two other bands entirely composed of gentlemen of the highest rank and of irreproachable character, who were named from the colour of their uniforms *Les Mousquetaires Gris et Rouges*, led by the Vicomte de Chateaunoir.

In the fury of their last attack, the gallant Prince Xavier was slain by the 51st Regiment, and the leader of the grey troop (for all these noblesse served on horseback) was left behind bleeding on the ground, though a desperate rally was *thrice* made by the energy of one Grey Mousquetaire to rescue and carry off the colonel. These noble rallies were made in vain ; for, after a third attempt, the Mousquetaires were swept from the plain of Minden by the terrible charge of the Scots Grey Dragoons, led by old Colonel Preston, the *last* soldier who wore a buff coat in the British service, and who had risen to command from being a kettle-drummer in the old Flanders War.

The faithful Mousquetaire fell in this flight, being pierced by a musket-shot from one of Lord George Sackville's Dragoons, and he lay all night on that sanguinary field, near the leader he had striven so valiantly and in vain to rescue.

A distinguished Highland officer, whose memoirs have been published, mentions that on the 2nd of August, the day after the battle, he rode over the plain, accompanied by Major Pringle of Edgefield.

"On one part of the field we saw a French officer,

who had been wounded in the knee, sitting on the ground, with his back supported by a dead horse. We accosted him, and offered any assistance in our power. He proved to be the commanding officer of *Les Mousquetaires Gris*, and was distinguished by several orders, which, with a handsome snuff-box, had probably excited the cupidity of some of the wretches who are never found wanting in the train of an army. We left him in high spirits, having undertaken to bring a cart or tumbril to carry him from the field; but with the hasty imprudence of young officers, we rode off together on this duty, instead of one of us remaining with the wounded man. It could not be more than ten or twelve minutes when we returned with the cart, and found—to our unspeakable concern—the murdered body of the poor French colonel (the Vicomte de Chateaunoir) lying naked on the ground."

Another officer adds, that near the corpse of the unfortunate colonel, which had been so ruthlessly stripped by the German marauders and death-hunters, lay, pistol in hand, the Mousquetaire, who had made such vigorous efforts to save him in the last charge of yesterday. He was still breathing, and after having his wound hurriedly dressed by a surgeon of the 51st, he was conveyed to the rear, in care of Major Pringle, who was a son of Lord Edgefield, a distinguished senator of the Scottish College of Justice. At the place where they found him, the adverse artillery had furrowed up the plain like a ploughed field by their shot, which lay so thick and half sunk in the turf, that they resembled an iron pavement, strown with all the destruction and débris of battle.

The Grey Mousquetaire was a tall and handsome

man, bronzed by the weather and scarred by battle. On the breast of his grey uniform glittered those decorations which few of the corps were without—the golden crosses of St. Louis and St. Lazare.

Pringle conveyed him to his own tent, for he knew well that the Mousquetaires were all men of no ordinary rank, and there he supplied him with wine and other comforts. As yet, he had not spoken; but as he gathered strength, he began to mutter and talk to himself in a strange language.

"Assuredly this man is not a Frenchman !" said Pringle, kneeling down to listen.

The Mousquetaire Gris was praying in the Erse tongue !

"What—are you a Scotchman ?" exclaimed the astonished major.

"A Highlander," sighed the other.

"I recognised your Gaëlic at once."

"Likely enough," responded the other, in a low voice; "the Gaëlic was the first language I heard, and, please God, it shall be my *last !* I spoke but the tongue I learned at my mother's breast !"

"And you are a Mousquetaire Gris ?"

"Yes—that grey uniform is all the inheritance which the dark day of Culloden has left me."

"Poor fellow !" said Major Pringle, with commiseration; "and you are—"

"Allan Robertson, of the house of Struan, who, thirteen years ago, was a captain in the Athole Regiment under his Royal Highness Prince Charles, whom God long preserve !"

"Hush—hush !" said Pringle, hurriedly; "remember that you are in the British camp."

"I care not," replied the other, with flashing eyes; "I have shouted his name at Preston, Falkirk and

Culloden, and why should I shrink from naming him here ?"

Major Pringle kept the Jacobite officer in his quarters, and in a few days he was able to sit up in a camp bed, and converse with case and coherence ; and many Scottish gentlemen of the army whose political sympathies were with the exiled race, frequented the tent, and supplied him with whatever he required and their own necessities could spare. He asked particularly about the wounds on the breast of his dead colonel, the Vicomte de Chateaunoir, and on being informed that they must have been done with a dagger, he became dreadfully excited, and exclaimed,

" Jules de Cœurdefer has murdered him !"

" Who ?" exclaimed Major Pringle and several officers who were present.

" A wretch most justly named Cœurdefer, who serves in the French army, to its disgrace ; a noble and an outlaw—a soldier and a robber ! a ribaud, with whom the Mousquetaires Gris et Rouges have had more than one sword-in-hand encounter."

Among the mass of papers and regimental memoranda, from which these legends are gleaned and prepared, I find this Chevalier Jules de Cœurdefer frequently mentioned as a prominent character during the early part of the Seven Years' War ; and some of Robertson's adventures with him during his service in the Grey Mousquetaires were very remarkable. His narrative was as follows.

" We, the Red and Grey Mousquetaires, by forced marches from ·Paris, quitted the gay Court of Louis XV., and joined the army of M. de Contades about the

end of May, crossed the Rhine with him at Cologne,
and on the same day the Free Band of the Chevalier
de Cœurdefer joined us, to the great annoyance of
the whole army; for our hitherto quiet and well-
ordered camp became a scene of incessant disquiet,
by drunken brawls, duels, and severe military punish-
ments; for as this *Franche Compagnie*, like the wild
Pandoors of Baron Trenck, subsist only by gambling
and secret robbery in camp, and by open plunder and
ruthless bloodshed in the field, you may imagine *our*
repugnance to co-operate with them; and our astonishment that leaders so strict as M. de Contades or
Prince Xavier of Saxony would tolerate their presence among us for a moment. Their ranks were
filled by men of all nations—runaway students, spend-
thrifts, cashiered officers, deserters, fugitive malefac-
tors—in short, by men ready for any desperate work,
and being deemed the cheapest food for gunpowder,
they had enough of it.

" Their captain, the Chevalier Cœurdefer, is the re-
presentative of an ancient but decayed family in Lorraine, who spent his patrimony among the gambling-
houses, the cabarets and bordels of Paris. Dismissed
summarily from the French line when a captain in
the Regiment du Roi for barbarously slaying a
brother officer, after severely wounding him in a
duel about a courtesan, he has now joined our army
against the Prussians, in the hope of winning himself
a new name by reckless bravery, cruelty, and outrage.
He is handsome and young, but without fear of God
or man; without religion, and without honour. Even
their chaplain—"

" What! they have a chaplain?" exclaimed Pringle,
laughing.

" Yes, a canon of Notre Dame, who was unfrocked

by the Archbishop of Paris for having an affair with
a citizen's wife in the Faubourg St. Antoine. He is
a burlesque on the clerical character, and fights—as I
was about to say—more duels than even the chevalier
his leader. One of this choice band plundered a
church at Cologne, and as sacrilege could not be tole-
rated, Prince Xavier made a great hubbub about it.
The thief had been seen; he wore the tattered uniform of the *Franche Compagnie*, and had huge *red
whiskers.* The chevalier paraded his men next day
for inspection. Bearing a piece of the true cross, the
holy fathers came along the line in solemn procession
to discover the culprit; but lo! every man was shaven
to the eyes, and not a vestige of whisker was to be
seen in the whole band of the Chevalier Jules.

"On the 2nd June, 1759, with the force of M. de
Contades, we joined the Maréchal Duc de Broglio
near Giessen, and left M. d'Armentieres with twenty
thousand men to oppose Prince Ferdinand of Brunswick, in the neighbourhood of the Wesel; and on
this important day we had an open rupture with the
Free Company of Cœurdefer, for when detailed together
to form the advanced guard of horse, the gentlemen
of the Mousquetaires Gris et Rouges flatly refused to
share a post of honour with a corps of outlaws. Then
the chevalier, flaming with irrepressible fury, flung
his glove in the face of our colonel, Henri the Vicomte
de Chateaunoir, with whom he had an old unfinished
feud, and a duel to the death was only prevented by
the determination of the maréchal duc, who bound
them both down by solemn promises to keep the
peace towards each other, at least until the close of
the campaign; but the villain Cœurdefer made a
vow of vengeance, swearing to 'lay the vicomte at his
feet, where he had laid many a better man;' and you

see how he has kept that vow, for by him or by his men our wounded leader was murdered on the field on the morning after Minden !"

"I do not understand," said Major Pringle, in whose tent this conversation took place one evening, when, with a few droppers-in, he and the now-convalescent Mousquetaire lingered over a few bottles of Rhenish wine ; "in fact, it seems to me a marvel how a gallant soldier such as the late Prince Xavier of Saxony could tolerate the presence of such a ruffian and bully as this Captain Cœurdefer."

"For various reasons ; he is brave——"

"Bravery is no strange quality in the French or Imperial armies, I think," said one of the 51st.

"Moreover, he is an expert forager, skilful in war, useful in council, and leader of two hundred troopers, who have only one virtue—their devotion to him. Besides, the brutal qualities he displays are not singular in the history of wars in Germany. We have had many such examples as he among the mixed races which make up the armies of France and Austria.

"In the last century there was the terrible Count Merode, a colonel of musketeers, whose name has become a proverb for all that is vile ; and there was the ferocious Jehan de Wart, a colonel of horse, who in Bavaria spared neither man, woman, nor child, when the lust of blood glowed in his fiery heart."

"Thank Heaven ! we have no such fellows among us," said the officer of the 51st, complacently.

"Sir," said Allan Robertson, with a cloudy brow, "you forget the nine of diamonds—the exterminating order of Cumberland, written on the night before we fought you at Culloden."

"But the assassination of your poor colonel,"

began Pringle, hastily, to change the turn the conversation was taking.

"Ah ! that was a frightful episode in this new war ; and yet believe me, my dear major, Cœurdefer has committed many such acts, and has always contrived to elude the hand of justice. Witness his vow to lay our colonel at his feet, where better men had lain. Liar that he is ! Chateaunoir was the first gentleman in France ! But true it is that, of the many who have lain at the feet of Jules, few have fallen in battle or fair combat."

"You seem to have serious cause for disliking him," said Pringle.

"Disliking !" reiterated Robertson, while his eyes sparkled and his pale face glowed with anger—"say abhorring him !"

"You had your sword," said the officer of the 51st.

"But it is the sword of a Mousquetaire," replied Robertson, sternly ; "the chevalier ranks with a field officer."

"True," said Pringle ; "you must pardon my friend, who forgets surely what discipline inculcates. And the cause of this animosity ?"

"Is a dark and painful story," sighed Robertson, as he drained his green glass of Rhenish, and tossed it on the turf floor of the tent.

"Let us hear it."

"Before the rising of the clans in 1745," began Robertson, "I was a student at the Scottish College of Pontamousson, where I learned Latin and the classics under the tuition of old Father Innes. I had then a dear friend named Louis d'Herblay, a native of Remiremont, at the foot of Mount Vosge in Lorraine. Louis was handsome, brave, and courteous ; an expert maker of verses ; a tolerable player on the guitar, and a smart handler of his sword, which he had seldom occasion to use, for he was beloved by every one; a successful love affair with Mademoiselle Annette, a pretty and sprightly girl, had put him in the best of humours with all mankind. Annette was the only daughter of the old Marquis de Chateaunoir, father of the vicomte of that title, Great Maréchal of Lorraine and Bar-le-Duc.

"Jules Cœurdefer, the spendthrift, gambler, and roué, was then, to our great regret, at college with us too, and having not yet come to his estates, his finances being far below his ambition and expenditure, to keep these equal he had betaken him to cards, dice, successful bets, to bullying some and cajoling others—and to every means his wild and wayward course of life permitted—a course which was the scandal of the good fathers of Pontamousson, and soon procured him the only favour he wished at their hands—expulsion.

"Between him and Louis d'Herblay there grew an aversion—a hatred that waxed stronger daily; an antagonism on his side, but on the part of Louis a cold and haughty bearing; for he despised the life and habits of Cœurdefer, whom he had thrice fought and thrice disarmed, when involved with him in tavern brawls beyond the college gates; for *within* these barriers no sword or other weapon was ever worn. But in the very spirit of a Venetian bravo, Jules was known, or suspected, to bear about his person a small *crystal poniard*, the most savage of all weapons for inflicting a wound; as the blade, when broken off at the hilt, remained like a deadly sting in the body of the victim. It was a weapon which could be used but *once* only, and then with terrible effect.

"I have mentioned that my friend D'Herblay had

a successful love affair. As a trophy of it, he wore at his breast an antique cameo of great size, set round with diamonds, and within it was the hair of Annette concealed by a secret spring. He was not rich, but was sufficiently wealthy and well born to render him an acceptable suitor even to the most wary of fathers; thus it had been arranged that, as soon as he left college, his marriage would be celebrated. Father Innes, our old preceptor, was to perform the ceremony; all the students congratulated Louis, and looked forward to his nuptials as to a *fête*—at least, all save Cœurdefer, who kept ever aloof from him, and smiled with the quiet covert smile of malice and hate, when D'Herblay or his affairs were mentioned in his presence.

"At last came the time appointed for Louis to leave the college, and I was to accompany him to Remiremont. He bade adieu to all the old Scottish priests of Pontamousson, and severally shook hands with all his brother students—all till he came to where Cœurdefer was lounging outside the gates smoking a huge German pipe; and D'Herblay, in the happy fulness of his honest heart, being unwilling to leave a foe behind him, approached and held out his hand, saying—

"'Farewell, M. le Chevalier, though we have not always been the best of friends, I hope we do not part as enemies. Here is my hand to you—my hand, in token of friendship and future amity.'

"Despite the honest frankness that beamed in the blue eyes of D'Herblay and the confiding generosity of his speech, the coarse Jules Cœurdefer gave him a sullen frown, and while rudely emitting a volume of smoke full in his face, with a sullen gesture of contempt, strode away.

"All the students muttered 'Shame!' and for a moment a cloud hovered on the usually smooth brow of D'Herblay.

"'Bah!' said he, turning to me, 'one who is so happy as I, can well afford to pity the wrath of one so poor in spirit and in Christian charity. Farewell, Jules,' he added, as we leaped on our horses; 'when next we meet, we shall part less sullenly.'

"'Yes—when *next* we meet, our parting *shall* be different,' replied Cœurdefer, looking over his left shoulder, with a black frown in his face, as we trotted from the college gates.

"'He means me mischief—pooh.! let the fool do his worst,' said Louis. We soon dismissed him from our thoughts, and laughing and chatting gaily, waving our hats to the old people, and kissing our hands to the young girls, we rode through the old familiar streets of Pontamousson, and took the road that led direct to D'Herblay's home, which lay more than twenty leagues distant. And now, gentlemen, observe that *within one hour* after we left the college gates, Jules de Cœurdefer, alone and unattended, also departed on horseback, ostensibly to return to his father's house on the French side of the Rhine.

"We cantered along the road to Nancy, between the yellow cornfields, feeling happy as boys in our new freedom, and singing together a song which Louis had composed in honour of Annette de Chateaunoir, and thus we pushed on without halting at the capital of the duchy, save for a few minutes at a jeweller's, where my friend bought a diamond bracelet for his future bride. Blaziers and Neufchateau were soon passed, and then we reached Epinal, which, in 1466, was bestowed upon the once independent princes of

Lorraine ; and their castle, now a ruin, crowns an eminence above it.

"Epinal is within ten miles of Remiremont, and there we were compelled by the state of our horses to halt, notwithstanding the impatience of my friend, to whom a night spent so near the residence of Annette seemed an age, and the ten miles that intervened a thousand leagues ; but we called for supper and made ourselves comfortable at an auberge. Louis assumed his guitar, and we sought to while away the time; and the hours flew quickly, for we had a thousand plans to form and things to talk of.

"Alas ! how little did we dream that Jules de Cœurdefer, like a bloodhound, was tracking us swiftly and surely, by Nancy, Blaziers, and Neufchateau, and had actually lodged himself in an auberge opposite ours, at Epinal.

"After sitting up late, we retired. Overcome by an excessive lassitude, induced by the long and arduous journey of the past day, I fell into a deep and profound sleep—so deep indeed, that the noon of the next day had rung from the church bells ere I awoke, and inquired for my companion. Thus, you may see, sirs, the difference between one who is a lover and one who is *not*.

"Louis had been up with the lark, as the aubergiste informed me, and full of impatience to visit his mistress, had mounted a fresh horse, and set forth alone, leaving a message for me to follow him to the mansion of the marquis, near Remiremont; adding, as an apology for his abrupt departure, that he was loth to rouse me from a slumber so comfortable and profound.

"I ordered my horse, paid my bill, and departed at leisure, for I had no hope of overtaking him. An

P

222 LEGENDS OF THE BLACK WATCH.

easy trot of ten miles brought me to Remiremont,
which is a pretty little town on the left bank of the
Moselle, and without difficulty I reached Chateaunoir, the fosse of which was filled by the river. The
edifice was ancient, surmounted by heavy turrets and
all built of *black* stone (hence its name), and it stood
embosomed among fine old trees.

" I sent up my name, and inquired for M.
d'Herblay.

" ' How—is he not with you, M. Allan ?' asked the
old marquis, with astonishment in his tone and
manner.

" ' No,' said I ; ' he quitted Epinal at least four
hours before me, leaving a message for me to follow
him hither.'

" ' Four hours before you, and he has not arrived
yet !'

" ' This is most perplexing, M. le Marquis !' said I.

" ' Oh, mon Dieu ! what can have happened ?' exclaimed mademoiselle, whom I now saw for the first
time, and who was a fair blonde, with a beautiful skin
and long dark eyelashes, which lent a softness and
inexpressible charm to her face.

" I could not reply. My heart misgave me ; for
knowing D'Herblay as I did, I feared that something most unusual must have occurred to prevent
his appearance at the chateau.

" Noon passed ; the sun verged westward, and still
he did not appear. I became seriously alarmed ; the
old marquis was perplexed and irritated ; while
Annette wept in silence.

" Horses were ordered at last, and with Chateaunoir,
his son the Vicomte Henri, afterwards Colonel of
the Grey Mousquetaires, and all his servants, I set
forth to search the roads and inquire for my friend.

For some time wo prosecuted this object in vain; but after much labour and anxiety, judge of ou horror, when in a secluded orangery, about two miles from Epinal, tho young vicomte found a man lying on the grass wounded, bleeding and dying, surrounded by a group of pitying and terrified vine-dressers.

"The damps of death were on the brow of this unfortunate, who proved to bo my friend, poor Louis d'Herblay.

"Ho was frightfully pale, having received several wounds—one of these in the bosom occasioned him the most exquisite agony. From this wound he had bled for some hours undiscovered, and now he was beyond all hope of recovery. Revived partially by our presence, by a cordial poured between his lips, and by the stoppago of the crimson tide which had soaked the soil whereon ho lay, in broken accents and at long intervals, ho related what had befallen him; and overy word he uttered there, so slowly, painfully, and laboriously, sank deeply in our hearts, for they wero too surely tho last words of tho dying.

"Loth to arouso me untimeously at Epinal, my kind friend had arisen, and softly descended tho wooden stair, saddled his horse, and left the auberge by dawn. Ho departed from Epinal at a canter, and in the overflowing happiness of his heart was singing merrily, when at a solitary part of tho road, ho heard the hoofs of a galloping horse, and a voico impetuously calling upon him to stop. Believing this follower was I, who had discovered his secret and hasty departure, ho turned to find himself confronted by a tall stranger, whose face was concealed by a black velvet mask, and whom he believed to be a brigand or assassin.

P 2

"'Monsieur,' said the strange horseman, in a voice which, by its varying tones, was too evidently disguised as his face, 'you are abroad betimes.'

"'As you also are,' replied Louis; 'but was it you, monsieur, who called upon me to stop?'

"'It was.'

"'For what purpose?'

"'That you shall shortly see.'

"'Shortly—nay, as soon as you please, for I am in haste.'

"'Indeed!' said the other scornfully and slowly.

"'What is your wish, sir?'

"'Simply, that you measure swords with me in this meadow.'

'"Why?' asked Louis, with astonishment.

"'I intended to have pistolled you through the back, *sans cérémonie*, at first; but my heart relented; thus, I mean to afford you a chance of saving your miserable life—though I must have your purse and valuables.'

"'You are, then, a robber.'

"'If one whose funds are down to zero, and who is desperate, be a robber, then I *am* one,' replied the mask, still in his feigned voice.

"'I am no•poltroon, yet I will gladly save your soul the commission of a double crime,' said poor D'Herblay, who was the very mirror of generosity; 'here is my purse, good fellow—pray accept it and be gone, for I have no time to trifle with you.'

The unknown coolly put the purse in his pocket and drew his sword, saying, with an ironical laugh—

"'I thank you, though I would have had it, at all events; but still,' he added, grinding his teeth, 'you must fight with me!'

"'Leave me until to-morrow,' said Louis; 'there

is one awaiting me at Remiremont—one expecting me to-day—whom I would not disappoint—a lady who loves me, monsieur.'

"The stranger laughed scornfully.

"'Let me see her but once again, and I shall meet you with joy.'

"The stranger laughed louder, and said bitterly—

"'Why not meet me now?'

"'I know not,' urged poor D'Herblay, who was anxious to ride on; 'but your presence chills my heart—I have a dark and solemn presentiment.'

"For a third time the other laughed ferociously, while his eyes sparkled through the holes in his mask, and he menaced D'Herblay with his sword, saying—

"'Fight—fight!'

"'To-morrow—I tell you, to-morrow.'

"'Never—be it now or never!'

"'I am too full of happiness to fight.'

"'Happiness!'

"'She whom I love—she whom I am to wed, expects me at Remiremont.'

"'She whom you love, and whom you hope to wed, shall never see you, but as a breathless corpse, fool!'

"'If I am slain, who will bear my last words to Annette?'

"'The spirits of the air or the demons of hell—I care not which,' was the fierce response.

"'Fool that I was to leave the auberge without my friend. Moreover, I decline to fight with a rascally *ferrailleur!*'

"This epithet, which is used in France to distinguish a person who, without provocation, delights in quarrelling and forcing others to fight, made this highway brawler tremble with rage.

" ' Coward !' he thundered out.

" ' Hah !' exclaimed Louis, leaping from his horse, and in his passion forgetting all but vengeance.

" ' Coward, come on !' reiterated his assailant.

"Louis pressed to his lips the cameo locket which contained the hair of Annette, and with a prayer to Heaven that he might be spared to see her, rushed upon his furious antagonist. A desperate duel began, and so ably were the voice and costume of the masker disguised, that never once did a thought of Jules de Cœurdefer cross the mind of D'Herblay. They had withdrawn from the roadway into an orangery, and taken off their coats and vests to afford them greater freedom. A perfect fencer, Louis stood erect, with his head upright, his body forward on a longe, all the weight on his left haunch—feet, hands, body, arm and sword *in a line*, and completely covered by his weapon.

"Their swords clashed and gleamed in the bright morning sun ; both were expert combatants, and most of their passes were skilfully made and as skilfully parried. The masker made a feint to the left, but changing the attack, suddenly ran his weapon through the sword-arm of Louis, fairly wedging the blade between the bones below the elbow, and covering his shirt with blood in a moment. Paralysed by this, his future defence was feeble. He received repeated wounds, and was at last laid prostrate on the earth, bleeding and senseless.

" ' Lie there, thou moonstruck fool !' exclaimed his ruthless conqueror, giving him a final stroke in the breast. Tearing away the cameo locket, he left the unhappy D'Herblay a dying man, for he expired in our arms as we were conveying him to Remiremont.

"On examining the wound in his breast, we found that it had been made by the blade of a *small crystal poniard*, which was purposely broken off from the hilt and left rankling in the orifice to insure by a mortal stroke the death of the victim !

" My first thought was of Cœurdefer, whom I knew to be the possessor of such weapons, which he had brought from Venice, where they are commonly used by the bravoes ; but the proofs I could adduce were too slight for me, a stranger and a foreigner, to accuse the son of a powerful baronial family ; thus the terrible suspicion remained locked in my own breast—a suspicion that grew less, however, when I remembered that the victor, like a common footpad, had taken the purse and locket of my poor friend.

"The grief of a kind, warm-hearted, and affectionate girl like Annette may be imagined. She wept little, but her sorrow was the deeper that it was unrelieved by any external manifestations. She was long inconsolable.

" Now came the war consequent to the League formed at Vienna, in 1757, to strip the King of Prussia of his dominions, and an alliance was formed by France, Austria, Russia, and Sweden, when Britain declared war against the former, and all Europe seemed to ' go by the ears' at once.

"The old Marquis de Chateaunoir marched as Colonel of Horse under the Maréchal d'Estrées, and fell at the passage of the Rhine. His son, the Vicomte Henri, became a soldier, too, and soon obtained the command of the Mousquetaires Gris, into which I, then a fugitive from the Scottish Highlands, was admitted by his request; but long before all this poor little Annette had become a canoness of Remiremont.

"This ecclesiastical establishment, by the peculiarity of its constitution, is one of the most singular in the church. It was founded by St. Romerick, a famous abbot, who lived in the days of Clotaire II., and who built his first convent on what was then a bare and desolate place, at the foot of Mount Vosge. All the ladies in it, the abbess excepted, take certain vows, reserving to themselves the right of quitting the convent and marrying if they please; and all must prove their nobility by four descents before admission. The abbess had both spiritual and temporal power under the Pope and Dukes of Lorraine.

" Annette was a canoness for three years, and lived in peace, viewing the world only as a place wherein to practise those little acts of kindness and Christian charity which the ladies of St. Romerick practised so freely as to make their establishment a boon and a blessing to that sequestered little city among the mountains. There her virtues, her attention to the sick, and her charity to the poor, excited the admiration of all, as her sorrowful story, and sad, grave manner won their sympathy. So three years glided away, until in an evil hour Jules de Cœurdefer came to visit his sister, who was the superior of this remarkable establishment.

" He saw Annette unveiled in the garden ; her pale beauty, her exceeding gentleness, and her loneliness raised a passion in his breast. Impetuous in all things, he at once besought his sister to intercede for him with Annette; and after many objections to engage in a task so unsuited to the nature of her office, the abbess, inspired by a natural regard for her only brother, and a desire to obtain for him the object

of his choice, whom she justly deemed a pearl among
women, and one whom she loved dearly and highly
esteemed, left nothing unsaid to urge his suit. M.
Jules became a regular visitor at the convent parlour,
and daily saw Annette in the presence of the abbess,
who, believing that his conversation and gaiety (for he
was fresh from Paris, and the camp of Maréchal
d'Estrées) might amuse and interest the lonely girl,
foresaw that in a second love affair she might gradually be drawn from the terrible memory of the first
and of its fatal end.

" They soon became intimate, and all Remiremont
rang with gossip; the old condemned the lax discipline of the abbess, and the young rejoiced that the
pretty canoness Annette de Chateaunoir was to become
the wife of the handsome chevalier.

" In submission to the stronger will of the lady
superior, and to the energetic mind of Jules, and perhaps dazzled a little by the brilliance, the splendid
uniform, handsome figure, and gay conversation of
that redoubtable personage, she passively admitted his
addresses. But this new lover's deep dark eye seemed
to exercise some mysterious and magnetic influence
over her; for, as the poor girl afterwards told me,
there were times when his glance seemed full of a
terrible fascination, and when she alternately loved
and felt a strange coldness—almost an involuntary
repugnance for him.

" She strove to conquer this emotion, the origin of
which she failed to fathom, and anxious, perhaps, to
forget the terrible sequel to her first love among the
gaiety proffered by the second, she consented to
receive the chevalier as her husband; and lest she
might retract, the ceremony was hurried on with a
haste on his part which the good-natured gossips of

Remiremont averred to be somewhat indelicate at least.

"His sister perceived the strange waverings and misgivings that agitated the mind of poor Annette, and on the marriage morning she embraced and kissed her tenderly.

"' Beware what you do, dearest Annette,' said she, ' lest you repent the hour you leave us. In marriage the love of the mind and character must be blended with and united to the love of the person, or there can never be any duration of tenderness or of mutual confidence. Oh, I pray Heaven, I may not have acted wrong in this affair !'

"The misgivings of the good abbess came too late.

"Full of hope, the gentle Annette smiled through her tears; full of love and triumph, the exulting chevalier led her away, and they were married. Before leaving the convent, Jules placed in her hand a case containing a complete set of brilliants—a tiara for her head, a necklace, bracelets, and rings. Among these jewels was a *cameo locket*, studded with the purest diamonds.

"On perceiving this well-known trinket, Annette grew pale, and tottered to a chair. It seemed to come like a signal from the grave of Louis d'Herblay to reproach her ! Her features became convulsed and her voice tremulous, for in a moment she recognised her own gift to Louis, previous to his last departure for Pontamousson, and there occurred to her a strange, but just and dreadful suspicion, that for a moment paralysed her and rendered her totally incapable of repelling the chevalier, who held her in his arms, and perceived at once, and with no little confusion, the misfortune or discovery which was impending.

"'Cursed fatality!' he exclaimed, through his clenched teeth.

"'Whence came this trinket, Jules? How came it into your possession? Speak!' she exclaimed, in accents of terror, and with the gestures of passion.

"'I do not understand you, dear Annette,' said he, finding that nothing but perfect confidence and a bold falsehood would carry him through this *malheur*. 'I had that locket made for me by a jeweller of the Rue St. Honoré, in Paris, many years ago, as a gift for my mother."

"'It is false all this; for, four years ago, I had it made here in Remiremont."

"'Annette!'

"'Has it any secret spring or clasp?' she asked.

"'No—none, I am assured,' he answered, boldly.

"'You are sure of this, Jules?'

"'I swear to you Annette,' he urged, becoming frightfully agitated, while the perspiration rolled like beads down his brow.

"'Swear not—you have lied enough already,' she exclaimed wildly. 'See, monsieur,' she added, pressing a spring and opening the locket by a secret hitherto unknown to Cœurdefer, 'it contains my miniature and a braid of my hair—mine, given in a happy, happy hour to Louis d'Herblay! O, Louis! look down on me from heaven, and see how fate has avenged thee! Away, chevalier—away; come not near me, and touch me not! If other proof were wanting that you were his murderer, it is here.'

"These words were rashly spoken, yet they stung Jules to the soul. She tore her bridal chaplet and veil from her brow, trampled on them with gestures of frenzy, and was borne away insensible in the arms of the canonesses.

"In one hour after that *dénouement* the exasperated chevalier had left Remiremont for the French camp—left it to return no more."

"And what of Annette?" asked some one.

"She took the black veil, and is now nun of the convent of St. Nicole, seven miles from Nancy. With that day's discovery began and ended the wedded life of Cœurdefer; and since then he has led a wild and reckless career, committing innumerable acts of daring, which by some strange fatality have passed as yet unpunished; but the assassination of D'Herblay—for that he *did* assassinate him, I have not the slightest doubt—is the blackest of his acts; unless, indeed, that other episode at Minden be a deeper and a darker one.

"The marriage prevented the Vicomte Henri alike from prosecuting him at common law as a felon, and from challenging him to a solemn duel, and so time passed on; but he hated my colonel—the handsome young Mousquetaire—with the hate of a tiger; hence I doubt not that by his hand, or the hands of some of his lawless troop at his behest, my leader perished on the field of Minden!

"France has not in all her army a more splendid soldier than that Mousquetaire Gris!

"After the junction of the French army under M. de Contades and M. de Broglio, as I have related, on their approach Prince Ferdinand retreated, first to Lippstadt, and afterwards to Ham, where he mustered all the forces in the Bishopric of Munster, and was joined by the soldiers of Imhoff, while we advanced and took possession of Cassel, Minden, and Beverungen.

"While we lay at Cassel, engaged in repairing and strengthening the fortifications, the vicomte, our leader, was engaged in two pieces of service, which savoured of the romance of the Middle Ages in Germany.

"There came to the colonel of the Mousquetaires, from the Lower Saxon side of the Weser, a certain old knight named Otto of Burgsteinfort, who though an adherent of the enemy, implored him as a soldier and a gentleman to attempt the rescue of his daughter, an only child, who had been carried off by a party of savage Uzkokes or Hungarian infantry, who had been subsidized by the King of Prussia, and formed a portion of the column commanded by Prince Ferdinand, but were more immediately under the orders of Count Hatzfeld in Munden, twelve miles distant on the Weser ; and these wretches, he added, had borne her into a forest in the Bishopric of Paderborn, where he dared not follow them, alone at least.   Pitying the distress of the old man, Chateaunoir left Cassel on this errand of mercy with forty gentlemen of the Mousquetaires Gris.   Of these forty I had the honour to be one.

"'Will not Count Hatzfeld do this service for you, baron ?' I asked.

"'No—though on my knees I prayed him ; I who never have bent my knee before to aught but a minister of God.'

"'Why ?'

"'Because our families are and have been long at feud.'

"'Good—I can understand that, for in my country we are not without hereditary hatreds.   Yet in this instance his conduct has been alike ungenerous and wicked.'

"'True ; thus I, a German, appeal to French chivalry,'

" 'In a happy moment, baron,' said Chateaunoir, 'and your appeal shall not be made in vain. This abduction——'

" 'Occurred three days ago.'

" 'Peste ! then we have no time to lose !'

" We crossed a range of mountains in the night, and entered the Bishopric of Paderborn, pushed on towards the forest, riding with such speed, that, to prevent our horses being knocked up, at a village near Borcholz, we refreshed them in the old Reiter fashion, by bathing their nostrils with vinegar, giving them water and wine to drink, and folding round their bits a piece of raw flesh sliced from a stray cow, which we shot, and cut up for the purpose.

" Otto, the knight or baron (for we named him both), acted as our guide, and such was the deadly treachery so frequently practised by those Germans, that we were not without fear that the whole story of the abduction might be a snare to lure away into ambush those who were considered by the King of Prussia as the right arm of the French general; and thus our colonel gave me express orders to keep by the old man's side, and on the first indication of treachery, or attempted flight, to pistol him without mercy !

" The harvest moon was shining full and yellow in her placid beauty high above the steep green mountains that look down on Liebenau ; but now it was on the wane, for the east was marked by the coming day, as in silence and circumspection we approached the fortress of the lawless Uzkokes. Every leaf was still, the sky was of the purest blue, and spread like a starry curtain behind the dark mountain peaks, and the sombre forest scenery was reflected like inverted trees of bronze in the calm lakes and tarns which we passed in our progress through this wild region of solitude and old romance.

" An old servant of the baron, who had been lurking about the forest in the vague hope of succouring his young mistress, now joined us, and threw himself at the feet of his master. For two nights and days this faithful fellow had been lurking in the vicinity of these terrible depredators, and now he acted most efficiently as our guide. His appearance, his tears, and enthusiasm dissipated our fears of a snare, and made me feel somewhat ashamed of having encouraged them.

"The Uzkokes, about twenty in number, were deserters from Count Hatzfeld's garrison in Munden, and had possessed themselves of an old and deserted hunting lodge of the Electoral Bishops, built at the foot of a rock; from thence they had been issuing from time to time, to plunder the peasantry, to rob wayfarers and to shoot deer.

" The sound of guttural voices in loud altercation, mingled with savage laughter, informed us that we were in the immediate vicinity of those enterprising worthies who had abducted the baron's daughter. Then we saw the gleam of a red wavering light between the stems and branches of the trees. This came from a huge fire around which they were all bivouacked, drinking, sleeping, or making merry, and being apparently without any proper watch or scout, as we were enabled to approach them by a forest path unchallenged and unseen. The reason of this seeming confidence was soon explained, when we found one of their number lying across the narrow way stretched upon his musket, either sottishly drunk or in profound slumber; but *which* we never had time to discover, for, quick as thought, the servant of the baron, a bloodthirsty Westphalian boor, dispatched him by one slash of his short and sharp *couteau de chasse.*

"The father was by my side as we advanced. Bareheaded, he was praying with his clenched hands pressed upon his breast. The poor old man was full of agony and terror.

"'They are twenty in number, you say?' asked Chateaunoir.

"'Exactly twenty, mein herr,' replied the old servant, wiping his hunting-knife on the grass with grim care before he sheathed it.

"'Then ten of *us* are enough for them,' replied our heroic young colonel; 'let the ten gentlemen next me dismount and take their pistols with them. You are sure, my friend, that your young mistress is still among them?'

"'Sure as I live, mein herr,' replied the boor.

The baron groaned.

"'See!' exclaimed a Mousquetaire, 'there is a white dress amid their circle.

"'*Christi kreutz !* it is my young lady!' whispered the servant, in a breathless voice.

"I placed my gloved hand on the baron's mouth lest he might utter a cry, and spoil all.

"'Where—where?' asked Chateaunoir.

"'At the foot of that elm-tree, and, *mein Gott !* she is tied to it with a cord.'

"Creeping forward after Chateaunoir (for he would allow no man to precede him) I saw a very remarkable scene.

"Around a huge fire of dried branches that crackled, sputtered, and blazed, casting a red and lurid glow on the gnarled trunks of the old oak-trees and on the leafy canopy formed by their twisted and entwined foliage overhead, were the twenty Uzkokes, all fierce-looking little men, of powerful, active, and athletic figures, with hooked noses, keen eyes, and wild in gesture. They were bearded to the cheekbones, and wore round fur caps and brown pelisses, or short jackets, and wide red breeches, ending in brodequins, or half-boots. They had each a short musket, slung across his body, with a crooked sabre, which was worn in front, so that the hilt came readily to the right hand. A few were asleep, snorting off the fumes of the midnight debauch, as they sprawled among staved barrels, broiled bones and broken dishes. The rest were engaged in a vehement dispute, while near them drooped the poor object of their contention, a pale-cheeked and slender young girl, secured to a tree by two broad buff waist-belts and a cord; her dress was disordered; her flaxen hair dishevelled and unpowdered; her face bowed down in her hands, which rested on her knees.

"This was the daughter of Otto of Burgsteinfort.

"Once she looked wildly up to heaven, and then bowed down her face again in hopeless misery. She was ghastly pale, and had a hopeless glare in her blue eyes. Beauty, if she really possessed it, seemed to have been quite scared from her.

"'*Morbleu!* how pale she is — 'tis quite a little spectre!' muttered the mousquetaires.

"'Hush, gentlemen,' said the vicomte, cocking a pistol and drawing his sword; 'we have come at a critical time. These wretches are all insanely drunk, and, if I understand their barbarous jargon aright, are now in vehement dispute as to whose property their fair prisoner shall be.'

"All seemed inflamed by the desire of possessing the prize by the strong hand; hence sabres were drawn, and a brawl, which might have saved us all further trouble, was about to ensue, when a corporal, who was leader of the gang, and evinced more brutality even than his comrades, swore 'that none should have her but the wolves,' and unslinging his musket, levelled it full at her head ; but at that moment a shot pierced his chest and he fell dead upon his face, with arms outspread upon the earth. Death had come to him from the ready pistol of Chateaunoir, who now led us on, and taking them by surprise, we cut down almost the whole party without resistance. Four who were asleep and dead drunk we hanged at our leisure, before mounting to return.

" We then, without loss of time, retraced our steps, lest we might be discovered and cut off by troops of Count Hatzfeld or Prince Ferdinand, and rode on the spur towards the Weser.

" To the grateful Baron Otto and his daughter we bade adieu within a few miles of |Hatzfeld's head-quarters, and sent the count an ironical message, complimenting him on his chivalry and gallantry to the fair sex. After this we reached our quarters in Cassel next evening, without the loss of a man, and so ended our adventure in the forest at Paderborn.

" The next affair to which I referred, is as follows :—

" We remained quietly in our new quarters for a few days until the Duc de Broglio devised an attack upon Munden, the fortifications of which were increasing under the eye of Count Hatzfeld. The Mousquetaires Gris et Rouges marched on this service, and early that morning, long before our trumpets sounded, I was roused by the din of the chopping blocks, of which every French troop has one, to cut straw for the horses before marching.

"With the dragoons of Brissac we formed the advanced guard of this expedition, which included the Regiments of Picardie and Normandie ; and here I may mention that our mounted comrades were not named from Brissac in Alsace, but from a little town of the same name in Anjou, which belonged to the ancient family of Cosse, one of whom, Charles de Cosse, was made a peer by Louis XIII., with the title of Maréchal Duc de Brissac.

"*En route* to the scene of our operations, the guide, a wild-looking denizon of the neighbouring forests, clad almost entirely in wolf's fur, and having a shock head of flaxen hair, which he seemed to comb on an average once in a year, left us in a wooded gorge to shift for ourselves, as he knew full well that the rocks and thickets on both sides were manned by his Prussian friends. We were thus caught in an ambush of infantry led by Count Hatzfield in person ! From both sides of the path there suddenly opened a destructive fire upon us. Night was just closing, and an immediate confusion ensued. After a short and feeble resistance the Dragoons de Brissac, believing themselves to be, as the French say, *écharpe*, or cut to pieces, fell back in a panic on our infantry, who were about a mile in the rear, and we, finding ourselves alike bewildered and unsupported, retired, leaving several of our comrades shot or unhorsed. Among these, unnoticed and unseen, was our Colonel, the Vicomte de Chateaunoir, whose horse had been killed by a musket-shot. The animal, after plunging thrice, fell heavily, and severely bruised the rider's right leg, which was crushed by its weight in his jack-boot, though the latter was lined by ribs of tempered iron. Thus he lay helpless and unable either to rise or extricate himself. Close by him lay a chevalier of the

Q 2

Golden Fleece, gorgeously attired, with silver aigui-
lettes on his shoulders. The blood was oozing from
a wound in his breast. Chateaunoir strove to staunch
it, and ultimately succeeded.

" ' Leave me, monsieur,' said the sufferer, who was
in great agony; 'leave me that I may die, and go to
that God who for you and me suffered more than I
this night endure !'

" With these pious words he became insensible, and
this chevalier, so daring and devout, was poor Prince
Xavier of Saxony, who was afterwards slain on the
field of Minden.

" The . moon rose above the mountains to light the
scene of this misfortune, and while stretched on the
ground, enduring great pain and thirst, Vicomte
Chateaunoir had the horror of beholding many of his
wounded companions butchered (even as he, perhaps,
was butchered at Minden !) by the sabres of some
prowling Jagers in search of plunder; and though he
lay still, feigning death, such would too probably have
been his own fate, had not a sudden torrent of rain
mercifully driven them into an adjacent wood for
shelter.   -

" Believing himself to be now altogether lost—for if
not rescued by his French comrades, he was certain
when day dawned to be slain by the Jagers or the
Westphalian peasantry—he lay bruised, sore, and helpless under the drenching rain, and was on the point
of becoming insensible from exhaustion and suffering,
when the tremulous light of a lantern gleamed along
the wet grass, and glinted on the scattered weapons,
the shot-riven soil, and the pale faces of the dead.
Two dark figures approached noiselessly, and then he
heard a female crying—

" ' Hatzfeld—Count Hatzfeld ;' and near him

there passed a young woman of great beauty, muffled to her chin in a mantle of furs, and attended by an old man bearing a lantern, the light of which, (while shuddering at the terrors it revealed), they turned from side to side on the faces of the dead and wounded among whom they threaded their way.

"'If you seek Count Hatzfeld, madame, you seek in vain,' said the vicomte, faintly.

"'Who spoke?' said the lady, pausing in terror.

"'I—a wounded Frenchman!'

"'And wherefore say you so, monsieur?' asked the lady, while her large dark eyes seemed to dilate with alarm ; 'is he wounded—slain?'

"'Nay, I hope not, as *you* are interested in his safety ; but he has simply fallen back with his victorious infantry towards the town of Munden.'

"'Thanks—thanks,' said she, turning away ; and then, seeing by the light of her lantern that the speaker was a young and very handsome man, she added—'Pardon my selfish anxiety, for Count Hatzfeld is my husband ; but you—who are you?'

"'To-night I am your humble servant, madame ; this morning I was colonel of the brave Mousquetaires Gris, under Louis XV.'

"'Your name——'

"'Henri, Vicomte de Chateaunoir.'

"'Who was the first to cross the Rhine at Cologne?'

"'I had that honour, madame.'

"'Oh, monsieur, I have heard of you very often.'

"'Then I would pray you, madame, a Prussian though you be, to give me but a cup of water ; for even under this falling rain I am dying of thirst.'

"The Countess of Hatzfeld hastened to give him

some wine from a flask borne by her attendant, and
she even proposed to remain beside him.

"'I would rather perish of cold and exhaustion, or
die by the knives and sabres of those rascally Jagers
or Uskokes, than have you remain here in such a piti-
less night as this, lady,' replied Chateaunoir. 'I am
a Mousquetaire Gris. I thank you, Madame la Comtesse ; but leave me to my fate. I have done my
duty to God and his Most Christian Majesty, and am
quite willing to leave the event to chance.'

"But this dame with the gentle eyes and black
tresses was one of the Douglases of Esthonia,* and
was resolved to leave the event in the hands of one
quite as fickle as fate, to wit, herself, and she pro-
tested that she would not and could not quit the
vicomte ; but with the assistance of her old valet,
whose silence and fidelity could evidently be relied
on, she succeeded in extricating him from his fallen
charger; she bound up the bruises of his limb, and,
supported partly by the hard paw of the old German
valet on one side, and by her soft arm on the other,
he was conveyed to an adjacent mansion, of which
the Prussians had taken possession. It stood about a
mile from the field ; and there the lady laid him on
a couch, and attended him with every care, while her
attendant   a cunning old fellow—kept watch, to announce when the count, a young and fiery soldier who
had vowed extermination to the enemies of the Great
Frederick, should return.

"When Chateaunoir found himself in a luxurious
bed, within a handsome apartment, hung with green
silk festooned by golden cords and massive tassels,

* Where the ruins of their castle are still to be seen on the
Douglasberg. They were descended from a Scottish Douglas
who served the Teutonic knights.

and having buhl toilet-tables, covered with Mechlin lace festooned with white and silver; large oval mirrors, lighted by rose-coloured candles in girondoles of glittering crystal, and vases of flowers between, he believed himself to be in a dream, the more so, as with half-closed eyes he saw a beautiful woman, with remarkably white hands, long tremulous eyelashes, and fine eyes, gliding noiselessly about his couch, and from time to time watching over his slumbers and recovery. So he thought,

"''Tis a spirit-woman, and this is some enchanted castle on the Rhine, or *under* it, perhaps. In Paris, I have often heard tales of such adventures in this land of diablerie, and seen them, too, in the theatres.'

"But the hands and arms of this 'spirit woman,' when they touched the vicomte were remarkably unlike those of a spectre or spirit; moreover, she had a bright roguish eye, and, by her manner, seemed not at all reluctant to receive compliments, or to indulge in a little innocent coquetry, being, as most pretty women are, charmed by the admiration she excited. She had resided long at Berlin, and as our young colonel was almost fresh from the King's antechamber at Versailles, she was charmed to find a chevalier so gallant in that sequestered district which lay between the Weser and the (then) wild forests of Paderborn.

"Three days slipped pleasantly away at that quiet old German chateau.

"On the evening of the 3rd, the galloping of horses was heard in the avenue, and Count Hatzfeld, still flushed by the success of his ambuscade, which, for a time, had completely delayed the advance of the Maréchal Duc de Broglio towards Munden, accompanied by a squadron of Blue Prussian Hussars, arrived at the mansion, and, without removing his soiled and blood-stained uniform, hastened to embrace his countess. Pale and confused, the latter had barely time to conceal the vicomte in a secret alcove, or ancient hiding-place which she had discovered, and which opened by a sliding panel at *the back* of the couch, whereon he had been reposing when Hatzfeld entered, and after a few gay words of greeting, threw aside his hussar cap, gloves, sabre, and rich pelisse, and with an exclamation of pleasure, satisfaction, and weariness, stretched himself on the same place and the same pillow where the vicomte had lain but a moment before!

"Trembling with apprehension, and paler than ever, the poor little countess sat near a mirror, dreading even the expression of her own face, and scarcely trusting herself to speak.

"And now scarcely a long, tedious, and terrible hour had elapsed, when a casual sound, or some vague suspicion excited by her peculiar manner, prompted Hatzfeld suddenly to unclose the long panel of the alcove, wherein lay the stranger almost side by side with himself. With a shout of angry astonishment, the count leaped up, and sprang to his lately relinquished sabre.

"'Stay,' exclaimed the countess, throwing herself upon his sword-arm; 'he is only a poor wounded man, whom I have saved and concealed.'

"'In my bed—or beyond it—could you find no more fitting place, madam?' exclaimed her husband, endeavouring to free himself from her impetuous grasp, while sombre fury and fierce suspicion sparkled in his eyes.

"'Hatzfeld—believe me—Hatzfeld, I speak the truth!'

" 'Swear that you do,' said he, menacing her white neck with the gleaming weapon.

" 'I swear it,' she exclaimed, 'by our Lady of Oetingen, I swear——'

" 'What?'

" 'That he is only a poor stranger.'

" 'And that you never saw him before?'

" 'Never before the night of the ambush.'

" 'And that he is——who?' queried the count, sternly.

" 'A mousquetaire of King Louis.'

" 'O Christi Kreutz! a soldier of King Louis!' reiterated the count; 'what matters it—Frenchman or Austrian—one can reach hell as soon as the other!'

" He made a thrust at Chateaunoir, who though weak from his bruises, sprang from the alcove, and would infallibly have been slain had not the countess hung upon her fiery husband's sword-arm, praying him by all he held sacred and dear to spare her the horror, the disgrace, and lifelong reproach of an act so cruel as this man's slaughter in her chamber; but she spoke to one who heeded and who heard her not.

" In his blind fury or suspicion, the count disdained to hear her, and coarsely strove to thrust her from him, bruising her tender breasts and hands, as she clung about him wildly. Though so faint that he could scarcely stand, Chateaunoir had now reached and drawn his sword; and how this matter might have ended, there are no means of knowing, had it not at this crisis been cut short by the ball of a field-piece passing through the house with a frightful crash, and then they heard the sharp shrill notes of the Prussian trumpets sounding *to horse*, as a party of the Duc de Broglio's Cavalry, who were again advancing towards Munden, approached the mansion, and seeing a squadron of Blue Hussars in the lawn with a standard displayed, had suddenly opened a fire on them from three pieces of flying artillery.

" Leaving our colonel to the care of his advancing friends, Hatzfeld had to depart on the spur for Munden, which was his head-quarters and nearest fortified post, while his fair young countess became the lawful prisoner of the Mousquetaires Gris. The vicomte treated her with every courtesy, and she was escorted with all honour to the quarters of the Duc de Broglio, whose timely approach had arrested an act of assassination.

" In his anger at Count Hatzfeld, and anxiety to remain with us, Chateaunoir, immediately on procuring a new horse, assumed once more the command of the Grey Musketeers, and marched at our head, on the expedition against the town of Munden.

" The sun was setting when we, who formed the advanced guard, came in sight of Munden, at the confluence of two streams, which there unite and are named the Weser ; and its current rippled in pink and gold as the tints of evening deepened on the laden barges that floated by the quays, on the spires of the churches, and the quaint architecture of the streets. The scenery was neither bold nor striking ; but the sun seemed to linger for a time ' at the gates of the west,' casting upward his rays through cloud and sky, diverging like the fiery spokes of a mighty wheel, and these continued to waver and play, to fade and gleam again from below the dark line of the horizon, long after the sun himself had disappeared from our eyes.

" As the last bright vestige of his flaming disc went down, a cannon—the solitary evening gun—boomed from tho fortifications of Munden, and tho Prussian standard was slowly lowered for the night; and this was to us a significant notice that as yet our approach was unseen.

"Munden we considered one of tho most important places on tho Weser. On one side it had eight solid bastions faced with stone, full of earth and impenetrable to cannon-shot. A half-moon lay before every curtain and the ditch was broad. The counterscarp, covered way and palisadoes were all in the best order, and the town was garrisoned by three thousand men, five hundred of whom were Irish, whose backs had never been seen by an enemy. Count Hatzfeld commanded tho whole, and his second was tho Baron O'Reilly, a soldier as resolute and determined as himself, consequently we had every reason to expect that broken heads would be numerous enough.

"If my warlike friends expect a detail of the siege and capturo of Munden, I regret that I can afford them but a brief note of tho operations, which were pressed by M. de Broglio with great vigour. Tho battalions do Picardie blockaded it on one side, while those of Normandie enclosed it on the other. M. de Contades broke ground before the strongest bastions, and M. do Broglio undertook to storm and destroy tho works and bridges on the Weser, while tho Vicomto de Chateaunoir, with tho Mousquetaires Gris et Rouges and tho cavalry, covered tho roads and collected supplies.

"The fire of our artillery, which was heavy, was neutralized by the elevation at which they were discharged, and by tho compactness of tho earthen parapets; but ultimately a breach was effected in two days, and a host of bravo fellows volunteered for the assault. Among these were all tho Grey Mousquotaires and about a hundred of the Dragoons of Brissac, dismounted. The honour of leading the stormers at midnight was assigned to the vicomte, who appeared in his brilliant state uniform, with all his orders sparkling on his breast.

" ' Is this wise, vicomte ?' asked the old Duc de Broglio.

" ' Wherefore, maréchal ?'

" ' You will be the mark of every musket to-night.'

" ' So much the better for others,' replied the gay noble ' Allow me to please myself, Monseigneur le Duc. I may as well be killed in my best coat to-night as have it sold at the drum-head to-morrow.'

" The second volunteer for the storming party was a mere child—a son of the Comte de Brille, who had been unjustly executed for losing a military post under General Lally, in India. The boy was serving as a private soldier under M. de Contades, and was burning for an opportunity to distinguish himself; thus when we advanced towards the breach mingling together pell-mell, men of all ranks and arms united in a mass, and falling fast on every side, with shot of every sort and size passing us with an incessant *hum* or *whistle*, tearing up the turf, shattering stones, and rending huge branches off the trees that grew on the banks of the river, the vicomte turned, with an emotion of pity, and said to the boy—

" ' M. de Brille, my young brave, return while there is yet time.'

" ' My father perished innocently on the scaffold in the Place de Grève, vicomte,' replied the boy, on whose pale cheek glowed the light of the fireballs, which filled the air above and sputtered in the muddy ditches below ; ' and I shall to-night redeem his coronet from the temporary tarnish it has suffered, or die. I, too, am a De Brille!'

· "'But the breach is just before us.'

"'Well!'

"'And you have no fear; pardon me, boy, I am your senior officer, and, believe me, your sincere friend.'

"'I thank you,' said he, haughtily; 'fear—I have none.'

"'Thou art a brave chick—Vive M. le Comte de Brille!' exclaimed the stormers, and the eyes of the lad flashed fire.

"'I know, vicomte,' said he, 'that at this moment my poor old mother, the widowed countess, is praying for me at home; and God,' he added, pointing with his sword to the starlighted heaven, 'will spare the widow's son!'

"'Bravo; forward, then, to the assault—to the assault! France and Vive Louis le Roi!'

"But he was *not* spared; he fell, pierced by a mortal wound. Like a swollen surge the stormers swept over him, and through the ghastly gap in the shattered rampart hewed a passage into the heart of the place, driving the foe before them. Count Hatzfeld was among the first who fell, for, after a brief encounter, Chateaunoir slew him at the third pass. After this the Prussians gave way, and the only resistance we experienced was from O'Reilly and his Irishmen, who took possession of a Lutheran church, where they fought like incarnate devils, swearing to blow themselves up, if they had powder enough, but never to surrender.

"By noon, however, they hoisted a white flag on the steeple, and agreed to leave the place with the honours of war, which we were glad to accord them.

By this time there were only two hundred left alive; and at their head the gallant O'Reilly marched out, with one standard displayed; it bore the Irish harp and Prussian eagle. One drum was beating before them; and, in the old fashion, each man had a bullet in his mouth and four charges of powder in his pouch.

"We cheered them heartily and saluted them with all the honours of war, and then the drums of the Regiment de Normandie were beaten before them down through that terrible breach, which was strewn with dead and wounded, and where the blood was battening in the sun or oozing and trickling between the stones; and from thence they crossed the Weser, and marched to Beverungen.

"On our advance towards the latter place, they were soon compelled to retire again; for, when we carried the town by assault, they retired from it on the Prussian side.

"My next service was on the field of Minden, where —but, gentlemen, you know the rest."

———

Such was the varied narrative of Allan Robertson, the Grey Mousquetaire.

On his recovery, being sick of exile and of the French service, he expressed a great desire to join any of our Highland regiments, even as a volunteer. His wish was warmly seconded by the officers of the 51st Regiment, and his hopes were realized beyond his expectations; for, by their desire and the recommendation of Prince Ferdinand of Brunswick, he was gazetted to an ensigncy in the Forty-second—the old Black Watch—then serving under General Amherst on the American Lakes; but before leaving the camp of the Allies, from whence he was first sent home in charge of sick and wounded soldiers, he had the satisfaction of seeing the strange career of his enemy, the Chevalier de Cœurdefer, terminated with abrupt ignominy.

At Fellinghausen—a severe battle, the name and results of which are now absorbed and forgotten in the greater glories of the previous encounter at Minden—the Free Company of the chevalier charged our 51st or Second Yorkshire Regiment, to which Allan Robertson had for a time attached himself as a volunteer. This occurred among those dense and ancient forests which surround Fellinghausen, and which, on this day in particular, rendered the operations of the cavalry on both sides almost futile.

Issuing from a jungle, heedless of the shells which exploded in the air or roared and hissed along the ground, and of the leaden rain that sowed the turf about them, the wild troopers of the Franche Compagnie fell *sabre à la main* on the 51st, who formed square in a trice, and by a withering fire swept them back in disorder. Then the Black Prussian Hussars, led by Count Redhaczl, a dashing noble, in his twentieth year, by a furious flank movement, cut them wholly to pieces. Beneath the sabres of the hussars a hundred men and horses rolled upon the earth, and many prisoners were taken. Among these were the Chevalier Jules, his chaplain, and a score of his troopers, all of whom were more or less wounded. They were immediately enclosed by the square of the 51st, and were soon after transmitted to the rear.

After the battle, the chevalier and his ghostly friend, the late canon of Notre Dame de Paris, were deemed such desperate characters that their paroles were not accepted, and they were placed in a secluded

house with the other prisoners, under a guard of
Keith's Highlanders, commanded by Captain Fother-
ingham, of Powrie, an officer who had covered himself
with distinction in the late battle. There they remained
for some time without Maréchal Broglio, who was
probably but too glad to be rid of them, making
the least effort for their ransom or exchange, until
Prince Ferdinand of Brunswick, to whom a report
was made on the subject, declared "that to supply
such fellows with rations was simply feeding what
ought to be hanged."

In an evil moment over their cups, the chaplain informed the chevalier that he had, concealed about
him, notes and gold to the value of fifty thousand
francs; the plunder of various persons and places.

"Fifty thousand francs!" said the chevalier;
"*mordieu!* with that sum I should soon gild over
the most watchful eyes and achieve my liberty."

This thought haunted him day and night, and
with one so unscrupulous the sequel may easily be
guessed.

One night the chaplain was roughly wakened by a
hand being heavily laid on his throat, and he found a
masked man standing over him, armed with a bayonet, and commanding him to yield his ill-gotten
wealth on pain of instant death !

A loud cry, cut short by a death-stab in the
throat followed, and, in less than a minute, the chevalier found himself a prisoner in the hands of the
startled quarter-guard, beside the dead body of his
comrade and with a blood-dripping bayonet, as a terrible testimony against him.

A court-martial next day made short work with
him, and he was sentenced to death—a doom which
he met with the most singular coolness and contempt.

His fate was announced to him at night, and he was chained to a tree lest he should escape before *reveille* next morning, when the sentence was to be put in execution. He conversed with his guards, smoked, laughed and sang catches, and was provokingly cool and gay to the last. On perceiving his old brother student, Robertson, loitering near him, he said,

" You have the odds of me to-night, *mon ami ;* but a Prussian bullet ere long may, perhaps, enable you to overtake me *en route* to the infernal regions."

" Be thankful, chevalier, that you end your life in camp, and not in Paris," replied the Mousquetaire, quietly.

" Wherefore ?"

" Because a soldier's death and a soldier's grave are a better fate than a felon's on the dissecting-table."

" Perhaps so—*peste !* unpleasant thought to have a parcel of medical *gamins* amusing themselves with one's intestines and arteries."

" Think, sir," said Allen, gravely and with pity, "you are to die to-morrow morning."

" Better then, than to-morrow night, if it is to be. *Allons !* comrade, another light ; for, *sang Dieu !* my pipe has gone out !"

So passed his last night on earth.

Grey morning came and the great-coated guard got under arms. The chevalier was unchained from the tree and marched to a secluded spot, where his grave, which the pioneers of the 51st had dug over-night, yawned in the damp mould among the bright green grass. He walked calmly round it and looked down with all the curiosity of an amateur or mere spectator. He then stood erect opposite the provost-marshal's guard, with a scornful smile and with folded arms,

"I thank you, M. le Prevot," said he, smiling gaily; "all is as it should be—'tis just my length; five feet ten inches."

The guard, or firing party, which was composed of twenty men of the 51st, were confounded, and, perhaps, disgusted by his unparalleled coolness. He declined to have his eyes bound up.

"Make ready!" said the provost-marshal, and his guard cocked their arms at the *recover*, according to the position of those days.

"*Pardonnez moi*," said the unmoved chevalier; "I have a little request to make of you, M. le Prevot."

"What is it, sir?"

"Don't bury that devil of a friar near me."

"You mean your victim?"

"*Peste!* so you name an avaricious monk, who wanted fifty thousand francs all to himself."

"Your chaplain."

"Yes—so don't bury him near me, I say."

"Why, chevalier?"

"He might trouble me in the night, for he has been a worse fellow in life than I, and is not likely to sleep so sound in that dark hole as poor Jules de Cœurdefer; so now with your permission, I shall end this scene myself. Once more, *soldats, appretez-vous armes!*"

The muskets were levelled at him, and steadily he looked at the twenty iron tubes before him.

"*Joue!*" he added rapidly, "FEU!"

The report of twenty muskets rang sharply on the still morning air, and pierced by eleven bullets the chevalier fell dead.

His body, shattered and covered by the blood that spouted from his wounds, was lowered, while warm,

into the grave by the pioneers of tho 51st; but
before they covered it up, an officer stepped forward
and took the cloak from his own shoulders to wrap
up his miserable remains.

He who performed this last act of kindness to the
earthly tenement of the wild and reckless spirit that
had fled, was Allan Robertson of "Ours," the *soi-
disant* Mousquetaire Gris.

VII.

THE LETTRE DE CACHET.

In the ancient church of St. Germain de Prez, at Paris, is a stone which bears the following inscription in English :—

M.S.

ADAM WHITE, OF WHITEHAUGH,

MAJOR IN THE ROYAL REGIMENT OF SCOTTISH HIGH-LANDERS, 1789.

R.I.P.

On that stone, or rather on its inscription, the following legend, compiled from the traditions of the regiment, was written.

Lately, every mess-table in the service rang with a romantic story that came by the way of Calcutta. It was reported and believed, that an officer of Sale's gallant brigade, who was supposed to have been killed at Cabul, thirteen years ago, had suddenly re-appeared, alive, safe and untouched. He had been all that time a prisoner in Kokan ; his name had long since been removed from the Army List ; and on reaching Edinburgh, his native place, he found that his wife had erected a handsome monument to his memory, was the mother of a brood of little strangers, and had become the "rib" of one of his oldest friends.

This reminds me of the adventures of Adam White

of Ours, who served with the **Black Watch** under
Wolfe and Amherst.

In the year 1757 three additional companies were
added to our regiment, which, the historical records
say, " was thus augmented to thirteen hundred men,
all Highlanders, *no others being recruited for the
corps.*" These new companies were commanded by
Captains James Murray, son of Lord George Murray,
the Adjutant-General of Prince Charles Edward
Stuart, James Stewart of Urrard, and Thomas Stirling,
son of the Laird of Ardoch. The two subalterns of the
latter were Lieutenant Adam White, of the old Border
family of Whitehaugh, and Ensign John Oswald, one
of the most remarkable characters in the British service—and of whom more anon.

White's father had been a major in the army of
Prince Charles; he had been wounded at the battle
of Falkirk, taken prisoner near Culloden, marched in
chains to Carlisle, and was hanged, drawn, and quartered by the barbarous laws of George II., while his
old hereditary estate was forfeited and gifted to a
Scottish placeman of the new régime.

Adam White was a handsome and dashing officer,
who had served under Clive in the East; and on the
9th of April, 1751, when an ensign, led the attack on
the strong pagoda named the Devil's Rock, when six
months' stores of Ali Khan's army were taken with
all their guards. Like many others who were ordered
on the American campaign, Adam White had left his
love behind him; for in those days a lieutenant's pay
was only a trifle more than that of the poor ensign—
for they (Lord help them!) when carrying the British
colours on the frozen plains of Minden, and up the
bloody heights of Abraham, had only *three shillings
and threepence* per diem.

Thus, for White to marry would have been madness; and as he had only his sword, and that poor inheritance of pride, high spirit, and pedigree, which falls to the lot of most Scottish gentlemen—for he was descended from that Quhyt, to whom King Robert I. gifted the lands of Stayhr, in the county of Ayr—poor Lucy Fleming and he had agreed to wait, in hope that his promotion could not be far distant now, when he had served six years as a subaltern, and the army had every prospect of a long and severe war with France for the conquest of North America. With the minstrel he had said—

> "Have I not spoke the live-long day,
> And will not Lucy deign to say
>   One word her friend to bless?
> I ask but one—a simple sound,
> Within three little letters bound,
>   Oh let that word be YES."

Lucy answered in the affirmative, and so' they parted

Lucy Fleming, the only daughter of a clergyman of the Scottish Church, lived at her father's secluded manse in Berwickshire, among woods that lie on the margin of the Tweed, in a beautiful and sequestered glen, where tidings of the distant strife came but seldom, save when the Laird of Overmains, and Rowchester, or some other neighbouring proprietor, sent "with his compliments to the minister" an old and well-read copy of the *London Gazette,* or more probably the *Edinburgh Evening Courant,* "sair thumbed by ilka coof and bairn;" for newspapers were few and scarce in those days, and the tidings they contained were often vague, marvellous, or unsatisfactory. But Lucy was only eighteen; and she lived in hope, while her lover in a crowded and miserable transport was ploughing down the North Channel, making a vain attempt to remedy sea-sickness by brandy and water, endeavouring to forget his melancholy among comrades who were full of bilious recollections of the last night's hock and champagne, and were seeking to drown their sense of discomfort in rough practical jokes, mad fun, and fresh jorums of *eau de vie.*

Done in the best style of Sir John de Medina, a famous foreign artist, who in those days resided in Edinburgh, and who now sleeps there in a quiet corner of the old Greyfriars Kirk-yard, a miniature of Lucy in a gold locket, with a braid of her black hair, was White's best solace; and for many an hour he lay in his swinging hammock, apart from all, gazing upon the soft features Medina's hand had traced. This miniature cost our poor subaltern half-a-year's pay; but the prize-money of Trichinopoli had paid for it; and now when rocking far, far at sea, oblivious of the ship's creaking timbers, the groaning of blocks, and jarring sounds of the main-deck guns, as they strained in their lashings; the whistling of the wind through the rigging; and the varied din of laughter, occasional oaths and hoarse orders bellowed from the poop, he abandoned himself, lover-like, to the sad and pleasing employment of poring over that little memento, until the dark hazel eyes seemed to smile, the red lips to unclose, the light of love and joy to spread over all her features, and her parting tears seemed to fall again, hot and bitterly from her cheek upon his; yet the last recollection of his dear little Lucy was her pale, wan face, with eyes red and swollen by weeping, as she stood on the stone stile of the old kirk-yard wall, when he bade her farewell, just as the lumbering stage from Berwick bore him away, perhaps—for ever.

In the same spirit did he brood over the thousand trifles that the lover treasures up in memory, and on none more than the love-music of Lucy's voice, which he might never hear again.

Never again !—he shrank from those terrible words, and, trusting through God's grace to escape the chances of the war that were before him, he endeavoured to reckon over the days, the weeks, the months, and it might be the years (oh what a prospect for a newly separated lover !) that must pass, before he should again see the little secluded kirk-hamlet, with its blue-slated manse, half buried among the coppice ; the Tweed brawling over its pebbled bed in front, under the white-blossomed hawthorns and green bourtree foliage ; the ancient church with its stone spire, its old sepulchral yews, and black oak pulpit, where for more than forty years the father of his Lucy had ministered unto a poor but pious flock.

He was an old and white-haired pastor, whose memory went back to those terrible times, when Scotland drew her sword for an oppressed kirk and broken covenant—

" When the ashes of that covenant were scattered far and near,
And the voice spoke loud in judgment, which in love she would
    not hear."

Adam White saw in fancy the dark oak pew, where on Sunday Lucy sat near her father's pulpit, and close to a gothic window, from which the sun, each morning in the year, cast the red glow of a painted cross on her pure and snow-white brow ; and so, with his mind full of these things, with a tear in his eye and a prayer of hope on his lip, " rocked on the stormy bosom of the deep," our military pilgrim went to sleep in his cot, as the Lizard light faded away, and word went round from ship to ship that Old England had sunk into the waste of sky and water, far, far astern.

By the many casualties of foreign service, Adam White, on joining the regiment in America, found himself junior captain.

It was now the spring of 1758, and George II. was King. Lieutenant-General Sir Jeffry Amherst, K.C.B., was proceeding on the second expedition against L'Isle Royale, now named Cape Breton, which had belonged to the French since 1713, and was deemed by King Louis the key to Canada and the Gulf of St. Lawrence.

Meanwhile, Major-General James Abercrombie of Glassa, a gallant Scottish officer, with the 1st Scots Royals, the Black Watch, the 55th, or Westmoreland Regiment, the 62nd, or Royal North Americans, and other troops, to the number of seven thousand regulars and ten thousand provincials, landed from nine hundred batteaux, and one hundred and thirty-five whale-boats, with all their cannon, provisions, and ammunition, on the 6th of July, at the foot of Lake George, a clear and beautiful sheet of water thirty-three miles long, and surrounded by high and verdant mountains. That district, now so busy and populous, was then silent and savage. No sound broke the stillness of the romantic scenery, or the depths of the American forest, but the British drum or Scottish pipe, as the troops formed in four columns of attack, and advanced against the Fort of Ticonderoga.

Our regiment, then styled "Lord John Murray's Highlanders," was commanded by Lieutenant-Colonel Francis Grant; his second was Major Duncan Campbell of Inveraw, and never did two better or braver

officers wear the tartan of the old 42nd. Viscount
Howe, a brilliant officer of the old school of puffs,
pigtails, knee-breeches, and Ramilio wigs, led the
55th.

Ticonderoga is situated on a tongue of land extending between Lake George and the narrow fall of water
that pours with the roar of thunder into Lake Champlain, a hundred feet below. Its ramparts were thirty
feet high, faced with stone, surrounded on three sides
by water, and on the fourth by a dangerous morass
that was swept by the range of its cannon and mortars.
The approach to this morass—the *only avenue* to the
fort—was covered by a dense abattis of felled trees of
enormous size, secured by stakes to the ground, and
having all their branches pointed outward.

The garrison, which consisted of eight battalions,
was five thousand six hundred strong; and as the
assailants advanced, it was the good fortune of our
hero, Adam White, to learn from an Indian scout
that three thousand French, from the banks of the
Mohawk river, were advancing to reinforce Ticonderoga. These tidings he at once communicated to
General Abercrombie, and orders were given to push
on without delay. The praise he obtained for his
diligence made the breast of our poor " sub" expand
with hope ; and with a last glance at his relic of Lucy
Fleming, he shouldered his spontoon, and hurried
with his company into the matted jungle.

The officer who commanded in Ticonderoga was
brave, resolute, and determined. Twenty-four years
before he had been a grenadier of the Regiment de
Normandie, and served with the army of the Rhine
under the famous Maréchal the Duke of Berwick. At
the siege of Philipsburg in 1734, the Prince of Conti
was so pleased by his intrepid bearing, that he placed

a purse in his hand, apologizing for the smallness of the sum it contained ; "but we soldiers, mon camarade," continued the prince, "have the privilege to plead that we are poor."

Next morning the young grenadier appeared at the tent of Conti, with two diamond rings and a jewel of great value.

"Monseigneur le Prince," said he, "the louis in your purse I presume you intended for me, and I have sent them to my mother, poor old woman ! at Lillebonne ; but *these* I bring back to you, as having no claim to them."

"My noble comrade," replied the prince, placing an epaulette on his left shoulder, "you have doubly deserved them by your integrity, which equals your bravery ; they are yours, with this commission in the Regiment de Conti, which, in the name of King Louis, I have the power to bestow."

"Bravo, prince, this is noble !"

"Bravo ! it equals anything in Scuderi !" exclaimed two officers, who were at breakfast with the prince.

The first of these was Maurice Count Saxe, general of the cavalry ; the second was the famous Victor Marquis de Mirabeau, the future political economist, who was then a captain in the French line.

In twenty-four years this grenadier became a general officer and peer of France by the title of Comte de Montmoriu ; and in 1758, he commanded the French garrison in Ticonderoga, where he left nothing undone to render that post impregnable. Thus a desperate encounter was expected.

Formed with the grenadiers in the reserve, the 42nd marched with muskets slung, and their thirteen pipers, led by Deors MacCrimmon their pipe-major, made the deep dark forests ring to that harsh but wild music, which speaks a language Scotsmen only feel ; and the air they played was that old march, now so well known in Scotland as the "Black Watch ;" and loudly it rang, rousing vast flocks of wild birds from the lakes and tarns, and scaring the Red men from their wigwams and camps in the dense forests of pine that covered all the then unbroken wilderness.

The day was hot—the sun being 96° in the shade ; the shrubs were all in blossom, and the wild plum and cherries grew in masses and clusters in the jungle, through which the heavily-laden columns of attack forced a passage towards Ticonderoga, leaving their artillery in the rear, as the officer commanding the engineers had reported, that without employing that arm, the works might be carried by storm.

While the reflection of all Lucy might suffer, should he fall, cost poor White a severe pang, he was the first man who sent his name to the brigade-major, as a volunteer to lead the escalade.

" But," thought he, "if successful, my promotion is insured ; and if I miss death, I shall, at least, be one step nearer Lucy."

Jack Oswald, who volunteered next, consoled himself by some trite quotation from Bossuet (he was always quoting French writers), that he had not a relation to regret in the world.

The country was thickly wooded, and the guide having lost the track through those hitherto almost untrodden wastes, the greatest confusion ensued. Brigadier-General Viscount Howe, who was at the head of the right centre column, suddenly came upon a French battalion led by the Marquis de Launay, who was in full retreat, and a severe conflict ensued. The viscount, a young and gallant officer, whom Abercrombie styles "the Idol of the Soldiers," fell at the head of his own regiment, the 55th, as he was calling upon the French to surrender. A chevalier of St. Louis rushed forward and shot him by a pistol ball, which pierced his left breast. The chevalier was shot by Captain Monipennie, and received three musket balls as he fell. The French were routed; many were slain, and five officers with one hundred and forty-eight privates were taken.

Meanwhile, the column of which the Black Watch formed a part, had been brought to a complete halt in a dense forest, where the rays of the sun were intercepted by the lofty trees; the guides had deserted, and the officer in command was at a loss whether to advance or retreat, when Adam White, who had been famous for beating the jungle and tigerhunting in India, found a war-path, and boldly taking upon him the arduous and responsible office of guide, conducted the troops through the wilderness; and thus, on the morning of the 8th July, the waters of Lake Champlain, long, deep, and narrow, appeared before them, shining in the clear sunrise, between the stems of the opening forest. Beyond rose the solid ramparts of that Ticonderoga which had proved so fatal to the British arms in the last campaign, faced with polished stones, grim with shady embrasures and pointed cannon, peering over trench and palisade; and over all waved slowly in the morning wind the white banner, with the three fleurs de lis of old France.

Fire flashed from the massive bastion, and then the alarm-gun pealed across the water, waking a thousand echoes in the lonely woods; and the drum beat hoarsely and rapidly the call to arms, as the heads of

the four British columns in scarlet, with colours waving
and bayonets fixed, debouched in succession upon the
margin of that beautiful lake; and there a second
time Captain White of Ours was warmly complimented
by General Abercrombie for his skill in conducting
his comrades through a country of which he was
totally ignorant.

"And if I live to escape the dangers of the assault,
believe me, sir," continued the general, "this second
service shall be recorded to your advantage and
honour."

But poor White thought only of his betrothed wife,
and far away from the shores of that lone American
lake, from its guarded fortress and woods, where the
stealthy Red man glided with his poisoned shafts, and
from the columns of bronzed infantry, wearied by
toil and stained by travel, his memory wandered to
that sweet sequestered valley, where the pastoral
Tweed was brawling past the windows of the old
manse; and to the honeysuckle bower, where, at that
moment, perhaps, Lucy Fleming, with pretty foot and
rapid hand, urged round her ivory-mounted spinning-
wheel; for, in those days of old simplicity, every
Scottish lady spun, like the stately Duchess of Lau-
derdale, so famous for her diamonds and her imperious
beauty.

But now the snapping of flints, the springing of
iron ramrods that rang in the polished barrels, the
opening of pouches and careful inspection of ammunition by companies at open order, gave token of the
terrors about to ensue; and old friends as they passed
to and fro with swords drawn to take their places in
the ranks, shook each other warmly by the hand,
or exchanged a kindly smile, for the hour had
come when many were to part, and many to

take their last repose before the ramparts of Ticonderoga.

" Stormers to the front !" was now the order that passed along the columns, as the arms were shouldered, and the companies closed up to half-distance, while the grenadier companies of the different corps were formed with the Highlanders, as a reserve column of attack ; for on them, more than all his other troops, did the general depend ; and a fine-looking body of men they were, those old British Grenadiers, whom Wolfe ever considered the flower of his army, though they wore those quaint, sugar-loaf Prussian caps, which we adopted with the Prussian tactics, and though their heads were all floured and pomatumed, with a smart pigtail trimmed straight to the seam of the coat behind, their large-skirted coats buttoned back for service and to display their white breeches and black leggings—their officers with triple-cocked hats and sleeve-ruffles, just as we see them in the old pictures of Oudenarde and Fontenoy.

As Colonel Grant had been wounded by a random shot, Major Duncan Campbell of Inveraw, a veteran officer of great worth and bravery, led the regiment, and Adam White was by his side.

The cracking roar of musketry, and the rapid boom-boom-booming of cannon, with the whistle and explosion of mortars, shook the echoes of the hitherto silent waste of wood and water, and pealed away with a thousand reverberations among the beautiful mountains that overlook Lake Champlain, as the British columns rushed to the assault ; but alas ! the entrenchments of the French were soon found to be altogether impregnable.

The first cannon-shot tore up the earth under the feet of Ensign Oswald, and hurled him to the ground ;

but he rose unhurt, and rushed forward sword in hand.

The leading files fell into the abattis before the breastwork, and on becoming entangled among the branches, were shot down from the glacis, which was lofty, and there perished helplessly in scores.

The Inniskillings, the East Essex, the 46th, the 55th, the 1st and 4th battalions of the Royal Americans, and the provincial corps, were fearfully cut up. Every regiment successively fell back in disorder, though their officers fought bravely to encourage them, waving their swords and spontoons; but the French held the post with desperate success. Proud of their name, their remote antiquity and ancient spirit, the Scots Royals fought well and valiantly. At last even they gave way ; and then the Grenadiers and Highlanders were ordered to ADVANCE.

While the drums of the former beat the "point of war," and the pipes of the latter yelled an onset, the reserve column, led by Inveraw, rushed with a wild cheer to the assault, over ground encumbered by piles of dead and wounded men, writhing and shrieking in the agonies of death and thirst.

Impetuously the Grenadiers with levelled bayonets, and the Black Watch, claymore in hand, broke through a bank of smoke, and fell among the branches and bloody entanglements of the fatal abattis.

"Hew !" cried White, "hew down the branches with your swords, my lads, and we will soon be close enough."

"Shoulder to shoulder ! Clann nan Gael an guillan a chiele," cried old Duncan of Inveraw ; but at that instant a ball pierced his brain, he fell dead, and on White devolved the terrible task of conducting the final assault. Oswald was by his side, with the King's colours brandished aloft.

Hewing a passage through the dense branches of the abattis by their broadswords, the Black Watch made a gallant effort to cross the wet morass and storm the breastwork by climbing on each other's shoulders, and by placing their feet on bayonets and dirk-blades inserted in the joints of the masonry. These brave men were totally unprovided with ladders.

White was the first man on the parapet, and while exposed to a storm of whistling shot, he beat aside the muzzles of the nearest muskets with his claymore, and with his left hand assisted MacCrimmon, the pipe-major, Captain John Campbell, and Ensign Oswald, to reach the summit; and there stood the resolute piper, blowing the *onset* to encourage his comrades, till five or six balls pierced him, and he fell to rise no more.

A few more Highlanders reached the top of the glacis, but they were all destroyed in a moment. White fell among the French, and was repeatedly stabbed by bayonets. And now the Grenadiers gave way; but still the infuriated Black Watch continued that bloody conflict for several hours, and "the order to retire was *three times* repeated," says the historical record of the regiment, "before the Highlanders withdrew from so unequal a contest."

At last, however, they *did* fall back, leaving, besides Adam White and Major Campbell of Inveraw, Captain John Campbell (of the fated house of Glenlyon, who had been promoted for his valour at Fontenoy), Lieutenants Macpherson, Baillie, and Sutherland; Ensigns Rattray and Stuart of Banskied, with three hundred and six soldiers killed; Captains Graham, Gordon, Graham

S

of Duchray, Campbell of Strachur, Murray, and
Stewart of Urrard, with twelve subalterns, ten sergeants, and three hundred and six soldiers, wounded ;
making a frightful total of *six hundred and forty-
eight* casualties in one regiment !

Oswald received a ball through his sword arm,
but brought off the colours, tradition says, in his
teeth !

The last he saw of his friend White was his body,
still, motionless, and drenched in blood, under the
muzzle of a French cannon, but whether he was then
alive or dead it was impossible for him to say.

Four hours the contest had continued, and then
Abercrombie retired to the south side of Lake George,
leaving two thousand soldiers and many brave officers
lying dead before Ticonderoga.

The regiment deplored this terrible slaughter, but
the loss of none was so much regretted as Inveraw,
Adam White, and old MacCrimmon the pipe-major ;
and as the shattered band retired through the woods
towards a bivouac on the shore of Lake George, the
pipers played and many of the men sang " MacCrimmon's Lament," which he had composed on the fall
of his father, Donald Bane, who had been piper to
MacLeod of Dunvegan, and was killed in a skirmish
with Lord Loudon's troops near Moyhall thirteen
years before, in the dark epoch of Culloden ; and the
effect of this mournful Highland song, as it rose up
sadly from the leafy dingles of the dense American
forest, was never forgotten by the spirit-broken men
who heard it :—

"The white mountain-mist round Cuchullin is driven,
The spirit her dirge of wailing has given;
And bright blue eyes in Dunvegan are weeping,
For thou art away to the dark place of sleeping.

Return, return—alas, for ever!
MacCrimmon's away to return to us never!
In war or in joy, to feast or to fray,
To return to us never, MacCrimmon's away!

"The breath of the valley is gently blowing,
Each river and stream is sadly flowing;
The birds sit in silence on rock and on spray,
To return on no morrow, since thou art away!
  Return, return, &c.

"On the ocean that chafes with a mournful wail,
The birlinn is moored without banner or sail,
And the voice of the billow is heard to complain,
Like the cry of the Tar' Uisc from wild Corriskain.
  Return, return, &c.

"In Dungevan thy pibroch so thrilling, no more
Will waken the echoes of mountain and shore;
And the hearts of our people lament night and day,
To return on no morrow, since thou art away!
  Return, return, &c."

For many a year after, this lament was used by the regiment as a dead march.

" With a mixture of grief, esteem, and envy, I consider the great loss and immortal glory acquired by the Scots Highlanders in the late bloody affair," says a lieutenant of the 55th, in a letter dated from Lake George, July 10. " I cannot say for them what they really merit; but I shall ever fear the wrath, love the integrity, and admire the bravery of these Scotsmen. There is much harmony and good regulation amongst us; our men love and fear us, as we very justly do our superior officers; but we are in a most d—nable country, fit only for wolves and its native savages."—*Caledonian Mercury*, Sept. 9, 1758.

For many a year after, Ticonderoga found a terrible echo in the hearts of the Highlanders; a cry for vengeance, as if it had been a great national affront,

s 2

went throughout the glens, and in an incredibly short space of time more than a thousand clansmen volunteered to join the regiment. So the King's warrant came to form them into a second battalion; and it was further enacted that "from henceforth our said regiment be called and distinguished by the title and name of our 42nd, or *Royal Highland Regiment of Foot,* in all commissions, orders, and writings. Given at our Court of Kensington, this 22nd day of July, 1758, in the thirty-second year of our reign." Blue facings now replaced the buff hitherto worn by the corps.

This warrant was issued while the survivors of Ticonderoga were encamped on the southern shore of Lake George.

In due time the tidings of this second repulse of the British troops before that fatal fortress reached the secluded manse on Tweedside; and from the cold and conventional detail of operations, as given in the official despatch of General Abercrombie, poor Lucy turned, with a pale cheek and anxious and haggard eyes, to the list of killed and wounded; and the appalling catalogue that appeared under the head of ' Lord John Murray's Highlanders " struck terror to her soul. Her heart beat wildly, and her eyes grew dim; but mastering her emotion, the poor girl took in the fatal roll at a glance, and in a moment her eye caught the doubly distressing announcement—

" *Wounded severely, and since missing, Captain Adam White.*"

"God help me now, father!" she exclaimed, and threw herself on the old man's breast; " he is gone for ever!"

. · " Missing !"

That term used in military returns and field reports to express the general absence of men dead or alive, struck a vague terror, mingled with hope, in the heart of Lucy Fleming. But then White was also *wounded*, and the dread grew strong in her mind that he might have bled to death, unseen or unknown, in some solitary place, with no kind hand near to soothe his dying agony or close his glazing eyes; and expiring thus miserably, have been left, like thousands of others, in that protracted war, unburied by the Red Indians—a prey to wolves and ravens, with the autumn leaves falling, and the rank grass sprouting among his whitened bones.

These thoughts, and others such as these, filled Lucy with a horror over which she brooded day and night; and it was in vain that her only surviving parent, the old minister,

"A father to the poor—a friend to all,"

sought to encourage her by rehearsing innumerable stories of those who had returned, in those days of vague and uncertain intelligence, after being mourned for and given up, yea, forgotten by their dearest friends and nearest relatives ; but in the first paroxysm of her grief and terror Lucy refused to be consoled.

The name of the missing man was still borne in the Army List; and by the slaughter of Ticonderoga he was gazetted to the rank of brevet-major, and Oswald to a lieutenancy.

Then weeks and months slipped away, but Adam White was heard of no more.

Every hope that inventive kindness could suggest, or the uncertainty of war, time, and distance could supply, were advanced to soothe the sufferer, who caught at them fondly and prayerfully for a time ;

but suspense became sickening, and day by day these hopes grew fainter, till they died away at last.

The colonel of the regiment, Lieutenant-General Lord John Murray (son of John Duke of Athole, who, after the revolution, had been Lord High Commissioner to the Scottish Parliament), an officer who took a vivid interest in everything connected with his regiment, spared no exertion or expense to discover the missing officer ; but, after a long correspondence with the Marquis de Montcalm, who commanded the French in America, M. Bourlemarque, who commanded near Lake Champlain, and the Comte de Montmorin, commandant of Ticonderoga, no trace of poor White could be discovered, as all prisoners had long since been transmitted to France.

At Chelsea, Lord John Murray appeared in the dark kilt and scarlet uniform of the regiment to plead the cause of its noble veterans who had been disabled at Ticonderoga ; and becoming exasperated by the parsimony, partiality, and gross injustice of the Government of George II., a monarch who abhorred the Scots and loved the English but little, he generously offered " the free use of a cottage and garden to all 42nd men who chose to settle on his estates." Many accepted this reward, and the memory of their gallant colonel—the brother of the loyal and noble Tullybardin, who unfurled the royal standard in Glenfinnan—was long treasured by the men of the Black Watch.

But this tale, being a true narrative, though enrolled among our regimental legends, will not permit of many digressions.

White's name disappeared from the lists at last; another filled his place in the ranks, and after a time even the regiment ceased to speak of him, in the excitement of the new campaign in the West Indies, where, in the following year, 1759, the most of his friends fell in the attack on Martinique or the storming of Guadaloupe ; and Jack Oswald, who was a strange and excitable character, becoming disgusted with the slowness of promotion, after being "rowed" one morning for absence from parade, sold out, left the service in a pet, became an amatory poet, and then a dangerous political writer, under the well-known *nom de plume* of Sylvester Otway.

Long, sadly, and sorely did Lucy Fleming pine for the lost love of her youth. The mystery that involved his fate, and the snapping asunder of the hopes she had cherished for years, the shattering of the fairy altar on which she had garnered up these hopes, and all the secret aspirations of her girlish heart, affected her deeply. She had all the appearance of one who was dying of a broken-heart ; and yet she did not so die. Many have perished of grief and of broken-hearts, but our fair friend with the black ringlets and the black eyes was *not* one of these.

In time she shook off her grief, as a rose shakes off the dew that has bent it down, and like the rose she raised her head again more beautiful and bright than ever ; for her beauty was now chastened by a certain pensive sadness which made her very charming ; and thus it was, that in the year 1761—three years after the fatal repulse of the British troops before Ticonderoga—she attracted especial attention at the Hague, whither her father, the amiable old minister, had gone for a season, leaving his well-beloved flock and sequestered manse upon the Scottish border, to benefit the health of his pale and drooping daughter. Being furnished with introductory letters from his friend Home, the author of "Douglas," who was then conservator of Scottish privileges at Campvere, the best society was open to them.

At the balls and routs of the Comte de Montmorin, the French resident, Lucy soon eclipsed all the blue-eyed belles of Leyden and the Hague. Enchanted by the charms of the beautiful brunette, their country-woman, a crowd of gay fellows belonging to the Scots brigade in the Dutch service followed her wherever she went ; and those who saw her dancing the last cotillion by M. Brieul of Versailles, the fashionable composer of the day, or the stately and old-fashioned *minuet de la cour*, with the bucks of Stuart's regiments or MacGhie's musketeers, might have been pardoned for supposing that poor Adam White of Ours, and the dark days of Ticonderoga, were alike forgotten—as indeed they were ; for Time, the consoler, was fast smoothing over the terrible memories of three years ago ; and again Lucy could listen with a downcast eye and a half-smiling blush to the voice that spoke of love and admiration.

Thrice the Comte de Montmorin asked her hand in marriage, and thrice she refused him ; but again monseigneur returned to the charge.

" Ah ! mademoiselle," said he, " I am lured towards you as the poor moth is lured towards the light—as an eaglet soars towards the glorious sun—soars, but to sink panting and hopeless down to earth again. Never did a Guebre worship the sacred fire with half the tremulous ardour I worship you ; for mine is a worship of the heart and soul—the love of father, lover, husband, and brother—all combined in one !"

" And so, M. le Comte, you *do* admire me," said Lucy, trembling.

"In that, Mademoiselle Fleming, I would only be as other men."

" Well—"

"I love you, mademoiselle."

"But so do many more."

"Mon Dieu! I know that too well; but none love as I do."

It was not in bombast like this that poor Adam White had wooed and won her love; yet in six months after her arrival at the Hague, to the dismay and discomfiture of six entire battalions of the Scots brigade—at least the officers thereof—she became the wife of M. le Comte Montmorin, Peer of France, Knight of St. Louis, and all the royal orders—he who in former days had been the trusty grenadier of Philipsburg and the resolute general at Ticonderoga; and though the old minister sorrowed in his heart for the brave and leal-hearted lad she had loved in other days, and who was buried in his soldier's grave so far away; and though he deemed, too, that the old manse by Tweedside would be lonely now, without her, as the count belonged to an ancient Protestant house in Lillebonne, and had a magnificent fortune, et cetera, he had no solid objection to offer; and so he pronounced the irrevocable nuptial blessing, and handed over his last tie on earth—the last flower of a little flock who were all sleeping "in the auld kirkyard at hame," to the titled stranger.

On the occasion the Scots brigade consoled themselves by giving a magnificent ball; and none danced more merrily thereat than the friend of the lost lover, Jack Oswald, late of Ours, who had been taken prisoner during some of his wanderings, and sent to France; but had made his escape in the disguise of a poissard, and was wandering home, viâ the Hague and Rotterdam.

"Poor Adam fell at Ticonderoga," said he, in a pause of the dancing—"I saw him knocked on the head—'tis well he lived not to see this day!"

"But the count is so rich!" said a disappointed man of the Scots brigade.

"Tush!" snarled Oswald, "the fellow is a mere Frenchman—a heartless fool, who would laugh in the face of a corpse, as old Inveraw of Ours used to say."

Let us change the scene to a period of thirty-one years after.

It is now the year 1789.

M. le Comte de Montmorin, a venerable peer, was then the secretary of state for the foreign department under Louis XVI. Madame la Comtesse, after being long the mirror of Parisian fashion, had become a staid and noble matron, with a son in the French Guards, and two marriageable daughters, the belles of Paris. The old minister, their grandsire, had long since been gathered to his fathers, and was sleeping far away, among the long grass and the mossy head-stones of his old grey kirk on bonny Tweedside. Another occupied his humble manse, another preacher his pulpit, and other faces filled the old oak pews around it.

The horrors of the French Revolution were bursting over Paris!

The absolute power of the crown of the Louis; the overweening privileges of a proud nobility and of a dissipated clergy, with their total exemption from all public burdens, and the triple tyranny under which the people groaned, had made all Frenchmen mad. A determined and fierce contest among the different orders of society ensued; the mobs rose in arms, and the troops joined them. A new constitution was demanded, and equality of ranks formed its basis; for the cry was,

"Vive the people! down with the rich, the noble, and the aristocrats!"

The flower of the French nobles either perished on the scaffold or fled for safety and for foreign aid; the King himself became a fugitive, but was arrested on the frontiers and brought back to Paris. The streets of that city swam in blood, and the son of Lucy Fleming, a brave young chevalier, perished at the head of his company in defending the beautiful Marie Antoinette, and his head was made a foot-ball by the rabble along the Rue St. Jacques. A thousand times Lucy urged her husband to fly, for Paris had become a mere human shambles, but the determined old soldier of Ticonderoga and Quebec stood by his miserable king, and coolly proceeded each day to the foreign office on foot; for the mobs systematically murdered every aristocrat who dared to appear in a carriage, sacrificing even the valets and horses to their mad resentment.

In July, a vast armed multitude assailed the Bastille, and foremost among the assailants was a Scottish gentleman—known by many as the notorious Sylvester Otway; by others as Jack Oswald of the Black Watch.

After quitting the regiment, this remarkable man (whose father was the keeper of John's coffee-house at Edinburgh) had made himself perfect master of the Greek, Latin, and Arabic languages; and he became a vegetarian, in imitation of the Brahmins, some of whose opinions he had imbibed during service in India. He became a violent political pamphleteer, and on the outbreak of the French Revolution repaired at once to Paris, where his furious writings procured him immediate admission into the Jacobin club, in all the transactions of which he took a leading part, and was appointed to the command of a regiment of in-

fantry, which was raised from the refuse, the savage
and infamous population of the purlieus of Paris; and
they marched sans breeches, shoes, and often sans
shirts, with their hair loose, and their arms, faces,
and breasts smeared with red paint, blood, and gunpowder.

At the head of this rabble, on the evening of the
14th of July, Oswald appeared with other leaders
before the walls of the terrible Bastille; and bearing
in his hand a white flag of truce, summoned the
governor, the Marquis de Launay, "to surrender in
the name of the sovereign people;" but that noble
proudly and recklessly despised this motley rout of
armed citizens, and opened a fire upon them. The
cannon taken from the Hotel des Invalides soon
effected a breach, and a private of the French Guards,
with John Oswald, the *ci-devant* lieutenant of the
Black Watch, were the two first men who entered the
place.   The poor garrison were all slaughtered or
taken prisoners; among the latter were De Launay,
his master-gunner, and two veteran soldiers, who were
dragged to the Place de la Grêve and ignominiously
beheaded.

The terrible Bastille, for centuries the scene of so
many horrors, and the receptacle of broken hearts,
was demolished, sacked, and ruined! The most active
in that demolition was the author of "Euphrosyne,"
and the "Cry of Nature"—the wild enthusiast, John
Oswald. Intent on releasing the suffering captives
who were believed to be immured there, he hurried,
sword in hand, from tower to tower, from cell to cell,
and vault to vault; through staircases and corridors,
dark, damp, and horrible, where for ages the bloated
spider had spun her web, and the swollen rat squat-
tered in the damp and slime that distilled from the
massive walls to make a hideous puddle on the floors

of clay, amid which tho bones of many a hapless wretch, forgotten and nameless now, lay steeping with their rusted chains.

In one of these, the darkest, lowest, and most pestilential—for it was subject to the tides of the Seine, where the oozing water dropped from the vaulted roof, where the cold slimy reptiles crawled, and where the massive walls were wet with dripping slime—he found a human being, almost an idiot, chained to a block of stone. He was old; his hair and beard were white as the thistle-down : he seemed a living corpse ; his aspect was terrible, for existence seemed a miracle, a curse in such a place ; and on being brought to upper earth and air by these blood-steeped men of the people, he became senseless and swooned.

Three other prisoners were found, and then, to its lowest vaults, the infamous Bastille was levelled—even to its base, and its records of tyranny, torture, suffering, human crime, and inhuman horror perished with it.

"The only State prisoners, where so many were supposed to have entered," says the *Edinburgh Magazine* for that year, "the only prisoners that were forthcoming in the general delivery amounted to four ! Major White and Lord Mazarine were two out of that number. The first gentleman, a native of Scotland, was in durance for the space of twenty-eight years ; he had never in that time been heard of by his friends, nor in the least expected thus to be enthralled. When restored to liberty, he appeared to have lost his mental powers, and even the vernacular sounds of his own language. The Duke of Dorset has taken him under his direct protection ; this is unasked, and therefore the more honourable."

So this miserable wreck, aged, pale, and wan, worn almost to a skeleton, nearly nude, with his limbs fretted by iron fetters, and all but fatuous; insane,

and with scarcely a memory of his native tongue or
past existence; in whose eyes the light of life and intelligence seemed dead, and who had forgotten the
days when he could weep or feel, was our long-lost
comrade, the soldier of Ticonderoga?

Inspired by just indignation, and determined to
unravel this terrible mystery, the Duke of Dorset
took him in a fiacre to the hotel of the Comte de
Montmorin, the only minister then in Paris, to demand the reason of this outrage upon the laws of war,
of peace, and of common humanity; but the official
of the unfortunate Louis could only shrug his shoulders, make the usual grimaces and apologies, and
plead, that as the records of the Bastille had perished
in the sack of that prison, it was totally beyond his
power to explain the affair; for not a scrap of paper
remained to show how or why this brave officer of
the Black Watch, who had been wounded and taken
prisoner in action in 1758, should have been found in
that dreadful place thirty-one years after. The Duke
of Dorset perceived, with surprise, that while speaking the Comte de Montmorin was ghastly pale, and
that his eyes were filled with terror. It would have
made a fine subject for a painter, but a finer still for
a novelist—the delineation of this interview, as it
took place in the drawing-room of the Hotel de
Montmorin on the morning after the demolition of
the Bastille.

The unfortunate victim of a government which had
long made that infamous prison an engine of tyranny,
was introduced by our proud and determined ambassador, who spoke for him in no measured tones; for
alas! the poor major could scarcely put three words
together, and for some hours seemed to have forgotten
the sound of his own voice.

In tho stately and now elderly French lady seated
on tho gilt fauteuil, between her shrieking and pitying
daughters, clad in her high stays, hooped petticoat,
and figured satin, with an esclavago round her neck,
and her white hair powdered and towered up into a
mountain of curls, flowers, and feathers, à la Marquise
do Pompadour, it was impossible for Adam White to
recognise tho once beautiful and black-eyed Lucy of
his youth—the simple Scottish girl of the quiet old
manse on Tweedside, for whom his sorrowing heart
had yearned with agony, in tho long and dreary days
of captivity, and in the longer watches of the silent
night, until love and youth and blessed hope all
passed away together.

It was as difficult for her to trace in that wan, aged,
and resuscitated man, the handsome young officer
who had left her side to fight Britain's battles under
Amherst and tho hero of Quebec. She was now a
white-haired matron, and he a wild-eyed, haggard
old man—old by premature years, for eight-and-
twenty in the Bastillo had crushed him by a load of
unavailing care and sorrow. How many seasons had
passed over that dark and vaulted solitude during
which his pained and weary eyes had never met
a friendly smile, or his ear welcomed a kindly
greeting.

Eight-and-twenty summers had bloomed and
withered, and eight-and twenty winters had spread
their snows upon the hills! In that long space of
time, how many had been wedded and given in
marriage, or been laid in their last homes?—how
many of the bravo and good,·tho noble and tho beautiful, had gone to " tho Land of the Leal," where there
is no dawning or gloaming, where tho sun shines for
ever, and tho flowers never die !

For eight-and-twenty years all the pulses of life had seemed to stand still; and now, under their changed aspect and character, and ignorant of each other's presence, ·Lucy Fleming and Adam White stood within the same apartment, without a glance of recognition. Weak, tottering, and frail, White was placed in a chair, and the countess brought wine to him from a side table. His aspect was that of a dying man; her eyes were full of pity, and her daughters wept to see this poor old man, whose wandering faculties were awaking to a new existence after the long and dreamless sleep of eight-and-twenty years, and to whom the upper air, the blessed sunshine, and the twitter of the happy birds, were all as strange and new as if he had never known them.

"Your name, monsieur le prisonnier?" asked her husband, coldly, and with averted eye.

"Adam White—yes, yes—I am sure it was so— Adam White; once a major in the 42nd Regiment of his Britannic Majesty George II.," he replied, with great difficulty and long pauses.

"George II. has been dead these twenty-eight years, sir," replied the Duke of Dorset, kindly placing an arm upon his shoulder, while, with outspread hands and eyes dilated with terror, the countess started back as if a spectre had risen before her.

"Dead! dead!" muttered the major. "I too have been dead, I think—and who now is on the throne?"

"His grandson, George III."

"Know you the crime for which you were arrested, monsieur?" asked the count, who did not seem to notice the agitation of the countess.

The sunken eyes of Major White flashed, but the

emotion died at once, for his heart seemed broken and his spirit crushed.

"Crime!" said he; "I was wounded and taken in the assault on Ticonderoga by the Comte de Montmorin."

"I commanded there, and I am he."

"This was thirty-one years ago—my God! oh, my God!"

"Be calm, dear sir," said the Duke of Dorset.

"And you have been all that time in the Bastille?"

"Yes, monseigneur."

"Horrible!" exclaimed the duke.

"You were arrested"—

"One night in the streets of Paris, near the Port St. Antoine, when I was at liberty upon parole, as a prisoner of war."

"When was this?"

"In 1761—three years after Ticonderoga."

"Ah, we had peace with Britain in 1763," said the count, averting his eyes, and endeavouring to assume a composure which he did not feel under the keen scrutiny of Dorset's eye. "And so we meet again — fortune has cast us together once more."

"Fortune—say rather fatality," replied White, as some old memory shook his withered heart.

"Did you ever hear how or why you were arrested?"

"Once, and once only—I was told—I was told that it was on the authority of a *lettre de cachet*, filled up by King Louis in the name of the Comte de Montmorin."

"It is an infamous falsehood!" exclaimed the count, passionately.

T

"Perhaps so," sighed White, meekly; "the man who told me so has been dead twenty-three years."

"And this arrest was"—

"On the anniversary of Ticonderoga—the night of the 15th of July, 1761."

"The 15th of July!" exclaimed the countess, wildly, and in a piercing voice; "on the morning of that very day my desk was rifled of your letters, and your miniature, Adam White!—O my friend—I see it all—I see this horrible mystery!"

White turned his hollow eyes and haggard visage towards her in wonder. He passed a hand repeatedly across his eyes, as if to clear his thoughts, then shook his white head, and relapsed into dreamy vacancy. After a painful pause, "That voice," said he, "is like one which used to come to me often—very often—in the Bastille; in my dreams it used to mingle with the rustle of the straw I slept on."

He smiled with so ghastly an expression that the Duke of Dorset grew pale with anger and compassion. He had gleaned from White the story of his life, and discovered in a moment that the countess was the Lucy Fleming of his early love; and that the count, on discovering the wounded and long-missing major to be in Paris in 1761, to preclude all chance of the lovers ever meeting again, had consigned him to the Bastille, there to be detained for life, as it was termed "IN SECRET."

"Monseigneur," said he, sternly, "I see a clue to this dark story; and believe me, that the king, whom I have the honour to represent, will take sure vengeance for this act of more than Italian jealousy, and for an atrocity which cannot be surpassed in the annals of yonder accursed edifice, which the mob of yesterday have happily hurled to the earth."

With these words he retired, taking with him Adam White, who seemed reduced to mere childhood, for recollection and animation came upon him only by gleams and at unexpected times. As they withdrew, the countess turned away in horror from her husband, and fainted in the arms of her terrified daughters.

The inquiry threatened by our ambassador was never made. Paris was then convulsed, and France was trembling on the brink of anarchy, even as the weak Louis trembled on his crumbling throne. The exertions of his Grace of Dorset to unravel more of the mystery, and the fears of the Comte de Montmorin, were alike futile, for next morning the poor major was found dead in his bed. He had expired in the night. The sudden revulsion of feeling produced by a release, after so many years of blank captivity, had proved too much for his weak frame and shattered constitution. He was buried in the church of St. Germain de Prez; and when Oswald's *sans-culottes* lifted the dead man from the bed, to lay him in the humble shell provided by the curé of the parish, there dropped from his breast a locket. It contained a miniature and a withered tress of black hair—the last mementoes left to him of all that he had loved in the pleasant days of youth and hope, and prized beyond even blessed hope itself, in the solitude and horror of the long years that had followed Ticonderoga. The ruffians who had desecrated the regal sepulchres of St. Denis respected the heritage of the dead soldier, so that the locket was buried with him; and there, in the ancient church of St. Germain, Oswald, the political enthusiast, interred his old and long-lost comrade with all the honours of war.

The stone which was erected in the church, and of

which I have given the brief inscription, is said, traditionally, to have been the gift of a lady—who, need scarcely be mentioned. How long this lady and the count her husband survived the disclosures consequent to the destruction of the Bastille, I have no means of knowing; but French history has recorded the fate of Jack Oswald.

His two sons left Edinburgh and joined him at Paris, where, to illustrate the complete system of equality and fraternity, he made them both drummers in his regiment, among the soldiers of which his severe discipline soon rendered him unpopular; and on his attempting to substitute pikes for muskets, the whole battalion refused to obey, and then officers and men broke out into open mutiny.

"Colonel Oswald's corps," continues the editor of the "Scottish Biographical Dictionary," "was one of the first employed against the royalists in La Vendée, where he was killed in battle. It is said that his men took advantage of the occasion to rid themselves of their obnoxious commander, and to despatch also his two sons, and an English gentleman who was serving in his regiment."

And thus ends another legend of the Black Watch.

VIII.

ADVENTURES OF CAPTAIN GRANT.

COLQUHOUN GRANT, a captain of one of our battalion companies during the Peninsular war, was a hardy, active, strong, and handsome Highlander, from the wooded mountains that overlook Strathspey. Inured from childhood to the hardships and activity incidental to a life in the country of the clans, where the care of vast herds of sheep and cattle, or the pursuit of the wild deer from rock to rock, and from hill to hill, are the chief occupations of the people ;—a deadly shot with either musket or pistol, and a complete swordsman, he was every way calculated to become an ornament to our regiment and to the service. General Sir William Napier, in the fourth volume of his "History of the Peninsular War," writes of him as "Colquhoun Grant, that celebrated scouting officer, in whom the utmost *daring* was so mixed with subtlety of genius, and both so tempered by *discretion*, that it is difficult to say which quality predominated."

In the spring of 1812, when Lord Wellington crossed the Tagus, and entered Castello Branco, rendering the position of Marshal Marmont so perilous that he retired across the Agueda, by which the general of the allies, though his forces were spread over a vast extent of cantonments, was enabled to victual the fortresses of Ciudad Rodrigo and Almieda, the 42nd, or old Black Watch, were with the division of Lieutenant-General Grahame, of Lynedoch. The service battalion consisted of 1160 rank and file, and notwithstanding the fatigues of marching by day and night, of fording rivers above the waist-belt, and all those arduous operations by which Wellington so com pletely baffled and out-generalled Marmont in all his attempts to attack Rodrigo—movements in which the sagacity of the "Iron Duke" appeared so re-markable, that a brave old Highland officer (General Stewart of Garth) declared his belief that their leader had the *second sight*,—not a man of our regiment straggled or fell to the rear, from hunger, weariness, or exhaustion; all were with the colours when the roll was called in the morning.

The information that enabled Wellington to execute those skilful manœuvres which dazzled all Europe, and confounded, while they baffled, the French marshal, was supplied from time to time by Colqu-houn Grant, who, accompanied by Domingo de Leon, a Spanish peasant, had the boldness to remain in rear of the enemy's lines, watching all their operations, and noting their numbers; and it is a remarkable fact that while on this most dangerous service he con-stantly wore *the Highland uniform, with his bonnet and epaulettes;* thus, while acting as a scout, freeing himself from the accusation of being in any way a spy, "for," adds Napier, "he never would assume any disguise, and yet frequently remained for three days concealed in the midst of Marmont's camp."

Hence the secret of Wellington's facility for circumventing Marmont was the information derived from Colquhoun Grant; and the secret of Grant' ability for baffling the thousand snares laid for him by the French, was simply that he had a Spanish love, who watched over his safety with all a woman's wit, and the idolatry of a Spanish woman, who, when she loves, sees but *one* man in the world—the object of her passion.

When Marmont was advancing, Wellington despatched Captain Grant to watch his operations " in the heart of the French army," and from among its soldiers to glean whether they really had an intention of succouring the garrison of Ciudad Rodrigo—a desperate duty, which, like many others, our hero undertook without delay or doubt.

Thus, on an evening in February, Grant found himself on a solitary mountain of Leon, overlooking the vast plain of Salamanca, on the numerous spires and towers of which the light of eve was fading, while the gilded vanes of the cathedral shone like stars in the deep blue sky that was darkening as the sun set behind the hills; and one of those hot dry days peculiar to the province gave place to a dewy twilight, when the Tormes, which rises among the mountains of Salamanca, and washes the base of the triple hill on which the city stands, grew white and pale, as it wandered through plains dotted by herds of Merino sheep, but destitute of trees, until it vanished on its course towards the Douro, on the frontiers of Portugal.

Exhausted by a long ride from Lord Wellington's head-quarters, and by numerous efforts he had made to repass the cordon of picquets and patrols by which the French—now on his track—had environed him, Grant lay buried in deep sleep, under the shade of some olive-trees, with a brace of pistols in his belt, his claymore by his side, and his head resting in the lap of a beautiful Spanish peasant girl, Juanna, the

sister of his faithful Leon, a warm-hearted, brave, and
affectionate being, who, like her brother, had attached
herself to the favourite scouting officer of Wellington,
and, full of admiration for his adventurous spirit,
handsome figure, and winning manner, loved him
with all the ardour, romance, and depth of which
a Spanish girl of eighteen is capable.

Juanna de Leon and her brother Domingo were
the children of a wealthy farmer and vine-dresser,
who dwelt on the mountainous range known as the
Puerto del Pico, which lies southward of Salamanca;
but the vines had been destroyed, the *granja* burned,
and the poor old agriculturist was bayonetted on his
hearthstone by some Voltigeurs of Marmont, under
a Lieutenant Armand, when on a foraging expedition.   Thus Juanna and her brother were alike home-
less and kinless.

The girl was beautiful.   Youth lent to her somewhat olive-tinted cheek a ruddy glow that enhanced
the dusky splendour of her Spanish eyes; her lashes
were long; her mouth small, and like a cherry; her
chin dimpled; her hands were faultless, as were her
ankles, which were cased in prettily embroidered red
stockings, and gilt zapatas.   With all these attractions she had a thousand winning ways, such as only
a girl of Leon can possess.   Close by lay the guitar
and castanets with which she played and sung her
weary lover to sleep.

Her brother was handsome, athletic, and resolute,
in eye and bearing; but since the destruction of their
house, he had become rather fierce and morose, as
hatred of the invading French and a thirst for vengeance were ever uppermost in his mind.   He had
relinquished the vine-bill for the musket; his yellow
sash bristled with pistols and daggers; and with

heaven for his roof, and his brown Spanish mantle for a couch, he had betaken himself to the mountains, where he shot without mercy every straggling Frenchman who came within reach of his terrible aim.

While Grant slept, the tinkling of the vesper bells was borne across the valley, the sunlight died away over the mountains, and the winding Tormes, that shone like the coils of a vast snake, faded from the plain. The Spanish girl stooped and kissed her toil-worn lover's cheek, and bent her keen dark eyes upon the mountain path by which she seemed to expect a visitor.

One arm was thrown around the curly head of the sleeper, and her fingers told her beads as she prayed over him ; but her prayers were *not* for herself.

Innocent and single-hearted Juanna !

Suddenly there was a sound of footsteps, and a handsome young Spaniard, wearing a brown capa gathered over his arm, shouldering a long musket to which a leather sling was attached, and having his coal black hair gathered behind in a red silk net, sprang up the rocks towards the olive-grove, and approached Juanna and the sleeper. The new comer was her brother.

" Domingo, your tidings?" she asked, breathlessly.

" They are evil ; so wake your Senor Capitano without delay."

" I am awake," said Grant, rising at the sound of his voice. " Thanks, dearest Juanna ; have I been so cruel as to keep you here in the cold dew—and watching me, too ?"

" Caro mio !"

" It *was* cruel of me ; but I have been so weary that nature was quite overcome. And now, Domingo, my *bueno camarudo*, for your tidings ?"

"I would speak first of the Marshal Marmont."

"And then?"

"Of yourself, senor."

"Bravo! let us have the Marshal first, by all means."

"I have been down the valley, and across the plain, almost to the gates of Salamanca," said the young paisano, leaning on his musket, and surveying, first, his sister with tender interest, and then, Grant with a dubious and anxious expression, for he loved him too, but trembled for the sequel to the stranger's passion for the beautiful Juanna. "I have been round the vicinity of the city from Monte Rubio and Villares to the bridge of Santa Marta on the Tormes—"

"And you have learned?" said Grant, impetuously.

"That scaling-ladders have been prepared in great numbers, for I saw them. Vast quantities of provision and ammunition on mules have been brought from the Pyrenees, and Marmont is sending everything—ladders, powder, and bread—towards—"

"Not Ciudad Rodrigo and Almieda."

"Si, senor."

"The devil! You are sure of this?"

"I counted twenty scaling-ladders, each five feet wide, and reckoned forty mules, each bearing fourteen casks of ball cartridges."

"Good—I thank you, Domingo," said Grant, taking paper from a pocket-book, and making a hasty note or memorandum for Lord Wellington.

"Ay—Dios mi terra!" said Juanna, with a soft sigh, as she dropped her head upon Grant's shoulder, and Domingo kissed her brow.

"Now, where is Maurico el Barbado?" asked the captain, as he securely gummed the secret note.

" Within call," said Domingo, giving a shrill whistle.

A sound like the whirr of a partridge replied, and then a strong and ferocious-looking peasant, bare legged, and bare necked, with an enormous black beard (whence came his soubriquet of *el Barbado*), sprang up the rocks and made a profound salute to Grant, who was beloved and adored by all the guerillas, banditti, and wild spirits whom the French had unhoused and driven to the mountains ; and among these his name was a proverb for all that was gallant, reckless, and chivalresque.

" Is your mule in good condition, Manrico ?"

" He was never better, senor."

"Then ride with *this* to Lord Wellington ; spare neither whip nor spur, and he will repay you handsomely."

" And how about yourself, senor ?"

" Say to his lordship that I will rejoin him as early and as I best may."

The Spanish scout concealed the note in *his beard* with great ingenuity, and knowing well that he could thus pass the French lines with confidence, and defy all search, he departed on his journey to the British head-quarters ; and the information thus received from Grant enabled the leader of the allies to take such measures as completely to outflank Marmont, and baffle his attempts upon Almieda and the city of Rodrigo.

" So much for my friend Marmont," said Grant, "and now, Domingo, for *myself.*"

" Read this," said Domingo, handing to him a document ; " I stabbed the French sentinel at the bridge of Santa Marta, and tore this paper from the guardhouse door."

It proved to be a copy of a General Order, addressed by Marmont to the colonels of the French regiments, " saying" (to quote General Napier) " that the notorious Grant, being within the circle of their cantonments, the soldiers were to use their utmost exertions to secure him ; for which purpose guards were also to be placed, as it were, in a circle round the army."

" Caro mio, read this to me," whispered Juanna.

He translated it, and terror filled the dilating eyes of the Spanish girl ; her breath came thick and fast, and she crept closer to the breast of her lover, who smiled and kissed her cheek to reassure her.

" Have you closely examined all the country ?" he asked Domingo.

" I have, senor."

" Well ?"

" There is but *one* way back to Lord Wellington's head-quarters."

" And that is—"

" At the ford of Huerta on the Tormes."

" Six miles below Salamanca ?"

" Yes."

" I will cross the ford, then."

" But a French battalion occupies the town."

" I care not if ten battalions occupied it—*I must even ride the ford as I find it ;* 'tis a saying in my country, Domingo, where I hope our dear Juanna will one day smile with me, when we talk of sunny Spain and these wild adventures."

" No—no—you will never leave Spain," said Juanna, with a merry smile. " Your poor Spanish girl could never go to the land of the Inglesos, where the sun shines but once in a year—not once every day, as it does here in beautiful Leon : but say no more of this, or I shall sing *Ya no quiero amores,*" &c., and, taking up her guitar, she sang with a winning drollery of expression which made her piquant loveliness a thousand times more striking :—

" My love no more to England—to England now shall roam,
For I have a better, fonder love—a truer love at home !
    If I should visit England,
      I hope to find them true ;
    For a love like mine deserves a wreath !
      Green and immortal too !
But, O ! they are proud, those English dames, to all who thither roam,
And I have a better, dearer love—a truer love at home !"·

"You have *me*, Juanna—dearest Juanna !" exclaimed Grant, tenderly, as he kissed her.

"And now for Huerta," said Domingo, slapping the butt of his musket impatiently ; "the moon will be above the Pico del Puerto in half an hour—vaya —let us begone."

Grant placed Juanna on the saddle of his horse, a fine, fleet, and active jennet presented to him by Lord Wellington, and led it by the bridle, while Domingo slung his musket, and followed thoughtfully behind, as they descended the hill with the intention of seeking the banks of the Tormes ; but making a wide detour towards the ford. The moon was shining on the river when they came in sight of Huerta, a small village, through which passes the road from Salamanca to Madrid. A red glow at times shot from its tile works, showing the outlines of the flat-roofed cottages, and wavering on the olive-groves that overhung the river, which was here crossed by the ford. While Grant and Juanna remained concealed in a thicket of orange-trees in sight of Huerta, Domingo, whose godfather was a tile-burner in the town, went forward to reconnoitre and make inquiries; and in less than twenty minutes he returned with a gloomy brow and excited eye.

" Well, Domingo, what news?" asked Grant, on whose shoulder the head of Juanna was drooping, for she was nearly overcome by sleep and fatigue.

" I have still evil news, Senor."

" Indeed."

" The French battalion occupies Huerta, and the main street is full of soldiers. Guards are placed at each end, and cavalry videttes are posted in a line along the river, patrolling constantly backwards and forwards, for the space of three hundred yards, and two of these videttes meet always *at the ford*, consequently, be assured, they know that you are on *this* side of the Tormes."

" The deuce!" muttered Grant, biting his lips. " M. le Maréchal Marmont is determined to take me this time, I fear; but I *will* cross the ford, Domingo, in the face of the enemy too! Better die a soldier's death under their fire, than fall alive into their hands."

" A soldier's death, and a sudden one, is sure to follow, Senor Capitano," added Domingo, gloomily, and poor Grant was not without anxiety for the issue. He thought of Juanna, and some recollection of the ignominious fate of the gallant Major André, when found beyond the American lines, under similar circumstances, may have flashed upon his memory.

" Do not weep, Juanna," said he to the Spanish girl, who strove to dissuade him from attempting the ford; " your tears only distress and unman me, when all my courage is wanted."

" Caro mio, if you love me, stay, for you cannot

deceive me as to the peril—it is great—and if taken, what mercy can you expect from Marshal Marmont?"

"But I will *never* be taken, alive at least," responded the Highlander, with a fierce and sorrowful embrace ; "'tis better to die than be taken, and perhaps have the uniform I wear—the uniform of the old Black Watch—disgraced by a death at the hands of a provost marshal."

The young Spanish girl caught the fiery enthusiasm of her lover, and nerved herself for the struggle, and for their consequent separation ; but Domingo had once more to examine the ground and so many points were to be considered, that day began to brighten on the Pico del Puerto and the Sierras of Gredos and Gata, before Grant mounted his horse ; and by that time, the French drums had beaten *reveille*, and the whole battalion was under arms at its alarm-post, a greensward behind the tile-works. Juanna and her lover parted with promises of mutual regard and remembrance until they met again.

"When will it be—oh, when will it be ?" she moaned.

"In God's appointed time—quando Dios sera servido," replied Grant. "Farewell, Juanna mia, a thousand kisses and adieux to you."

"Bueno—away !" said Domingo, taking Grant's horse by the bridle—"away before day is quite broken !"

As they hurried off, Juanna threw herself on her knees in the thicket, and prayed to God and Madonna for her lover. She covered her beautiful head with that thick mantle usually worn by the women of Leon, to shut out every sound ; but lo ! there came a loud, yet distinct shout from the river's bank, and then a confused discharge óf firearms that rang sharply in the clear morning air.

"O Madonna mia!" exclaimed the Spanish girl, and with a shriek she threw herself upon her face among the grass.

Meanwhile Grant had proceeded in rear of the tile-works, close by where the French regiment was paraded in close column at quarter distance, and so near was he, that he could hear the sergeants of companies calling the roll; but a group of peasants assembled by Domingo, remained around his horse, with their broad sombreros and brown cloaks, to conceal it from the French, along *whose front* he had to pass to reach the ford. From the gable of a cottage, he had a full view of the latter—the Tormes brawling over its bed of rocks and pebbles, with the open plain that lay beyond, and the two French videttes, helmeted and cloaked, with carbine on thigh, patrolling to and fro, to the distance of three hundred yards apart, but meeting at the ford.

"Their figures seem dark and indistinct, in the starry light of the morning," said Grant.

"But we know them to be dragoons," said Domingo.

"Si, senores," added the brother of Manrico el Barbado; "from this you may perceive that their helmets and horses are afrancesado."

"Frenchified—yes; now when I whistle, let go my horse's head, and do you, my good friends in front, withdraw to give me space, for now the videttes are about to part, and I must make at dash at it!"

At the moment when the patrols were separated to their fullest extent, and each was one hundred and fifty yards from the ford, Grant dashed spurs into his horse, and with his sword in his teeth and a cocked

pistol in each hand, crossed the river by three furious
bounds of his horse. Receiving without damage the
fire of both carbines, he replied with his pistols, giving
each of the dragoons a flying-shot to the rear, but
without injuring either of them. There was an in-
stantaneous and keen pursuit; but he completely
baffled it by his great knowledge of the country, and
reached a cork-wood in safety, where he was soon
joined by Domingo de Leon, who, being attired as a
peasant, and unknown to the French, was permitted
to pass their lines unquestioned.

Marmont's rage on Grant's escape was great; the
sentinels at the ford were severely punished, and the
officer commanding the regiment in Huerta was
deprived of his cross of the Legion of Honour. Grant
was not satisfied with the extent of his observations,
for he became desirous of furnishing Lord Wellington
with still further intelligence.

From the conversations of French officers whom he
had overheard, he made ample notes, and proved that
means to storm Ciudad Rodrigo were prepared; but
he was resolved to judge for himself of the direction
in which Marmont meant to move, and also to see his
whole division on the line of march. For this purpose he daringly concealed himself among some coppice on the brow of a hill near the secluded village of
Tamames, which is celebrated for its mineral springs,
and lies thirty-two miles south-west of Salamanca.
There he sat, note-book in hand, with Leon, smoking
a cigar, and lounging on the grass, while his jennet, un-
bitted, was quietly grazing close by, and the whole of
Marmont's brilliant division, cuirassiers, lancers, infantry, artillery, and voltigeurs defiled with drums beating, tricolours waving, and eagles glittering through the
pass below; and Grant's skilful eye counted every cannon

U

and reckoned over every horse and man, with a cor-
rectness which astonished even Lord Wellington. The
moment the rear-guard had passed, he mounted, and
although in his uniform, rode boldly into the village
of Tamames, where he found all the scaling ladders
left behind. With tidings of this fact, and the strength
of Marmont's army, he at once despatched a letter to
Wellington, by Manrico el Barbado, who, as before,
concealed it under his nether-jaw; and this letter,
which informed the allies that the preparations to
storm Rodrigo were, after all, a pompous *feint*, allayed
their leader's fear for that fortress, and to Marmont's
inexpressible annoyance, enabled him to turn attention to other quarters,

Fearless, indefatigable, and undeterred by the
dangers he had undergone, Grant *preceded* Marmont
(when that officer passed the Coa) and resolved to
discover whether his march would be by the duchy of
Guarda upon Coimbra, the land of Olives; or by the
small frontier town of Sabugal, upon Castello Branco,
which stands upon the Lira, a tributary of the Tagus,
and still displays the ruins of the Roman Albicastrum
from which it takes its name.

Castello Branco is a good military position; but to
reach it, a descent was necessary from one of those
lofty sierras that run along the frontier of Portuguese
Estramadura, and are jagged by bare and sunburned
rocks, or dotted by stunted laurel bushes. From
thence, he traversed a pass, at the lower end of which
stands the town of Penamacor in the province of
Beira, thirty-six miles north-east of Castello Branco.
There, our adventurous Highlander, accompanied by
Manrico el Barbado and the faithful Domingo de
Leon, concealed himself in a thicket of dwarf-oaks;
and there a very remarkable adventure occurred to

him, while waiting the approach of the French, whose
advanced guard he hourly expected to see in the dark
mountain pass below. Their horses were • beside
them.

Wrapped in their cloaks, the captain and his two
Spanish comrades, after a supper of broiled eggs—
huevos estrallados — sat by a fire of leaves and
withered branches, and after sharing a bottle of vino
de Alicant, composed themselves to sleep—a state of
oblivion soon obtained by the two sturdy paisanos ;
but Grant remained unusually restless, thoughtful
and awake. His mind was full of other times and
past events—of distant scenes and old familiar faces.
He thought of his home, .of the regiment, and of
Juanna, whom he had left at Huerta ; and as the red
sunset deepened into night upon that lofty mass of
rock which is washed by the Eljas and crowned by the
picturesque houses, the strong fortifications, and the
three churches of Penamacor, the light and shadow
blended into one, and darkness came broadly and
steadily on ; then a strange and mysterious sensation
of sadness stole over him—a solemn melancholy which
he strove in vain to account for and dispel.

At last, when about to drop asleep, about ten
o'clock, he started up, for a broad blaze of light illu-
mined all the citadel of Penamacor. He saw its solid
ramparts and the sharp spires of its three churches
standing in black and bold relief against the unwonted
glow that filled the sky above the city ; he heard the
clanging of an alarm-bell, the hum of voices, and the
tread of feet, as two vast and dark columns of infantry debouched from the pass and began to descend
the mountains towards the bridge of the Eljas.

"The enemy—the enemy !" he exclaimed. "Up,
up, Domingo—Manrico, awake !"

Roused by his voice they sprang to his side; but lo! at that moment, the light faded away from the citadel; the sounds of the alarm-bell, the hum of distant voices, and tread of marching feet died away; the columns vanished, and the hollow way from the pass to the river was lonely and silent as before, in the clear light of the star-studded sky!

Of all these alarming sights and sounds, Manrico and Domingo had seen and heard nothing!

"It was a dream!" said Grant, as he threw himself on the sward in alarm and perplexity, while his heart beat wildly and strangely—and for the remainder of that night sleep never closed his eyes. The three wanderers passed the whole of the next day lurking in the oak woods that overhang the pass of Penamacor, and Domingo, who, after sunset, ventured into the town for some provisions for supper, returned to say that *no* lights had been burned, and *no* alarm had been given last night, as *no* fear was entertained of the approach of Marmont.

Night again drew on, and the three companions were all alike watchful and awake.

The hour of ten began to toll from the bells of Penamacor. At the first stroke Grant felt a nervous sensation thrill over his whole body, while the same solemn melancholy of the same time last night again weighed down his heart.

At the tenth stroke, lo! a brilliant light flashed across the sky. It shot upward from the citadel of Penamacor! Again, as before, the crenelated battlements and the sharp spires of the three churches stood darkly out from the blaze, which was streaked by the ascent of hissing rockets; again the alarm-bell sent its iron clangour on the wind, but mingled with the boom of cannon; again came the hum of voices, and again two dark and shadowy columns debouched from the black jaws of the mountain gorge and descended towards the bridge of the Eljas; but this time there came horse and artillery; the uplifted lances and the fixed bayonets gleamed back the starlight, while the rumble of the shot-laden tumbrils rang in the echoing valley.

"Madre de Dios! the enemy!" exclaimed the two Spaniards, starting to their muskets.

"What! do you, too, see all this?" exclaimed Grant, wildly, as he smote his forehead; for now he had begun to distrust the evidence of his own senses, and a horror that these mysterious visions, known in Scotland as *the second sight*, were about to haunt him, made his head reel.

"See them—yes, senor, plain as if 'twas day," said Domingo.

"O! senor capitano, 'tis the French—the French! the ladrones los perros!" exclaimed Manrico, rashly firing his musket at three or four soldiers, whose outline, with shako and knapsack, appeared on a little ridge close by. Four muskets, discharged at random, replied, and in a moment the three scouts found themselves fighting hand to hand with a mob of active little French voltigeurs.

The latter recognised the Highland uniform of Grant, and finding him with two Spaniards, knew him at once to be the famous scouting officer, for whose arrest, dead or alive, Marmont had offered such a princely reward, and uttering loud shouts, they pressed upon him with bayonets fixed, and muskets clubbed.

Strong, active, and fearless, he hewed them down with his claymore on all sides. He shot two with his pistols, and then hurled the empty weapons at the heads of others, and, with Leon, succeeded in mounting and galloping off; but Manrico was beaten down, and left insensible on the mountain side.

"Grant and his follower," says General Napier, "darted into the wood for a little space, and then, suddenly wheeling, rode off in different directions; but at every turn new enemies appeared, and at last the hunted men, dismounting, fled on foot, through the thickest part of the low oaks, until they were again met by infantry detached in small parties down the sides of the pass, and directed in their chase by the waving of the French officers' hats on the ridge above. (Day had now broken). Leon fell exhausted, and the barbarians who first came up killed him, in spite of his companion's entreaties."

"My poor Juanna, what will now become of you?" exclaimed Grant, on seeing his faithful Domingo expiring under the reeking bayonets of the voltigeurs; and now, totally incapable of further resistance, he gave up his sword to an officer, who protected him from the fury of his captors. He was at last a prisoner !

A few days after this, Manrico, covered with wounds and with one arm in a sling, appeared sorrowfully before Lord Wellington, to announce that Grant, "el valoroso capitano," had been taken, after a desperate conflict in the pass of Penamacor. Lord Wellington was greatly concerned for the safety of his favourite officer, and the greatest excitement prevailed in the ranks of his regiment, for Colquhoun Grant was well beloved by the soldiers of the Black Watch. To the guerilla chiefs Wellington offered a thousand dollars for the rescue of Grant, and his letters proclaiming this reward were borne by Manrico and the broken-hearted Juanna through some of the wildest and most dangerous parts of the frontier; but Marmont took his measures too well, and kept his valuable prisoner too securely guarded, for rescue or escape to be thought of.

The officer who had captured him, M. Armand, was a young sous-lieutenant of the 3rd Voltigeurs (the same who had destroyed the *granja* of Leon the farmer); but he had a heart that would have done honour to a marshal of the empire; and, with all kindness and respect, he conducted him to the quarters of the Marshal Duc de Raguse.

The latter invited the captive to dinner, and chatted with him in a friendly way about his bold and remarkable adventures, saying that he (Marmont) had been long on the watch for him; that he knew his companions, Manrico the Bearded, Leon and his sister Juanna (here Grant trembled), and that all his haunts and disguises were known too.

"Disguises—pardon me, M. le Maréchal," said Grant, warmly—"disguises are worn by spies; I have never worn other dress than the uniform and tartan of my regiment."

"Vrai Dieu! the bolder fellow you!" exclaimed the Duc de Raguse. "You are aware that I might hang you; but I love a brave spirit, and shall only exact from you a special parole, that you will not *consent* to be released by any partida or guerilla chief on your journey between this and France."

"Monseigneur le Duc, the exaction of this parole is the greatest compliment you can pay me," replied Grant, who, on finding matters desperate, gave his word of honour, and was next day sent towards the Pyrenees with a French guard, under M. Armand, his captor. Grant, without suspicion, was bearer of a treacherous letter to the Governor of Bayonne, in

which he was designated by Marmont " a treacherous
spy, who had done infinite mischief to the French
army, and who was not executed on the spot out of
respect for *something resembling a uniform* (*i.e.,*
the Scottish dress) which he wore; but he (Marmont)
desired that at Bayonne Grant should be placed IN
IRONS, and sent up to Paris." (*Peninsular War,*
vol. iv.)

On the first night of his march to the rear, M.
Armand halted in a grove of cork and beech-trees,
within a mile of Medellin, on the Guadiana—the
birth-place of Cortes, the conqueror of Mexico; but
as a guerilla chief with 5000 desperadoes held possession of the town and bridge, our lieutenant of Voltigeurs, with his prisoner and escort, were forced to
content themselves with such shelter as the light
foliage of the wood afforded.

The night was pitchy dark; the blackness that involved the sky, the mountains, the vale through which
the Guadiana wound, and the wood where our travellers
bivouacked, was palpable, painful, and oppressive;
but at times it was varied by the red sheet lightning
which shot across the southern quarter of the sky,
revealing the lofty Sierra, whose sharp peaks arose afar
off like the waves of a black sea, and the stems and
foliage of the cork and beech-trees in the foreground.

On this night occurred the most horrible episode
of Grant's military adventures.

After having drained their canteens of Lisbon wine,
and discussed their ration of cold beef and commis-
sariat biscuit, Grant and Armand, the voltigeur, lay
down fraternally side by side in their cloaks to
repose; their escort lay close by, long since asleep;
for Grant had given his parole that he " would not
attempt to escape," and such were their ideas of mili-

tary honour and value for a soldier's word, that these brave Frenchmen never doubted him.

Just as the two officers were about to sleep, they became aware of various cold and dewy drops, or clammy creeping things, that continued to fall upon them from the beech trees overhead.

"Sangbleu!" exclaimed the lieutenant of Voltigeurs; "we are all over creepers or cockroaches, and they drop like rain from this old beech upon us."

"Let us seek another tree, my friend," said Grant, drowsily; "one place is the same as another to me now."

"Diable! let us shift our camp then—but do you smell the lightning? It must have scorched the grass."

"Why?"

"There is a stench so overpowering here on every breath of wind."

Moving a few paces to their left, they lay down at the root of another beech tree; but there the same cold dewy drops seemed to distil upon them like rain; yet the night was hot, dry, and sultry; and ever and anon there fell those hideous creepers, whose slimy touch caused emotions of horror.

"Tudieu!" shouted the Frenchman, springing up again; "I cannot stand this! We had better have beaten up the guerillas in their quarters at Medellin. Holo, Corporal Touchet—flash off your musket, and let us see what the devil is in these trees!"

Roused thus, the corporal of the escort cocked his piece; and as he fired, the two officers watched the beeches in the sudden and lightning-like gleam that flashed from the muzzle.

Lo! the dark figure of a dead man swung from a branch, about twelve feet above them!

"Ouf!" said the voltigeur, with a shudder of horror.

"These beeches bear strange nuts," said Grant, as they hastily left the wood, and passed the remainder of the night on the open sward in front of it. When day dawned, Grant went back to examine the places where they had first attempted to sleep. The corpses of a man having a voluminous beard, and a woman with a profusion of long and silky hair, were suspended from the branches; and, as they swung mournfully and fearfully round in the morning wind, the crows flew away with an angry croak, and a cry of horror burst from the lips of Grant on recognising Manrico el Barbado and—*Juanna de Leon!*

*　　　*　　　*　　　*

Three weeks after this, Colquhoun Grant saw the long blue outline of the Pyrenees undulating before him, as he approached the frontier of France, a country for which he had now the greatest horror; and during the whole march from Medellin towards Bayonne, the young subaltern of Voltigeurs experienced the greatest trouble with his prisoner, on whom that frightful episode in the cork wood had left a dreadful impression.

In his hatred and animosity to France and everything French, Grant, from that hour had resolved, that though he could not with honour attempt to escape while in Spain, he would spare no exertion or trouble, no cunning or coin, to leave France, and return once more to find himself sword in hand before the ranks of Marshal Marmont, whom he now viewed as the assassin of that poor maiden of Leon.

As they approached Bayonne, he took an early opportunity of deliberately tearing open the sealed letter which the marshal had given him for the Governor of that fortress, and made himself master of its contents. Instead of finding its tenor complimentary and re-commendatory as he had been told, he saw himself therein designated as a "dangerous spy who had done infinite mischief to the French army," and who should be marched in fetters to Paris, where no doubt tortures such as those to which Captain Wright was subjected in the Temple, or a death on the scaffold awaited him! The contents of this letter more than released him from any parole.

"Oho, M. le Duc de Raguse, is this your game?" said Grant, as he tore the letter into the smallest bits, and buried them in a hole. "Let me see if I cannot make a Highland head worth a pair of French heels."

Arrived at Bayonne, Lieutenant Armand presented him to the governor and bade him adieu. Then Grant confidently requested, in the usual way, to be furnished with a passport for Verdun, the greatest military prison in France. This the governor at once granted him, little suspecting that he meant to commence an escape the moment he left the garrison. Aware that, guarded as all the avenues from Bayonne and the Pyrenean passes were by French troops of every kind, flight towards Spain was impossible, he resolved to make the attempt in the *opposite*, and consequently less to be suspected, direction. The moment he left the governor's quarters, Grant quietly put the passport in the fire, and repairing to the suburb of St. Esprit, which, from time immemorial has been the quarter of the Portuguese Jews, he sold his silver epaulettes and richly-laced Highland uniform, to a dealer in old garments, and received in lieu the plain frogged surtout, forage cap, and sabre of a French staff-officer; he stuck the cross of the Legion of Honour at his button-hole, and after promenading along the superb quay, after repairing boldly to the " Eagle of France," an hotel in the Place de Grammont, he ordered an omelette and a bottle of vin ordinaire with all the air of a Garde Imperiale and sat down to dinner.

Inquiring of the waiter "if there were any officers in the house about to proceed to Paris?" he was told that " M. le General Souham was about to leave that very night." Grant procured a card, and writing thereon *Captain O'Reilly, Imperial Service*, sent it up, and was at once introduced to old Souham, who was just about to start, and was in the act of buckling on his sabre.

" Captain O'Reilly," said he, frowning at the name, and glancing round for a French Army List, but fortunately none was at hand.

" Of what regiment?"

" Lacy's disbanded battalion of the Irish Brigade."

" Ah ! And in what can I serve you, monsieur?"

" Allowing me to join your party about to proceed to Paris."

" You do me infinite honour, M. O'Reilly."

" Thanks, general."

" From whence have you come?"

" The banks of the Coa."

" Sacre ! the banks of the Coa !"

" Yes; I am attached to the staff of M. le Duc de Raguse."

" Ah ! old Marmont. Peste ! he is my greatest friend. M. Armand of the 3rd Voltigeurs brought me a letter from him, in which he says that a dear friend of his would join me on my way to Paris."

" How kind of brave Marmont," said Grant; " he never forgets me."

"So he has captured the notorious Scaramouche, Captain Grant?"

"Yes; a wonderful fellow that!"

"Quite a devil of a man; allons, let us go; you have a horse of course?"

"No, M. le General."

"One of mine is at your service."

"Mille baionettes! You quite overwhelm me."

In half an hour after this, Grant, with Souham and two other French officers had crossed the wooden drawbridge of Bayonne, and left the citadel of M. Vauban with all its little redoubts in their rear, as they all rode merrily *en route* to Paris; Souham by the way telling twenty incredible stories of Wellington's prince of scouts, the Scottish Captain Grant. In a house of entertainment in the Rue Royale at Orleans, Grant fortunately made the acquaintance of a man who proved to be an agent in the secret service of the British Government. This person furnished him with money and a letter to another secret agent who lived in an obscure part of Paris, where he arrived, still disguised as an officer in the suite of General Souham, and as such, for a time, he visited all the theatres, the gardens, the operas; and all splashed and travel-stained, as fresh from the seat of war, was presented to the great Emperor, who patronizingly spoke to him of the probability of restoring Lacy's Irish Regiment, " by recruiting for it among the Irish in the prisons of Bitche and Verdun, in which case his services would not be forgotten," &c., "and his promotion to a majority would be duly remembered," &c. &c. Grant could not foresee that in *three* years after this, the old Black Watch, after raising the cry of "Scotland for ever" at Waterloo, would make the Tuileries ring to their Highland pipes, and that he would actually compose the well-known parody—

"Wha keep guard at Versailles and Marli,
   Wha, but the lads wi' the bannocks of barley?"

He spoke French with fluency, having been a pupil of the famous Jean Paul Marat, when that notable ruffian taught French in Edinburgh, where, in 1774 he published a work entitled "The Chains of Slavery."

Grant thanked the Emperor, and thinking that the daring joke had been carried quite far enough, he doffed his French uniform, sabre and all, and making a bundle thereof, flung the whole into the Seine one night. Then, attiring himself in an unpretending blouse, he repaired to the house of the secret agent, presented his letter, and obtained more money to enable him to reach Britain.

"Monsieur is in luck," said the agent; "I have just ascertained that a passport is lying at the foreign office for an American who died, or was found dead this morning."

"How is your American named?"

"Monsieur Jonathan Buck."

"Very good—thanks! From this very hour I am Jonathan Buck," said the reckless Grant. He reloaded his pistols, concealed them in his breast, and repairing to the Foreign Office, demanded his passport with the coolness of a prince *incog.*

"Your name, monsieur?"

"M. Jonathan Buck," drawled Grant through his nose.

The passport was handed to him at once, and long before the police could ascertain that Monsieur Buck had departed this life at 9 A.M., and yet had received his papers at 9 P.M., on the same day, our hero had left Paris far behind him, and was travelling post towards the mouth of the Loire.

On reaching Nantes, he repaired at once to Paimbœuff, twenty miles further down the river, where all vessels, whose size was above ninety tons, usually unloaded their cargoes; and there he boarded the first vessel which had up the stars and stripes of America, and seemed ready for sea. She proved to be the *Ohio*, a fine bark of Boston, Jeremiah Buck, master.

" 'Tis fortunate," said Grant through his nose, as he was ushered into the cabin of the Yankee; " I am a namesake of yours, captain—Jonathan Buck, of Cape Cod, seeking a cabin passage to Boston."

" All right—let me see your passport, stranger?"

" Here it is, skipper."

" Well, for a hundred and fifty dollars, I am your man," drawled the Boston captain, who was smoking a long Cuba; " but it *is* darned odd, stranger, that I have been expecting *another* Jonathan Buck, my own nephew, from Paris; he is in the fish and timber trade, and hangs out at old Nantucket; but he took a run up by the dilly to see the Toolerie, the Loover, and all that. Well, darn my eyes, if this is not my nephew's passport!" exclaimed the American suddenly, while his eyes flashed with anger and suspicion. "Stranger, how is this?"

In some anxiety, Grant frankly related how the document came into his possession, and produced the letters of the secret agent, proving who he was, beseeching the captain, as a man come of British blood and kindred, to assist him; for, if taken by the French, the dungeon of Verdun or Bitche, or worse, perhaps, awaited him.

The Yankee paused, and chewed a quid by which he had replaced his cigar. Full of anxiety, yet without fear, Grant summoned all his philosophy, and recalled the words of Bossuet, "That human life resembles a road which ends in frightful precipices. We are told of this at the first step we take; but our *destiny* is fixed, and we *must* proceed."

Natural sorrow for the loss of his relative, and the native honesty of an American seaman, united to open the heart of the captain to our wanderer, and he agreed to give him a passage in the *Ohio* to Boston, from whence he could reach Britain more readily than from the coast of France, watched and surrounded as it was by ships and gunboats, troops and gens d'armes, police, spies, passports, &c. Believing all arranged at last, Grant never left the ship, but counted every hour until he should again find himself in Leon, the land of his faithful Juanna, with his comrades of the Black Watch around him, and the eagles of Marmont in front.

At last came the important hour, when the anchor of the *Ohio* was fished; when her white canvas filled, and the stars and stripes of America swelled proudly from her gaff-peak, as she bore down the sun-lit Loire with the evening tide; but now an unlooked-for misfortune took place. A French privateer, the famous *Jean Bart*, ran foul of her, and, by carrying away her bowsprit and foremast, brought down her maintopmast too. Thus she was forced to run back to Paimbœuff and haul into dock.

For our disguised captain of the 42nd Highlanders to remain in the docks, guarded as they were by watchful gens-d'armes, was impossible; thus, on being furnished by the skipper of the *Ohio* with the coarse clothes of a mariner, and a written character, stating that he was "Nathan Prowse, a native of Nantucket, in want of a ship," he stained his face and hands with tobacco-juice, shaved off his moustache, and repaired to an obscure tavern in the suburbs of Paimbœuff, to find a lodging until an opportunity offered for his escape. Under his peajacket he carried a pair of excellent pistols, which he kept constantly loaded; and a fine dagger or Albaceto knife, a gift of poor Domingo de Leon.

As ho sat in the kitchen of this humble house of entertainment, his eye was caught by a printed placard above the mantelpiece. It bore the imperial arms, with the cipher of the Emperor, and stated that "the notorious spy Colquhoun Grant, a captain in a Scottish regiment of the British army, who had wrought so much mischief behind the lines of le Maréchal Duc de Raguse, in Leon, and who had been brought prisoner to France, where he had broken his parole, was wandering about, maintaining a system of espionage and Protean disguises; that he had, lastly, assumed the name, character, and passport of an American citizen, named Jonathan Buck, whom he had wickedly and feloniously murdered and robbed in the Rue de Rivoli at Paris; that the sum of 2,000 francs was hereby offered for him dead or alive; and that all prefects, officers, civil and military, gensd'armes, and loyal subjects of the Emperor, by sea and land, were hereby authorized to seize or kill the said Colquhoun Grant wherever and whenever they found him."

With no small indignation and horror, tho Highlander read this obnoxious placard, which contained so much that wore tho face of truth, with so much that was unquestionably false.

"So Buck, whose papers I have appropriated, has been murdered—poor devil!" was his first reflection; "what if tho honest skipper of tho *Ohio* should see this precious document and suspect *me?* In that case I should be altogether lost."

He retired from the vicinity of this formidable placard, fearing that some watchful eye might compare his personal appearance with the description it contained; though his costume, accent, and the fashion of his whiskers and beard altered his appearance so entirely that his oldest friends at the mess would not have recognised him. He hastily retired upstairs to a miserable garret, to think and watch, but not to sleep.

When loitering on the beach next evening, he entered into conversation with a venerable boatman, named Raoul Senebier, and an exchange of tobacco pouches at once established their mutual good-will. Grant said that " he was an American seaman out of a berth, and anxious to reach Portsmouth in England, where he had left his wife and children."

The boatman, an honest and unsuspicious old fellow, seemed touched by his story, and offered to row him to a small island at the mouth of the Loire, where British vessels watered unmolested, and in return allowed the poor inhabitants to fish and traffic without interruption.

" I can feel for you, my friend," said old Senebier; " for I was taken prisoner at the battle of Trafalgar, and was seven years in the souterrains of the *Château d'Edimbourg*, separated from my dear wife and little ones, and when I returned, I found them all lying in the churchyard of Paimbœuff."

" Dead—what, all ?"

" All, all, save one—the plague, the plague !"

" Land me on the isle, then, and ten Napoleons shall be yours," said Grant, joyfully, and in twenty minutes after, they had left the crowded wharves, the glaring salt-pans which gleam on the left bank of the Loire, and all its maze of masts and laden lighters, as they pulled down, with the flow of the stream and the ebb-tide together. The fisherman had his nets, floats, and fortunately some fish on board ; so, if over-hauled by any armed authority, he could pretend to have been at his ordinary avocation. They touched at the island, and were told by some of the inhabitants that not a British ship was in the vicinity, but that a French privateer, the terrible *Jean Bart*, was prowling about in these waters, and that the isle was consequently unsafe for any person who might be suspected of being a British subject; so, with a heart that began to sink, Grant desired old Raoul Senebier to turn his prow towards Paimbœuff.

Morning was now at hand, and the sun as he rose reddened with a glow of Italian brilliancy the tranquil banks of the Loire, and the sails of the fisher-craft that were running up the stream. No vessels were in sight, for terror of the British cruisers kept every French keel close in shore ; but suddenly a large white sail appeared to the southward, and in the lingering and ardent hope that she was one of our Channel squadron, Grant prevailed upon Raoul to bear towards her. The wind became light, and all day the two men tugged at their oars, but still the ship was far off, and yet not so distant but that Grant, with a glistening eye and beating heart, could make out her scarlet ensign ; when evening came on, and a strong current, which ran towards the Loire, gradually swept the boat towards the coast of France, and just as the sun set, old Raoul and the fugitive found themselves suddenly close to a low battery, a shot from which boomed across the water, raising it like a spout beyond them. Another and another followed, tearing the waves into foam close by.

"We must surrender, monsieur," said Raoul, wring-

x 2

ing his hands; "and I shall be brought in irons before M. le Prefect for aiding the escape of a prisoner of war."

"Call me your son," said Grant; "say we were fishing, and leave the rest to me."

"I have a son," said Raoul; "he escaped the plague by being where he is now, on board the *Jean Bart.*"

They landed under the battery; a little corporal in the green uniform of a Voltigeur, with six men, conducted them with fixed bayonets before the officer in command. He was a handsome young man, and Grant in a moment recognised his former captor and companion, M. Armand, the sous-lieutenant of the 3rd Voltigeur Regiment.

"Milles demons! is this you, monsieur?" exclaimed Armand, who knew Grant at once.

"Exactly, Monsieur le Lieutenant," replied Grant, with admirable presence of mind; "'tis I, your old companion, Louis Senebier, captain of a gun aboard the *Jean Bart*, from which I have a day's liberty to fish with my father, old Raoul of Paimbœuff, whom you see before you here; but understanding that a rascally British cruiser is off the coast, we were just creeping close to the battery when monsieur fired at us."

"Is this true, M. Senebier?" asked Armand, with a knowing smile.

"All true; my son is said to be very like me," replied the old fisherman, astounded by the turn matters had taken.

"Like you? Not very, bon! But you may thank heaven that I am not M. le Prefect of the Loire. Leave us your fish, M. Senebier, and be off before darkness sets in. See," he added, with a furtive but

expressive glance at Grant; "see that you keep your
worthy father clear of yonder British ship, which will
just be abreast of the battery and two miles off about
midnight."

Armand placed a bottle of brandy in the boat, and,
while pretending to pay for the fish, pressed Grant's
hand, wished him all success, and pointed out the bearings of the strange sail so exactly, that the moment
darkness set fairly in, Raoul trimmed his lug sail and
ran right on board of her; for her straight gun streak,
her taper masts, and her snow-white canvas shone in
the moonlight above the calm blue rippled sea, distinctly in the clear twilight of the stars.

"Boat ahoy!" cried a sentry from the quarter;
"keep off, or I shall fire."

"What ship is that?" asked Grant, in whose ears a
British voice sounded like some old mountain melody.

"His Britannic Majesty's frigate *Laurel*, of thirty-
six guns."

"Hurrah!"

"Who the devil are you?"

"A prisoner of war just escaped."

"Bravo!" cried another voice, which seemed to be
that of the officer of the watch; "sheer alongside,
and let us see what like you are. Stand by with the
man ropes—look alive there!"

Grant shook the hard hand of Raoul Senebier,
gave him five more gold Napoleons, and, in a
moment after, found himself upon the solid oak deck
of a spanking British frigate. Now he was all but
at home, and his Proteus-like transformations and
disguises were at an end. A single paragraph from
the "History of the War in the Peninsula" will suf-
fice to close this brief story of Colquhoun Grant's

adventures, of which I could with ease have spun three orthodox volumes, octavo.

"When he reached England, he obtained permission to choose a French officer of equal rank with himself to send to France, that no doubt might remain about the propriety of his escape. In the first prison he visited for this purpose, great was his astonishment to find the old fisherman (Raoul Senebier of Paimbœuff) and his real son, who had meanwhile been captured, notwithstanding a protection given to them for their services. But Grant's generosity and benevolence were as remarkable as the qualities of his understanding; he soon obtained their release, and sent them with a sum of money to France. He then returned to the Peninsula, and within four months from the date of his first capture, was again on the Tormes, watching Marmont's army! Other strange incidents of his life could be told," continues General Napier, "were it not more fitting to quit a digression already too wide; yet I was unwilling to pass unnoticed this generous, spirited, and gentle-minded man, who, having served his country nobly and ably in every climate, died not long since, exhausted by the continual hardships he had endured."

But his name is still remembered in the regiment by which he was beloved; and his adventures, his daring, and presence of mind, were long the theme of the old Black Watch at the mess-table, the bivouac, and the guard-room fire.

IX.

THE STORY OF DICK DUFF.

DICK DUFF, the lieutenant of our light company in 1812, was one of the happiest and most lively fellows in the British service. He sang and was merry from morning till night, and was occasionally uproarious from night till morning ; and not even all the horrors of the retreat from Burgos could repress his flow of spirits. Moreover, he was the terror of innkeepers, and made the lazy hostaleros and keepers of posadas attend to his various commands with a celerity that astonished themselves ; for Dick Duff could swear with marvellous fluency in Spanish and five other foreign languages ; he had served at Malta, in Egypt, and Holland ; and was wont to boast that he had acquired the whole vocabulary of oaths. This was highly necessary, Dick was wont to allege, "lest in a casual war of words with any ragamuffin on whom one might chance to be billeted, an officer and gentleman should have the disgrace of being put down by the sauce piquant of a rascally foreigner."

Dick had joined the service as a full private in the year 1800, having been forced into the ranks by his chief or landlord.

He was the second son of a respectable sheep farmer on the mountains of Mull, where his forefathers had resided for ages. His elder brother,

Hamish, when a child, had been swept out to sea (while playing among the fisher-boats on the beach), and was drowned, to the grief and dismay of his parents, to whom a wandering Scottish priest, Father John of Douay, had foretold his birth, and predicted his future usefulness and greatness in the church. His mother, an old Catholic of the house of Keppoch, looked upon this elder child as blessed by Heaven, and in the fulness of her heart she gladly dedicated it to the then oppressed church of her forefathers, in token of which she had unavailingly tied to his neck a valuable *amulet.*

Their landlord, like many other Scottish feudatories in the year 1800, became desirous of appearing a person of importance in the eyes of the Government; to this end he resolved to raise a kilted regiment among his tenants, and on procuring a letter of service, immediately called upon them for their sons.

These tidings caused some consternation in Argyleshire, a county from which every war, prior to 1800, had swept at least *four thousand* of its best men, few of whom ever survived to return.

The aged father of Dick appeared with others before their feudal tyrant, who threatened to deprive every parent of his farm, if his sons delayed or declined to volunteer for service; and this can easily be done, as the Highland crofter has seldom a written lease to show, believing that the old hereditary cabin of his forefathers is his, as much as the air he breathes or the heather he treads on.

"Duncan Duff," said the laird, who had already donned the uniform of colonel, " I am raising a regiment for the King's service, and must have your son Dick; he is a stout, active fellow, and here is the bounty."

The old man wrung his hands, and said—

"Sir, my son is the only prop of my last days. I am getting old, and may not be able to work long at my little croft."

"Oh, don't trouble yourself about your croft," sneered the laird.

"If my only son goes to battle, what will become of *me ?*"

"The parish will attend to *that,*" was the cruel reply.

The eyes of the old Highlander flashed fire, but reverence for his chief repressed the mingled threat and curse that rose to his tongue.

"Please yourself, Duncan," resumed the feudatory; "I have only to warn you that another person has made my factor an advantageous offer for your farm, and your son's enlistment or his disobedience will materially influence me in considering the said offer."

"My croft, sir ! have not I and my fathers been here under your family for four hundred years and more; and is not our blood the same ?"

"Stuff! I tell you that I must have a thousand men, and cannot spare your son."

"I had another son, sir—a poor child who was drowned in his infancy; had he lived, one should have gone to battle and one remained—but God deals hardly with me."

"I care not," was the dogged reply; "men I want, and men I shall have !" for the letter of service gave the laird an opportunity to nominating all his officers, nearly fifty in number.

So Dick became a soldier in the laird's regiment, and as the old man could not remain on his little farm alone, he became a soldier too, in his sixtieth year, and on the long dusty marches in Holland, poor

Dick was often seen carrying the knapsack, firelock, and canteen of his brave old father, whom he buried with his own hands after he was killed by the French at the battle of Alexandria, where he, and twenty others, perished in a rash attempt to rescue their chief, the colonel, who was there wounded and taken prisoner. Dick's promotion was rapid, and after passing through the intermediate ranks, he found himself, by his own merit, a lieutenant in the Highland regiment of this obnoxious laird in the year 1808; and his reason for leaving it and exchanging into ours, was a mishap that occurred to him in Glasgow.

His corps had been quartered for a year in the barracks of the Gallowgate in the capital of the west, and Dick, who was decidedly of convivial, and scandal whispered of somewhat nocturnal, habits, and having, moreover, a high appreciation of the virtues of Glasgow punch, was in the habit of going home every night in the happiest mood of mind; and on more than one occasion was assisted by the friendly arm of the watchers and warders of the civic guard, or of the corporal of the patrol. The regiment marched for Edinburgh, changing quarters with the brave old Pompadours, who were so called from the colour of their facings resembling Madame's gown; but Dick, having obtained a month's leave between returns, resolved to enjoy himself a little longer among his old haunts, and remained behind, exulting in freedom from duty and the seclusion of mufti.

A week after the regiment marched, Dick Duff found himself about midnight propped against a lamppost in the High-street, with very vague ideas of his own name, rank, and residence, and seriously weighing in his own mind whether the pavement and row

of lamps extending to the right, or those that lay to
the left, led to the barracks ; for his faculties were so
cloudy, that he had become utterly oblivious as to
the circumstance of his being on leave, in plain
clothes, and living at a west-end hotel.

After long and serious pondering, Dick instinctively
discovered the right way by old habit, and proceeded,
somewhat deviously, of course, through the delightful
locality known as "the Sautmarket," and along the
Gallowgate, until he found himself before the dark
gate of the barracks, and heard the familiar step of
the great-coated sentry pacing slowly to and fro in-
side. Here he kicked with vigour, and struck up his
favourite mess-room song—

> " Who knows but our girls—
>   (We have known stranger things !)
> When once they've got feathers,
>   May make themselves wings ;
> And like swallows in winter,
>   May soon take their flight ;
> And for lovers of ' ours,'
>   Bid their husbands good-night."

"Hallo ! gate—gate !" shouted Dick, sprawling
against it with outstretched hands.

"Who comes there ?"

"Friend—particular friend of yours, my boy—
very."

The drowsy sergeant of the guard unfastened the
barrier, and sulkily passed a lantern once or twice
across the face of the visitor, till it was knocked out
of his hand by Dick, who exclaimed—

"D—n it, sir, what d'ye mean ?—light me to my
quarters."

" I beg pardon, sir," said the sergeant, who thought
Dick might be one of the staff ; but the lantern was

extinguished, so our friend resumed his song, and stumbled on alone to the old staircase, with which he was quite familiar; and ascending by mere force of habit to his room, found the door-handle on the right as usual, and entered.

"All right," muttered Dick, "all right. Here's the bed-post—and the candlestick should be *here.*"

But he could neither find candle nor matches, and resolving to "row" his man in the morning, he threw off his clothes, tumbled headlong into bed, and was soon sound asleep.

Now it happened that the proprietor of the afore-said quarters was the officer of the main-guard, who as the next day proved Sunday, was to come off duty at eight o'clock a.m., and duly at the hour of seven his servant entered to prepare a fire and lay break-fast. Hearing a vehement snore proceed from his master's bed, the servant drew back the curtains, and, to his no small surprise, discovered the dark, sun-burned, and well-whiskered visage of a stranger, whom he immediately awoke; but not without con-siderable difficulty and after reiterated efforts.

"Who are you," grumbled Dick; "and what the devil do you want?"

"What do *you* want here?"

"Where, old fellow?"

"In my master's bed."

"Master's bed, you scoundrel!" stuttered Dick; "how dare you intrude into an officer's room? be off, or I shall send you to the *shop* in a minute." And so, Dick Duff, believing that he had settled the little mistake satisfactorily, again composed himself to sleep, while the servant hurried to the main guard to acquaint his master that "a thief was in possession of his bed and quarters." These tidings promptly brought up the officer with his sword in his hand, and a file of the guard at his heels.

Dick was once more roused, and wrathfully, too, from his slumbers, to find by his bedside two soldiers and an officer *cap-à-pie* in a strange uniform.

"What do you mean, fellow, by this unwarrantable in-in-in-trusion?" asked Dick, with great dignity.

"Who are you, sir?" asked the officer in a louder key.

"You'll soon find that out—off with you, sir, or by heavens I'll parade you where you won't like it. I have a pair of saw-handled pacifiers that are the deuce for hitting at fifteen paces."

"What the devil are you about in my quarters?"

"*Your* quarters?"

"Yes, sir, *my* quarters," thundered the Captain of Pompadours.

"Come, now—I like that."

"D—n it, sir?"

"Don't get excited, old fellow; is not this number three stair, four room?"

"Yes, of course it is."

"Then allow me to insinuate, sir, that you are drunk —very drunk, in uniform too—disgraceful; consider yourself under arrest. Sir, these quarters are *mine*— you will retire, if you please."

And Dick, who was still very groggy, again addressed himself to sleep. Trembling with anger, the Pompadour for a moment doubted the evidence of his own senses; but seeing all his own luggage and property in the room, and being certain that his brain was not turning, though the cool impudence of Duff confounded him,

"Coporal of the guard," said he, in a stifled tone of anger, "handcuff this insolent fellow, and march him to the cells."

"Handcuff—the devil !" shouted Dick.

This imperative order made him spring up, and at that moment, the recollection of the change of barracks, his month's leave, and the last night's potations, flashed upon him. Unhappy Dick was sobered in a moment, and his countenance fell, and he turned to explain—to apologize ; but the Pompadour would listen to nothing. Our friend was iguominiously hauled from bed, hastily dressed, roughly handcuffed, and despite all his assertions that he was "an officer —an officer and a gentleman," &c. &c., he was marched to the guardhouse, into which he would have been thrust, had not a staff-officer, the friend with whom he had supped overnight, passed in at that moment and recognised him.

The officer explained, Dick expostulated, the Pompadour was sulky ; but after fiery threats, mutual apologies and expressions of friendship for life were exchanged, and Dick dined that evening at the mess, of which he was made an honorary member ; but the story "found vent," with a hundred absurd additions ; and Dick was so quizzed about it by the small wits of his own corps, that he exchanged into Ours, and joined us about the time Corunna was fought.

But before the battalion embarked, he fell into another scrape by inserting in the Edinburgh papers the following advertisement !—

"Vive l'amour ! any fair dame of spirit, maid . . . . or widow, who would wish to see the world, and will join her fortunes with those of a gallant officer, about to embark for the seat of war—age 25, height five feet ten inches by one foot ten across the shoulders

—good looking decidedly, may have her offers carefully considered, by forwarding her name and qualifications to the President of the Mess Committee."

But for the hurry of embarkation, old Sir David Dundas, he of the "Eighteen Manœuvres," who then ruled at the Horse Guards, would have made this piece of impertinence a dear joke to Dick Duff.

The latter, at Torres Vedras was severely wounded in the left leg, and given over for a time to the care of a pretty patrona, who was so kind to him, and like Corporal Trim's Beguin, fomented the wounded part so tenderly, that Dick remained so long on crutches, we thought he would never get off them or be well; tell one night getting tipsy at the quarters of his friend Garriehorn of the Grenadiers, he walked home, he never knew how, *without them;* and as he had been heard singing his invariable and inevitable song,

> ' " Who knows but our girls,
> (We have known stranger things)," &c.

in the Plaza of Torres Vedras, he was obliged to report himself ".fit for duty" next day, despite the tears of his patrona.

After serving at Busaco, Fuentes d'Onor, Badajoz, and Salamanca, his battalion, with Stirling's old Highland Brigade, endured all the horrors of the retreat from Burgos.

At the siege of the latter, the task of storming the famous hornwork, which had a hard sloping scarp of twenty-five feet, and a counter-scarp of ten, was specially confided to the 42nd Highlanders, who assailed the bastion after darkness had set in, and rushed on with great gallantry. Dick Duff was the first man up on the first ladder; and his feather bonnet was literally blown off his head by a volley of balls; every man by his side was bayonetted; and as each poor fellow in his fall knocked down others, the loss was terrible!

Sword in hand, Major Cox entered the gorge; Major (afterwards General Sir Robert) Dick led the regiment on *en masse*, and the hornwork was immediately captured; but two lieutenants and thirty-two rank and file were killed; four officers, one volunteer, and one hundred and sixty-four Highlanders were wounded. Captain Donald Williamson expired that night of his wounds. Lane, the poor gentleman volunteer, was severely wounded and became senseless; but revived, on finding two of the Cameron Highlanders gently abstracting a gold watch worth fifty guineas from his pocket.

"I beg your pardon, my lads," said he; "but I am not quite done with this."

"We beg yours, sir," answered they; "but we thought you dead, and supposed we might take it, as well as others."

They carried him carefully to the rear; and as they were returning, two stray shots killed them both. Lieutenant Gregorson was killed, and found stripped naked, by Lieutenant Orr, who buried him in a trench. In the gorge of this hornwork, so fatal to the Black Watch, their old Quartermaster Blanket, had both his legs carried away; so he might fairly have sung,

> "O now let others shoot,
> For here I leave my *second legs*,
> And the *Forty-second Foot*."

He lived long a prisoner at Bitche and Verdun, and by his fiery temper and wooden pins was named by the French *le Diable Boiteux*.

In this siege the regiment had other losses ; but the concentration of the enemy's forces, and the advance of superior numbers, obliged the Duke of Wellington to retire into winter quarters on the frontiers of Portugal ; and the fatigues and privations incident to this retrograde movement, fell on no regiment more heavily than on our friends of the Black Watch.

On a gloomy afternoon in the month of November, pressed by the enemy's cavalry, who were vastly superior to the British, the brigade of which the 42nd formed a part, entered the ancient and pleasant city of Valladolid, all drenched and bedraggled by fording the swift Pisuerga ; for the French, to impede our previous advance, had blown up the principal arch of the bridge.

Dick Duff was taken prisoner by the French hussars in a taberna, at Villahoz, by the treachery of the keeper, a well-known Spanish rogue, named Antonio Morello. By his captors and the hostalero he had been stripped nude, but made his escape and rejoined the regiment (just as it was entering Valloria) clad only in a pair of short scarlet pantaloons, which he had taken from a dead Frenchman of the line, and his aspect created no small surprise in the ranks—but I cannot add merriment, for our soldiers were then at the lowest ebb of misery and desperation. During this terrible retreat the rain had been incessant, and poured pitilessly down on the wet, dripping sierras and rough muddy mule roads traversed by our troops, whose sufferings and privations were indescribable.

The baggage was generally far in the rear, and the troops were without tents or other means of shelter from the inclemency of the weather. The *vivas* that greeted the British advance were no longer heard—

Y

gloom, sombre desperation, and scowling famine were in every eye. The arrears of pay were in many instances beyond parallel. Many regiments had not received a penny for nine months—nine months of constant fighting! (How many tradesmen in England would have worked for that period without wages?)

The officers were reduced to about a shirt each; most of the men had only the collars or wrists of their linen remaining — many had not a vestige. "Their jackets were so patched," says an officer of the Gordon Highlanders, in his narrative, "that I know nothing to which I can so aptly compare them as parti-coloured bed-covers; for there were not fifty in my own regiment but had been repaired with cloth of every colour under the sun."

So admirably is the kilt adapted for marching and activity, that the Highland corps were the only battalions *without stragglers.*

Hollow-eyed and gaunt, bearded and grisly, emaciated and miserable in aspect, footsore and shoeless, their jackets turned to black and purple, their feather bonnets reduced to quills, and all trace of pipeclay long since washed out of their belts, yet heavily laden with knapsacks, great-coat, blanket, havresack, wooden canteen, camp-kettle, sixty rounds of ball-cartridge, their arms and accoutrements covered with mud and mire—after many days' of incessant alarm, halting and forming square to repel the enemy's cavalry, who at times charged into the rivers up to their very holsters—the Black Watch defiled along the quaint old streets of Valladolid, with their pipes playing a fiery *spaidsearach Gaelhealach,* or Highland march; but it failed to rouse either the spirit or bearing of the men.

As our troops were retreating, their entrance excited no enthusiasm in the sullen and ungrateful Spaniards. They gazed apathetically from under their heavy eyebrows and broad sombreros, as battalion after battalion defiled past, nor manifested the smallest interest until some Highland regiment approached, when cries of—"Look at the Scots," broke from every quarter.

"*Mira los Escosses! Viva los valiantes! Viva los Escosses—los hombres valerosos.*"

Others, who knew the number of the Black Watch, varied the cry with—

"*Viva la Regimento Quarenta Dos!*"

Through streets of old and decaying houses the regiment defiled to the Plaza Mayor, while the bells of San Benito, St. Paul, and the Scottish College were tolled mournfully. All the balconies there were covered with tapestry; and amid a profusion of crimson velvet, a portrait of Ferdinand VII. was hung in the great Plaza. There the battalion dispersed in search of billets; the officers to inquire if the baggage had come up; to sigh for camp-beds and portmanteaux, that might be stuck in the mud twenty miles off; or to swear at stupid servants or drunken bat-men, who had let them fall into the hands of pillagers and paisanos.

Wellington and his aides-de-camp had taken up their quarters in the Scottish College, the rector of which, an old Highlander, though sick and dying, welcomed them warmly.

Dick Duff, Garrichorne, the captain of Grenadiers, and Colquhoun Grant, the famous scouting officer, whose adventures are already, we hope, familiar to the reader, made their way straight to a posada, previous to entering which an "examination of ammu-

Y 2

nition" took place, and among four purses two duros
could only be mustered.   At this time, many officers
actually sold their silver epaulettes to the Jews of El
Campo *for bread.*'

"Ugh!" said Dick ; "this comes of one's paymaster
being nine months in arrear !   and yet, though we
have scarcely a tester among us, we are fighting for
an island which, according to the learned Bochart,
was named by the Phœnicians emphatically—*the land
of tin!*"

An arched door gave admittance from the street to
the lower story of the posada, where the horses and
mules were generally stabled ; from this, an open
ladder gave access to the common hall ; a second
ladder led to the sleeping apartments, which were
minus carpets, bells, plaster, and almost without windows or furniture ; but, as Dick said to the grumbling
captain of Grenadiers, no one looks for such things in
a Spanish inn.

Several Spanish officers were already in the public
room, all travel-stained and splashed with mud, but
wrapped in their cloaks, and all with their feet planted
on the only brassero, round which they sat in a circle,
smoking and making themselves as comfortable as circumstances would admit ; while the host, an old and
sour-visaged Asturian, with clumsy hands and enormous shoulders, superintended the cooking of various
edibles, which simmered and sputtered in stone jars
on the flat hearth, the fuel piled upon which cast a
lurid glow from under the broad impending mantelpiece on his swarthy visage, his stealthy eyes, and
black grisly beard.   This fellow was repulsive in aspect; but his wife, *la patrona,* was a pretty paisana,
not much above eighteen years of age, dressed in the
picturesque costume of the country, and having her

handsome legs encased in the tightest and brightest of scarlet stockings. She welcomed us with smiles of the utmost good humour that two brilliant eyes and a mouth filled with the finest teeth could express.

"All right, Garriehorne," said Dick, in his bantering way; "here is one of the beautiful sex—come esta senora, how handsome you look to-night; 'pon my soul, I feel quite inclined to fall in love with you. Senor Patron—what is in the crocs, old fellow ?"

Displeased by Dick's mode of addressing his young wife, the host affected not to hear.

"What can you let us have for supper, senora ?" asked Garriehorne, unbuckling his sword, "hot castanos and garlic, of course, with Xerez and ripe grapes."

"Ripe grapes in November," growled the sulky patron; "what the devil are you talking about, senor oficial?—*Ninas y vinas son mal de guardar!*"

"Which means—"

"That ripe maidens and ripe grapes require vigilance to keep long," said the pretty patrona, with a waggish smile. "We have a fine guisado in this croc, senor."

"A guisado!" exclaimed Dick. "By Jove, the very thought of it makes me more hungry than ever."

"What is it made of?" said the captain of Grenadiers, doubtfully.

"Don't you know — everything! hare, rabbit, chicken, pheasant, claret and water, bacon, salt, garlic, onions, pepper, pimentos, Valdepenas butter, a bunch of wild thyme—"

"The deuce! what more ?"

"A little oil, and then it would add glory to the wedding of Camacho," said Dick.

"The senor caballero is quite a Spanish cook,"

said the pretty patrona ; " but," she added, with a·
furtive glance at Dick's pair of French pantaloons,
" I hope we shall not lose—"

" Lose—not at all, my dear senora. You shall be
paid in gold as pure as your wedding ring."

" If we have it," added Garriehorne, aside.

" So serve up the guisado. Its odour is exquisite !
By Jove, we four Hannibals have here found our
Capua ! But, Senor Patron," continued Dick, speaking with his mouth very full, " you are singularly like
an ugly fellow whom I met yesterday—what is your
name ?"

" Morello."

" The devil it is ! that name proved an unlucky
one to me lately."

" Where, senor ?"

" At Villahoz."

" I have a son there—"

" Keeper of a venta ?"

" Si, senor."

" The villain ! he betrayed me to the French for
ten dollars."

" Likely enough of Antonio," said the young wife ;
" he is my step-son, and proves mala, mala—very
bad."

" Step-sons frequently do in a step-mother's eyes,
my dear patrona."

" He hates his father—"

" The unnatural wretch !"

" Hates him for having married *me*."

" In that I almost agree with him," said Dick.

" But he hates me, too."

" Hates you—so young, so charming !"

" Yes, senor, and daily vows to have revenge ; believing that I have cheated him out of his birthright."

" Dick, what are those fellows round the brassero jabbering about ?" asked the grenadier.

" Oh, they are mere cazadores, who say we should not have given up Madrid, or Burgos either, without a battle."

" Faugh ! don't speak of Burgos; I am sick of shelling, storming, and mining. A. battle, indeed ! but, perhaps, they know better than Lord Wellington."

" A pretty woman that patrona is, ugh !" added Dick, as he drew off his boots. " See how muddy and deep the path that leads to glory and Portugal is ! There are three inches of the mud of immortality, at least."

By this time our friends had finished the guisado, which proved excellent, and a huge leathern bota of Xerez had been passed rapidly from hand to hand. They became comfortable—then jolly. Dick sang his usual song, and they all retired to pass the night in a crazy garret, and to thank Heaven that they were not for out-picquet on the Burgos road, and that they were to halt and not march all the next day.

Exhausted by toil, and perhaps somewhat overcome by their potations, and what our old friend Sancho Panza would term " the blessed scum" of the hot and savoury guisado, Colquhoun Grant and Garriehorne fell into a sound sleep on the hard floor, with plaids around them, and their swords at hand ; but poor Dick Duff's restless disposition kept him long awake.

He thought of the young and pretty patrona, with her taper legs and melting black eyes ; of her scowling old spouse, and the rascal, Antonio Morello, who yesterday had so nearly procured him—the said Dick Duff—three inches of a French bayonet, or a three years' sojourn at Bitche or Verdun on parole. Then, as the moon shone brightly, he rose and looked out upon the scenery, where the bright flood of her silver light fell aslant on the spires of the churches, and gilded with a white lustre the pinnacles and little square belfries of the convents. On one side lay a narrow street which led to the Plaza Mayor; on the other, spread a wilderness of flat roofs, from amid which the huge cathedral, begun, but never finished, by Philip II., reared its dark outline; beyond, lay the beautiful plain watered by the Esqueva, stretching away in the moonlight and the haze it exhaled. All was silent and still, and no one seemed abroad save one man, whom Dick perceived to be reconnoitring the posada with stealthy eyes and steps. He placed a short ladder against one of the lower windows, which opened in two halves. He pushed the lattice open and entered.

"Is this fellow a thief or a lover?" thought Dick; "if an affair of gallantry, it is no business of mine. Bah! what is there to steal from a Spanish posada? and to interfere with the nocturnal rambles of some loving stableboy or amatory muleteer would be rather an insane proceeding on my part."

With these reflections he resumed his place on the floor, and was about to drop asleep—for on service all curiosity becomes blunted; the value of property and the risk of death but of little consequence—when a cry pierced his ear.

A cry! it was a wild and despairing one, that rang terribly along the wooden corridor; a struggle—the stamping of feet—the explosion of a pistol, with the fall of a body heavily on the floor followed; and then all became still save the barking of the *perro de caza*, or house-dog, in the yard. Duff's first thought was of the enemy—that their cavalry were in the town—

and that the picquets had been repulsed on the
Burgos road. Then he thought of the intruder.

"Up, Grant," said ho; "get your sword, Garrichorne—the French or the devil are at work here!"

"Help, senores caballeros—help!" cried a piteous
voice in the corridor.

"Is that you, senor patron?"

"Si, senor—'tis I and the senora patrona—open,
por amor de Dios—the posada has been attacked by
thieves."

"By thieves"—

"Yes; and by the holy of holies, I have had the
narrowest of escapes," he added, dragging in his young
and pretty wife. Both were in their night dresses;
both were breathless and ghastly pale.

"What was the meaning of that pistol-shot?"

"You shall hear, senor—you shall hear," replied
the host, staggering to a seat. "Dios mio! I was
sound asleep, my day's work has been a severe one,
so many noble caballeros have been about the house
all day long. I was asleep; but the senora patrona
saw a man in our room; he carried a pistol in one
hand, a lantern in the other. Her cries awoke me,
and I sprang from my bed to reach my Abaceto knife,
which usually lies on a stool close by; when lo!
there was a flash in my eyes, a pistol-ball grazed my
right ear, and buried itself in the pillow I had just
left! Santiago! my knife was in my hand; I became blind! I rushed upon the would-be assassin;
once, twice, ay, thrice, my knife was buried in his
heart; at first there was a cry of agony, then I heard
the breast-bone crack, as, with a heavy sob, he was
dead. Ouf!" he added, as a light was brought;
"see how my right hand and arm are drenched in
blood."

He flung the knife on the floor, and it sounded like a knell.

"Grant, look to the poor patrona," said Duff. "Come, Garriehorne, the man may not be dead yet."

"O, senor, I warrant him dead enough; my first stab went straight to the heart," replied the hostalero, grinding his teeth with savage energy.

Proceeding along the dingy corridor, they reached his bedroom, where a man, in a pool of thickening blood, lay prostrate on the floor.

"He is quite dead," said Garriehorne.

"Grant, turn the poor devil over, and let us see what like he is," said Dick Duff.

He was turned on his back, and a hoarse cry burst from old Morello, on recognising in the relaxed jaw and fixed eye-balls of the corpse the features of—— *his son Antonio !*

*   *   *   *   *   *

"Come, gentlemen, let us quit this place," said Dick, with a shudder; and, as they issued into the empty streets, daylight was beginning to struggle through their sinuous windings, while the merry rat-tat of the British and Portuguese drums was heard, as they beat *reveille* in El Campo, the market-place, and before the old royal palace, where Anne of Austria first saw the light, and which, to the fourth story, was full of allied troops. The inlying picquets (always turned out in those days an hour before daylight) were standing under arms, looking pale, wan, and drowsy in their dark great-coats, in the Plaza Mayor. This place was square, and surrounded by an arcade, within which are shops, and the brick houses have balconies of gilded iron at all the windows. At a corner of the old palace our ramblers passed under a curious projecting clock, like that of

Strasbourg; but being a loyal old Spanish clock, of true Castilian origin, it had never gone since the French entered Spain.

"Senor," said Dick Duff to a Spanish cazadore who passed, and who seemed, like himself, to be on the look-out for a place of entertainment, "what house is that?"

"You mean the house without windows?"

"Si, senor, and which has only those little holes to admit light through its high walls."

"The Holy Office, senor."

Dick shrugged his shoulders and quickened his pace.

"And is that place opposite the convent so famed for its pretty nuns?"

"Which, senor?"

"The convent of the Bleeding Heart."

"No, senor," said the don, with a dark look; "it is the monastery of the Bloody Nose."

"You seem to be a wag, my friend—well, and what place is that which the staff are just leaving?"

"El Colegio de los Escosses."

"Bravo—the Scots College!" said they altogether; "muchos gratias, senor—we shall go there."

And just as Wellington, cloaked and muffled, with a telescope slung over his shoulder, his blue cape and cocked hat covered by oiled skins, trotted into the Plaza Mayor, followed by his aides-de-camp, one of whom was Prince Leopold, now King of the Belgians, Dick Duff and his comrades presented themselves at the arched doorway of the ancient Catholic seminary.

"A college of priests!" said Dick; "I would infinitely prefer a convent of nuns—but we cannot choose, unfortunately."

" Now, Duff," said Garriehorne, " you must behave with propriety."

"Oh, you shall see ; I am arranging my face to a most becoming length."

While they were speaking the door unfolded, and a grave, dark-complexioned priest, clad in a long black satann, appeared before them. His mild glance of anxious inquiry expanded into a kind smile when he saw the tartans and plumed bonnets of the visitors ; for he was a Scotsman, and in those days, anterior to the Catholic emancipation, the Scottish clergy of the ancient faith were all but outcasts, and usually exiles from their own country ; thus the poor man's heart filled and his eyes glistened, as he stretched out his hands inviting them to enter, and led them through the garden towards the main building of the college.

This Scottish college at Valladolid was founded by the family of Semple, one of whom, Robert, known as the great Lord Semple, was long ambassador from James VI. of Scotland to Philip II. of Spain ; a service on which he acquitted himself with reputation and honour to his country, while his rigid adherence to the Catholic Church won him the respect of the Spaniards.   The revenue of this college is about 1000*l.* per annum, and the edifice was anciently a house of the Jesuits.   Its lands are to be held of the Spanish crown *while vines shall continue to grow on them,* and in its cellars is a jolly wine-tun capable of holding eighteen thousand bottles—the mention of which made Dick Duff's eyes twinkle with delight. Its chapel had a crucifix which grew out of a thorn-tree to convert a Jew, but is now in the cathedral ; and still better, it had a valuable library, wherein hangs a portrait of the founder in rich robes carrying a baton, and another of his lady, Agnes Montgomery, daughter of Hugh, Earl of Eglinton. Six miles from the city, the college has a handsome country mansion, which Wellington occupied for one night during the Burgos retreat.

The ancient faith in Scotland was then all but extinct. A few wandering priests, braving the severe penalties of the Scottish law, lurked in the wildest parts of the Highlands, and, protected by the gentle ties of clanship, administered the rites of the Roman Church to its scattered adherents. At Glenlivat, in the eighteenth century, a little academy was maintained by them almost in secret; there philosophy and divinity were taught to boys of talent, after which they were sent abroad to the Scottish colleges of Rome, Douay, Ratisbon, or Valladolid, from whence, as Jesuits or secular priests, they returned to preach once more unto the clans the faith in which their fathers died.

All these odds and ends of information *anent* this Scoto-Spanish establishment were told to the military visitors by Father John Cameron, in a low and gentle tone, as if he feared to wake some one, and all the Scottish priests and students, who crowded about the Highland officers in the little refectory, where wine and fruit were freely proffered, spoke in the same remarkable manner, stopping ever and anon as if to listen for a passing sound; while gravity and anxiety were impressed on every face.

Rattling Dick Duff had so completely adopted the bearing of a modest, quiet, and seriously-disposed young man, that the heart of Father John Cameron, a priest well up in years, was quite won; and Dick began to feel some compunction, while telling him with the utmost gravity, that "a natural abhorrence of gaiety and military uproar, with a love of retirement and of cloistral seclusion, &c. &c., had brought him and his companions, Captain Garriehorne and Colquhoun Grant, the famous scout who so tormented the Duc de Raguse, to visit them;" but he added, "what the devil is the matter? Is any one dead or hidden here—what's the row, that you all speak in whispers, as if the walls had ears?"

"It is a strange story," said the old priest, Father Cameron; "our beloved rector, without an apparent ailment, believes himself at the point of death. It is a sad narrative to me, for I loved the rector as a younger brother; although many years his senior (more than I dare reckon now), his talents and his piety made him superior to us all. He believes that the day, the hour—yea, the moment of his departure *is fixed:* it is a solemn, a terrible presentiment—but you, as soldiers, will be inclined to smile at it and me."

"Nay, sir," replied Dick, "you wrong us there; for on service we see every day the most terrible fulfilment of presentiments. I had a brother drowned upon the 16th of November—my father ever said it was *our fatal day*, and had been so for ages. He was wounded by my side on the 16th of November, when our Highlanders stormed one of the West India Isles, and on the 16th of November he was killed near the city of Alexandria, and with my own hands I buried him the day before we marched towards the Nile. Poor old man!"

"And there was poor old Major Wallace of Ours," said Grant, "who had always a presentiment that he would die on the 18th of March, the day he was wounded as an ensign at the blockade of Alexandria in 1801, and on the 18th of last March we found him dead in his tent, killed by a random shot, when we were covering the siege of Badajoz."

"Ay," sighed the priest, "there was poured forth the hot blood of many a gallant heart."

"So you see, my dear sir, that solemn presentiments are to be found in the camp as well as in the cloister," added Dick, draining his wine-horn, with a thoughtful smile. .

"Our reverend rector is powerfully possessed by the idea that he will not outlive the 16th of this month of November, the day on which his patron——"

The priest hesitated.

"Don't hesitate, my dear sir," said Dick ; "for I am come of an old Catholic stock—say on."

"The day on which his patron-saint died, and for a year past this conviction has become stronger in his mind as the time approached ; yet he is a halo man and well, though somewhat more feeble than he was wont to be. His patron is Margaret, Queen of Scotland, who died on the 16th of November, and this day is the *fifteenth*. A month ago, he felt this presentiment come more strongly, mysteriously, and solemnly upon him ; so that he could no longer attend to his duties as rector, but spent his whole time in abstemious fasting and earnest prayer, as one preparing for a great change. He dismissed all the professors, students, servants, and other inmates to a country house which we possess, six miles from the city, telling us to enjoy ourselves for a brief space, as a dark day of mourning was at hand.

"Impressed by the solemnity of his manner, we set out for the place, and remained there anxiously waiting to hear tidings from him, for he is dearly loved by us all, and by none more than me. A week elapsed, but we heard nothing from Valladolid ; at last, I turned back, being his dearest friend, and moreover, the oldest priest in the college—for I can remember the days when Charles of the Two Sicilies sat on the Spanish throne, and I was one of those who chanted the *De Profundis* by the grave of Charles Edward Stuart ; I can remember when the spires of seventy convents towered over Valladolid, for in El Campo every alternate house was a religious one ; and *now* there are but sixteen and *only* twenty-four convents. Well, gentlemen, I came back to inquire, and soon saw enough to fill me with alarm. In our absence the rector had hung the college chapel with black ; he had moreover raised the pavement before the shrine of St. Margaret, and after measuring his own height, had there dug a grave for himself, eight feet deep, and as I crossed the aisle, its ghastly depth in the black and bone-impregnated earth that lay piled on each side, struck me with awe and terror. I searched for the rector, but was unable to find him in any of the dormitories, refectory, library, or garden. At last, barefooted and bareheaded, clad in sackcloth, and girt by a cord of discipline, I found him kneeling near the grave he had dug ; he was praying earnestly, and never did the divine Murillo conceive a head more noble, or a face more expressive of piety, enthusiasm, worship, and prayer, in all its glory, than those of our rector as I saw him at that moment, with his eyes uplifted from a book of vespers towards the crowned statue of the Scottish Queen, around which twelve little lights were sparkling ; and I could hear the words that came from his pale lips, though they fell faintly and slowly,

"'Deus, qui beatam Margaritam, Scotorum Reginam, eximiâ in pauperes charitate mirabilem effecisti : da, ut ejus intercessione et exemplo, tua in cordibus nostris charitas jugiter augeatur.'

"When I approached, he fainted. I had him at once conveyed to bed and applied restoratives ; but so low had his strength and system ebbed by excessive fatigue, prayer, and fasting, that we have scarcely a hope of recovering him, and the conviction that he shall die to-morrow, on the 16th November, the anniversary of his patron's death, seven hundred years ago, is so vividly impressed upon his mind, that knowing its breadth of thought and unyielding energy of purpose, a solemn sadness has come upon us all, and we wait in terror the issue of this gloomy presentiment."

The military visitors were deeply impressed by this strange and fantastic story ; and on Father Cameron requesting them to visit the couch where the rector lay, in the hope that their Highland garb might rouse some old or other emotions in his breast, they at once assented and followed in silence to his chamber.

Under cloisters arched and old, they were led through the ancient chapel, where many a stern Jesuit who had heard Loyola preach, and where many a poor priest of the Scottish mission, were at rest from their labours ; and past the newly-dug grave where a stone already bore the name of the rector, cut by his own hand. Duff paused for a moment and read thereon,

M.S.

Don Iago de Santa Margareta ; Rector del Collegio de los Escosses ; Valladolid. Requiem a Dios por el.

"Mater Salvatoris, ora pro nobis !" muttered Father Cameron, as he hurried past, and led them into the gloomy little apartment, in which the further to mortify his flesh, the rector had taken up his quarters.

z

It was square, and floored with red tiles; on the dull and discoloured walls were two or three Murillos and Alonzo Canos ; in the window, around which the naked vines had clambered, lay a skull before a crucifix ; around were shelves laden with books, many being old tomes of Scottish theology ; and there were many old engravings of the House of Stuart in ebony frames, Prince Charles, James VIII., and Cardinal York.

Dick Duff took all this in at a rapid glance, and then his eyes rested on a thin, wan, and emaciated figure that lay on a plain and uncurtained Spanish bed in a corner of the apartment. The rector's eyes were closed and his hands were clasped. He scarcely seemed to breathe, and yet he was praying earnestly. His profile was sharp and thin ; he did not seem to be much above forty years of age; yet the hair that clustered round his high and intellectual temples was prematurely silvered over.

"Heavens !" exclaimed Dick, in a suppressed voice, and with a start of terror, "how like my poor old father he looks just now !"

"Like your father ?" reiterated Garriehorne.

"Yes—yes: he is the poor old man's image—just as he lay dead at Alexandria, when I rolled him in my blanket and buried him in the sand, digging his grave with my bayonet—God rest him !"

"The rector's history is a strange one," said Father Cameron ; " but we know not his name, therefore wo call him James of St. Margaret."

"But how came he here ?"

"Listen," replied the priest in a low voice, and they all drew aside. "Many years ago I was at sea, flying for safety from Argyllshire, having been hunted from parish to parish, because I had dared to say mass in

secret to our people—for to perform the offices of
our faith in Scotland was then to commit a crime.
Our vessel was running seaward down the Sound of
Mull, when a boat was discovered adrift, without sails
or oars; and in that boat we found a little child—a
boy—asleep, or worn by terror and the tossing waves
into a dreamless torpor. He was brought on board,
and to me the discovery of a boy floating thus upon
the sea, like Amadis de Gaul or Florizel in their
baskets, as we read in the old romances; or like
Moses or Judas Iscariot, as we may read in the
writings of the Fathers, seemed of great import—tho
more so, as I found an amulet, or reliquary, at his
neck, wherein was a relic of St. Margaret, with a prophecy written by one whom I knew, for I was then
but a youth—yea, knew well——"

" Father John of Douay?" exclaimed Dick Duff.

" Yes; John Macdonald of Douay—how know *you*
that?"

" Ask me not—ask me not, sir—but proceed."

" Yes, written by the most reverend father, John
of Douay (who was butchered by the French in Flanders), foretelling that . this child would yet become
great in the church, and would serve God at His
altar long and faithfully——"

" This was in the year 1772?" exclaimed Dick, who
had listened breathlessly.

" It was, sir. The poor child could tell me nothing
of his parents, and knew only that his name was ·
Hamish—that he had seated himself in an old boat
upon the beach, and fallen asleep, after which he was
awaked by the rough rocking of his new cradle, as it
tumbled on the waves, which had risen and floated it
out into the Sound. He wept for his mother long
and passionately; but I brought him hither, and in

the bosom of our Mother Church he soon learned to forget his earthly mother, who is now, perhaps, awaiting him in heaven——"

"For her wish has doubtless been mysteriously fulfilled," said Duff, incoherently. "Eternal Power! if this should be the case! Tell me, good sir, is there a scar——"

"Upon his left side?—yes."

"The mark of a stag's-horn, which gored him on the rocks of Loch-na-Keal."

"Yes, yes."

"Then this child whom you found floating on the sea, and who has lived to become the Rector of your College, is my *brother*, Hamish Duff, for whose supposed drowning in the Sound of Mull, our poor mother died of grief on the sixteenth of November."

"The *sixteenth* of November! the very day on which he has so long believed he is himself to die."

Dick threw down his plumed bonnet and hastened to the bedside with his eyes full of tears and a wild expression in his face.

"O how like our old father he looks!" he exclaimed, as he turned down the coverlet.

There was no motion; he placed a hand on the rector's heart; but there was no pulsation. He was dead—dead, but still warm.

At that moment the clock of the college tolled the half-hour *after* twelve!

Thus as he had so long foretold and foreseen, but by what mysterious intuition or presentiment, Heaven alone knows, he had actually passed away on the early morning of the sixteenth day of November.

*   *   *   *   *   *

The French cavalry were still pressing on, and the

jaded allies were still in full retreat; thus the Scottish fathers of the ancient college hurried the funeral by the next noon, that the Lieutenant of the Black Watch might lay his brother's head in the grave; and accordingly the rector was lowered into the tomb which his own hands had formed before the shrine of St. Margaret, the Patroness of Scotland; and Dick Duff was a changed man, and a grave man too, during the remainder of that horrible retreat, on which so many of our brave soldiers perished of starvation and fatigue; and which Lord Wellington continued without delay, until the Ebro and the Douro were far in his rear; and his harassed army found winter quarters on the frontier of Portugal.

Father John Cameron lived to a good old age, and died Catholic Bishop of Edinburgh, where he now lies interred before the altar of St. Mary's Chapel.

X..

THE FOREST OF GAICH;

OR, THE CAPTAIN DHU.

AFTER the Flemish campaign, under his Royal Highness the Duke of York, and the terrible retreat to Deventer—a retreat in which the sufferings of our troops rivalled those endured by the French after Moscow—the 42nd Highlanders were encamped during the spring of 1795 at Hanbury, in England, under the command of General Sir William Meadows, when their strength, which had been weakened by their recent operations against the French republican armies, was greatly augmented by volunteers from various Highland fencible corps, which had been raised in the preceding year. Among others, they were joined by the two entire flank companies of the Grant Fencibles, or old 97th Regiment, which had been raised to the number of thirteen hundred men by Sir James Grant of Grant, Bart. (locally known as the *Good* Sir James), almost entirely among his own name and clan in Strathspey, a district which has long been famous for its stirring music and the military spirit of its people. These volunteers, in the month of September, set out on their march through Badenoch to join the 42nd, under the command of Captain MacPherson of Ballychroan, who had been appointed to the corps, the colonel of which was then Major-General Sir Hector Munro, K.B.

Evan MacPherson was generally known in that wild and mountainous district named Badenoch as the Captain *Dhu*, or Black Officer, in consequence of his raven-coloured hair, his swarthy complexion, and dark eyes, and, perhaps also, from the peculiarities of his character, which, though brave to recklessness, was stern, severe in discipline, and at times mysterious, savage, and vindictive.

The captain swore high, drank deep, and gambled as if he had the mines of Peru among the glens of Ballychroan. These qualities, together with his great strength and stature, rendered him more feared than loved in the district of Badenoch, where it was currently believed that he was in league with the devil, and where the story of his terrible end is yet remembered with a shudder by the people round the winter hearth. There are many yet alive in Strathspey who saw and knew Black Evan, and remember the events which I am about to record.

From Speyside he marched his volunteers through Glentromie, and, following the course of the river which gives that valley its name, entered the wilder and more romantic parts of Badenoch, between the Stoney Mountain and Drum Ferrich, till about nightfall, when, to the great bodily discomfort and greater mental discomposure of the soldiers, who dared not complain save in whispers to each other, he halted in the haunted Forest of Gaich, a wild and uninhabited tract of country on the northern slope of the mighty Grampians.

There he ordered them to pile arms, and have a fire lighted in a place which he indicated, near a well, deemed holy, as the water of it had been blessed

by St. Eonaig of old. On this, a white-haired sergeant, Hamish Grant, from Brae Laggan, respectfully
ventured to suggest that the fire might burn equally
well elsewhere.

MacPherson, who was not accustomed to be trifled
with or have his orders disputed, stormed and swore
terribly, according to his wont, both in Gaëlic and
English.

"Good will never come of it," said the sergeant,
moodily.

"Let evil come if it may, and welcome be it !" responded MacPherson, scornfully ; " let the old fellow
who blessed the well come from his grave at Kil-
maveonaig, and, if he chooses, I'll give him a jorum
of its water flavoured with Ferintosh."

Muffled in their grey great-coats, or in their plaids
of the bright red Grant tartan, the soldiers sat or lay
in groups near the fire, which burned cheerfully, and
shed a wavering glare along the green mountain slope.
The night was calm, and the stars shone brightly overhead ; no moon was visible yet, and scarcely a breath
of wind stirred the light foliage of the silver birches.
Attracted by the unwonted light of the fire, the dun
deer were visible at times, but for a moment only,
as they peered from their lair among the feathery
bracken leaves, and then fled to distant parts of the
forest.

The soldiers sung Gaëlic songs to while away the
time, and each shared with his comrade the contents
of his canteen and havresack ; for, having just left
their homes in Strathspey, all were amply provided
with bread and cheese, beef, venison, and plenty of
good usquebaugh ; thus, though the place of their halt
was weird, wild, and—all save the little runnel that

trickled down the heather slope—unholy, the night seemed likely to pass merrily enough.

Apart from all his men lay Evan MacPherson, of Ballychroan, who on this night was unusually sullen, gloomy, and taciturn; so much so, that the soldiers, all of whom knew him well, remarked that a *tarnc-coill*, or black cloud, was upon him; for at times he had his dark or melancholy hour.

" And how could he be otherwise ?" said old Sergeant Hamish, in a whisper, as he took a huge *sneishen* from the silver-mounted mull of Corporal Shon Grant, his own cousin, " only seventeen times removed," as Bailie Jarvie has it. "Oich ! oich ! who but he would have halted in the Forest of Gaich, and at night too ?"

" I'll sleep with one eye open, at all events," replied the corporal, impressively, with a wink.

" And I with both my ears," said Duncan Bane, the piper ; "for, by the horns of the devil—"

" Whisht ! Oich, don't name *him* here, for he is, perhaps, nearer than we know of; but what were you about to say ?"

" That we shall be lucky if we pass the night without hearing the scream of Comyn's eagles as they fly towards the Tarff."

" It is said, they pass through the forest from Benoch Corrie Va always at midnight," said Donald Bane Grant, or Fair-haired Donald the piper, in a whisper.

Some of the younger soldiers laughed ; but the older shrugged their shoulders, and took an additional dram and *sneishen*, as they thought of all the Forest of Gaich had witnessed in other times.

In a previous legend, the fate of the Red Comyn

has been mentioned ; but this forest was the death-scene of his father, the equally traitorous Black Comyn ; and it was to the story of his terrible death the soldiers referred.

"He was killed," said one, "by a fall from his horse, which a weird woman had bewitched."

"Not at all," said the sergeant, bluntly ; for he was well versed in all the oral literature of his native hills.

"How then—how ?" asked several.

"His death happened thus," began the sergeant in Gaëlic. "The Black Comyn was a fierce tyrant, who dwelt in the black Castle of Inverlochy, to which he added the great round western tower, that still bears his name ; and there he and his wife, who was the Lady Marjorie, daughter of John Baliol, King of Scotland, were a terror and a grievance to the whole country by their exactions, extortions, and severity. Every one in Badenoch knows the story of his conceiving a love for two pretty girls whom he saw reaping in a field near Croc Barrodh, and whom, because they fled from him, he ordered his Lowland men-at-arms to strip nude as they came into the world, and in that condition he compelled to finish the reaping of the field in the light of open day, while he and his friends mocked them, and looked on.

"Two days after this, he was at the Cell of St. Eonaig, in Blair Athole, where he tarried at a way-side cottage to obtain a draught of beer. The baron was thirsty, and he drank deep ; the day was hot—he had ridden far, and the beverage was cool, sharp, and refreshing.

"'This beer of yours pleases me much,' said he ; 'whence get you it, dame ?'

"'I am my own brewer,' replied the cottager; 'but the malt is brought from St. John's Town.'

"'And the water?'

"'From yonder stream.'

"'The Alduehcarlinn?'

"'Yes.'

"'Good! I shall have such beer made in my Castle of Inverlochy, if it cost me a thousand lives and fifty thousand silver crowns!' said Comyn, wiping the white froth from his coal-black beard with his steel glove.

"'Then you must make a road over the Grampians,' said the woman.

"'And a road I shall make, dame,' he exclaimed.

"The woman laughed covertly, and bitterly uttered a curse under her breath; for she was the mother of one of the young reapers whom he had so recently dishonoured. Now this woman was a witch, and the beer she had given the Lord of Badenoch was brewed under a spell; thus, whoever drank thereof became her victim and the instrument of her will.

"The Black Comyn resolved that whatever might be the result, he would have beer of the same kind in his Castle of Inverlochy; but to procure the ingredients a road was necessary, and he at once ordered one to be made. Then thousands of men were soon seen at work, with axe and shovel hewing a path from the lonely little cell of St. Eonaig, through the dense fir woods of Craig Urrand, building a bridge across the Bruar in Athole, and digging a way straight to this Forest of Gaich; and thus far it was made when the work was stopped by witchcraft.

"Daily the Black Comyn came to survey the road and to watch its progress over hill and glen, and wood and water, and many observed that daily two eagles hovered above his head, but high in mid-air, where the arrows of his best archers failed to reach them ; for these screaming eagles were witches, the mother of the two pretty reapers—the beer woman of St. Eonaig, and another cailloch who dwelt by the Lochy, and who came hither to scheme out vengeance and to destroy the Black Comyn's road, lest when finished it might prove an easy avenue for the Perthshire clans to march into Badenoch.

" By the day of St. Eonaig the road had been made nearly to Gaich, and the dun deer, roused from their lair, were flying before the workmen, when the screams of the two giant eagles were heard overhead ; the men were dispersed or rendered powerless by a spell, while all their horses and oxen took to flight, as if possessed by the demons which entered the swine of, old, and rushing headlong over the precipices were destroyed.

" Comyn beheld this sudden catastrophe with emotions of astonishment and rage, which were soon changed to fear, when the flapping wings and shrill cries of the furious eagles rang close in his ears, and with dusky wings outspread, and monstrous beaks open, he saw them descending swoop upon him.

" He turned his fleet horse, and goring him with his spurs, fled he knew not whither.

" The infernal birds pursued him closely, and the summer sun cast their shadows like flying clouds upon his path. He crossed the ridge of the Grampians, and galloped downward at a frightful pace towards Craignaheilar ; but there they overtook him, though he cowered upon his horse's mane, and implored God to save him ! His entreaties were in vain, for God seemed to have abandoned the Black Comyn to the fiends, even as He abandoned his son the Red

Traitor to the dagger of Bruce; and now the eagles, plunging their beaks and talons in his flesh, tore him limb from limb, and scattered the reeking fragments of his body in the wilderness. One of his legs was still dangling in the silver stirrup when his terrified horse fell dead on the banks of the Tarff.*

"And once in every hundred years," concluded the sergeant, "his spirit is said to ride from Gaich, followed by the screaming eagles."

"And here, too," said the corporal, glancing about him and stirring the embers of the fire, "has been seen many a time, as I have heard my mother say, the great Black Cat of the Woods—the king of all cats."

"Aire Dhia!" exclaimed the sergeant, uneasily; "that is the devil himself."

"Cat or devil, I care not which," said the corporal; "but we all know the story of the Laird of Brac na Garacher, who fought in the wars of Montrose, and when hunting here in Gaich, on Yule Eve, shot a black cat of enormous size, and just as he approached, cautiously, to examine the scratching brute, to his astonishment it opened its red mouth and addressed him in very good Gaelic, begging that he would have the Christian charity to inform the cats at home of his untimely end. You may be sure that Brac na Garacher lost little time after that in making his way out of the forest and reaching home, where he related what had happened, and all the family laughed at him, saying, there was nothing in the world like good Campbelton whiskey for making even a cat speak!

"But lo! the moment his story was concluded, a

* "At a place still named *Lechois*, or *one foot*, according to Mr. Scrope. See his work on "Deerstalking."

little black kitten, that sat by the hearth, sprang with a fierce bound to the back of a high arm-chair, with its tail bushy like a fox's brush, its cars flat on its head, its yellow eyes glaring with rage, its back erect, and its little body swollen to all appearance thrice its usual size. There it sat for a minute spitting and howling like an evil spirit, and then vanished up the chimney! This event silenced the laughers, and sorely disturbed the mind of the laird, who resolved to consult with the minister about it on the morrow, and, in the meantime, to drink deep before going to bed. About midnight he was awakened by a sound, and, by the dim rays of his night-lamp, saw a black mass hovering over him.

"It was the huge black cat he had shot in the Forest of Gaich!

"Its eyes shone like those of a snake, its fierce claws were extended towards him, its red mouth was open, and its hot breath came balefully upon his cheek, as slowly, surely, and deliberately, it descended from the roof of his bed upon him, and clutching at his throat, lacerated and strangled him to death!"

"And I have heard from my father, who was *out* with the Prince, God rest them both!" said the piper, "that on the same night of Brae na Garacher's death, when the minister of Kingussie was riding home by the skirts of this forest, he passed a mighty multitude of cats. They covered all the sides of the hills, and swarmed among the rocks and trees, like mites in an old cheese. On reaching home, he found that every cat in the village, and all the adjacent cottages, had disappeared, and gone towards the Forest of Gaich, from whence they never returned."

Just as this third veracious story was concluded by Donald Bane the piper, he, the sergeant, and others who yet lingered by the watch-fire, as if in that place, so weird and lone, they were loth to commit themselves to sleep, were startled by the presence of a man —a stranger—who suddenly appeared among them, without any one having seen or heard him approach —appeared as if he had sprung from the ground.

His aspect was remarkable, and had something alike impressive and terrible about it. He was dressed like a Lowland peasant; but his complexion was dark as that of a mulatto. His hair, beard, and whiskers were of raven blackness; the latter appendages, which he wore in great profusion, grew close up to his keen and restless eyes, which glared from under the shadow of his beetling brows and broad round bonnet, like those of a polecat from under a bush; but his grey plaid, the folds of which were full and ample, rose high upon his breast and concealed his mouth.

His eyes, which had all the fascinating glare of the fierce bright orbs of the rattle-snake, leisurely surveyed the quailing soldiers one after another in silence, and then he grinned, as if pleased by the startling impression his sudden appearance created, and spreading his strong, brown, swarthy hands over the flames, thrust them almost *into* the fire, without seeming to feel the heat in any way oppressive.

"Who are you?" asked the sergeant, firmly.

"One whom you may perhaps know well enough by-and-by," replied the other, with a grimace.

"Are you a Lowlander?" asked the corporal.

"Dioul!" growled the other; "did such pure Gaëlic as mine ever come from the tongue of a bodach in brecks? But speak out, my friends; of what are you afraid?"

"I fear nothing human," replied the sergeant; "but I fear God, and hate the devil and all his works."

" What wrong has the devil ever done *you ?*"

" He put it in the heart of a vile Cateran to draw his dirk on me at the Inverness cattle tryst in August last."

" Nay, sergeant, it was not the poor devil who caused this, but your hot Highland whiskey and temper to boot. Yet I do not think you have much to complain of, as you well nigh slew him afterwards."

" The devil ?"

" No—the Cateran, as you call him. As for the devil, he, poor fellow, is very much maligned on earth, I assure you."

" 'Twas only a dab with a dirk I gave the Cateran, and he gave me another."

" A dab—a severe wound ?"

" Bah ! I would let any honest man do as much to me, for a good dram, any day ; like true Highlanders, we parted after the first blood drawn."

The dark man gave one of his ferocious grins, as he said,

" You parted—true; but how fared it with your assailant ?"

" He was lodged by the meddling provost and bailies in the bottle dungeon in the middle arch of Inverness Bridge."

" Yes—confined there, with nothing between him and the rain and wind of heaven but an iron grating —a narrow hatch of steel ribs, over which the wayfarers tread, and there he is yet."*

" All this is the provost's fault, *not* mine. *We* march by daybreak," said the sergeant, who had imbibed a strange mistrust and fear of this nocturnal visitor ; " whither go you ?"

* This *oubliette* perished with the old Bridge of Inverness.

"To a warmer place than even the warmest West Indian Isle," was the significant reply of the other, with a withering glance of malevolence and irony; "but it was not to talk with you I sought the Forest of Gaich to-night. My man is here!"

With these strange words, the tall dark man strode to the foot of a tree. There, muffled in his cloak and fast asleep, or to all appearance so, Captain MacPherson was lying with his head pillowed on the root of a gigantic larch, and when shaken roughly by the shoulder, he started up with one of his terrible oaths, but grew pale on beholding the person who aroused him. On recovering himself partially,

"What errand brings you here to-night?" he asked, in a low and stifled voice.

"To see *you*," was the brief reply.

"But why now, fiend?"

"Where so fitting a place as the Forest of Gaich?"

"True—true! fool—madman that I was! What lured me to halt here?"

"What lured you?"

"Yes."

"Shall I tell you?" grinned the other.

"Yes."

"Fatality."

"Alas! alas!"

"Come," said the visitor, fiercely, "for time presses."

"Hurry no man's cattle," grumbled MacPherson; "so begone, fiend, for I go not with you to-night."

"You will not?"

"No!"

The dark stranger laughed till the very hills seemed

A A

to echo; and that weird sound made the marrow freeze in the bones of the old sergeant, who was listening.

"Come," continued the visitor, "lest I drag you hence."

"Drag!" reiterated the captain, with a furious malediction.

"Yes, drag; for you are powerless as a suckling, and your will is mine."

For a moment their swarthy eyes glared like live coals upon each other. At last those of the Captain Dhu lowered, and he said, in a broken voice,

"Go to the place of tryst, and I shall be with you."

"When?"

"In the snapping of a flint," he groaned, while the perspiration rolled over his pallid brow.

"Ha! ha! Nay, I go not without you."

"Then the curse of God—the bitter, blighting curse that marked the front and withered up the soul of Cain—be on you!" exclaimed the captain, maddened with fear and rage. "Hound of hell, lead on—I follow you! Stand by your arms, men. Sergeant, at your peril, see that no man follows us!"

The swarthy man grinned again on hearing this outburst and these orders; and while the startled soldiers gazed in each other's faces with blank astonishment at the progress and issue of a conversation so strange, and at the aspect of one before whom this terrible officer, the Captain Dhu—he so stern and stormy, so fierce and unyielding—seemed to quail and bow, he and his weird-like visitor went from amidst them, and together sought a lonelier and more sequestered part of the forest.

They remained absent for some time. The whole

party of soldiers were now awakened, and muttered strangely among themselves; while, regardless of the orders he had received, old Sergeant Hamish Grant, impelled by an irresistible and, perhaps, laudable curiosity, crept slowly forward on his hands and knees; but he had not proceeded far thus, when he heard the voices of the captain and his nocturnal visitor—the former in tones of entreaty, and the latter in those of authority and fierce derision. Creeping on a few paces further, with a drawn bayonet in his hand, he beheld a sight which, when he considered the proud and stern character of his leader, filled him with blank wonder.

The waning moon was now visible; it shone out for a moment from behind a mass of crapelike cloud. The dark figures of MacPherson and the stranger were distinctly seen. The place of their meeting was a green fairy ring, covered with rich grass, which waved solemnly in the breeze. Close by it towered three gigantic granite blocks, spotted with green lichens, silent, grim, and lonely, for they were Druidical obelisks; and in the middle of this circle of Loda lay the "mossy stone of power," the altar of other times. MacPherson was on his knees; the dark man towered over him, threatening and commanding, but what he said, the trembling sergeant knew not, though all around was deathly still, save the trembling of the wiry pine foliage; for at times a tremulous motion will agitate a wood, even when the breath of the wind has passed away. Wan, white, and ghastly, the rays of the sinking moon poured over Benoch-corri-va aslant, and threw the shadows of the Druid stones, and of those who lingered there, far beyond the ancient circle.

A cloud passed over her face, veiling everything for a moment.

A A 2

When again the still white moonbeams fell on the fairy ring and the Druid stones, no one was there.

The place was lonely and silent.

Full of terror and awe, the sergeant rushed back to the bivouac to tell what he had seen ; but for a time his lips were sealed, for he heard the voice of the captain, who had reached the night-fire before him, ordering the whole to stand to their arms and prepare to march.

Evan MacPherson was deadly pale ; his manner was wild and excited ; but the strictness of discipline, and the. known severity of his character, alike forbade inquiry or remark.   The arms were unpiled in silence, knapsacks were strapped on, and just as the light of daybreak began dimly and faintly to eclipse the waning moon, the Strathspey men proceeded on their march, which lay across the Grampians, and through Glen Bruar towards Blair Atholl.

A dead silence pervaded the ranks : if any spoke, it was in a whisper, and each man suggested to his comrade that Evan Dhu of Ballychroan had sold himself to the Evil One. If further proofs were required than those afforded by this night-interview, Sergeant Hamish Grant and the piper, Donald Bane, were ready to aver on oath that in every place around the fire and across the forest towards the fairy ring whereon the foot of that mysterious visitor had trod, the grass was scorched and withered.   Their clansman, the corporal, who was somewhat sceptical on this point, suggested that these black spots might have been caused by the birch and pine sparks from their watchfires, but old Hamish indignantly repelled the idea ; and the future career of Evan of Ballychroan more than corroborated all that was averred to have taken place on that eventful night, in the haunted Forest of Gaich.

About the end of September, MacPherson, with his Strathspey men, joined the regiment, which embarked on the 27th October for the West Indies, forming part of the expedition of twenty-two thousand one hundred and fifty-nine infantry, and three thousand and sixty cavalry, led by Sir Ralph Abercrombie, and destined to reduce the isles of St. Lucia, St. Vincent, and Trinidad. Tempestuous weather succeeded the embarkation, and on the 29th the wind blew a hurricane, which drove many of the Indiamen and transports from their anchors, dismasted some, and bulged others on the beach. The expedition was thus delayed until the 11th November, when again the whole fleet, consisting of three hundred sail, put to sea; but the flagship *Impregnable* was stranded on a sand-bank, and unable to proceed; other disasters succeeded; the *Middlesex*, with five hundred of the Black Watch on board, had her bowsprit and foretopmast carried away by the *Undaunted* when off the Isle of Wight, and was thus left astern of the whole squadron; which had no sooner cleared the British Channel, than it was dispersed by another dreadful tempest, which totally disabled the *Commerce de Marseilles*, a hundred-and-twenty-gun ship (French prize), having the 57th Regiment on board, and caused the loss of several transports and many hundred lives. The admiral was driven back to Portsmouth, and his fleet, after being long tempest-tossed, and scattered over the stormy winter sea, reached Barbadoes in detail.

In the Black Watch, this strange series of disasters were secretly but unanimously attributed to the malevolence and interference of the Devil. The mysterious meeting in the Forest of Gaich was remembered, and Evan of Ballychroan was viewed with anything but favour by the soldiers under his command; yet he did his duty bravely and cheerfully, and was stern and severe as ever when any fault or dereliction of orders occurred. The superstitious dread with which his mountaineers regarded the events of the voyage need not excite surprise, when we remember that, about the same period, the crew of one of his Majesty's crack frigates flatly refused to sail until the captain thereof sent his black tom-cat ashore, or had its ears and tail docked, to alter its feline aspect.

But this long succession of mishaps by sea, and upon the events which preceded the voyage, were forgotten by the Strathspey men, when, on the 9th of February next year, the *Middlesex* ran into one of the harbours of Barbadoes, and the clear brilliant sky and blue waters of the Caribbean Sea were beaming around them; and then the charming greenness and fertility of this place, the most eastern of these lovely Indian isles, made all long for the shore, eager to disembark, and to escape the vertical heat of a tropical sun blazing on the decks of a crowded transport.

Brigades were now detailed to attack and reduce the principal isles of the West Indies. General Whyte, with the brave 39th (*"Primus in Indis"*), the Sutherland Highlanders, and the old 99th, sailed against Demerara and Berbice, which he captured almost without resistance; while Brigadier-General Moore (the future hero of Corunna), with our old friends the 42nd and other troops, sailed to favour the French in St. Lucia with a visit, and found themselves off the Pigeons' Isle on the 27th April, when they were ordered to land at a little sandy bay, into which the bright blue water ran in glittering ripples, under shadowy foliage of the most luxuriant and brilliant green.

The landing was made by the troops in four divisions, at four different points; and the first man who leaped ashore was Evan MacPherson of the Black Watch. His company followed with a loud hurrah! and when the four united columns advanced against Morne Fortunée, the principal military post in the island, on officers desirous of leading the forlorn hope being requested "to enclose their cards to the brigade-major," the first on the list for this perilous work was the Captain Dhu!

This caused his men to consider and have serious doubts of the affair during the halt in Gaich; for, as Sergeant Grant said, a man who had really sold himself to the Devil would have chosen some less dangerous trade than soldiering; and, moreover, would not have been in such a deuced hurry to risk promotion to a warmer climate than the West Indies.

"But how if his life be charmed," suggested the corporal, "and his skin proof to shot and steel? we have heard of such things in the Highlands. Like Claverhouse, he may have his *appointed time*."

"Lambh dhia sinn!" exclaimed the sergeant; "so have we all."

But the corporal's opinion was not given without finding due weight; and it caused the unfortunate captain to be more closely watched than ever.

Ere nightfall the troops were all under arms, and on the march to assault the great fort of the island; and when, as usual in such cases, old Rawlins the quartermaster was made custodier, *pro temp.*, of all the rings, watches, and purses of the officers, that they might be safe with him in the rear, it was remarked that MacPherson retained his own valuables.

372 LEGENDS OF THE BLACK WATCH.

"Ballychroan is a cool fellow," said the officers;
"he has quite made up his mind to escape scathe-
less."

The eve of the tropical sun is brief and beautiful;
in the forcible lines of Scott—

> "No pale gradations quench his ray,
> No twilight dews his wrath allay;
> With dislike battle target red,
> He rushes to his burning bed;
> Dyes the wild waves with bloody light,
> Then sinks at once—and all is night!"

So sank the disc of the West Indian sun into the
burning Caribbean sea, and sudden darkness veiled
the march of the troops, while the pipes of Donald
Bane, and other kilted minstrels of the Black Watch,
woke the echoes of the fertile valleys and green cocoa-
groves, as the corps formed the avant garde of the
midnight movement, which brought the troops close
to Morne Fortunée, in the attack on which Mac-
Pherson charmed all by his rashness and headlong
bravery.

By a mistake of the black guide, General Moore
found himself entangled with the French outposts two hours before the other columns came up.
An immediate encounter ensued. The 53rd Regiment drove back the enemy; and here Evan Mac-
Pherson, ever foremost in danger, leaving his own
ranks, pushed on with the English corps, as the dis-
patch of Lieutenant-Colonel Abercrombie, its commander, relates; and after a hand-to-hand conflict,
slew the French Republican general, piercing him
through the body with such force that the long fluted
blade of the Highland claymore would not come
forth; so that he had actually to place his feet upon

the corpse before he could withdraw his weapon. Spurning the body off his sword, he uttered one of his old ferocious oaths of passion and blind fury.

The outpost was carried; by daybreak the other columns came up, and with the loss of fifty grenadiers Morne Fortunée was completely invested.

After this, five companies of the Black Watch, the Black Rangers under Malcolm of Lochore (a Fifeshire gentleman, who had a powerful presentiment that he would that day close his earthly career), the 55th Regiment, and the Light Company of the 57th, were ordered to assault the battery of Seeke which was close to the outworks of Morne Fortunée, and, by a dangerous flank-fire, enfiladed the approach thereto.

As they advanced to the attack, MacPherson, being senior volunteer for the forlorn hope, led the stormers. He seemed wild with excitement; his cheek was red, and his dark eyes sparkled with a fiery glow.

Followed closely by six men carrying a scaling-ladder, with his sword clenched in his teeth, and bearing in his arms one of those huge grass-bags which are often used in such affairs to prevent stormers from being hurt by falling into the trenches, and which, for this purpose, are filled with freshly cut grass, he rushed forward at the head of the forlorn-hope-men, nearly all of whom were swept away by a rolling fire of grape, canister, and musket-shot. He tossed his grass bag into the trench, and seizing the ladder, shook off the dying men who clung to it, and with his own powerful hands he erected it at once against the slope of the stone bastion, uttering shouts of rage and triumph as he ascended.

Pell-mell a cheering mass of the Black Watch and 55th men intermingled followed him.

The fire concentrated upon this point was terrible; it seemed the very crater of a volcano, vomiting flame and missiles, and bristling with points of steel. Lieutenant James Frazer of the Black Watch, and Donald Bane, now the pipe-major, fell dead. The former was caught in the arms of Sergeant Grant just as he was falling over the bastion, and many more were killed and wounded. MacPherson received several cuts and scars; but he seemed to be regardless alike of danger and pain. On the old sergeant falling in the embrasure stunned by a blow from a musket-butt, the captain snatched the halbert from his hand to replace his claymore which had been broken on a musket-barrel, and armed anew, he hewed a passage into the battery, which was carried in triumph; but not until the brave Malcolm of Lochore was slain by a grape-shot (thus fulfilling his solemn presentiment) and many of his Rangers had perished by his side.

MacPherson's bonnet had been denuded of its gay plumage by musket-shot, his plaid and uniform had been cut and pierced by sabres and bayonets; yet he had but three wounds of consequence, and when he presented to General Moore the tricolour which he had pulled down from the battery, the brigadier said,

"By my soul, Captain MacPherson, you seem to bear a charmed life."

To this the captain replied only by one of his strange laughs, as he tore a Frenchman's tricoloured sash into strips to bind up the wounds in his sword-arm, for he had received two bayonet-stabs and a sword-cut in the affair.

But though the battery of Secke had thus fallen, Morne Fortunée was yet untaken; and when the

Vizie, a fortified ridge under its guns was to be mined and carried by assault, MacPherson again volunteered for service in the front.

The local features and scenery of these isles, torn as they were by convulsions of nature into deep gorges covered with bosky thickets, or invaded by abrupt cliffs and bluffs, made the operations of the troops, who were cross-belted for weeks consecutively, severe and harassing. The hardihood and power of endurance which are characteristic of the Scottish Highlanders, rendered the Black Watch of the greatest service, while, on the other hand, the cavalry of the expedition were soon totally unfit for duty, and the 26th Light Dragoons gradually disappeared altogether.

"St. Lucia presents a chequered scene of sombre forests and fertile valleys, smiling plains and towering precipices, shallow rivers and deep ravines;" but the chief of all its hills are the huge pyramidal Pitons, two sugar-loaf shaped masses of rock, which from their base in the blue ocean to their summits in the sky are ever covered with waving foliage of the most brilliant green. The steep and rugged nature of the country and its pathless woods, where of old the painted Carib lurked, presented innumerable difficulties to the soldiers and seamen, who had to drag the battering guns from the beach into position against Morne Fortunée; but on the 17th May a sufficient number were in readiness to open a fire against the Vizie, or fortified ridge, which had been strengthened by palisades, earthworks, and bastions of stone, on which the French had mounted some of their heaviest guns.

It was proposed to undermine one of these bastions, and Evan MacPherson, who had volunteered for the engineering department, discovered—no one knew how—an arched place almost immediately under it; and he at once resolved to turn this vault to the best advantage. It was small and domed with stone, having been an oratory hewn out of the hill-side in the days of the Sieur de Rousselan, a French Governor of St. Lucia, who died in 1654, and who was much beloved for his gentleness even by the fierce Caribs, one of whose women he had married.

Here, for three nights preceding the seventeenth of May, the Captain Dhu, with ten soldiers of the 27th Regiment, worked to lay a mine, which, when fired, would blow the whole upper work, with its men, cannon and shot into the air. In the dark they crept to and fro on their hands and knees, reaching the place unmolested it is true, but not *unseen;* for on the third night they were attacked by the French, and a terrible close combat with bayonets and pistols took place in the dark. Most of MacPherson's men were slain and cruelly butchered by the infuriated French; but him they could neither kill, capture, overcome, or drive out of the vault.

Plying his broadsword with both hands, he swept aside the charged bayonets and clubbed muskets like dry reeds by a winter brook; the wounds he inflicted were terrible! Lights were now brought, and in the red blaze of torches, and the ghastly green glare of fire-balls, his tall and muscular form was seen towering over a pile of fallen men who encumbered the slippery and gory floor, towering like an infernal spirit or destroying angel, his sword-blade and his eyes flashing together, his swarthy cheek a deep red, and his black hair waving in elf-like locks.

" *C'est le diable !*" exclaimed the French, and precipitately retired, leaving the vault, but only to adopt measures more surely to destroy him. Piles of straw, damp hemp, tar-barrels, and powder were flung in. Then fire was applied, and thus all the miserable wounded were suffocated or burned alive, with the corpses of the dead. Even the Captain Dhu did not come forth after this; and at midnight his regiment, with the 27th or Inniskillings, and the 31st or Huntingdonshire Foot, commenced the attack on the fortified ridge of the Vizie without him; and his company was led by Lieutenant Simon Frazer, who was afterwards so severely wounded at the capture of St. Vincent.

Six days the fighting continued, and an unceasing fire was exchanged between the British battery and the fort, until the 27th Regiment, by a desperate exertion of bravery, effected a lodgment within five hundred yards of the French works, where they repulsed a furious sortie of the enemy, and maintained their ground almost over the very place where the miners had been destroyed. This movement proving successful, the French capitulated on the twenty-sixth May, and from that day the Isle of St. Lucia became a British colony, after the loss of one hundred and ninety-four officers and men killed, and five hundred and fifty-four wounded, according to the nominal return; but that document was in error by one; for among those returned as slain six days before the capitulation, was the Captain Dhu.

When the interment of the dead took place, the fatal mine was explored, and it presented a dreadful scene, being full of dead soldiers, half scorched, roasted, decomposed, and covered with black festering wounds, while the pavement was so slippery with blood and hideous slime, that the fatigue party could scarcely bear out the remains of their comrades to their hastily-made graves under the fatal guns of Morne Fortunée.

The 27th found old Bill Hook, the corporal of their Pioneers, literally burned to a mere piece of charcoal; and the remains were alone identified by a brass tobacco-box which the deceased was known to possess.

One body, fearfully blackened by smoke, and having the uniform scorched off it, a sword in its fingers calcined by the fire to a mere stripe of rusty iron, was borne out and laid upon the grass in the bright sunshine; and then with a shout of astonishment old Hamish Grant and others recognised the famous Captain Dhu!

"It is MacPherson, Black Evan of Ballychroan!" they exclaimed; and the whole regiment crowded to gaze on what they believed to be the remains of this brave but terrible fellow.

"Quick—let us bury him!" said some of the soldiers.

But louder cries of astonishment rose from all, when he began to move and breathe; and then, like one awakening from a long trance, opened his eyes and gazed wildly about him.

For six days he had survived the horrors of that dark and terrible vault! The surgeons were promptly on the spot, and no means were left untried to restore MacPherson.

"Oich! oich!" muttered the Strathspeymen; "leave him to himself—the hour of his end is not yet come." Sergeant Grant, who was ordered to see if the vault was now cleared of dead bodies, entered it slowly and with some reluctance; but in a moment after he came forth with a bound, as if he had been shot from a mortar, leaving his bonnet behind him; his grey

hair was on end, his eyes dilated, and his usually nut-
brown and weather-beaten cheek was deadly pale
with terror.

"What the devil is the matter now?" asked several
officers.

"The Devil himself is the matter," gasped the
sergeant.

"How—what have you seen?" asked General
Moore, laughing.

Hamish could not explain himself in English; but
to the Black Watch who crowded about him he related that, on entering the *black-hole*—for so they
named the mine—he had seen in the further end
thereof the figure of a man, and believing he was
some Frenchman who had found concealment there,
he drew his sword and approached. Then a pair of
bright, fierce, and terrible eyes, glaring like those of an
owl or snake, met his gaze; and while secret awe and
horror filled his soul, he found himself confronted by a
man who was of giant stature, and whose face was darker
than that of a mulatto, with a beard of raven blackness, and wearing a grey plaid and Lowland bonnet.

He was the stranger whom they had seen in the
Forest of Gaich!

He uttered a shrill laugh, which rung round the
vault, and for a moment rooted the poor sergeant to
the bloody pavement; then the soldier, wild with
terror, rushed into the light of day.

The story that a Scottish sergeant had seen the
Devil in the mine occasioned great laughter in the
camp, for no trace of his Satanic majesty—not even
the print of a cloven hoof—could be found, when the
31st Regiment demolished the whole fabric next day,
after dismantling the Vizie.

    '   *   ◆   ●   ●

After the capture of Morne Fortunée, a marked change came over the Captain Dhu. He was subject to fits of profound melancholy and abstraction, and to gusts of passion and fury, when he drank deep and became almost mad, exclaiming that he was tormented by fiends—that the atmosphere was full of flame—that hell was yawning under his feet, and so forth. His excesses soon impaired his health so severely, that he was sent home with invalids, on a year's leave of absence, with a constitution broken by war, wounds, and the wine-bottle; and with a temper soured and furious, none knew by what.

The transport *Queen Charlotte,* in which he sailed from St. Vincent, was wrecked in the Irish Channel; and of three hundred souls who were on board, the Captain Dhu—though but the ruins of what he had been in bodily strength—alone escaped, being cast ashore, lashed to a spar; and after many strange and perilous adventures among the Irish, who were then in arms against the government, in the winter of 1799, he found himself at home in his native place, the beautiful valley of the Spey: and now we have reached the last chapter in his mysterious history—an event which is still locally remembered by the Grants and others in Strathspey as the DARK DEED in the Forest of Gaich.

On the 11th of January, 1800, being the day preceeding Yule, he summoned a party of gillies, and announced his intention of proceeding up the mountains to hunt the red deer in that place.

The Badenoch men looked at each other with perplexity and fear—as, from time immemorial, the Eve of Yule has been the epoch for all mischief, devilry, and witchcraft in the Highlands; and the scene of the proposed hunting was just the place that men might be supposed to avoid at such a time.

"To hunt on Yule Eve—and in the Forest of Gaich !"

Irresolute and unwilling alike to offend or obey, they gazed at each other in silence.

"Go not forth to hunt to-day," said old Hamish Grant, the sergeant, who, being discharged after long service, was an occasional visitor at the house of his old leader.

"And why not to-day?" thundered Black Evan, with a terrible oath.

"Can you ask ?"

"What day is it in particular ?"

"The Eve of Yule."

"Would you refuse to fight the enemy on Yule Eve ?" asked the captain, scornfully.

"No, Ballychroan," replied the sergeant, proudly ; "for on that day in the year '76 I fought with the Americans on the Delaware."

"And what is Yule to me ?" exclaimed the captain, as he drank a deep draught. "Ha ! ha ! what is that to me ? Go I shall, though the fiend—the accursed fiend—came up from hell with all his legions to bar the way. Go I shall, Hamish ; and go I must ?"

"This is most strange !"

"Fatality compels me," said the captain, mournfully and wildly. "Oh, how few could comprehend the misery of a conviction like this ! Fain would I give up *existence* if I could receive oblivion in exchange, but not life—*this* life at least. Fain would I rest in my grave, Hamish ; but in the grave, even of a saint—yea, under the altar-stone of Iona—I could not find repose."

D D

"I do not understand all this," said the old sergeant, solemnly; "so let us consult the minister about it."

"The minister—bah!"

"You never feared death, Ballychroan?"

"Death—no! for he has everywhere eluded me. You have seen me rush into the breach amid a thousand dangers, and escape them all. I have flung myself upon the levelled bayonets, and among the uplifted swords of the enemy; but the bayonets became pointless, the swords blunted, the bullets harmless as snow-flakes! In the dark vault of the Vizie, the flames spared me; even the ocean itself repelled me, when three hundred brave men went down into its greedy gulf; and, like he who wanders for ever—he who mocked his Saviour on the ascent to Calvary—I seem to bear a charmed life; but yet, like that more happy wretch, I cannot live for ever. No, Hamish, no—my days are numbered!"

"Go not forth to-day," reiterated the old soldier, grasping the arm of the excited captain.

"Bah!" he responded, and drained another glass of whiskey.

"What did Kenneth Ower foretel two hundred years ago?"

"That when a *black* Yule overtook a *black* Laird of Ballychroan, the race would cease."

"Well—you are the first of your family who have the name of Evan *Dhu*—and you have no son."

"Thank Heaven, no! I care not for predictions, and Kenneth Ower Mackenzie, the Brahn prophet, was a fool."

"He foretold strange things though."

"Such as, that oats would replace the fairies on the hill of Tomnahourich, and that ships with sails

unfurled would pass and repass it; but the green
bracken and the purple heather wave yet on the
Fairies' Hill, and we have heard nothing of the
ships."*

"Kenneth Ower never spoke in vain," said the
white-haired sergeant.

"I am too old a soldier to be terrified by silly predictions," exclaimed the captain, wrathfully; "so enough
of this. Set forward, men—away to the forest! Let
us drink, dance, and hunt while we may!"

And quaffing off a huge jug of alcohol, with a
party of gillies, whom he had made half tipsy, he
departed towards the Forest of Gaich.

Of all that band of hunters, not a man ever came
down from the Grampians again!

On that night, when the whole atmosphere seemed
calm and still, a terrific tempest, sudden as the discharge of a cannon, swept over the mountains. For
hours the forked lightning played and flashed over
Benoch-Corri-Va and the haunted Forest of Gaich,
while the thunder-peals made the old women in every
cottage and clachan totter down on their knees to
mutter a prayer for deliverance from evil and danger,
as the electric salvos hurtled over the great wooded

* The captain spoke in 1800. "Tomnahourich, the far-famed
Fairies' Hill, has been sown with oats," states the *Inverness
Advertiser* of 1859; "according to tradition, the Brahn
prophet, who lived 200 years ago, predicted that ships with unfurled sails would pass and repass Tomnahourich; and further,
that it would yet be placed under lock and key. The first part
of the prediction was verified by the opening of the Caledonian
Canal, and we seem to be on the eve of seeing the realization of
the rest by the final closing up of the Fairies' Hill." In what
succeeds I have closely followed local and oral tradition; but the
black officer was *not* the last of his race, as he left a daughter,
who, I believe, was married in England.

B B 2

valley, through which the swollen Spey, the most
furious of the Scottish rivers, laden with the spoil of a
hundred forests, swept with a ceaseless roar to the
German Ocean.

Over Gaich, the sky seemed all on fire.   It was an
expanse of crimson flame streaked with forky green
flashes; and against this steady flush the huge Grampians stood strongly forth in sombre outline.

With night this storm passed away.

Three days after, some shepherds who, in pursuit
of their scattered flocks, ventured into the wilderness
of Gaich, saw a sight, the memory of which causes₁
many yet to shudder, as they tell to their grandchil-
dren around the winter hearth the story of the Captain Dhu.

A lonely shieling, in which he and his twenty gillies took refuge, had been destroyed by a thunder-
bolt.   Its rafters and stones were scattered over the
forest, with the corpses of its inmates—every man of
whom had been *torn limb from limb*, and scattered
far apart, as if by the hands of some mighty fiend!

Such was the startling end of the Black Captain
and his companions.

His evil reputation, the weird locality of his hunting,
and the equally weird character of this tempestuous
night, have fixed the idea deeply in the minds of the
peasantry that Evan Dhu, of Ballychroan, decoyed
these twenty Badenoch men into Gaich Forest for the
sole purpose of delivering them to the fiend, in con-
formity with some terrible compact; for the whole
scene of the catastrophe bore evidence of their destruction by some infernal agency, rather than, as others
averred, the levin brand of Heaven.

At times, on the returning Eve of Yule, those who
have been belated in the forest suddenly find them-

selves in the midst of an invisible company of rois-
terers, whose laughter, shouts, imprecations, and
impious songs, fill the poor loiterers with affright; for
though the voices seem close to the ear, no one is
visible: and these unearthly bacchanalians are supposed to be the spirits of the doomed captain and his
companions.

On other occasions, screams, yells and entreaties
for mercy—wild, and thrilling, and heartrending—
with the hoarse, deep baying of infernal dogs, are
swept over the waste on the wind. But since that
terrible catastrophe on Yule Eve, 1800, none pass
willingly through the Forest of Gaich alone !

NOTES.

I

In the story of Farquhar Shaw, the formation of the Highland Watch has been fully detailed; but the following is the Letter of Service by which the Independent Companies of the *Reicudan Dhu* became the 43rd, and afterwards the 42nd Regiment of the Line :

"George R.—Whereas, we have thought fit that a Regiment of Foot be forthwith formed under your command, and to consist of ten companies, each to contain one captain, one lieutenant, one ensign, three sergeants, three corporals, two drummers, and one hundred effective private men ; which said regiment shall be formed out of six Independent Companies of Foot in the Highlands of North Britain, three of which are now commanded by captains, and three by captain-lieutenants :

"Our will and pleasure therefore is, that one sergeant, one corporal, and fifty private men, be forthwith taken out of the three companies commanded by captains, and ten private men from the three commanded by captain-lieutenants, making one hundred and eighty men, who are to be equally distributed into the four companies hereby to be raised ; and the three sergeants and three corporals draughted as aforesaid, to be placed to such of the four companies as you shall judge proper; and the remainder of the non-commissioned officers and private men, wanting to complete them to the above number, to be raised in the Highlands with all possible speed, *the men to be natives of the country, and none other to be taken.*

" This regiment shall commence and take place according to the establishment thereof. And of these our orders and commands, you and the said three captains and the three captain-lieutenants, commanding at present the six Independent Highland Companies, and all others concerned, are to take notice, and yield obedience thereunto accordingly.

" Given at 'our Court of St. James's this 7th day of November, 1739, and in the 13th year of our reign. By His Majesty's command.

(Signed)   " WM. YONGE.

" To our right-trusty and well-beloved cousin
John Earl of Craufurd and Lindsay."

Letters of service usually contain the *special conditions* under which troops are levied. It is worthy of remark that such are carefully *omitted* in the foregoing.

II.

HIGHLAND SOLDIERS.

In the war between 1755 and 1762, sixty-five thousand Scotsmen were enlisted, according to the " Scots Magazine " for 1763, and of these a great proportion were Highlanders, whose services were extremely ill-requited.

NOTES. 389

"Were not the Highlanders put upon every hazardous enterprise where nothing was to be got but broken bones, and are not all these regiments *discarded* now, but the 42nd?" says a writer in the *Edinburgh Advertiser* of 6th July, 1764. "The Scots colonel who entered the Moro Castle* is now reduced to half-pay; while an English general, whose avarice was the occasion of the death of many thousands of brave men, is not only on full pay, but in possession of one-fifth of the whole money gained at the Havannah—what proportion does the service of this general, who received £86,000, bear to a private soldier who got about fifty shillings, or an officer who received about £80?†

"The 42nd regiment consisted of two battalions and three companies, in all 2800 men, and now (in 1764) there remain only about ninety privates alive of the whole."

A passion for military glory and adventure, with the old patriarchal love of the chiefs and gentlemen who officered the Highland regiments, drew our mountain peasantry in great numbers into their ranks. "Thus we find," according to General Stewart, whose work has been quoted in the text, "that the whole corps embodied in the Highlands amounted to twenty-six battalions of fencible infantry, which, in addition to the *fifty battalions of the line*, three of reserve and seven of militia, formed altogether a force of EIGHTY-SIX HIGHLAND REGIMENTS embodied in the course of the four wars in which Britain had been engaged since the Black Watch was regimented in 1740. From a first glance, allowing 1000 men to each

* Lieutenant-Colonel James Stuart, who afterwards commanded at Cuddalore, in 1789.
† Lieut.-General the Earl of Albemarle received £122,697 10s. The writer is in error.

of these eighty-six regiments, would appear to come near the truth; but on a closer view it will be found to be far short of the actual number—several of the regiments had in the course of their service treble or quadruple their original number in their ranks. Thus the 71st, the 72nd and the 73rd, during the thirty-one years they were Highland (*i.e.* kilted), had at least 3000 Highlanders each, and other regiments had numbers in proportion to the length and nature of their service, both in tropical and temperate climat

"From the commencement of the late war," according to another and equally careful writer, "the Island of Skye alone had furnished no fewer than 21 Lieutenant-Generals and Major-Generals; 48 Lieutenant-Colonels; 600 other commissioned officers and 10,000 foot soldiers; 4 Governors. of British colonies; 1 Governor-General; 1 Adjutant-General; 1 Chief Baron of England; and 1 Judge of the Supreme Court of Scotland."

The game laws and expatriation of the people have now reduced the Highlands and Isles to a wilderness, or nearly so; the clans, whose memory is so inseparably connected with the military history of Scotland in modern times, and with the memory of days gone by, are swept to Australia, or the wilds of that Far West which is now the new home of the Celtic race.

According to Wilson—

Time and tide
Have washed away like weeds upon the sands,
Crowds of the olden life's memorials;
And mid the mountains you might as well seek
For the lone site of fancy's filmy dream.

III.

THE LETTRE DE CACHET.

Of Major White's companion in misfortune, referred to in the legend bearing the above title, the *Edinburgh Magazine* for 1789 supplies the following information :—

"The Earl of Mazarine is an Irish peer; he was nearly stopped at Calais, on Friday, on his way here. He was with two other gentlemen, his companions in misfortune, and being all extremely mean and shabbily dressed, were suspected of being bad persons, and no one seemed desirous of embarking in the packet with them. He was at length obliged to declare himself. The people in the packet thought him mad. On landing at Dover, his lordship was the first to jump out of the boat, and in gratitude to Heaven for his deliverance, immediately fell on his knees, and kissing the ground thrice, exclaimed—

"God bless this land of liberty!"

This was one of the last episodes in the history of the terrible Bastille.

THE END.

ROUTLEDGE, WARNE. & ROUTLEDGE'S

NEW AND CHEAP EDITIONS

OF

Standard and Popular Works.

To be obtained by Order of all Booksellers, Home or Colonial.

THE STANDARD EDITION OF THE

NOVELS AND ROMANCES OF SIR EDWARD BULWER LYTTON, BART., M.P. Uniformly printed in crown 8vo, corrected and revised throughout, with new Prefaces.

20 vols. in 10, price £3 3s. cloth extra ; or any volumes separately, in cloth binding, as under :—

	s.d.		s.d.
RIENZI: THE LAST OF THE TRI-BUNES		ERNEST MALTRAVERS	3 6
	3 6	ALICE; OR, THE MYSTERIES	3 6
PAUL CLIFFORD	3 6	THE DISOWNED	3 6
PELHAM: OR, THE ADVENTURES OF A GENTLEMAN	3 6	DEVEREUX	3 6
		ZANONI	3 6
EUGENE ARAM. A TALE	3 6	LEILA; OR, THE SIEGE OF GRA-NADA	2 8
LAST OF THE BARONS	5 0		
LAST DAYS OF POMPEII	3 6	HAROLD	4 0
GODOLPHIN	3 0	LUCRETIA	4 0
PILGRIMS OF THE RHINE	2 6	THE CAXTONS	4 0
NIGHT AND MORNING	4 0	MY NOVEL (2 vols.)	8 0

Or the Set complete in 20 vols. £3 11 6

,, ,, half-calf extra . . 5 5 0

,, ,, half-morocco . . 5 11 6

"No collection of prose fictions, by any single author, contains the same variety of experience—the same amplitude of knowledge and thought—the same combination of opposite extremes, harmonized by an equal mastership of art ; here—lively and sparkling fancies ; there, vigorous passion or practical wisdom—these works abound in illustrations that teach benevolence to the rich, and courage to the poor; they glow with the love of freedom ; they speak a sympathy with all high aspirations, and all manly struggle ; and where, in their more tragic portraitures, they depict the dread images of guilt and woe, they so clear our judgment by profound analysis, while they move our hearts by terror or compassion, that we learn to detect and stifle in ourselves the evil thought which we see gradually unfolding itself into the guilty deed."—*Extract from Bulwer Lytton and his Works.*

The above are printed on superior paper, bound in cloth. Each volume is embellished with an illustration ; and this Standard Edition is admirably suited for private, select, and public Libraries.

The odd Numbers and Parts to complete volumes may be obtained ; and the complete series is now in course of issue in Three-halfpenny Weekly Numbers, or in Monthly Parts, Sevenpence each.

A CHEAP RE-ISSUE OF THE LIBRARY EDITION OF

BULWER LYTTON'S (SIR E.) NOVELS AND TALES.

Uniformly printed in crown 8vo, and bound, with printed cloth covers and Illustrations.

LIST OF THE SERIES:—

Price 2s. 6d. each.

RIENZI.
PAUL CLIFFORD.
PELHAM.
EUGENE ARAM.
ZANONI.
ERNEST MALTRAVERS.

ALICE.
DISOWNED.
DEVEREUX.
LUCRETIA.
LAST DAYS OF POMPEII.

Price 9s. each.

NIGHT AND MORNING.
CAXTONS.

HAROLD.
MY NOVEL (2 vols.)

Price 1s. 6d. each.

PILGRIMS OF THE RHINE. | LEILA.

Price 3s. 6d. boards.

THE LAST OF THE BARONS. |

Price 2s. boards.

GODOLPHIN.

"England's greatest novelist."—*Blackwood's Magazine.*

THE RAILWAY EDITION OF

THE RIGHT HON. B. DISRAELI'S NOVELS.

In fcap 8vo, price 2s. 6d. each, boards.

THE YOUNG DUKE.
TANCRED.
VENETIA.
CONTARINI FLEMING.

CONINGSBY.
SYBIL.
ALROY.
IXION.

In fcap 8vo, price 2s. each, boards.

HENRIETTA TEMPLE. | VIVIAN GREY.

"We commend Messrs. Routledge's cheap edition of the right hon. gentleman's productions to every one of the 'New Generation' who wishes to make himself master of many suppressed passages in history, the every-day doings of the faërie realms of politics and fashion, and the profound views of a clear-sighted statesman on the tendencies and aspects of an age in which he has played, and is still playing, so conspicuous a part."—*Morning Herald.*

"Mr. Disraeli's novels sparkle like a fairy tale—the dialogues are wonderfully easy, and characterized by 'a turn of phrase that is peculiar to men of fashion, now that the wits' are defunct. His tales, too, abound in knowledge of the world, introduced in a natural and unobtrusive manner."—*Literary Gazette.*

UNIFORM ILLUSTRATED EDITIONS OF MR. AINSWORTH'S WORKS.

In 1 vol. demy 8vo, price 6s. each, cloth, emblematically gilt.

TOWER OF LONDON (The). With Forty Illustrations on Steel, and numerous Engravings on Wood by George Cruikshank.

LANCASHIRE WITCHES. Illustrated by J. Gilbert.

JACK SHEPPARD. Illustrated by George Cruikshank.

OLD ST. PAUL'S. Illustrated by George Cruikshank.

GUY FAWKES. Illustrated by George Cruikshank.

In 1 vol. demy 8vo, price 5s. each, cloth gilt.

CRICHTON. With Steel Illustrations, from designs by H. K. Browne.

WINDSOR CASTLE. With Steel Engravings, and Woodcuts by Cruikshank.

MISER'S DAUGHTER. Illustrated by George Cruikshank.

ROOKWOOD. With Illustrations by John Gilbert.

SPENDTHRIFT. With Illustrations by Phiz.

STAR CHAMBER. With Illustrations by Phiz.

"It is scarcely surprising that Harrison Ainsworth should have secured to himself a very wide popularity, when we consider how happily he has chosen his themes. Sometimes, by the luckiest inspiration, he has chosen a romance of captivating and enthralling fascinations, such as 'Crichton,' the 'Admirable Crichton.' Surely no one ever hit upon a worthier hero of romance, not from the days of Apuleius to those of Le Sage or of Bulwer Lytton. Sometimes the scene and the very title of his romance has been some renowned structure—a palace, a prison, or a fortress. It is thus with the 'Tower of London,' 'Windsor Castle,' 'Old St. Paul's.' Scarcely less ability, or rather, we should say, perhaps more correctly, scarcely less adroitness in the choice of a new theme, in the instance of one of his latest literary productions, viz., the 'Star Chamber.' But the readers of Mr. Ainsworth—and they now number thousands upon thousands—need hardly be informed of this; and now that a uniform illustrated edition of his works is published, we do not doubt but that this large number of readers even will be considerably increased."—*Sun.*

In 1 vol. demy 8vo, price 14s. cloth gilt.

MERVYN CLITHEROE. With Twenty-four Steel Engravings, from designs by Hablot K. Browne.

"'Mervyn Clitheroe,' like all Mr. Ainsworth's tales, abounds in action; the story never lingers; and certainly, in none of the long list of creations that bear his name, has he produced more vivid scenes or more just representations of life."—*Literary Gazette.*

GENERAL SIR CHARLES NAPIER'S ROMANCE.

In 1 vol. post 8vo, price **7s. 6d.** cloth extra.

WILLIAM THE CONQUEROR; a Historical Romance.

By General Sir CHARLES NAPIER; edited by his brother, Sir WILLIAM NAPIER.

"The real hero of the book is Harold, and the real moral of his fate is one illustrative of the consequences of leaving England comparatively defenceless, not because she had not, when William landed at Pevensey, plenty of stout hearts to defend her, but because those stout hearts were not incased in well-disciplined bodies. Had Sir Charles Napier seriously entered the field of literature as a rival of our best novelists, he would have taken rank very near to Sir Walter Scott."—*Globe.*

"There is a fine manly spirit in Sir Charles Napier's romance, which raises it above the level of ordinary fiction; it breathes of war and adventure; in a word, it displays that genuine sympathy with action which is the true foundation of romance, and which certainly does not appear with any surpassing strength in the imaginative literature of the day."—*The Times.*

"This is precisely the sort of romance we should have expected from a Napier—full of fierce contests and bold encounters, impetuous, graphic, and concise; every page tells of a battle-field or feat of arms of high emprise, not unmingled as in the deeds of ancient chivalry, with the softening influence of woman's love."—*Examiner.*

In 1 vol. price **5s.** cloth extra, or **5s. 6d.** in 2 vols.

SIR GUY D'ESTERRE. By SELINA BUNBURY, Author

of "Coombe Abbey," "Our Own Story," &c.

"All romance is the story of 'Sir Guy d'Esterre,' by Miss Selina Bunbury. It is a tale of the time of Irish war and tumult, in the reign of Elizabeth; of the Ireland from which Spenser fled to die. The period is well chosen, and Miss Bunbury has a quick fancy at command. Her romance will give pleasure to many readers."—*Examiner.*

In post 8vo, price **7s. 6d.** cloth extra.

THE DAY AFTER TO-MORROW; or, Fata Morgana.

Edited by WILLIAM DE TYNE (of the Inner Temple).

CONTENTS:—Prologue—Carberry Lodge—The World's Workshop—Government by Representatives—The Commons' House—The House of Peers—The Throne—The Printing House—The Church—The Law—The Centres and the Great Centre—The Foreign States—The Inner Life—The Public Service—India—The Earth as seen from the Moon.

"This is a remarkable book, and will make a sensation."—*Newcastle Chronicle.*

In 1 vol. demy 8vo, price **6s.** cloth.

COUNT OF MONTE CRISTO. By ALEXANDRE DUMAS.

Comprising the Château d'If, with Twenty Illustrations, drawn on Wood by M. Valentin, and executed by the best English engravers.

"'Monte Cristo' is Dumas' best production, and the work that will convey his name to the remembrance of future generations as a writer."

In 8vo, cloth extra, price **2s. 6d.** gilt back.

FANNY, THE LITTLE MILLINER; or, The Rich and

the Poor. By CHARLES ROWCROFT, Author of "Tales of the Colonies," &c. With Twenty-seven Illustrations by Phiz.

In 2 vols. 8vo, **12s. 6**d. cloth, emblematically gilt ; or the
2 vols. in 1, price **10s. 6**d. cloth extra, gilt.

CARLETON'S TRAITS AND STORIES OF THE IRISH PEASANTRY.

A New Pictorial Edition, with an Autobiographical Introduction, Explanatory Notes, and numerous Illustrations on Wood and Steel, by Phiz, &c.

The following Tales and Sketches are comprised in this Edition :—

Ned M'Keown.	The Donah, or the Horse Stealers.
The Three Tasks.	Phil Purcell, the Pig Driver.
Shaue Fadh's Wedding.	Geography of an Irish Oath.
Larry M'Farland's Wake.	The Llanham Shee.
The Battle of the Factions.	Going to Maynooth.
The Station.	Phelim O'Toole's Courtship.
The Party Fight and Funeral.	The Poor Scholar.
The Lough Derg Pilgrim.	Wildgoose Lodge.
The Hedge School.	Tubber Derg, or the Red Well.
The Midnight Mass.	Neal Malone.

" Unless another master-hand like Carleton's should appear, it is in his pages, and his alone, that future generations must look for the truest and fullest picture of the Irish peasantry, who will ere long have passed away from the troubled land, and from the records of history."—*Edinburgh Review.*
" Truly—intensely Irish."—*Blackwood.*

In fcap 16mo, price **1s.** sewed wrapper.

THE NEW TALE OF A TUB. By F. W. N. BAYLEY.

Illustrated by Engravings reduced from the original Drawings by Aubrey.

" Fun and humour from beginning to end."—*Athenæum.*

G. P. R. JAMES'S NOVELS AND TALES.

Price **1s.** each, boards.

Eva St. Clair.	Margaret Graham.

Price **1s. 6**d. each, boards.

Agincourt.	Forest Days.	One in a Thousand.
Arabella Stuart.	Forgery.	Robber.
Arrah Neil.	Gentleman of Old School.	Rose D'Albret.
Attila.		Russell.
Beauchamp.	Heidelberg.	Sir Theodore Brough-
Castelneau.	Jacquerie.	ton.
Castle of Ehrenstein.	King's Highway.	Stepmother.
Delaware.	Man-at-Arms.	Whim and its Conse-
De L'Orme.	Mary of Burgundy.	quences.
False Heir.	My Aunt Pontypool.	Charles Tyrrell.

C

G. P. R. JAMES'S NOVELS & TALES—*continued.*

Price 2s. each, boards; or in cloth gilt, 2s. 6d.

Brigand.	Henry Masterton.	Woodman.
Convict.	Henry of Guise.	Gipsy.
Darnley.	Huguenot.	Leonora D'Orco.
Gowrie.	John Marston Hall.	Old Dominion.
Morley Ernstein.	Philip Augustus.	The Black Eagle; or,
Richelieu.	Smuggler.	Ticonderoga.

*** Mr. James's Novels enjoy a world-wide reputation, and, with the exception of Bulwer Lytton, no author is so extensively read. His works, from the purity of their style, are universally admitted into Book Clubs, Mechanics' Institutions, and private families.

ROUTLEDGE'S STANDARD NOVELS.

In fcap 8vo, price 2s. 6d. each, cloth gilt.

This Collection now comprises the best Novels of our more celebrated Authors. The volumes are all printed on good paper, with an Illustration, and form, without exception, the best and cheapest collection of light reading that is anywhere to be obtained.

The following are now ready :—

1. Romance of War. By James Grant.
2. Peter Simple. By Captain Marryat.
3. Adventures of an Aide-de-Camp. By James Grant.
4. Whitefriars. By the Author of "Whitehall."
5. Stories of Waterloo. By W. H. Maxwell.
6. Jasper Lyle. By Mrs. Ward.
7. Mothers and Daughters. By Mrs. Gore.
8. Scottish Cavalier. By James Grant.
9. The Country Curate. By Gleig.
10. Trevelyan. By Lady Scott.
11. Captain Blake; or, My Life. By W. H. Maxwell.
13. Tylney Hall. By Thomas Hood.
14. Whitehall. By the Author of "Whitefriars."
15. Clan Albyn. By Mrs. Johnstone.
16. Cæsar Borgia. By the Author of "Whitefriars."
17. The Scottish Chiefs. By Miss Porter.
18. Lancashire Witches. By W. H. Ainsworth.
19. Tower of London. By W. H. Ainsworth.
20. The Family Feud. By the Author of "Alderman Ralph."
21. Frank Hilton; or, The Queen's Own. By James Grant.
22. The Yellow Frigate. By James Grant.
24. The Three Musketeers. By Alexandre Dumas.
25. The Bivouac. By W. H. Maxwell.
26. The Soldier of Lyons. By Mrs. Gore.
27. Adventures of Mr. Ledbury. By Albert Smith.

ROUTLEDGE'S STANDARD NOVELS—continued.

28. Jacob Faithful. By Captain Marryat.
29. Japhet in Search of a Father. By Captain Marryat.
30. The King's Own. By Captain Marryat.
31. Mr. Midshipman Easy. By Captain Marryat.
32. Newton Forster. By Captain Marryat.
33. The Pacha of Many Tales. By Captain Marryat.
34. Rattlin the Reefer. Edited by Captain Marryat.
35. The Poacher. By Captain Marryat.
36. The Phantom Ship. By Captain Marryat.
37. The Dog Fiend. By Captain Marryat.
38. Percival Keene. By Captain Marryat.
39. Hector O'Halloran. By W. H. Maxwell.
40. The Pottleton Legacy. By Albert Smith.
41. The Pastor's Fireside. By Miss Porter.
42. My Cousin Nicholas. By Ingoldsby.
43. The Black Dragoons. By James Grant.
44. Arthur O'Leary. By Charles Lever.
45. Scattergood Family. By Albert Smith.
46. Luck is Everything; or, Brian O'Linn. By W. H. Maxwell.
47. Bothwell; or, the Days of Mary of Scotland. By James Grant.
48. Christopher Tadpole. By Albert Smith.
49. Valentine Vox, the Ventriloquist. By Henry Cockton.
50. Sir Roland Ashton. By Lady Catharine Long.
51. Twenty Years After. By Alexandre Dumas.
52. The First Lieutenant's Story. By Lady Catharine Long.
53. Marguerite de Valois. By Alexandre Dumas.
54. Owen Tudor. By the Author of " Whitefriars."
55. Jane Seton; or, the Queen's Advocate. By James Grant.
56. Philip Rollo; or, the Scottish Musketeers. By James Grant.
57. Perkin Warbeck. By the Author of " Frankenstein."
58. The Two Convicts. By Frederick Gerstaecker.
59. Deeds, not Words. By M. Bell.
60. Feathered Arrow. By F. Gerstaecker.
61. Con Cregan; or, the Irish Gil Blas.
62. Old St. Paul's. By W. Harrison Ainsworth.
63. Prairie Bird. By Hon. C. H. Murray.
64. Petticoat Government. By Mrs. Trollope.
65. Ladder of Gold. By R. Bell.
66. Maid of Orleans. By the Author of " Whitefriars."
67. The Greatest Plague of Life. By Mayhew.
68. The Millionaire. By D. Cottello.
69. Colin Clink. By C. Hooton.
70. Brigand. By G. P. R. James.
71. The Convict. By G. P. R. James.
72. Darnley. By G. P. R. James.
73. Gowrie. By G. P. R. James.
74. Morley Ernstein. By G. P. R. James.
75. Richelieu. By G. P. R. James.
76. Henry Masterton. By G. P. R. James.

ROUTLEDGE'S STANDARD NOVELS—*continued.*

77. Henry of Guise. By G. P. R. James.
78. Huguenot. By G. P. R. James.
79. John Marston Hall. By G. P. R. James.
80. Philip Augustus. By G. P. R. James.
81. The Smuggler. By G. P. R. James.
82. Woodman. By G. P. R. James.
83. The Gipsy. By G. P. R. James.
84. Henrietta Temple. By Disraeli.
85. Vivian Grey. By Disraeli.
86. Will He Marry Her? By John Lang.
87. Leonora D'Orco. By G. P. R. James.
88. One Fault. By Mrs. Trollope.
89. Salathiel. By Dr. Croly.
90. Secret of a Life. By M. M. Bell.
91. Old Dominion (The). By G. P. R. James.
92. Rory O'More. By Samuel Lover.
93. The Manœuvring Mother. By the Author of "The Flirt."
94. The Half-Brothers. By Alexandre Dumas.
95. The Ex-Wife. By John Lang.
96. The Two Frigates. By the Author of "The Green Hand."

AINSWORTH'S (W. Harrison) WORKS.

In fcap 8vo, price **1**s. each, boards.

St. James's. | James II. (Edited by.)

Price **1**s. **6**d. each, boards.

The Miser's Daughter. | Windsor Castle.
Rookwood. | Crichton.
Spendthrift. | Guy Fawkes.

Price **2**s. each, boards.

Tower of London. | Lancashire Witches.
Old St. Paul's. | Flitch of Bacon.

"A cheap edition of Mr. Ainsworth's novels is now being published, and that fact we doubt not will enable thousands to possess what thousands have before been only able to admire and covet."

AUSTEN'S (Miss) WORKS.

In fcap 8vo, price **1**s. **6**d. each, boards.

Mansfield Park. | Persuasion, and
Emma. | Northanger Abbey.

"Miss Austen has a talent for describing the involvements, and feelings, and characters of every-day life, which is to me the most wonderful I ever met with."— *Sir Walter Scott.*

BULWER LYTTON'S (Sir Edward) WORKS.

In fcap 8vo, price 1s. each, boards.

Leila; or, the Siege of Granada. | Pilgrims of the Rhine (The)

In fcap 8vo, price 1s. 6d. each, boards.

Lucrotia.
Pelham.
Devereux.
Disowned (The).
Last Days of Pompeii (The).
Eugene Aram.

Zanoni.
Godolphin.
Paul Clifford.
Alice; or, the Mysteries.
Ernest Maltravers.

In fcap 8vo, price 2s each, boards.

My Novel. 2 vols.
Harold.
Rienzi.

Caxtons (The).
Last of the Barons.
Night and Morning.

"Now that the works of England's greatest novelist can be obtained for a few shillings, we can hardly imagine there will be any library, however small, without them."

CARLETON'S (W.) TALES AND STORIES.

In fcap 8vo, price 1s. 6d. each, or in cloth, 2s.

Three Tasks, Shane Fadh's Wedding, &c. (The).
Fardarougha the Miser.

Poor Scholar, Wildgoose Lodge, &c. (The).
Tithe Proctor (The).

Emigrants (The).

"Unless another master-hand like Carleton's should appear, it is to his pages, and his alone, that future generations must look for the truest and fullest picture of the Irish peasantry, who will ere long have passed away from the troubled land and the records of history."—*Edinburgh Review.*

CROWE'S (Mrs.) WORKS.

In fcap.8vo, 1s. 6d. each, bds.
Light and Darkness.
Lilly Dawson.

In fcap 8vo, 2s. each, bds.
Susan Hopley.
Night Side of Nature (The).
Linny Lockwood.

"Mrs. Crowe has a clearness and plain force of style, and a power in giving reality to a scene, by accumulating a number of minute details, that reminds us forcibly of Defoe."—*Aberdeen Banner.*

COOPER'S (J. F.) WORKS.

In fcap 8vo, price **1s. 6d.** each, boards, or in cloth, **2s.**

Last of the Mohicans (The).
Spy (The).
Lionel Lincoln.
Pilot (The).
Pioneers (The).
Sea Lions (The).
Borderers, or Heathcotes (The).
Bravo (The).
Homeward Bound.
Afloat and Ashore.
Satanstoe.
Wyandotte.
Mark's Reef.

Deerslayer (The).
Oak Openings (The).
Pathfinder (The).
Headsman (The).
Water Witch (The).
Two Admirals (The).
Miles Wallingford.
Prairie (The)
Red Rover (The).
Eve Effingham.
Heidenmauer (The).
Precaution.
Ned Myers.

"Cooper constructs enthralling stories, which hold us in breathless suspense, and make our brows alternately pallid with awe and terror, or flushed with powerful emotion: when once taken up, they are so fascinating, that we must perforce read on from beginning to end, panting to arrive at the thrilling *dénouement.*"—*Dublin University Magazine.*

DUMAS' (Alexandre) WORKS.

In fcap 8vo, price **2s. 6d.** each volume, cloth boards.

The Vicomte de Bragelonne. 2 vols.
Count of Monte Cristo. 1 vol.

"The 'Vicomte de Bragelonne,' which has been much inquired for, is the completion of those celebrated tales, the 'Three Musketeers' and 'Twenty Years After.' In this series of works, A. Dumas has selected a most eventful period in the history of France—the days of Richelieu, Mazarin, and the early manhood of Louis the Fourteenth. The author's principal aim has been to develop a personage particularly belonging to this period. The Gascon soldier and adventurer, D'Artagnan, is but what a Raleigh was in history and a Quintin Durward in fiction. Rashly brave, astute, shrewd, indefatigable, almost invincible—before his various qualities difficulties are but chimeras, obstacles thin *air.* In a word, the 'Vicomte de Bragelonne' maintains the character of its two predecessors, and the three form the most interesting and suggestive works we have read for many years."

Price **2s.** each, boards, or in cloth, gilt, **2s. 6d.**

Three Musketeers (The).
Twenty Years After.

Marguerite de Valois.
The Half-Brothers.

EDGEWORTH'S (Miss) WORKS.

In fcap 8vo, price **1s.** each, boards, or in cloth, **1s. 6d.**

The Absentee.
Ennui.

Manœuvring.
Vivian.

"Sir Walter Scott, in speaking of Miss Edgeworth, says that the rich humour, pathetic tenderness, and admirable tact that she displayed in her sketches of character, led him first to think that something might be attempted for his own country of the same kind with that which Miss Edgeworth fortunately achieved for hers."

GERSTAECKER'S WORKS.

In fcap 8vo, price 1s. 6d. each, boards, or in cloth, 2s.

Wild Sports of the Far West (The). | Pirates of the Mississippi (The).

Price 2s. boards or 2s. 6d. cloth.

Two Convicts (The).
The Feathered Arrow.

Price 1s. boards.

Haunted House (The).

"Our author appears to delight in recounting the stirring incidents of bush life and wild prairie. When nature soars in her grandest moods, the spirit of man partakes of something of the illimitable. It is this feeling, combined with the love of adventure, that prompts many to quit the home of their fathers, and to go forth in quest of the strange, the wonderful, and the wild."—*Devonport Telegraph.*

GORE'S (Mrs.) WORKS.

In fcap 8vo, price 1s. 6d. each, boards, or in cloth, 2s.

Heir of Selwood (The).
Dowager (The).
Pin Money.

Self; or, the Narrow, Narrow World.
Money Lender (The).

"Mrs. Gore is one of the most popular writers of the day; her works are all pictures of existing life and manners."

GRANT'S (James) WORKS.

In fcap 8vo, price 2s. each, boards, or in cloth gilt, 2s. 6d.

Harry Ogilvie.
Frank Hilton.
Yellow Frigate (The).
Romance of War (The).
Scottish Cavalier (The).

Bothwell.
Jane Seton.
Philip Rollo.
Adventures of an Aide-de-Camp (The).

"The author of 'The Romance of War' deserves the popularity which has made him, perhaps, the most read of living novelists. His tales are full of life and action, and his soldier spirit and turn for adventure carry him successfully through, with a skill in narrative which even the author of 'Charles O'Malley' seldom shows."

M'INTOSH'S (Miss) WORKS.

Price 1s. boards.

Charms and Counter-Charms.

Price 1s. 6d. boards.

Violet; or, Found at Last.

"Miss M'Intosh's style reminds the reader forcibly of Miss Edgeworth and Mrs. Opie; all her books inculcate high moral principles, and exalt what is honourable in purpose and deep in affection."

MARRYAT'S (Captain) WORKS.

In fcap 8vo, price **1**s. **6**d. each, boards.

Peter Simple.
Midshipman Easy (Mr.).
King's Own (The).
Rattlin the Reefer. (Edited.)
Jacob Faithful.
Japhet in Search of a Father.
Pacha of Many Tales (The).

Newton Forster.
Dog Fiend (The).
Valerie. (Edited.)
Poacher (The).
Phantom Ship (The).
Percival Keene.
Naval Officer (The).

"Marryat's works abound in humour—real, unaffected, buoyant, overflowing humour. Many bits of his writings strongly remind us of Dickens. He is an incorrigible joker, and frequently relates such strange anecdotes and adventures, that the gloomiest hypochondriac could not read them without involuntarily indulging in the unwonted luxury of a hearty cachinnation."—*Dublin University Magazine.*

MAXWELL'S (W. H.) WORKS.

In fcap 8vo, price **1**s. **6**d. each, boards, or in cloth, **2**s.

The Stories of Waterloo.
Captain O'Sullivan.

Wild Sports and Adventures.
Flood and Field.

In fcap 8vo, price **2**s. each, boards, or in cloth gilt, **2**s. **6**d.

Luck is Everything.
Bivouac (The).

Hector O'Halloran.
Captain Blake; or, My Life.

"Maxwell's tales are written in a bold, soldier-like style, free and energetic."—*Edinburgh Review.*

PORTER'S (The Misses) WORKS.

In fcap 8vo, **2**s. each, boards.

Scottish Chiefs (The).
Pastor's Fireside (The).

In fcap 8vo, **1**s. **6**d. each, boards.

Recluse of Norway.
Knight of Saint John (The).
Thaddeus of Warsaw.

"Miss Porter's works are popular in every sense of the word; they are read now with as much pleasure and avidity as when they were originally published."

"ROCKINGHAM" (The Author of).

In fcap 8vo, **1**s. **6**d. each, boards.

Rockingham; or, the Younger Brother.

Electra. A Tale of Modern Life.

Price **1**s. boards.
Love and Ambition.

"All the works of this author bear the imprint of a master-hand, and are by no means to be confounded with the daubs thrown together in the circulating library."—*Times.*

ROUTLEDGE'S ORIGINAL NOVELS.

In Fancy Boarded Covers.

1 THE CURSE OF GOLD. (1s.) By R. W. Jameson.
2 THE FAMILY FEUD. (2s.) By Thomas Cooper.'
3 THE SERF SISTERS. (1s.) By John Harwood.
4 PRIDE OF THE MESS. (1s. 6d.) By the Author of " Cavendish."
5 FRANK HILTON. (2s.) By James Grant.
6 MY BROTHER'S WIFE. (1s. 6d.) By Miss Edwards.
7 ADRIEN. (1s. 6d.) By the Author of " Zingra the Gipsy."
8 YELLOW FRIGATE. (2s.) By James Grant.
9 EVELYN FORESTER. (1s. 6a.) By Marguerite A. Power.
10 HARRY OGILVIE. (2s.) By James Grant.
11 LADDER OF LIFE. (1s. 6d.) By Miss Edwards.
12 THE TWO CONVICTS. (2s.) By Frederick Gerstaecker.
13 DEEDS, NOT WORDS. (2s.) By M. Bell.
14 THE FEATHERED ARROW. (2s.) By Frederick Gerstaecker.
15 TIES OF KINDRED. (1s. 6d.) By Owen Wynn.
16 WILL HE MARRY HER? (2s.) By John Lang.
17 SECRET OF A LIFE. (2s.) By M. M. Bell.
18 LOYAL HEART; or, the Trappers. (1s. 6d.)
19 THE EX-WIFE. (2s.) By John Lang.
20. ARTHUR BLANE. (2s.) By James Grant.
21. HIGHLANDERS OF GLEN ORA. (2s.) By James Grant.

BY MISS EDGEWORTH.

In fcap. 8vo, price One Shilling each, boards ; or, in cloth, 1s. 6d.

THE ABSENTEE.	MANŒUVRING.
ENNUI.	VIVIAN.

"Sir Walter Scott, in speaking of Miss Edgeworth, says, that the rich humour, pathetic tenderness, and admirable tact that she displayed in her sketches of character, led him first to think that something might be attempted for his own country of the same kind with that which Miss Edgeworth fortunately achieved for hers."

BY LADY CATHARINE LONG.

In fcap. 8vo, price Two Shillings each, boards; or, in cloth gilt, 2s. 6d.

SIR ROLAND ASHTON.	THE FIRST LIEUTENANT'S STORY.

BY WASHINGTON IRVING.

In fcap. 8vo, price One Shilling each, boards; or, in cloth, 1s. 6d.

OLIVER GOLDSMITH.	KNICKERBOCKER'S NEW YORK.
LIVES OF MAHOMET'S SUCCESSORS (The).	WOOLFERT'S ROOST.
SALMAGUNDI.	

BY THE MISSES WARNER.

In fcap. 8vo, price Two Shillings each, boards ; or, in cloth, 2s. 6d.

QUEECHY.	WIDE, WIDE WORLD (The).

Price Eighteenpence, boards.	Price One Shilling, boards.
HILLS OF THE SHATEMUC (The).	MY BROTHER'S KEEPER.

ROUTLEDGE'S STANDARD NOVELS,
Price Two Shillings and Sixpence each.

VOL.		AUTHOR.
52	THE FIRST LIEUTENANT'S STORY	Lady Catharine Long.
53	MARGUERITE DE VALOIS	Alexandre Dumas.
54	OWEN TUDOR	By the author of " Whitefriars.'
55	JANE SETON; or, the Queen's Advocate	James Grant.
56	PHILIP ROLLO; or, the Scottish Musketeers	James Grant.
57	PERKIN WARBECK By the author of" Frankenstein."
58	THE TWO CONVICTS	Frederick Gerstaecker.
59	DEEDS NOT WORDS	M. M. Bell.
60	FEATHERED ARROW (THE)	Gerstaecker.
61	CON CREGAN	Lever.
62	OLD ST. PAULS'	Ainsworth.
63	PRAIRIE BIRD	Hon. C. A. Murray.
64	PETTICOAT GOVERNMENT	Mrs. Trollope.
65	LADDER OF GOLD	R. Bell.
66	MAID OF ORLEANS By the author of" Whitefriars."
67	THE GREATEST PLAGUE OF LIFE	Mayhew.
68	THE MILLIONAIRE	D. Costello.
69	COLIN CLINK	C. Hooton.
70	BRIGAND	G. P. R. James.
71	THE CONVICT	Ditto.
72	DARNLEY	Ditto.
73	GOWRIE	Ditto.
74	MORLEY ERNSTEIN	Ditto.
75	RICHELIEU	Ditto.
76	HENRY MASTERTON	Ditto.
77	HENRY OF GUISE	Ditto.
78	HUGUENOT	Ditto.
79	JOHN MARSTON HALL	Ditto.
80	PHILIP AUGUSTUS	Ditto.
81	THE SMUGGLER	Ditto.
82	WOODMAN	Ditto.
83	THE GIPSY	Ditto.
84	HENRIETTA TEMPLE	Disraeli.
85	VIVIAN GREY	Ditto.

www.ingramcontent.com/pod-product-compliance
Lightning Source LLC
Chambersburg PA
CBHW030818110726
47900CB00006B/1656